Blue, the Novel

Barry McMahon

Blue, the Novel is a work of fiction. Any resemblance to people living or dead is purely coincidental. Names that are familiar are used to highlight the absurdity of a situation or to enhance the fictional aspects of the story. This novel is the text-only version of Blue: An Artist's Novel, a work in series, including illustrations by the author which is at once novel and graphic novel.

DEDICATION

To artists everywhere who dream of worlds beyond and within.

INVITATION

To Jim Carrey:
I hope you read this book and are able to visualize yourself in the leading roles of Blue and Tommy when we make the movie. I believe this is the perfect role for you because it is about an artist who becomes enlightened and powerful. When I was in my early twenties, my mother called me on the phone to ask me if I had ever heard of a guy named Jim Carrey. I had been watching you on In Living Color and thought you were the most amazing performer. She said, "He stole your shtick! His comedy is what you used to do when you're just walking around the house being funny." I told her that was the greatest compliment I had ever received. So, I believe that you, playing a fictionalized version of me, would be a fitting extension to this novel.

If you like the idea of starring in the picture and want to produce the movie, please send me an email: Barry@BarryFineArts.com. Look up some of my other creations at BarryMcMahon.com.

CONTENTS

ACKNOWLEDGMENTS

Thank you John Taylor.
Wherever you may be in this universe, I hope we meet again.

1 BIRTH

"Blue!" the doctor said, horrified, "Utterly and completely, blue! Like midnight. I haven't spanked a baby in years, but hell!" Sam Morgan wasn't usually one to panic but he smacked that baby's ass as hard as he could, as much out of fear as anything else.

He was completely freaked out at the sight of it.

The nurses stood around with their mouths agape while Sam uselessly speed-bagged the inert newborn like a heavyweight champ afraid of losing his edge.

He turned and thrust the lifeless form into the arms of a nurse too slow to back away as the others had, terrified that they might be given the unseemly task of disposing of the corpse.

"Run," Sam directed, "NOW," he added with urgency as he yelled, "to Emergency!"

The nurse responded quickly, a cute young woman who made the uniform look like it was a costume from a fantasy shop, altogether far too hot for prime time while being absolutely decent in every way.

If Sam wasn't busy trying to get the first breath out of this tiny little baby he would have offered to share his last with Nurse Neitzel.

"Hurry," he urged her once again as they rounded the corner at the end of the hall.

A passing gurney split the caregivers in two, blocking the doctor behind, as Nurse Neitzel continued around the corner bumping directly into a thin, quiet, deeply-wrinkled, African man in colored dress, accidentally pressing the baby between herself and the old man.

The old man looked at the baby, then into the nurse's eyes which told him of the newborn's condition.

He placed his hand upon the baby, looking kindly at the nurse who paused. With his other hand, he gently stroked the hand of the woman who lay still upon the gurney. She looked up at him from eyes that had not opened in days and smiled.

As she did, the man fell to the floor, nearly tripping Nurse Neitzel. He died. So did the old woman. The nurse regained her balance to hear Dr. Morgan shouting, "we have to keep going!"

He instructed the other nurse, who had been pushing the gurney, to attend to the fallen man.

Nurse Neitzel's eyes finally move to the baby who was now awake, alive and smiling up at her.

The baby is named Blue.

2 NIGHTMARES

Blue's alarm clock was his best friend and his worst enemy.

He counted on the thing to wake him up, rescuing him from countless horrors that unfolded, nearly nightly during his slumber.

Unfortunately, setting it meant that it was bedtime and bedtime meant more dreams. Even his "Happy Dumm-Dumms" pajamas couldn't protect him from the sadness and uncertainty that haunted every nightmare.

Blue wished for normal nightmares.

A dragon, swooping down from the sky, breathing fire and clawing at him, from the smoky aftermath of its own exhalation, would have been a welcomed experience. At least a dragon can be fought. You could lunge at him with your sword or take a swing at him with your stick, for example. That sounded like fun to Blue.

How about a plane crash or maybe a disaster at sea, he asked himself regularly, reasoning that he could always find a parachute or a life preserver.

There was actually something he could do about it.

He would be able to react. That was it. That was the horror of the nightmare.

He had thought about it long enough to understand the root of the nauseating emptiness he felt upon waking. There wasn't a single thing he could do. Not for himself, and often, even more frustratingly, he couldn't help them.

They were an interesting group. It can be said with a degree of certainty that you would never meet such a group ever in your life, even if you lived to be as old as Blue's great-grandmother who at the age of eighty-five, still played tennis with women half her age. In fact, it is unlikely that you would ever meet any of the beings with whom Blue had become familiar.

There is the man who is sometimes a woman, who sits in a room, at a desk, waiting to teach Blue something every night.

The man who is sometimes a woman goes by many names, among them are Sophocles, Aristotle, Buddha, Jesus Christ, Mohammad, Confucius, Mother Theresa, Cleopatra, Queen Victoria, Sir Isaac Newton, William Shakespeare, Carl Jung, John Lennon, Count Lev Nikolayevich Tolstoy and Abe Vigoda.

The room in which the man who is sometimes a woman sits is at the top of a rather lengthy staircase. Inexplicably, the man who is sometimes a woman is able to greet Blue every night to tell him what they are going to study that evening.

The subjects are just as varied as are the personas of the man who is sometimes a woman, and contrary to assumption, not all lessons are taught by the most likely persona. For instance, Confucius was preparing a lesson on applied physics while Karl Marx planned to show Blue how to make home-made ice cream. Planned is truly the operative word here and this is, ultimately, the source of the frustration.

Between Blue and the accumulated knowledge of humankind's existence stands a seventy-five foot tall, living peanut.

Anyone would be terrified of a seventy-five foot tall, living peanut if it could breathe fire, fly around or smash things up a bit.

Blue's peanut simply blocks the doorway to the man who is sometimes a woman.

There is nothing simple about it, really. Blue has been trying to reason out why he has been blocked, night after night, for years. He has asked the peanut and the peanut has responded.

The peanut doesn't know.

The peanut only knows that Blue is not allowed to pass him, Blue is not permitted to reach the man who is sometimes a woman.

The other piece of information that the peanut was able to provide would have been great news if Blue hadn't already tested it to his own dissatisfaction. The peanut told him that he is not allowed to hurt Blue. Hurt is defined as "to cause bodily injury to; to injure."

Blue felt that the giant peanut hurt him. To this day, you could not convince him otherwise, that being scooped up, ingested and eventually vomited to the location from which you had been previously scooped, could be viewed in any way other than that of being hurtful. Blue told the peanut that shortly after pulling himself up from a pool of extra chunky bile.

The giant nut asked him if he had any broken bones. Blue said, "no."

The nut asked whether Blue had any cuts or bruises. Blue said, "no."

The nut asked Blue if he felt as though he may be suffering from internal bleeding, light-headedness or blindness. Blue said, "no."

"Then you are not hurt," the peanut informed him. Blue stared at the nut in quiet desperation.

"You threw me up! You could have just swallowed me for good. It would all be over. This whole stupid thing would end!" Blue cried out in disgust.

"I am sorry," the peanut frowned, "I think I am allergic to you."

"Allergic to me?! You CAN NOT be serious," Blue moaned through clenched teeth, "then why eat me?"

The peanut sat dejectedly in front of the doorway. "I have to stop you, I cannot hurt you, I have no shoe box to keep you in, I must eat you."

The peanut had a point. A very meaningless point but one which made total sense to a peanut and when that peanut is seventy-five feet tall, that is good enough.

The other "regulars" in Blue's nightmare cast of characters included the yeti, the clown, Chunk, Glurp and the Light Wizards.

The yeti was always moping around. He would lumber through any number of dreams, passing right between Blue and any fun he might be having or person he might be interested in spending time with.

During one particularly wonderful dream, Blue was finally talking with Angelina, a very lovely young girl in Blue's fourth grade class. She was everything Blue loved about fourth grade. She ran like the wind, sang like a bird, caught flies with her bare hands then let them go because she wouldn't hurt them. Angelina made up jokes that were actually funny. She didn't just recite jokes she read from a joke book or overheard from an older brother, like Matthew Burger always did. She made them up herself. She remembered everything she read, could perform complex math problems in her head and knew where almost everything in the world was, like cool buildings, countries, states, capitals, natural wonders and best of all, amusement parks.

Blue could never speak to her in real life. He was too shy.

The one time he tried, a bird unloaded on him from a tree above his head just as he uttered her name. She had only just looked at him when the mess hit. Blue reached his hand up to feel for what had hit him and there across all of his fingers the payload was smeared. Angelina looked on, stunned but empathetic with her fingers pressed slightly against her own mouth, silencing a gasp so laden with pity it made Blue blush and run.

In this particular dream, however, Angelina was smiling at Blue with admiration. In this particular dream, Blue had heard the bird move in the branches above his head. In this particular dream, Blue stepped directly sideways just as the payload dropped. Without even looking, he raised one foot up, like a crane in the water, letting the splash of excrement splatter the exact spot where that foot had been a fraction of a second earlier. He froze in that position long enough to show how perfectly he had timed the whole event, then strode toward Angelina with an uncharacteristic suavity that captivated even her.

Blue moved in close, Angelina's breath became shallow, expectant, she wanted to talk to him, to Blue!

Suddenly, a large limousine pulled up directly adjacent to the sidewalk where Blue approached Angelina. The back door flew open and out rolled a yeti.

As he rolled, his head struck the concrete directly between them.

Blue and Angelina looked down in awe. The seven-foot tall creature turned and looked up at them, slowly moving, re-positioning himself, preparing to stand. He did so with great effort. He turned toward Angelina, his belly to her face, and moaned. She gazed up at him with sadness. His butt was right about chest high to Blue who leaned around the yeti's massive girth to steal a look at Angelina. She too, leaned to look at Blue. At this, the yeti fell to the ground, sitting cross-legged between them and began to cry. He promptly tugged at Blue, forcing the boy to look more closely at his skinned knee.

It is very hard to tell that a yeti's knee is skinned so the yeti made sure that Blue saw the skinned knee by pulling Blue down hard enough and close enough that Blue skinned his own knee, elbows and chin in the maneuver.

Blue pried himself up to his knees and looked up to Angelina, who had vanished.

This is how it usually went with the yeti.

Generally, what happens for the next five hours or so is that Blue spends all of his time trying to comfort the yeti, to no avail, since the yeti is implacable. On this night, the yeti forced Blue to hug him and sing him to sleep on the bench just feet away from the place where Blue was going to talk to Angelina. The very bench where Blue thought he might steal his first kiss.

Yeti breath is bad, but yeti gas is worse. The yeti had this habit of farting while sleeping that was like clockwork. He would start to fall asleep, spooning Blue while Blue tried to sing even though the oppressive weight of the yeti's arm was crushing the very breath with which he was trying to sing right out of him, so he wheezed out the words as if singing his last breath away. The yeti liked the way it sounded and Blue knew that so he endured the pain of it rather than suffer the consequences of a wakeful yeti.

When the yeti, whom Blue called Walter, wouldn't or couldn't sleep, he complained. He listed everything that was wrong with the world because of mankind's stupidity.

It is one thing to have to suffer the lamentations of an insomniac yeti, it is quite another to attempt to counter his requiem with optimism when everything he says is essentially correct. So, one night, Blue tried commiserating. Optimism was truly a survival technique. Optimism followed by singing, and yes, succumbing to the clockwork habit was a means of survival.

Blue welcomed the farting in comparison to the overwhelming depression resulting from commiseration.

The clock worked like this. Walter fell to sleep. Within minutes Walter began to scratch his behind. This gave Blue the chance to slide out from the spoon of Walter's embrace. After the scratching, Walter always sat up, bolt upright, directly perpendicular to whatever surface he and Blue had been spooning on. He would open his eyes, survey the area until he saw Blue, motion to Blue that he must come to him, whereupon he would take Blue's hand, pulling him into a spooning position behind himself. When Walter felt as though Blue understood his job, namely spooning Walter back to sleep, Walter would sleep. Blue would know Walter was asleep when Walter began to fart, and the clock struck one.

Blue was often relieved by the farting because it meant two things. One was that Walter was now asleep and because of his massive build, Blue's feet were closer to the gas than any other part of his body. The other thing that the farting meant was that by the time the clock struck twelve, which it always did after the farting started and the clock striking began, Blue's alarm clock would ring.

When Blue awoke from his nightmare with Walter he always felt the same way, hollow, empty, frustrated and demoralized. Then, a brief wave of optimism would wash across his mind and settle in his heart.

In that moment he was a pure boy. He was Blue, alone, awake, alive. He was at peace, breathing in the morning, thinking of nothing.

3 FRANK

Within minutes he would hear his father's footsteps, outside his bedroom door and the feeling of peace would vanish.

His mind would begin to fill with thoughts, kicking the lid closed on the iron crate in which he hid his heart.

"Get out here, Blue, time to eat, and I gotta leave so don't make me late," Blue's dad, Frank, would say, every day, all the time.

Blue couldn't remember a day he had made the old man late. In fact, Frank would be the only one who said a word in the morning, unless his sister decided to make some stupid joke that always had a color in it like, Hey Blue, you're looking a little green around the gills this morning." Then she'd laugh and say, "get it? green around the gills, and your name is Blue?," then she would punch him.

Frank would laugh and kiss her on the forehead and then he'd start listing all of his jobs for the next five days and if they were lucky he'd get another one by next week, so he could make even more money which wouldn't be enough to pay the bills because he had to spend so much on the stupid kids, *not you, Lisa, you're worth every penny, blah, blah, blah...*

That thought took about a second to pass through Blue's mind.

Unfortunately, it took about fifteen minutes to play out, in reality, on this particular morning. This time, however, it was punctuated by some good news from Lisa. She was going to have a recital this evening where she was going to perform "Greensleeves" which she had been practicing so beautifully for the past month on the "family's" organ which only she was allowed to play.

The good part, was that the practicing would finally stop, at least for a short while until Lisa got another song to learn.

"Oh, Blue, you're looking white as a ghost!" Lisa punched into Blue's gut as they left the house and his father gently guided his head toward the wood paneled Country Squire station wagon using the hard metal thermos on which Blue had spent his paper route earnings, for Father's Day.

Nearly daily, Frank would talk about how nice it was of Lisa to get up early on Father's Day to brew him a nice thermos full of nice coffee because she was the best and nicest daughter a father could ever have.

Blue couldn't shake the memory of the sound of the freeze-dried crystals being scooped into his gift after his sister commandeered it.

Pouring the boiling water that he had prepared only seconds earlier over the crystals, Lisa closed the thermos, warning him that it was her idea and danced out of the kitchen to present the gift to Frank.

Blue thought himself silly to have put so much tape on the label that said "to: Dad - Happy Father's Day - from: Blue.

If she had thought about it, Lisa would have written her own name on it or ripped off the label, but she was too concerned with making a display of herself to cover all the bases. Upon presenting the thermos to Frank she boasted, "I made you coffee daddy!"

Frank looked down and started reading loudly, "to: Dad – Happy Father's Day - from," suddenly his voice dropped about ten levels as he finished, "Blue."

Quick as a wink his voice shot up again, he held Lisa up in his arms and shouted, "My little angel made me coffee!"

That memory only took a second to flash through Blue's mind, but the smell of those mountain grown, freeze-dried crystals hung in the air and decided to ride along with them all the way to school.

4 GLURP

Nightmares have a way of sticking with a person, especially if they are recurring nightmares, particularly if they are nightmares wherein a strange, yellow, humanoid creature continually engages in dramatic displays, seeking attention, remaining dissatisfied, regardless of how much attention he truly is paid.

Glurp is just such a creature and it is in Blue's nightmares that he repeatedly performs. He is a singer, a dancer, a juggler and a mime. He walks the tightrope, leaps motorcycles over buses, dances with wolves, carries a six-gun, with which he can shoot *"Lincoln off a penny,"* swims underwater without coming up for air, ever, and makes a Crème Brûlée which is to die for.

Glurp also seems to know every word that was ever uttered and is not the least bit concerned others may not want to hear them. If there is a prompt, his quick quotation will follow, regardless of propriety or decorum. He quotes Gandhi in the same breath as Hitler and Martin Luther King with Nixon. He is both articulate and recklessly self-indulgent in word and deed. Glurp is powerful. He makes even the heaviest object seem light as a feather, the most insurmountable task as easy as pie.

Glurp is incredibly insecure.

Blue has always found him to be incredibly annoying. Amazing, but annoying. If you asked Blue what he thought of Glurp, he wouldn't be able to tell you, exactly. But if you asked him if Glurp was insecure, he would answer you emphatically, "NO."

Blue was in awe of Glurp's many talents. In fact, when Blue first met Glurp, both of them were only seven years old and Blue was enamored. Blue had just finished wiping the last bit of chunky bile off of his sleeves and was turning to face the seventy-five-foot-tall peanut when two large round spots appeared before his eyes. They came closer to his face, obscuring his vision until all went black.

He actually felt the spots bump up against his face. As he reached up to feel what the spots were made of, they were removed from his eyes, enabling him to see, no more than five inches away from his own face, a very oddly shaped, yellow head.

"Peanut butter cup?," said the yellow head. There stood Glurp, in all his glory, green shirt, tight black pants and big eyes on a very yellow head, holding two peanut butter cups in his hands, the spots before Blue's eyes.

He would have smelled the peanut butter if he hadn't been drenched in it a moment earlier. Blue couldn't think of anything more revolting than the thought of eating a peanut butter cup at that moment. It was about the funniest thing that had ever happened in one of his dreams and well worth a rather hearty laugh which Blue was more than willing to muster.

The more he laughed, the more he thought about how funny it really was and the funnier he thought it was the more he laughed until, finally, tears began to stream down Blue's face, as much out of pure relief as anything else.

"Whatsa Matta?!" Glurp teased, "Don't you think I'm funny? Goin' to have yourself a big blubberin' sob over a little candy?"

Blue shook his head and held up his index finger, asking for a second to compose himself.

"Who are you?" he asked.

"Glurp's the name," Glurp responded, "but you can call me Glurpendomulous Nobfidium Exparthenamius McGililily Finnegoshion the Third. How's about you?"

"I'm Blue"

"Of course you are, and why not, after all, how many times does a guy get eaten and spit back out by a seventy-five-foot-tall peanut?!"

"Somewhere in the neighborhood of about a hundred by now, I'd say," said Blue. "You see it just keeps happening over and over and over again. In fact, if you hadn't come along, it would probably be happening right about now. But really, my name is Blue."

"Well, Blue, it looks like I came along at just the right time," Glurp gestured over his shoulder," look, no more Mr. Nut!"

"You're right," said Blue, "thank you Glurpe-n-d-o..."

"You can call me Glurp"

Blue saw Glurp pretty regularly after their first meeting, almost nightly, in fact, at first. Over the years, however, Glurp's appearances in Blue's dreams became more sporadic. He always seemed to show up when Blue felt stuck and needed someone or something to change the course of his dream. Glurp was incredibly good at that.

Blue didn't always have bad dreams. Sometimes he had very good dreams that went bad, like when Walter showed up, while others were simply reflections of his daily routine. As Blue grew older, his dream to nightmare ratio shifted toward the positive and dreams filled his night with opportunity, wonder, escape, and even love. Actually, Glurp was sort of responsible for Blue's first kiss.

As Blue got older, Mr. Nut became larger and considerably more menacing. He seemed to forget the rule that stated that he wasn't supposed to hurt Blue. Since he didn't remember where the rule came from and Blue never knew who defined the rules, Mr. Nut took it upon himself to determine how we was going to handle Blue on any given day.

On this particular day, Mr. Nut was violent. He decided that before ingesting Blue, he would peel Blue. He would crack open his shell and eat out his insides like a peanut. He lifted Blue high into the air and held him up to the light of the sun, between his index finger and thumb, inspecting him for just the right spot to crack him open. He decided that pinching him between the fingers and thumb would be the best approach.

As he did so, Blue doubled over, tucking his elbows in and covering his head with his hands, bracing himself against the nutty giant. As Blue folded forward, the hooded jacket he was wearing popped out at the waistline like a cracked shell. Mr. Nut was delighted to see how nicely the edge of the "shell" presented itself to him. He held Blue by the legs with one hand and grabbed at the coat with the other. He peeled the coat off Blue who slipped out of his grip and began to fall toward the ground.

The moment before Blue hit the ground a street merchant pushed his cart, loaded with bananas directly under him. With a squishy thud, Blue landed safely in the cart. Before he could fathom what had just occurred, Blue was being pulled by the arm, out of the cart and off the banana pile.

"Nice of you to drop in," Glurp chuckled, " I've banana few bad spots before but there is nothing a peeling about this situation of yours!"

Blue dove to the ground and rolled under the cart as soon as his feet hit pavement. "Get down," he whispered emphatically, trying to protect Glurp who stood over him nonchalantly peeling a banana and laughing.

"You really don't get it do you," he said to Blue, "I suppose you have to go through this every time you come here but for me, it's a bit comical."

What Glurp was alluding to, was the fact that any time that he appeared, whatever was bothering Blue disappeared. It always took Blue a little while to recognize the situation because it was after all, for Blue, a dream.

Compared to many people, Blue was actually quite good at identifying that he was in a dream state and acting accordingly. Still, Blue had a heck of a time with the peanut. Once the peanut decided he was going to get violent, Blue lost all sense that he was dreaming. It became a fight for his life and Blue felt real fear.

Blue had the exact same problem when it came to girls. He was petrified of girls. Not that girls would hurt him physically, or even emotionally for that matter, but that he would fail with them. He was pretty sure that he was destined to be alone because the only woman he ever loved in his life, his mother, was dead. Blue loved his mother completely, without ever knowing her.

She died giving birth to Blue.

Frank never let Blue forget it. Every time that Blue did something that Frank didn't like, he would tell Blue that his mother would have been disappointed in him, angry with him or hateful toward him for the supposed transgression.

Blue didn't believe Frank. In fact, he knew that Frank was lying, not because of anything anyone ever told him, people never discussed his mother with him for fear of hurting his feelings, people other than Frank that is.

Blue knew Frank was lying because Blue knew his mother. The bond he felt with her went beyond an earthly knowledge of who she was or what she was like. He could feel her emotions within him, he saw things the way she would have seen them.

Frank is why Blue was afraid of girls. He believed that he had to steer clear of any relationships with girls because that would only lead to pregnancy, babies and death.

Glurp considered it his personal mission to erase that way of thinking completely from Blue's mind. This is how Glurp annoyed Blue. This is how Blue learned from Glurp. This is what Glurp did.

Glurp told outrageous stories of love. Madly passionate encounters with various women, separately and together. Glurp may as well have been Wilt Chamberlain for all of the globetrotting he claimed to have done.

Courtship was not at all what Glurp was about. Glurp did have dreams, Blue would find, and apparently, they all had to do with sex. Glurp was after women for a good time. He liked to party. His idea of a party was performing various sexual acts countless times regardless of who they occurred with in as many places as he could think of, then talking about them.

This is when Blue started to get annoyed. Most annoying was that he and Blue spent a great deal of time together with a variety of Blue's friends, real friends of Blue. They would go to parties where Billy, Blue's best real friend, Edgar, Tricia, Justine, CapMan and the lovely and luscious Brianna would hang out, sharing music, stories and movies, talking politics, religion and art. In Blue's dreams, these parties were everything that Blue wished a party would be. The atmosphere was always just right. If Blue wanted to listen to music, the music was the main event. If he wanted to talk politics, everyone there seemed to have an opinion and they were eloquent enough to express it. If he wanted to see a movie, they had a big screen, an awesome sound system and unlimited popcorn. There was always just the right number of people at each gathering and everyone seemed to be having a good time. Everything was just right, Blue was happy.

Precisely at the moment that Blue felt this way, Glurp would arrive.

It occurred to Blue that Glurp not only rescued him from dire situations within his dreams, but also denied him some very pleasurable experiences or things that made him truly happy in his dreams.

Glurp was fantastically gregarious. He could find his way into any conversation instantly. The problem was that as soon as he did, he tried to take the conversation over. It wasn't enough that he had engaged Blue's friends, he had to own them. They had to become his friends and if that was at Blue's expense, so be it.

Glurp had the annoying habit of making Blue appear stupid. The most frustrating thing about it being Blue's dream was that he often had to accept the dream situation. He was only able to do what was possible within his own dream. He found himself unable to remember or recite facts, excerpts from novels or poems, song lyrics, lines from movies, any of the bits of trivia or threads of conversation he was accustomed to sharing in wakeful life with his friends, while in this dream state where Glurp was around.

Another truly annoying habit of Glurp's was to tell Blue as well as Blue's male friends that they were thick. He would attempt to reinforce that idea by flicking them on their skulls with his unusually rigid fingers.

Then his eyes would turn to the ladies. His chest would swell, his posture become more erect as he sauntered his way toward them. On any given night, the women in Blue's circle of friends would react differently to Glurp's advances. While it was often difficult to stomach the discourse as it unfolded it nonetheless served to provide great insight into the human condition, or what made women tick.

At least that's what Blue thought.

Glurp made the girls feel sexy.

He scared them.

He pleased them and made them cry.

Glurp said some incredibly romantic things that made the women blush, smile or just plain crawl up on his lap. Blue sat by and watched everything, powerless within his dream state. Although Blue had no memory from dream to dream of the events which happened between Glurp and his friends, he had very vivid memories of the dreams while he was awake.

Blue began to experiment with his understanding of women, derived through the exploits of Glurp.

Brianna was the loveliest person whom Blue had ever seen. She walked with a slight shift in her hips, just enough to say sexy without being blatantly sexual. When Blue watched her walk his thoughts drifted far away from any fears he had, and his heart felt light. He remembered something he had heard Glurp say to her one night in a dream and decided to say it to her for real.

"I wish that I could be your guardian angel, not just because I think that you deserve to be protected, so I can see if you walk like that everywhere you go. I don't believe that you do, because the way it affects me makes me think that it can only be for me." Blue whispered to Brianna when their other friends were busy watching CapMan add another one to his "Wall of Fame," a beer bottle cap collection so expansive that it was no longer a single wall but many walls. Most remarkable was the fact that every cap was from a bottle that he had consumed himself.

"Whooeee! Yes!"

Normally, the fact that CapMan had just announced his decision to extend the collection to the ceiling for lack of wall space would have been just the thing to elicit such a response from Blue, however, that wasn't the cause of the outburst. Blue played it off like it was but that was because he felt embarrassed, elated and downright giddy over something so extraordinarily wonderful that he had no intention of making it public. That was, not until he had time to process and enjoy it for himself. Brianna had, only seconds earlier whispered back, "Well, Blue, it is only for you."

He couldn't believe it. Blue felt as though he had stolen a line from Glurp to trick Brianna into accepting how he felt for her. It seemed a bit false to use a line from an imaginary friend who resembled a large Lemonhead with legs, but there was something different going on. In fact, this blissfully romantic episode was only the beginning of a realization and transformation for Blue that would prove to be a major turning point in his life.

Until now, Blue had been rather non-committal. He was attending college with an "undeclared" major. He had always been an artist in his own mind and, by the looks of it to everyone else, a fairly good one.

However, he didn't really commit to it until he started creating art about his dreams. The moment he discovered that Glurp's words worked on Brianna, he began to explore his dreams, openly, within his artwork. Blue imagined Brianna waiting for him in bed, Glurp was out of his subconscious and jumping off the page. Blue's first kiss, his sexual appetite, his fears and his ambitions were drawn, painted and collaged right alongside Glurp, Mr. Nut and Walter for all his friends, his teachers and even his lovely Brianna to see. As Blue translated his dreams to his art the nightmares became less frequent. Glurp showed up only occasionally and Walter and Mr. Nut disappeared altogether. By the time Blue graduated from college, Glurp was just a childhood memory.

Brianna would prove to be Blue's first love. She also became the first woman to break his heart. She ended up sleeping with a friend of a friend who was really cool, and she was quite sure that Blue would like him.

5 BOSTON

Blue never bothered to find out. In fact, he moved as far away as possible in an easterly direction without falling into the ocean.

Blue loved Boston.

He did what any young enterprising rising star of art would do. He worked in a frame shop/ and a restaurant and spent his money on all the wrong things. He confused his social life with art and dabbled in too many disciplines for any self-respecting gallery to accept him.

He was an artist.

Like any good artist, Blue surrounded himself with other artists, his friend Billy eventually joined him in Boston where they shared an apartment with two musicians. Billy and Blue had a few shows together. At one show they made a collaborative work, casting one another's faces and making hand-made paper likenesses which each decorated for the other. Then they painted one another's faces and sat in front of the art. Billy spent most of the night making fun of the people who struggled to get the concept while Blue fantasized that some high-powered agent would come in and recognize that he and Billy were the next Rauschenberg and Johns.

Blue was always trying to play music but wasn't very good at it, but his roommates were. So, Blue became a roadie. The great thing about being a roadie was that you got in to the shows for free and you got to travel.

On a weekend trip to Vermont, Blue saw a very amazing thing that would prompt him to create a painting which he still hangs onto today, even after countless offers from would-be collectors.

The bands were playing in Lake Champlain, Vermont, home to Champ, the Lake Champlain monster. Champ had been photographed and seen by many but never very clearly and not in any verifiable fashion. Photos were always blurry, and the eyewitness accounts fell short of convincing or credible to those who demanded the facts.

Blue was always a bit gullible and really wanted to believe in things like sea serpents, ghosts, flying saucers and the supernatural.

The show went late.

It was an awesome show. People had to be kicked out of the bar to get them to leave. Blue was wet with sweat from head to toe. Moving amplifiers was nothing compared to dancing full tilt for hours on end, but Blue did both. He was pretty high by the end of the night, after loading up the last of the gear, sliding the high hat into what little space was left for it between the Marshalls and the battered case that still managed to protect the most beautiful hollow-bodied Rickenbacker bass Blue had ever laid eyes on.

Blue's roommate, JW, asked him to paint a fire-breathing Godzilla monster on the pick guard and a crazy little Cap'n Ahab chasin' down the Great White Moby Dick on the back of the body but Blue refused because the Ric was so damn beautiful.

JW said it would just make the Ric that much better and after Blue turned famous, the guitar would be worth even more. JW was a good friend and a good roommate. Blue painted the guitar and it was in fact way cooler after the paint job, particularly when JW would pop it up from his hip where he slung it low while playing, displaying the back of the body.

Blue had painted the chase scene upside down facing JW so when he popped it, the crowd would see the crazy little Ahab character mercilessly lunging after Moby with spear in hand. True Genius!

Still rushing from an awesome show, relentless dancing and the adrenaline pumping from being the only roadie for all three bands, Blue, who was always sober, didn't drink, smoke, chew, shoot, inhale or swallow anything remotely mistakable for hallucinogenic, was high as a kite on life. He dropped the van at the house where all three bands were crashing for a night of Spinal Tap and beer and went for a walk around Lake Champlain.

He sat by the side of the lake, alone and at peace.

He closed his eyes.

When he opened them, a small island appeared, fifty feet out into the lake. The island moved slowly toward him. Instead of running in fear, Blue sat on the edge of the shore in a lotus position and waited as the island grew and grew nearer to him. When the island was approximately twenty-five feet away from Blue, and shore, a large boulder rolled right up to Blue and stopped, inches away from his crossed legs.

The boulder opened its eyes.

Blue laughed, quietly, to himself.

The boulder narrowed its eyes and lifted from the ground with a sound that was remarkably similar to a musing human, a sound like "hmmm." The boulder moved slowly past Blue followed by a long neck and the island which sprouted a tail as it left the lake and began walking down the middle of the street.

Blue was sure that this must be Champ, and he followed the creature.

Within a few seconds, Champ reached a stoplight which he very carefully ducked under as he continued down the street. The town was dark except for the stoplights, streetlamps and the sporadic glow of interior lighting, softened by the curtains drawn against the night, leaving Blue alone with Champ as they made their way through town to an open field where Champ rolled in the grass and lay on his back as if looking up at the moon, which seemed to be gazing right back down at the two of them. Blue followed Champ's lead and lay down his head on a pillow of clover, breathing in the scent of its white little flowers, falling fast asleep.

Suddenly, Blue is startled.

He sits up and looks around, quickly trying to understand what all of the commotion is about. Soldiers are storming past him on both sides. As quickly as they arrived, they are gone.

All except one. He appears to be someone of rank and importance although Blue, never concerning himself with military issues other than to abhor them, is impotent to recognize the rank and therefor suitably unimpressed. The officer, whose skin is pale and translucent, points toward the open field and orders Blue to join the ranks of the soldiers or get out.

Blue finally adjusts to being awakened enough to see what is happening around him. The soldiers have fallen into rank in the distant field. A young girl is innocently tossing a beach ball up and down only a few yards away while just beyond her, Champ is quietly surveying the troops.

Blue notices some tanks lined up in the field, their cannons trained on the peaceful Champ.

"What on Earth are you doing here?," Blue demands, his sense of urgency and outrage immediately apparent to the officer.

"I am here to kill that," the officer responds as he points at Champ, "and I'd suggest you run along, little man, before you get yourself caught in the tussle." The officer then turns toward the girl and says, "come along Cynthia, daddy is going to kill the nasty beastie now."

The girl stops throwing the ball, "I want my lolly now," she responds, "you told me I could have a lolly, remember?" She continues, singing the last syllable, "and I want to go back to the beach," she finishes as she kicks the beach ball directly at her father.

He catches it and says, "of course, my little darling," and pulling a rather large lollipop from a pocket which didn't seem to exist seconds earlier, hands it to the little brat saying, "and we'll be back to the beach in no time, just as soon as I eliminate this," he pauses to find just the right word, "thing!"

"You can't do that!" Blue shouts.

"I can, little man. Now shut up and get out of my way or I'll have you thrown in prison." The officer ordered.

Blue realized he was going to get nowhere with the soldier, so he ran up onto a large boulder right next to Champ and tried to get the "monster's" attention.

"Champ, Champ! Hey Champ, you have to listen to me, they are going to kill you!," Blue yelled. Champ simply turned his head and gently nuzzled his forehead into Blue's chest.

"NO!" Blue added in earnest, "You don't get it, you have to run away, they are going to kill you!" Blue reached out to Champ, but the monster just rolled over like a puppy wanting to play, his belly to the open sky and sunshine overhead.

Blue jumped down from the rock, waving his arms to the soldiers and yelling, "Don't shoot, DON'T SHOOT, can't you see he's harmless?," as he ran up to Champ and hugged his massive neck, just under his smiling chin. Blue was fairly certain that Champ was smiling, and this made his plight seem even more urgent, ridiculous and morally charged.

"You can't kill my friend!" he yelled at the top of his lungs.

At that moment, all guns opened fire on Blue and Champ.

Blue felt his chest burst open just before he saw a large missile of some sort detonate as it struck Champ in the belly. Blue and Champ were terminated instantly. Blue's head fell directly next to Champs large eye which looked at him lifelessly as Blues vision went blank.

A second later, Blue woke up.

He was lying on the beach. He felt as though someone had just stroked his cheek. He slowly opened his eyes. Startled, he sat upright. Champ was looking down at him, his large nostrils, directly over Blue's head. Blue didn't know what to do. He was so relieved that he wanted to hug Champ, but he couldn't be sure what had happened. He wondered if this was really the first time he was actually seeing the monster or if, in fact, it was happening at all. He patted Champ on what he thought must be the nose and smiled. Blue began talking to Champ. He told him everything that had just happened, and the monster just stayed right there and listened.

"I can't believe you're alive," Blue whispered, "I can't believe I'm alive."

He hugged Champ as best he could. It was more like laying up against Champs head, with feeling. "I want you to go back into the water," he directed Champ, then reconsidered and politely asked the creature, "please, I think that something bad will happen to you if you don't," he added.

Champ raised his head from the beach slowly. He tucked his forehead into Blue's chest and turned away gently as if saying goodbye to an old friend.

Blue sat on the beach and watched as Champ moved slowly back into Lake Champlain. He watched Champ swim for a while until, finally, the monster who was his friend dove under the water and did not come back up. Blue's head was resting on his own forearm, his body stretched out on the sand facing the lake. The breeze across the water was cool and soothing. Blue again returned to sleep.

"Nurse! I'm gonna need some coffee in here, STAT!" Blue heard from above. He opened his eyes to see JW leaning over his face with bedhead and a mischievous grin.

"Get me ten CCs of the good stuff and hold the cream, this one's flat-lining!" JW held a coffee over Blue and continued, "It took us a little while to find you, but I think it's still hot. We thought you were dead!"

"So did I," Blue responded as JW's face came into focus and the dancing girls faded into the sky.

"What the hell are you doing sleeping out here man?" JW asked.

"It's a long story," Blue said, "let's just forget it. I want to get home." Blue said as he got up from the sand.

JW gave him the coffee as Tricia gave Blue a little kiss on the cheek. JW lived in Blue's apartment, was a good friend, and had a girlfriend who walked around the apartment naked all the time. There were four men living in the apartment and not even one of them ever asked her to get some clothes on.

Back at the house where the bands had been sleeping, everyone piled in the van. Blue was driving and JW was riding shotgun. "Hold on a second," JW said to Blue. He reached over and pulled something from Blue's collar and handed it to him saying, "good morning sunshine." It was a single white clover flower.

Blue wondered about that flower daily for the next couple of weeks. He was sure it meant that what seemed like a horrible nightmare had actually happened which threw his mind into a spin about the reality of Glurp, Walter and Mr. Nut, but he had no intention of taking a trip down "Nightmare Memory Lane."

It did make him consider however that there was more to his reality than met the eye, particularly the wakeful eye. The painting, "Defending Champ" did for Blue what the works that dealt with Glurp, Walter and Mr. Nut had done earlier in his life. It relieved his mind, made him feel better about his nightmares and eased his fears. Drawing and painting in general was very therapeutic for Blue and he remained active artistically, despite a reluctance to submit his work to galleries for consideration. He had a hard time with the whole process of the "art world" and the steps he would have to go through to display his work, sign with an agent or gallery or both, in his mind "package himself for sale."

Instead he came up with a brilliant idea. He would create artwork where he could be entirely expressive, creative and distinctive, unchained to any one style, free to explore his own unique vision AND be able to sell his work for lots of money, gain adoring fans and live in luxury.

Blue decided to illustrate comic books.

Before Blue came to the realization that this idea of his was seriously flawed on a variety of levels, while he was still fully enthusiastic, hopeful and committed, he managed to convince his friend, John Tanner, to write the story. The two of them worked tirelessly, generating ideas, sketching out concepts, developing characters and trying different artistic approaches. Ultimately, they created "Leer." The comic grew from a single issue to a graphic novel, or at least it was supposed to, it just never did.

However, nothing worth doing should ever be left undone.

6 REBOOT

Blue spent the next twenty-five years of his life doing an awful lot of leaving things undone.

He had many relationships that started gloriously and ended without ceremony. He never seemed to get any better at relationships regardless of their number. What he did get good at was art. Blue had managed to continue painting his entire life and picked up even more skills along the way, but he felt unsatisfied. His lack of commitment to any one thing had become a disadvantage rather than a positive mantra of exploration and self-improvement. He began to see how fulfilling one's purpose by seeing something meaningful through to its completion goes hand in hand with making a commitment. He had learned that making that commitment could be an anchor rather than a prison, a place of safety and power rather than a dungeon. His need to break free from Frank's influence on him could only be satisfied by realizing his own purpose, by making a commitment to himself first.

"So, after over twenty-five years I'm going to finish "Leer,"" Blue said to himself as he stepped among the pages he penned so long ago. "I have to find them all but where on Earth did I put them?" he asked himself as he dumped out boxes of notebooks, sketchpads, receipts, bills, unpaid traffic violations, unopened wedding and graduation invitations, REAL comic books and pornography.

"Pornography? where the hell did that come from?" Blue inquired of his own memory because it was true, Blue never did buy any pornography. It wasn't because he didn't like to look at naked women. He really liked looking at naked women, and that's what he spent the next twenty minutes doing, thoroughly forgetting about the fact that he was trying to organize all of the "Leer" drawings into one place. After he finally got finished jerking himself around and got back down to re-establishing his priorities, Blue finally found the original "cover" image for "Leer."

*

A letter to the reader from Barry McMahon, the guy telling this story:

To say that Blue owes everything to John Tanner when it comes to the creation of "Leer" would be an overstatement but as a witness to much of the discussion regarding the creative process for the graphic novel, I have been asked to share my perspective.

Blue, John and I were sitting around Blue's studio one hot summer night. I had just pounded my eighth St. Pauli Girl in a row after we all polished off a whole Bar-B-Qued chicken each and John was nursing his second. Blue never drank, as I recall, and it is for that reason that I was stunned that he asked me to write this foreword. Regardless, I was sufficiently impressed with the conversation of that evening to have managed to allocate a reasonable chunk of permanent memory to it.

Blue had, to that point in time, never struck me as the comic book illustrator type. I will admit that I have no idea what that type is, I just didn't think Blue was it. I mean, he was such an "artist" type artist. He always talked about Rauschenberg and Johns, Jim Dine and Kurt Schwitters, Duchamp, Dali and of course Pablo. Blue loved to call him Pablo because everyone else called him Picasso and Blue hardly did anything like everyone else.

So, when he stood up and looked John directly in the eye and said, "I need your help," I couldn't believe it. Blue never asked for help with anything. I knew this was going to be something unusual for Blue. He told John that he wanted to write a comic book, as he put it, "More correctly, I want you to write it so I can focus on the artwork."

John became immediately excited by the proposition. He leaped into an interview about plot, characterization, setting, tone, genre, the works. Blue had very little to say about any of that. He said, "John, I just said, I don't want to write the comic book, I want to illustrate it."

I could not imagine a more dynamic duo to create a comic book than Blue and John. Both men are talented beyond their disciplines yet work tirelessly and respectfully within them. However, neither one is encumbered by dogmatic constraints.

The first few months of work were exhilarating to witness. At first, Blue handed John completely finished pages full of unusual and provocative imagery. The concept being that Blue would create a story-less piece and John would fill in the story.

The work was spectacular.

The imagery was bizarre and unpredictable and the stories were sheer poetry.

Unfortunately, none of it held together at all. I told them that they should scrap the comic book idea and make a coffee table manuscript or collection out of the art and poetry but neither would have it.

Both men were committed to the idea that they were going to be like Miller and Moore, bringing something different, something new to comics, while recognizing the greatness of heroes like Stan Lee. So they changed their approach.

John decided to take a few weeks to write, no meetings, no discussions and no ideas from Blue.

I was in the room when John delivered the first twelve pages of "Leer" to Blue. I can still remember the expressions on his face as he read all the way through the pages, three times. Blue's expressions changed from anticipation, to laughter to intense agreement and approval, but in the end his face displayed nothing but awe and admiration for the words that John had bestowed upon him.

The same admiration and respect was written on John's face just one week later when Blue uncovered the first of the drawings for the comic book.

This awe swap continued for months until Blue announced that he was going to submit the work to a variety of publishers.

John wanted to have more written, but Blue felt that it was important to get a reaction before they spent too much time barking up the wrong tree.

Blue confessed to me later that he probably should have aimed a bit lower with his first comic book rather than making a dozen submissions to the largest, most well established, most influential and least interested publishers he could find.

I probably don't have to mention any names here, so I won't, but the point that I must make is that Blue and John were turned down cold. The standard response was. "Thank you for your submission to..., However, we do not accept unsolicited manuscripts for publication." The response that kept Blue going, gave him hope, and doubled his workload was in addition to the line above, one publisher said... "The manuscript you have submitted is not in the proper format for production..."

"That's what we're doing wrong!," Blue beamed to John as he laid the rejections out in front of him. "All I have to do is redraw all of the drawings in the proper format!"

This is the kind of guy that Blue is. He had just spent months working on the most incredible drawings, real works of art, for the book, and he was ready to redo every single one of them.

John suggested that Blue try different publishers with the same drawings, but Blue didn't want to risk that "Leer" might go unpublished.

So, Blue did the drawings over again, in the proper format.

John continued writing, and in the process discovered that the comic book "Leer" was going to have to be a graphic novel. John simply had too much to say about Leer, Edgar Van and Mona for one comic issue or even three for that matter.

Blue had several sketches created for the new pages and, in fact, had more than the original set completed, in proper format, when the inevitable happened.

Life.

Blue's girl dumped him, and John had a Doctoral thesis to write. Blue left town to avoid the heartache of daily visual reminders and John went on to teach something other than writing.

Now, twenty-some years later, Blue has begun to put the pieces back together again and plans to finish "Leer." After a thorough search for John which yielded no fruit, Blue has decided to finish it himself.

Enjoy,

Barry

*

Blue had an interesting dilemma in front of him. He knew enough about the characters in *LEER* to draw them for the rest of the story, he just didn't know what he should have them do or say. To make matters worse, he was trying to piece together a story that had been unfinished - twice.

Finally, after much deliberation, he decided to assemble all of the images he had from the first two tries so he could get the story going in his head, maybe then the rest would just come to him, he thought. He had forgotten about the flood in the basement. Several of the original black and white pages had been ruined by a leak in his basement walls and all that he had left were some less than perfect Xerox copies he had made twenty-five years earlier.

"It's just going to have to be good enough," he said to himself as he imitated Jerry Lewis as the original *Nutty Professor.*

Blue drank his beer, a habit he had acquired with a vengeance, like it was the formula in the movie and instantly transformed into the suave and charismatic *Buddy Love,* but he was alone in his studio and felt rather silly about the whole thing inside of a minute.

As he looked around at the copies of pages he had spent so much time drawing he felt a mixture of sadness at the loss of the originals and excitement at the opportunity to create a new and improved *LEER.* He kept looking for any scraps of information he could find that would help him further the story that John had originated while musing about where this hero might go and what adventures might be in store for him.

He knew that it would be difficult to pull it all together aesthetically, considering that the black and white images were simply meant to replace the colored images, but he felt as though his ideal readers would want to see everything. After all, a graphic novel would really just be a very short novel without the graphics, so a graphic novel with two sets of graphics must be even better, a graphic, graphic novel!

"What to keep and what to kill, that really is the question, isn't it?," Blue thought to himself as he looked through the stack of notes, sketches and rewrites from the early days of "Leer."

The more he looked at everything, the less he wanted to kill any of it. Blue found himself marveling at the sheer amount of time that he and John had put into "Leer" to no avail, bolstering his ambition to see the project through. He decided to include it all.

His studio was already littered with every kind of art supply, collage element and "another man's treasure" one could imagine but Blue had become adept at finding everything just the way he had scattered it, out of necessity. It wasn't that Blue was messy so much as he was chaotically productive. When he spread the stack out on the floor, Blue began a sort of dance, leaping from notes to sketches, over to a large ink and colored pencil rendering on an over-sized topographical map and back again.

"I'm going to confuse the hell out of everyone who tries to read this," Blue said to himself as he landed with his legs splayed wide across a large drawing and a row of a half-dozen inked pages in succession.

"Anybody who can't figure out the story can go back to reading "Archie,"" Blue imagined hearing John snicker into his ear.

He turned so suddenly that he nearly fell on the drawing of the ice that Leer broke through over twenty-five years earlier.

John was nowhere in sight, but Blue felt him there. If he found out that John was dead, it would have made sense to him. The paranormal evangelists would identify the chilling feeling as his dear friend's presence, possibly attempting to contact him from the great beyond. It wasn't that kind of chill. It was more like exhilaration, a palpable feeling of shared purpose, as if John were actually there, helping Blue to make the right decisions, nothing buried, nothing burned.

Blue spent a few days trying to assemble the pieces of "Leer" together.

After the initial rejection letters, he had scrapped the idea of photographic reproductions with text bubbles overlaid by hand and Xeroxed on a color copier. Now, twenty-plus years later, with scanner and personal computer technology being what it is, Blue is entertaining the idea once again. He reasons that the print industry has developed step by step with other industries, utilizing the latest hardware and software innovations, making it possible to use much of what was rejected so many years ago. The biggest drawback Blue was running into was that there was simply no way he could meld the first version with the second. Finally, he decides not to try.

"I'm going to use it all. I'm going to just lay it out there, mix it all together and let everybody figure it out for themselves. People are smart. If Leer is dreaming about Mona in color on one page and black and white on another, so what. Hell, I thought he was dreaming about Catherine Kent! And maybe I'm getting ahead of myself. Too bad, there's just way too much good shit in here to waste it by trimming the fat. This is like good fat. This is Porterhouse fat, charbroiled and sizzlin'." Blue concluded.

Again, Blue's friend John snickered into his ear, "That's not really good fat either, Blue. Avocados. Avocados are good fat, not Porterhouse."

Blue shook his head as if John's voice was a heavy deposit of water in his ear.

He plunged his fingers into his ears and twisted them in alternating directions. Blue felt as though he might lose his balance as he listened for the voice once more and that's when he saw it, a large, beat-up envelop with coffee cup stains on the outside. He recognized the envelop as coming from his short-lived career as a librarian, a job he had during the time that he and John were working on *LEER*.
He grabbed the envelope and unwound the red string from the buttons securing the contents. Inside were several Xeroxed pages of *LEER*, in varying states of disrepair. At the top of the stack was page two where Arnold tries on the mask. The paper had yellowed but the lines were good. Blue scanned the image into his computer and cleaned it up a bit until he felt satisfied that it was good enough to put in the book.

And only the living
seeing with their eyes and listening with their ears
can find their way back
The drums. Bellowing out a compromise. Peace for the dead, life for the living.
Simple, serene. She is at peace with the world.
But behind the mask, I can hear her breathing.

Blue was running into an issue caused by the two different versions of *LEER.* In California, during the time it had taken Blue to recreate a few of the pages, replacing black and white images for their color counterparts, John had rewritten several pages for the new graphic novel. The page numbers didn't always seem to match up with the action so it was a puzzle to reunite images with the associated text.

"I'm just going to have to add some text here and there to merge these stories into one," Blue said to himself as he mixed color pages with black and white and arranged them in an order he thought made sense. "Something simple like *meanwhile back in New York* should do the trick," he reasoned as he waited patiently for his 6100 Power Macintosh to load the enormous TIFF files into Photoshop 4.0.

"You have to learn to stop rushing through everything," Edgar Van told the boy patiently. "Oh, alright, just take a break, a short one, and don't

try to cram a whole day's worth of running into five minutes, Rachmaninov demands proper breathing."

The boy ran off as fast as his legs could carry him which was surprisingly fast considering his girth.

"The world continues to become smaller," Van ponders as he turns the globe with the hands of an artist, playing the topographical braille with his fingers as if stroking the strings of a harp. "My holdings become larger exponentially each day but what good does it do me when those who hear are not truly listening and those who do listen become that which I loathe most of all, the devoted."
"You were different, more capable, truly gifted and absolutely independent, but now you're gone."
"He's not going to let you leave here, y'know," the perfect little pretty in pink sister taunts the pudgy little superhero as he attempts his getaway.

"He can't catch me when I'm flying!" the boy responds as he rushes up to the balcony. Now he is free. He dashes up the stairs and leaps onto the railing, a risky move but when you possess his powers, it's easy. Faster and faster he runs along the rail until...

Falling is only a little different from flying really, one just bears a little more intent.

The boy falls helplessly toward the marble floor, too quickly for fear to overtake surprise.

"Joshua!," Van yells as he deftly grabs the large golden candlestick and hurls it in a single motion, like a javelin, toward the falling boy, and just as quickly as he fell, he is saved. The candlestick neatly pierced the fabric of his cape in precisely the right spot for Joshua to land with his sorry ass sitting directly in a rather large and surprisingly comfortable chair roughly two hundred years older than anyone he had ever known.

"So much for not being able to catch you," Joshua's sister Shannon remarked dryly as the boy sat dumbfounded, staring up at the candlestick which saved his life, embedded deep in the masterfully stained woodwork of the church.

Blue gathered all of the notes he could find, the early typewritten pages from John, and the artwork he had produced, even the rough sketches. There were a few gaps in the sequence, but one thing was becoming very clear. Arnold loved to party, was wild about Bea, and absolutely adored Edgar Van. Leer had something special going on, a sort of sixth sense and in Arnold's estimations was a little too serious, and Mona knew Leer. Blue was still trying to sort out how Catherine Kent fit in, but for the moment, he assumed she died seventeen years before the death of Arnold's father which meant that Arnold had now lost both his sister and his father and all he cared about was seeing the most "preshas" Edgar Van!

Blue decided that the best way to find the truth was to lay out everything, only then could the story rise up from the pages, only then could the secret of *LEER* be revealed.

"Traveling blind, just like Leer," Blue thought to himself. "Can't tell if I'm remembering or inventing at this point but I guess it doesn't matter much. After all, Leer is just a fictional character. John didn't really give me enough to go on except I know that Leer's arrival in New York is something of a homecoming. Guess we'll see what happens as we stumble through the dark together."

Blue decides to keep searching his studio for lost pages of text even while he realizes that twenty-five years can bury even the best of things pretty deep.

"The suitcase, if only I could find that old, brown, buckled suitcase. I kept everything in there, that and the travel bag. Never should have switched to boxes. Oh well, Welcome Home, Leer, let's see if we can figure out why you're here! And where the rest of you might be," Blue cries out as he holds up chosen pages from what he has already found.

Blue remembered working at the Mark Hopkins in San Francisco as well as at the Meridian in both Boston and SF, and the incredible haughtiness of the staff, especially the concierge in Boston. The thing that constantly amused Blue about working with those people is that they all had a certain shell of superiority about them. They were the finest in the hospitality industry. Nobody could compare with their impeccable presentation and sophistication, their refined sense of service. In short, nobody ran and got shit for you quite as nicely as they did. But just try to break in there. Try to become one of the elite if you were just a fine art grad from the Midwest capable of pronouncing about fifty words in any language other than English solely because you watched enough cartoons to pick up the exaggerated accent of a great French lover or a macho Spanish bullfighter from Mel Blanc. So, when it came time for a message to be delivered to our friend Leer, Blue had no trouble at all coming up with a suitable delivery scene. The concierge at Leer's hotel would be visited by three spirits. They all just happened to be in one body. The body of a clown. This clown was obnoxious, silly and a little spooky. He was a bit of a showboat, perhaps a trifle too rude toward the concierge, but he got the job done. He delivered a letter, special delivery for Leer.

Blue spent a couple of days looking for missing page sixteen and in the process waded through twenty-plus years of documents, photos and artwork ranging from brilliant to barely recognizable as coming from his own hand.

So, page sixteen of version "whatever" of Leer was lost and if it looked anything like page 28, no great loss. A bigger problem was staring Blue in the face. He had some nicely laid out pages with half-decent drawings going, but the supporting text was lost. Blue prided himself on keeping the most useless piles of trash with an unshakable commitment to the notion that he would one day spin them into gold. John's words were not trash, yet apparently, Blue had disposed of them somewhere between the East and West coasts of the USA, and he was in no position to panhandle the entire country. Pages seventeen through thirty shared similar characteristics to one another, they were drawn, to varying levels of completion but were essentially text free.
They remained that way...

Blue has been staring for days at the stack of pages for which John left him no text. He prefers to think about it that way, even though, somewhere in the back of Blue's mind, he realizes that he probably lost the text himself. He paces back and forth across his studio repeatedly and then it occurs to him, there is an old box tucked away in the old safe. The safe is a beautiful old metal safe with thick walls of steel and a variety of little compartments for storing little treasures. Nothing is truly safe in the safe. There is no door. The landlords left the safe in the studio because it was just too heavy to move, plain and simple. As Blue thinks again about the various ways they could have managed to bring the safe up to the fourth-floor studio, he searches all of her compartments for any missing pages, any scrap that might fill in the gaps in the story of Leer.

No luck.

He did find his autographed picture of Ann Margaret.

Blue had been a scenic painter on a movie she was in that was shot in his town many years back. He always thought that she was pretty hot while he was growing up but by the time he actually got to meet her, she was old. The funny thing about this particular moment is that Blue, standing in his studio, eyesight failing, knees creaking slightly, stood staring at the photograph of the actress and thought, "She actually is pretty damn hot!." He carefully placed her photo back into the drawer and continued looking for the missing pages.

Blue found another envelope from his old library job and opened it excitedly. There inside, he found several typed pages that had been missing. The text that had been written follows...

Four dead cats, impaled through their necks into fenceposts by the side of the road are silhouetted by the sunset. The television tells the tale.

"In local news, residents of the sleepy Long Island town of Greenbriar were at a loss to explain the grisly display found lining the highway yesterday morning. One local official, when asked to comment, noted that the number of dead cats--four--matched exactly the number of shopping days left until Christmas." On one of the posts, a note reads "You figure it out"

A television blasts the news in the "Home of the Immortal Beloved," an orphanage owned and operated by millionaire philanthropist Edgar Van... ""MUTE," the nation's radical anti-obscenity faction denied responsibility for the brutal act... But repeated their call for the arrest of Edgar Van" "KaaK" the television is turned off remotely by Mr. Van himself.

"Yo, Nuncle!" Arnold says as he pulls a primitive mask from in front of his face.

"No Picture, No Pleasure!"

"I try to limit the gore here." Van responds as he stands amidst a mass of children seated on the floor.

"No doubt, Uncle Edgar, but the mask--what a beast!"

"I told you," Edgar Van sternly responds, "the mask is off limits!"

"Yeah, well, y'know, I couldn't see any colors but it was still plenty bright."

Van holds a finger to his lips as he utters Arnolds name in an attempt to silence him.

"And I could see their hate, Nuncle, when they said your name."

"Arnold!" Van raises his voice and motions toward the door, "The angels?"

Arnold is working to open a crate while Edgar Van looks on. "You know sir, I'd like to stay on here after we've fixed up the chapel.

Van wonders, "And you're not going to your father's funeral?"

"I told you, Uncle Edgar, I don't fly. I don't even like standing on ladders. I especially won't fly to jungle land," Arnold takes a drag on his cigarette, "Not for some guy I only remember from newspapers." He takes another long draw on his smoke, "Ashes to ashes, y'know. Even fathers have to die."

Van reaches a hand toward Arnold and extinguishes the cigarette between his index finger and thumb with a squeeze. "You have a few things to learn Arnold. These are dangerous times. The mask, the children, we are all vulnerable."

"Right, Nuncle, Vulnerable."

"Your father's friend called again," Van calmly continues a subject he knows Arnold would rather avoid.

"Leer?" Arnold muses, "He's almost as whacked as the old man was."

"He's arranged to come to New York after the cremation." Edgar tells his nephew.

"What a picture that will be, eh Nuncle? Steamy jungle town. Blind man barbeques the corpse of ex-ambassador." Arnold holds the head of a statue of an angel and strikes a pose, as if in Hamlet, ""Alas, poor Arnold," my drawing

teacher says to me. "Your father was, in the end, a savage. You should be thankful Arnold, that from your father you will inherit nothing." But he gave me life, eh Nuncle? That'll be Leer's great wisdom for me. Nothing like a little pagan ritual to shed some light on things." Arnold laughs to himself as he sparks up his torch to mend the broken statue.

"December 24th, not yet morning. Camped in the shadow of Gunung Agung - bodies stir - the headman tells me, they're ready. All around me the trees resonate. Off right, a stream glows. Van Der Waals forces. Nothing really dies." Leer is extremely bright, but tormented.
"Rumors and superstition, I hear them from the Press, from the Governor, from the Board of Regents, There are rumors, Mr. Leer, that you haven't always been blind. You're a public figure, Leer, with nothing to hide. But we have no record of your childhood." He hears the voices of his past. "We've heard rumors that when you were seventeen...Accusations"

"My heart won't let me speak," Leer recalls, "with nothing to feed on, they become frantic," he reminds himself, "they scratch and slither like lizards in a bowl."

"The villagers have a custom. What to keep and what to burn. My oldest friend, William Kent.

But nothing really dies. Nineteen years ago, I saved her life. She stood there wet, coughed up by the ocean."

"Catherine Kent," she said.

"I watched her lips move. Then something about a light. She laughed – started to draw letters in the foam."

"Kent," she said. "K-E-N-T, now you'll never forget."

"Never." Leer reminds himself once again, "I rub at my eyes to wash away the oldest pictures. For seventeen years now, her spirit has followed me. Even here, to her father's burial." Leer takes a ring from his pinky finger. "What to keep and what to kill?

Drowned.

Nothing to burn. But she's dead just the same. An end to Catherine Kent

Today I bury both."

Blue finds more pages from a different time in the project, he wonders
if John meant it to truly represent another timeline...

"What I can say for sure these days
Wouldn't fill a shoebox.
The fear of it. Can't remember
what I -- my name. My name is Mona
Damino. I live in New York City."

"When Leer gets back I'm going to
charge him extra." Arnold says to himself " Noldo feeds his
cat, Noldo gets his mail, but
coming uptown before noon turns
Noldo's head to pudding.
Boy—o. Do my eyes deceive me?
Look here Angel."

"Insane. I'm not a killer, I'm just
out of my head. My name --
remember who I am." I am Mona.

"Van at the Garden! Such fine
stealables. We'll live like kings
tonight, my Love, and Leer be
damned."
Arnold fans himself with the tickets he has taken from Leer's mailbox.

"Oh Arnold. Van tickets!" Bea swoons.

"No rain, no snow —- unnatural.
World ready to crack from the cold.
The railing creaks and I swing my
head around, thinking that it's
Leer. Hunting me down.

Been running for too long, for all
of my life. Can't think, can't
forget. My name is Mona Damino."

"Christmas soon, eh Noldo?" Garry Nelson runs a newsstand,
Footsteps away from the busy subway.

"I'm feeling the Big Jolly already,

Sir Garr. Going to Madison Square
Garden to hear the pashon man.
Grief shall be ours, dear girl, for
robbing Leer blind. Noble and
joyous grief." Arnold and Bea are
intoxicated with anticipation.

Mona overhears Arnold in disbelief,
"I hear his name everywhere.
Hunting me down. Damn the fear of
it. Damn you, Leer."

Mona turns the corner as a street performer performs his version of a Smith's
tune, "Kindness is nice and kindness can stop you, from doing all the things in
life you'd like to..."

"How ya' doin' today go-jus?!" Another news vendor smiles as Mona picks up a
newspaper.

"So, ask me ask me ask me."

"Just makin' talk sister. Is that a crime now too?" the seller asks as Mona reads
the headlines...

Mute Declares War followed by Ex-Ambassador Kent's Death Causes Rift in
Already Unstable Foreign Relations

"Because, if it's not love, then it's the bomb that will bring us together."

Mona drops the paper back onto the top of the stack and the vendor is
disappointed on both counts. He decides to read the lead article.

By John Taylor, UPI
New York City. Today, Cornelia Pozer, National Director of Mothers Undoing
Teenage Excess, called for stronger measures to block the Edgar Van concert
scheduled for Christmas Day. Noting that "The cause is now in its eleventh
hour" with little chance of success in the courts, Pozer refused to rule out the
use of violence in pursuing the groups objective.
"Our children want to do what's right," said Pozer. "but with all his talk about
passion, he's tearing their heads apart [sic]. Our children get curious, and then
he's got them. But I will promise you that we will triumph. We will banish this
Pied Piper and he will never return."
Although the group claims to have wide support, sales of tickets to the concert
would indicate otherwise. In fact, since MUTE's most recent call to arms, sales

of all Van related items, both within the city as well as nationwide, have sky-
(cont. pg. 5A)

Meanwhile, in a record store across town, a woman asks for directions to Mr.
Edgar Van's music. The young man at the counter indicates an area by the
window where she can find the records if they are still in stock. She thanks the
young man graciously.
Her next action is to spray the entire display with a fire extinguisher, ruining the
display and forcing people out of the store. She is hauled away smiling by New
York's finest.

Back in Bali...

Leer nimbly races through the jungle,
A blind man with the skills of a ninja.
"The sky comes in
close. Heat like I've
never felt before,
hard to breathe.

Muscles fan out, pull
back, and I could just
as well be running at
the bottom of the
ocean.

Except for the sounds.
Drums bellowing out
from the crest of
Gunung Agung. The
tramp and pummel of a
hundred feet behind
me, branches lashing
back against arms and
wooden faces. Ahead,
the crashing of waves
where the jungle ends,
sweet song to a blind
man's ear. A place to
get to.

Run. Like I'm running
for my life.

*Bamboo resonates off
left. Here, than long
gone. Gecko lizard
rushes across my path.*

And then nothing.

*Almost nothing. Two
hydrogen, one oxygen.
Two to one.*

*Van der Waals forces.
Good enough for this
distance.*

*Two to one. More like
fifty to one. All the
faces of a lifetime,
features distorted by
time but pressing closer.
Familiar masks, bending
low and speaking in my
ear.*

*I take hold of the wooden
covering, tear away the
closest mask.*

*The memory
breathes out, thick and
hot. Living.
The face...
CRASH*

*The face is my own.
Swallowed up. That first
time -— when I was nine years old
death was as big as a whale*

*And icy cold. I
struggled, kicked against
the blackness, turned my
head looking for a window
or a door. The skates*

pulled me down.
My lungs emptied.
What left me then was the
illusion of life. Death
was more credible. I
opened my mouth and
sucked it in.

And now...
The carcass. Less than a
mile from this clearing
to the water.

They have a custom here.
A man dies and they bless
his body in smoke and
fire. Then they climb
Gunung Agung.

Down the slopes of the
volcano they run, through
the jungle to the sea.
Fast and reckless they
run, and the spirit of
the dead man runs with
them, refusing at first
to give up his place
among the living.

Defiance, though, can't
avert his fate. The
running and the drums
confuse him. He loses
his way in the jungle.

And only the living
seeing with their eyes
and listening with their
ears
can find their way back.

The drums. Bellowing out
a compromise. Peace for
the dead, life for the

living. Simple, serene.
She is at peace with the
world.

But behind the mask, I
can hear her breathing.

Seventeen years
since I saw her alive.

Seventeen years
since I saw anything at
all.

And suddenly nothing
seems right. As if the
dead
once lost and confused
have found their way
back." Leer senses far beyond his immediate surroundings.

Night soon, then the
dreams will start again.
Falling, down through
black sky, but I can't
turn over. Twist my head
to see, can feel the
earth rushing up to meet
me.

New name, new owners.
"Home of the Immortal Beloved"
Same rickety balcony.

I'm not a killer. Must
go back to where I buried
the truth. Take me back
to...

Yes?
Ah. You must be Ms.
Damino. I'm so glad to
meet you.

Welcome Home.

Outside of Madison Square Garden
A line of police, keeping
picketers at bay.
Arnold talking to Bea.

Up front, near the stage, he's
wide-eyed, wigged out with
excitement. You can see
some of the crowd, some of
the stage with Van and
silhouettes of musicians.

The crowd is
hooked.

Close up of Van
playing, looking powerful
and a little wild.

Arnold is really
worked up. Behind them,
the crowd starts to push
forward.

Now the crowd is really
pushing, Van working to a
climax, lasers, strange
lighting.

Glint of a knife, a masked
man.

"Inside the Garden, Bea-girl.
In front of Edgar Van God and
every Slack that knows a good
sound. This is how it was in the
beginning, Bea-love. Adam got
some tickets from a blind
man's mailbox, took his pearl-girl Eve, took
her to hear the Prince of
Majesty, the Fine Divine
The most preshas EDGAR VAN

To get me out of this Garden
now, my Pearl-Girl..."
"All the fairies in heaven..."
"Would have to drag me through
the gates..."

Blue assembles the pages and remembers. The timeline is all wrong. The first images he drew matched up to the text in the typed pages John had provided, but they didn't fit with the new storyline. Was Arnold Edgar Van's nephew or his greatest fan? Was John hinting at alternate timelines? And where was page sixteen?

Suddenly a wave of nausea overcame Blue. He began to sweat profusely even though the air in the studio was pleasant and cool. He became dizzy and suddenly went cold. He looked down at his hands which had turned blue. Blue doubled over in pain, his stomach on fire. He began to vomit. As he did, he distinctly heard the Beatles singing "Help." Blue caught a glimpse of himself in a mirror. He had turned blue all over. Blue stumbled backwards and fell into a work table. As he tried to hold himself up, he capsized a large cardboard box, spilling the contents upon himself. Books and papers poured out from the box, hitting Blue in the face. He was losing consciousness. At the precise moment that Blue's head hit the floor, Leer, page sixteen, fell upon him.

He instantly felt better. Blue recognized Mona in the opening panels. It was as if none of the nausea or even the complexion change had occurred, his head felt no pain, Blue was fine.

Blue was happy to discover that an old woodcut of Robert Fripp he created in college was also in the capsized box.

Blue was ecstatic that he had recovered the missing sixteenth page for a couple of reasons. Primarily, he was pleased to have discovered a black and white rendering that was at least similar to the original colored panels from the initial drawings and perhaps more importantly, he no longer felt like he was about to die. In fact, he felt exhilarated. Blue was fairly certain that Mona was the key to the "Leer" story as John had been writing it which meant that she couldn't be dead. He was so puzzled over the Mona Damino - Catherine Kent relationship that he had been immobilized when it came to drawing for the book. Now, he was certain that Mona was, in fact, Catherine returned. This did two things for Blue. It gave him a place to go back to and a means to move the story forward. Blue felt rejuvenated. He felt strangely healed and supported by the appearance of that sixteenth page, by Mona.

He couldn't seem to get the Beatles out of his head. For days he walked around humming "Help," "A Hard Day's Night" and "Across the Universe" over and over again with occasional meanderings into "Come Together" and countless other great Beatles tunes. Frankly, Blue was stunned that he actually knew so many Beatles tunes by heart. He had nearly forgotten all of the hours he spent as a child running over to the Codwalluper's house to listen to the Beatles, Stones, Beach Boys and the Kinks while dreaming of getting completely naked with Ginny Maplethorpe, Nathan Codwalluper's best friend. Nathan was George's brother. George was Blue's friend. Blue was pretty sure that Nathan was gay even though Blue didn't really understand "gay" very well back then and had no idea what a fag hag was, or how completely Ginny fit the MO.

The point is that Blue really knew an awful lot of Beatles tunes and spent a few days humming them and being an unabashed punster decided that the aural hallucination of the song "Help" during his near-death experience was an indication that he should include beetles in his book.

He had been assembling the second half of the book into its proper order ever since the vomiting episode. What Blue affectionately and privately referred to as his barfmitzvah. It would indeed prove to be a turning point in both the story and his own life.

The second half of the book was comprised predominantly of sketches. Some were so loose that he could barely remember what they were meant to depict, and even if he recognized the images, he was often clueless as to their meaning. For now, he had beetles.

Blue began drawing where page thirty left off. He hadn't filled in the missing text for half of the book, but he was pretty sure that he could double back and fill in the details. The only thing he had to do now was figure out a transition. "When in doubt, turn to the news," Blue jokes to himself as he draws another frame into an already overcrowded page, his usual uncontrollable impulse to decorate the page so the story it tells keeps telling long after the ride into the next scene.

This time the story is the bug bites, a sudden plague of bug bites popping up all over the city, causing itching like the poison oak which drove him insane in the days before the "madness."

The "madness" is any time between the current time and sometime in the past upon which Blue is willing to look at with esteem. Blue refers to the madness mostly as that period during which he has been guided or influenced by unseen forces telling, revealing or indicating to him in some way the proper path for him to follow, like the Mona incident, however, not all of the instances turn out so positively.

Blue begins to talk himself through another difficult moment. "So there's Van, Mona, Arnold, MUTE and the butler, I don't know if I'll ever get what was going on there, some chic who seems a bit uptight, the ominous butler, a horny teenager who might be dead, or was it the ever vigilant "Maintenance Man" who perished in the explosion?"

Blue snickers as he tries to make his drawing happen twice as fast as it normally takes. "People want results, masked men better fly!, thanks for that wisdom, Frank, and by the way, How's that lottery retirement plan working out for ya?" Blue sneered to himself.

"And forget about writing,' Frank continually said, "never make people read!"

"I guess he'd be pretty unhappy with me right now, eh Mr. Leer? Jackass was probably right though, after all, I'm the one crazy enough to be talking to a 20 year old recycled comic book character!" Blue smiles as he deftly adds another line from his 3B Prismacolor pencil to his awesome new page for "Leer."

7 NEW STUFF

Blue spent the next five minutes laughing to himself about how fucked up he is.

He had come to the realization that he had absolutely no clue why he was even born. His spent most of his time, of late, trying to convince his friends and himself that art is a calling as much as the priesthood or social work is a calling and that there is importance to even the most indefinable of motivations behind an aesthetic.

What made him laugh was that the very next action he took was to draw a superhero janitor who was really out to clean up the streets.

"Some calling."

Somewhere, in Blue's mind, there was a very sound reason for his creation, "Maintenance Man," to make an appearance in a totally unrelated story he had started more than twenty-five years before.

He decided it was best to stick to the work at hand, and for the moment, that was Leer.

The longer Blue thought about the various parts comprising his life's oeuvre, the more sense it all seemed to make and the less chance he had of explaining it to anyone else.

A wise friend of his once told him that it wasn't his job to do that. "You can only be responsible for yourself. Create the work that you feel is right for you to create at the time that you are creating it and it will be right for the path that you are on. You cannot control how others view your path any more than you can control the path of others."

Blue's friend William always said things that seemed so patently obvious that it made Blue ill but were so brilliantly and appropriately timed that it made Blue's skin tingle.

Blue continued drawing, starting the next page with the punctured skin of a patient, wounded by the beetle plague. He was about to breathe life into a character he hadn't drawn in years. He began with a note about the setting.

"Can't Buy Me Love," by the Beatles is muzaking its way through a hospital in Minneapolis.

Blue drew a pretty, young nurse.

"I hate the Beatles," Tonya is a late-night nurse, she is tearing off strips of sheet fabric to fashion a bandage, the hospital ran out, too many beetles, too many bites, not enough bandages, "can't buy me love?! Bullshit!," she flirts with the patient who she clearly thinks is cute, wealthy or both, "You can buy me love anytime! New dress, new shoes, a handbag, diamonds, pearls, a shiny new car, and travel, first-class, any place in the world my precious little heart desires." She pouts, "them stupid Beatles! No wonder I never get what I want!"

"Don't blame the Beatles," Leer says as he enters the room and walks toward Tonya. Leer stops in his tracks, sensing another presence. "Oh shit. It's you!" Leer turns, smacking his forehead in amazement pointing straight above his head.

"Blue!" Leer shouts.

"Keep drawing! No Matter what, keep drawing," Leer asks, demands, expects, "Oh and, sorry about the house, it really won't matter in the end, or the beginning for that matter."

Blue continued drawing Leer, unsure if he was hallucinating, had fallen asleep at the drawing board or simply died. He tried to remember how much water he had to drink that day. The studio could get pretty damn hot. Still, he couldn't get over the fact that a character in his book was just talking to him, so he decided to listen to Leer and continued drawing.

8 TRANSITION

"Ahhh... It's funny when you try to explain an inexplicable thing, at least by human standards this can't be explained. Anyway, good to see you Blue." Leer said as he climbed out of the frame right as Blue put the finishing touches on his sunglasses. "Nice touch, by the way, Blue," Leer smirks as he pulls the glasses off. "That whole blind superhero thing works well in the comics, but you know as well as I do that I see as well as you do, maybe better!"

"Holy shit!," vomits Blue. "John, John Tanner? Fuck man! I thought you were dead...or corporate! "Blue stands in disbelief for a moment, "DUDE! It is SO FUCKIN' COOL to see you. What the hell, man? You just walked out of this fuckin' comic that I...me - I - just finished DRAWING!" Blue stutters-shouts-explodes in disbelief.

Then he drops to the floor and pleads, "If I draw a new iPad in your hand will it really be there, and perhaps more importantly, will all of the available apps be preloaded? No seriously, this calls for a celebration, how about I draw a six-pack, chilled to perfection. Damn, I have absolutely nothing to offer you, I mean you just crawled out of paper you must be parchment, parched I meant." Blue laughs to himself.

Leer smiles, "Actually," he confides, "we aren't staying."

"We? Who's We? - You and me?" Blue asks cautiously.

"Yeah," Leer laughs and in a single motion puts his sunglasses back on and grabs Blue by the shoulder, pulling him back from an infinite drop, as a star cruiser obliterates Blue's house and everything in it except for the small patch of floor which Blue and Leer still occupy. It was as if the entire house exploded on impact leaving only enough of the structure to keep Blue and Leer from falling. In fact, it was so sudden that Blue didn't even feel it. What he did feel was the cruiser, inches away from his face, radiating an intense energy.

Blue reached up to the cruiser and gently placed his fingers upon the hull of the ship. The surface seemed to silently hum, buzzing rapidly like the vibrator Blue found under the bathroom sink just days after his sister Lisa returned from her "Girl Scout" camping trip.

Frank never seemed to put together the fact that Lisa continued to go on "Girl Scout" camping trips all the way through college and never once received a merit badge. What she did do was use every penny that Frank ever earned in any way she pleased right up until the day that Blue moved out.

She probably continued to do so but Blue never bothered to find out.

In fact, the only thing larger than Blue's disregard for the father and sister he left behind was this cruiser. It was so large that at least a hundred thousand mobile homes could perform parking ramp ballet maneuvers for a week, inside of it, and never recognize a single turn. Blue knew very little about mobile homes and even less about parking ramp ballet. What Blue did know about mobile homes is that many of them are actually quite luxurious. This he learned from a photographer friend who currently resides in a Trekkie commune somewhere in the Badlands of South Dakota.

"Watch your step" Leer smiles as a sliding door suddenly materializes and slides open in front of Blue.

Blue steps forward, banging directly into the side of the ship.

The door laughs. "Okay, sor-r-r-ry," says the door," c'mon in," suddenly the door appears and slides open again.

Just as suddenly, and completely pissed off, Blue marches directly into the side of the ship.

The door laughs again.
Blue is furious. He looks in the direction of the laughter and says, "Fine, I don't have to go anywhere. I am probably just dreaming anyway, so I will just stay right here, in my broken home and wait until you go away and I wake up!"

The door giggles.

Leer clears his throat, loudly. "Sorry Mr. Leer," the door opens, continuing, "safe passage to all who enter through this door, guaranteed by All That Is."

"See Blue, it's like the man says, sure hope Moses knows his roses." Leer shouts," Thank you kindly angel Gabriel!" Then the two men step into what can only be described as a black hole of doom where everything gets sucked into the void.

A constant feeling of falling accompanied by the urge to vomit and an insatiable hunger. Blackness, seemingly endless blackness filled with nothing but hunger. For days upon days, a light-less drop through empty space with an empty stomach, in silence.

"Hey," whispers Leer into Blue's ear, "how's your head?"

"My head?," asks Blue.

"Yeah, well it looks different," adds Leer.

"What do you mean different?," Blue asks, suddenly realizing that he is no longer hungry.

"You don't have a nose," Leer responds.

"What?" Blue puzzles.

"You don't have a nose" Leer responds again.

"What do you mean I don't have a nose? I can smell you for cryin' out loud!," Blue nervously snaps.

Leer holds up a small mirror to Blue.

"Man!," Blue exclaims, "I look pretty good as an emoji!"

Leer and Blue experience a series of physical changes in rapid time.

"This is a little hard to grasp at first but all you have to do is go along with everything that happens to you." Leer laughs as he becomes a serpentine creature, part dragon, part sea serpent who dives in and out of the water pulling Blue at breakneck speed toward a volcanic island looming in a pitch-black sea. Blue is on Leer's back, riding his serpent companion like a horse.

"I can tell I'm really in for it now, Leer." Blue shouts to a silent Leer. The transformation is complete for him. He has become the serpent.

Blue barely squeezes a breath in before the serpentine Leer dives deep, deeper than any ordinary man would dare to dive. Fortunately, Blue is no ordinary man. In fact, he is no longer a man at all. The ancient folk called them Avastrana, "of the water" for lack of a better translation - Blue had become the translation, part sea creature, part ninja warrior.

He moved with the serpent as if it were an extension of himself, guiding it with a tight grip on Leer's gills which turned out from the corners of the serpent's mouth which was huge, open and feeding on the thousands of smaller fish which had grouped in the deepest part of this undersea ravine where the pair glided through the icy waters as if they had been doing so all their lives. Blue heeded Leer's advice and trusted his instinct to let the sea creature, who had moments earlier been his friend, feed. In his bones, or whatever they had become, he felt an overwhelming certainty that the bond he shared with the serpent was critical to his own survival, as he felt this, the gills wrapped gently around his forearms, becoming a second skin. Now rider and serpent were one.

Together, the companions raced through the open sea, covering an incalculable amount of distance in a seemingly insignificant length of time.

Just as suddenly, they were swimming through a tunneled maze, so narrow Blue could feel the walls brush against his back, his head tucked in so close to the serpent that he could hear its breath more clearly than he could hear the water rushing past his ears. They reached an opening in the maze. In front of, and above them, were numerous tunnel entrances. They were surrounded by sheer rock walls, above them only blackness. A blackness filled with giant worms. From each of the tunnels, converging on the central shaft that Blue and Leer managed to find in the seemingly endless maze, emerged giant worms. Unlike a common nightcrawler, these worms had big, lifeless eyes and mouths full of razor-sharp teeth. Suddenly the worms oozed from the tunnels, hurling themselves toward Blue and Leer.

Blue arched backward, his feet and lower legs, already entwined with the skin of the serpent. He stretched fully backward, then snapped forward instantly like the spark from a match bursting into flame. His head swung forward as his arms, now glowing, flared forward, bringing with them pure energy that rolled from his joints, through his limbs and out the tips of his fingers, searing liquid laser light. Blue and Leer spun upward, a relentless, twirling rocket of light, slicing through miles of underwater shafts, presumably leading upward while becoming increasingly redundant. Another attack from three sides, then four, then five.

"Why not thirty?" Blue thought, he could just as easily slice through a hundred gummy attacks. "This has to end," Blue thought to himself again but felt that Leer agreed, unspoken, still strongly entwined, swimming forcefully onward.

Blue thought for all of one moment.

Differently.

Blue thought radically differently from the thinking it took to remain doing what he was doing. He thought radically differently from the way he ever would have thought before and stepped off of Leer's back. Without thinking as radically differently as Blue was thinking, it would be impossible to understand what stepping off meant at that exact point in time.

Fortunately, Leer knew exactly what it meant to think radically differently and was not the least bit surprised that Blue had decided to do so at that moment. He was no more surprised at Blue's decision than he was by the fact that he, himself, was wildly popular in Affergarten. Leer wasn't particularly surprised to be wildly popular anywhere since he could speak nearly every language known to man, and a few unknown to man, had the uncanny ability to define precisely the last hue you had envisioned, or might envision if asked, and his hair was pure white. Absolutely white. Sometimes these things don't come across too well in comic books, but his hair was brilliant white. It was so white that you would have to add white to the white paper to make it white enough if you were trying to draw a picture of Leer for a friend.

White.
We have already established the whiteness of Leer's hair. But let's take a moment to examine the whiteness of Leer's face, and Blue's for that matter. First, we must take a step backward. Or, rather, sideward, which is exactly what Leer did at precisely the right moment because that is what Blue did, making it essential that Leer did the same. Leer performed the action with a grace that can only be described as thoroughly graceful. If he had done it any other way he would have ended up dead.

"You look positively dead!," Blue laughed, "white as a ghost."

"So do you," replied Leer as both men disembarked the star cruiser, gracefully, nonchalantly sidestepping their way off the ship and onto the "deck" which was still the remnant of Blue's house, as the cruiser continued its journey at the speed of light without so much as slowing down even just a little to let them off.
"Happens every time," yawned Leer, stumbling yet unfazed by the abrupt exit. "The color will come back in no time. The yawning helps with the exit adjustment. Have you seen enough?"

"No," Blue quietly responded, "just thinking," his breathing as regular as ever. Then he reached up his hand. Blue was quickly ripped off his broken floor by a goozlesnorp, a surprisingly majestic bird-fish-lady, whose body was part woman, part fish, and, yes, part bird. As she pulled him from the platform, Blue reached down with his other hand and snatched Leer by the back of his shirt, at once lifting him from the floor and swinging him up onto the back of the goozlesnorp. She flew synchronously to the will of Blue who was catapulted by the combined motion of Leer and the flight path of the goozlesnorp to her back. The bird-fish-lady, Leer and Blue relaxed into one being, gliding upon the air, high among the clouds.

Neither Blue nor Leer could tell you precisely how long it took to lose all sense of time, motion, thought, physical existence or feeling. What they could tell you is that time seemed endless. Well, endless aside from one fact. It was over within the blink of an eye.

When asked about this very moment at a moment some considerable time later, or perhaps before, during the Third Tribunal of Intergalactic Shit or TOIS, pronounced [toiz] both men testified in exactly the same manner. "I closed my eyes, no, actually, I blinked, yes, I blinked, and when I opened my eyes..."

The Tribunal only gets together when a human exceeds expectations after discovering its power.

It has only happened two other times, which is irrelevant because only humans bother to consider time to be of any great importance. They only bothered to name the tribunal the Third Tribunal of Intergalactic Shit because humans seemed to need it to be named the first time it happened, which is also irrelevant, or more precisely, incorrect. In fact, the TOIS only happened or will ever happen three times in the history of everything. But even that is immaterial because incidents in the actual universe, not the one humans understand, are timeless. They exist in and of themselves, rather than as a part of something in particular, such as a lifetime, or a planet's history. Even the name of the tribunal itself is something of a universal joke since a tribunal is purely a human concoction. Still, it sounds official to a race where words are still something of importance.

The "third" tribunal was initiated and conducted by a Fanderstan by the name of Nertz, an amoeba of radiant energy with an afro of cosmic jellybeans at its core. The tribunal was broadcast throughout the entire universe instantly, telepathically, in human terms, that is. The fact is that humans can't comprehend what was broadcast instantly. There is no human word for it and if there was one, no human could speak it. Nertz was conducting the tribunal on behalf of a great many other "beings" throughout the universe that became interested in Blue due to a specific instance.

Blue had been expected to guide Leer.
Blue had, in fact, done precisely that.
But Blue had done it in his own way.

The beings that felt a need for the tribunal were accustomed to knowing everything that a human would do, well in advance of it being done. They had seen evolutions of grand scope in human terms that barely made them notice but what Blue was capable of was new for a human, especially for his first day of "discovery."
Nertz would bring up this day a total of 517 times during the tribunal to see if the stories would change. Leer and Blue continued to recount the occurrences of the day in the exact same way but neither one of them could explain why things happened as they did.

Nertz finally determined that it was not his job to figure it out either. He was simply leading the tribunal in an effort to reveal how Blue had managed to do what he had done and to determine whether or not he might ever do it again. This was the part that the other beings found most disconcerting. What happened during that blink of an eye would determine the fate of a society.

9 RESURRECTION

"Hey Bmphf, grrmp, gmmn, mmnnn, ahh,HEY, Biwwy!" Mike Masterson finally bellowed past the triple-decker submarine he was forcibly sinking with both hands somewhere off the coast of gluttony, his large but lagging maw unable to keep pace with his insatiable zeal for cold cuts slathered in ultra-sauce, thousand island dressing supercharged with high-fructose corn syrup and some unspellable chemical that, while legal, left nicotine back in kindergarten at addiction school. "Biwwy, we're on the news!" Officer Masterson loved to sit in his squad car with the radio tuned to the local news, hoping to "catch himself" on the sight of the latest breaking story. Lieutenant Billy Hurst rarely got in on the act, but he jumped into the passenger seat of the squad car because today's crime scene was different.

Masterson could barely reach the knob past his lunch bag, pinned between his belly and the steering wheel. He turned up the volume, ."..and now, apparently, both men are dead. The initial report attributes the deaths to gangland violence. Police and fire vehicles surround the ambulances, now hearses at the sight of this grizzly double homicide. The paramedics worked as though their very lives depended upon saving the two slain gang bosses, and that may not be very far from the truth. Tommy Levito and Victor Alonso controlled nearly every illegal operation in the city and owned, controlled or persuaded more than half of the city's legal enterprises. Medical crews pronounced the rivals dead only moments ago and have just closed the doors on the lives of both men for whom the only certain future is a five minute trip to the city morgue."

"By Farb," both officers reverently added as they bowed their heads, "Course I doubt he'll have much use for them," Masterson chuckled as both men eyed the ambulances as if even their futures were inextricably linked the lifeless cargo inside. Masterson turned off the radio, one hand on the knob, the other on his sub.

Suddenly, the rear doors on both ambulances burst open from inside. Tommy Levito and Victor Alonso jump down from the back of the vehicles and survey the crowd of police and fireman, gangsters, pimps, hookers, junkies, skateboarders and librarians all assembled for the spectacle, nearly every single one of them breathless and all of them stunned.

Leer was entirely drenched in blood from the nose down and Blue had a hole in his gut the size of a grapefruit.
The two men looked at one another and smiled.
Tommy's hole closed itself instantly and only Victor's clothes revealed any sign of injury. Both men turned toward the crowd which remained silently in a state of shock. Blue began to snicker, then Leer quietly laughed to himself. The laughter of Tommy and Victor grew until both men were nearly in tears. Within a minute the entire population on the scene was laughing along, whether out of nervousness, relief or sheer infectious joy.
Tommy and Victor stood within a couple of feet of one another. No one had budged in the last several minutes after the laughter subsided. A feeling of wonder hung in the air, but it felt like wonder that had been rained heavily upon and was hungry and confused. Leer and Blue had begun to understand that they were important men, or rather Victor and Tommy were, and the sense that everyone was watching to see what their next move was going to be was palpable. Actually, Blue and Leer didn't even know their own names at this point to say nothing of the fact that they had no understanding of how the men, whose bodies they now stood in, died. Leer had jumped a couple of times before but never by goozlesnorp and never into someone else's deceased body, and Blue was still half expecting Glurp to show up.

Instead, a woman walked toward them from the front line of the crowd which was still fanned out, motionless around them, satisfied to spectate as she walked with determination toward the risen pair. As soon as she drew near enough to be seen clearly, both men instantly recognized her. Blue turned to look at Leer who returned the gaze with an expression which told Blue that she was, in fact, the spitting image of Mona Damino, or Catherine Kent, but she looked different, both in attire and demeanor. Now, was clearly not going to be the right time to clear up the little Mona vs Catherine mystery. In fact, this only added complexity to it.

"Well, I am going to have to have this thing checked out, the woman said as she played with her firearm, surveying it, then eyeing up Blue's gut. She looked a little too much like Siouxsie Sioux for either Blue or Leer to handle without a slight bit of laughter, only she thought they were laughing at her joke about the piece. She was cocky, forceful and outrageously sexy, if not intimidating, particularly to Blue as she stepped in close and in a single motion nuzzled the barrel of her firearm up under his chin while pulling Leer in close, grabbing his shirt and clenching it into her fist. "Did you guys forget you hate each other?" She eased her grip on Victor as if checking herself. It didn't take long for Leer to sense the situation. He knew that he, Victor, was one of the two men in charge, leaving Blue, or Tommy, to be the other and for the moment at least, hot little "Siouxsie" was on his side. Leer took a chance on his read and putting one hand on her shoulder stepped in to gently but firmly push her gun hand down, away from Blue's chin. "Hey now, easy does it, nobody should have to die more than once in a day, not even him." Leer safely suggested.
He was as much saving Blue as he was trying to leave the conversation open, for information seeking purposes. It worked.
"I just can't believe you don't want me to plug Tommy again for you, Victor, and we even have the stiff shuttle handy to cart his ass away," the woman added with a disdainful look at Blue.

She was still trying to sort out her feelings about what had just happened by doing the thing that came easiest to her, swinging her gun around and threatening somebody.
Everyone in the crowd had just watched as Tommy Levito and Victor Alonso fought hand to hand for three hours - Actually Tommy mercilessly beat Victor to a pulp because Tommy was that much better a fighter, yet Victor refused to go down. Max, the hot Siouxsie look-alike couldn't bear it any longer, so she blasted a hole in Tommy's stomach, the size of a grapefruit. Tommy hit the pavement just as Victor keeled over. Both men were dead. Everyone was stunned.
At the moment of their deaths, everything changed. Nothing was certain. The cops didn't know what to do because half of them got regular dough from one of the stiffs on the ground, if not both. The crowd volleyed stares across to one another trying to gauge their next

move. The crony volleyball tournament ended before it began however as neither side could figure out who would serve. The captains were gone. The bosses were dead. Both stiffs were in the ambulances before anyone knew what hit them. As the crowd began to realize that Tommy and Victor were dead the faintest breath of hope seemed to sigh its way through the crowd of cops and cronies. For a moment, Max thought about running. She could just go. She could live in a small town, no more Victor, no more guns - Freedom.

But now, here she was again, ready to blast another hole, ready to do whatever Victor wanted.

"Maxie!, darlin', angel of my dreams," drooled old Petey McGoogle as he sauntered up behind the woman with the gun.

"Max! McGoogle, my name is Max!" she replied as she shoved her gun directly up under his balls.

"All right. all right, Max, I beg your pardon, Max, for Farb's sake, no reason to go off halfcocked," the old letch grinned mischievously. "It's nice to see you hangin' with the boys, always knew you'd take up with one of 'em, kinda thought it would be Tommy, not Victor. Funny how life plays tricks on ya' ain't it sugar?" McGoogle kept rambling despite the razor-sharp glare Max was burning back, directly into his, droopy, drunken looking eyes. " 'Course you couldn't have a piece of Tommy even if you wanted him now could ya, 'siderin' the old family history and all, too many of your relatives' relatives got a thing against Tommy's great, great somethin' or another, ain't that right?"

Max continued glaring at McGoogle, but he had hit upon a truth that only she knew. She had always wanted Tommy. Sure, she was Victor's girl, but the dirty old coot was right, she would have been all over Tommy if there hadn't been the bad blood between the families. This was Rat Town and things seemed to hang in Rat Town like a bad odor. Plus, it turns out that anything that ever happened in Rat Town, McGoogle either knew about it, heard about it, knew it was coming, was there, or caused it. So McGoogle spent most of his time talking about whatever he knew was going to cause the biggest headache for everyone around him because that's how he got his kicks.

"So, as I was sayin' seems Tommy's great, great somethin' or another, well he offed, sweet little Maxie's, "Cah-Humm," pardon me, Max's great, great somethin' or another over Tommy's great, great somethin' else, if you savvy the sadness, so he's kinda like your brother, ain't he hot rocket?"

This time Max gets in real close with her whole body, so close it excites the old man until he feels the steel of her blade pressed tight up against his jugular.

McGoogle laughs his lowest laugh which is still an octave too high for manly and looks up over her shoulder saying, "Ah, to die with you would be orgasmic, you pretty little witch!"

Without turning her head, Max knew what he was getting at, "You must mean Bitch, because I get the distinct impression that you brought yours. Her eyes still glued to McGoogle, she relaxes her grip upon the knife and eases it away from McGoogle's throat, saying, "Hello Krunk, how's the weather up there big fella?" Krunk is perhaps the single most lovable bad guy imaginable. He is about twelve feet tall and looks like a toddler's toy. His massive hands can pound just about anything to rubble and he eats nearly anything. In fact, he will eat anything and will do whatever McGoogle tells him to do. Max knew this about Krunk and slowly stepped away from McGoogle.
"Looks like you're going to have to find a little snack elsewhere, M'bucko," McGoogle says as he pats Krunk about thigh high, "One time he ate three different women for me. They just wouldn't cooperate. The fourth one finally agreed that I WAS the guy she was planning to meet at the airport for a little "layover." Turns out, she decided to stick around long enough to pop out a few mini McGoogles before Krunk finally did eat her. Never dawned on me 'til then that Krunk might have a problem detecting sarcasm. Still, I been thinkin' it might not be a bad idea to start me another family," McGoogle salivates in Max's direction. Blue is just disgusted by McGoogle, so he steps in between Krunk, McGoogle and Max with a peremptory "How's it goin' Krunk, McGoogle, came to see the show?" Krunk towered over them, his eyes fixed on Max, his face puppy-like and smiling in a relieved, I don't have to eat you smile.

"So you're not really dead, 'eh Tommy boy?," quipped McGoogle, "and by the look of things, you seem to be steppin' up to protect and serve the very witch who blasted a hole in you less than an hour ago!"

Tommy laughed then spoke with a firm tone in his voice, "Look, I'm not exactly sure what just happened, but I am pretty damn sure that there is not a thing that you can do to me that is any worse, no offense Krunk. Now Victor and I have some serious talking to do - ain't that right Victor?"

Leer moved his eyes upward from surveying the body he is in as it transformed from badly beaten to perfectly healthy and replied, "apparently, we do."

"Max, I didn't kill your great, great somethin' or another, but you DID kill me. It just didn't work. So, that makes us even," Tommy smiles as he turns to Victor and puts his arm around him like the two of them were old friends, walking off to share a secret, which they were, it's just that nobody else knew it.

So much for freedom, Max thought to herself. Now she was really in love. She blasted a Farb-Damn hole in him and he smiles and calls it even. What the Fuck got into Tommy and how was she going to get her hands on some. Better yet, wrap her legs around some. She wanted him inside of her - her thoughts - her feelings - her every minute, but there was no way in varst that she was going to let him know it.

"Krunk very happy he no have to squash and eat lady Max!" Krunk nervously approached with something very tiny, barely held between his huge fingers. It was a little black ponytail holder. Max casually removed it from Krunk's massive hand and tied up her hair. "Thanks, big boy, she winked, then spun her way toward the cops who had bleachered themselves on their squad cars with oversized submarine sandwiches and energy drinks.

Max zeroed in on Colin Dugan, a skinny young cop who reminded her of a ferret. He had spent a little too much time getting into her business of late and she couldn't pass up the opportunity to amuse herself. "So, Colin, you gotta be shittin' your pants right now. The two of them actually talking?! She struts in close and whispers in his ear, "Probably about YOU!"
"Okay Leer, where are we?" Blue whispered even though the two men were clear across the way from anyone who might give a damn and

even further away from those who didn't, considering half of Rat Town showed up minutes after the tenderizing process had begun on Victor's face.

"Hang on Blue," Leer interrupted, punctuating the disruption with the barrel of small pistol he found in his pocket, "I suggest you quickly pull out that piece that's hanging off your hip and put it to my head." If anyone had been watching closely enough they would have seen that Victor clearly had the drop on Tommy but Blue recovered quickly enough to make a good show of it to the casual observer, which is all who were left watching. Anyone who really cared was too busy trying to find the right person to talk to, the right thing to talk about and the right attitude to bring to the conversation. Everyone was startled at the resurrection, bewildered by the laughter and perplexed at the vision of Tommy and Victor walking off like old friends. What they were seeing now was more like it. Tommy and Victor, guns to each other's heads, talking about God knows what. Correction, Farb knows what.

"And what the hell are we doing here?" Blue continued.

"I have no idea, Blue," Leer confided, "Actually, no one does. I mean, seriously, when you start making these jumps you can't control it, schedule it, make a reservation or even entertain the thought of guiding your journey in any appreciable way, UNLESS you are a Quanji, which I am not, Leer pauses...but I think you might be."

"What's a Quanji, "Blue asked as he pushed the barrel of his gun harder into Leer's temple.

"Look Blue, I appreciate your enthusiastic performance but the gun is real. If you shoot me here, I'll be just as dead as anywhere else, so let's put them down. I think we've got them snowed." Both men tuck their guns away and the crowd relaxes once again.
No one wanted to make the wrong move, so people decided to leave the area.
"A Quanji is what the Dolmari call the navigators or drivers. The Dolmari are your spirit guides, and yes, you have them whether you believe in them or not. Of course, they can't do much for you if you choose not to believe, but given the circumstances, you'd better start believing, and fast," Leer urged as Blue tried to figure out just how much of this he was

willing to swallow.

"Why don't we just hop onto another Goozlesnorp, all I had to do was just hold up my hand like thi..." Blue said as he raised his hand. Leer quickly pulled it down then followed through with a headlock instructing Blue against such behavior, "You don't want to do that, Blue, the places that you end up in can get pretty bizarre when you continue to wing it without a specific destination, Quanji or not!"
Blue didn't know how to tell Leer that he was having strange feelings, from the moment Leer arrived, that the two of them had a destiny to fulfill, but not as themselves.

"So what the hell are we supposed to do now, John? Leer? Victor? SHIT! I don't even know what to call you!" Blue stood up to Tommy's full height, his frustration boiling over inside his muscular build. Victor's headlock snapped open like a little pistachio shell, dropping Leer to the ground. "Don't call me anything if you can help it," Leer suggested as he lifted himself back up to standing. "Call me whatever your thugs call me but play it cool as long as possible. We have no idea what sort of shit these guys were into. Bad enough to get them killed at least. Besides, I can't get over how much Max reminds me of Catherine. If we get through this I can tell you all about Catherine, Mona, even old Edgar Van but for now, we've got enough to handle right here. Anyway, you'll catch onto this parallel universe thing before you know it, especially if you are a Quanji."

Blue was pretty certain that he had become a Quanji, he just wasn't entirely sure that he wanted to be one. Even though he felt completely drawn to this body, he was having trouble accepting that he was going to have to live in it.

"How are we supposed to figure that out if I'm a Quanji if you won't let me put my hand up? Blue quipped, "I've got a destination in mind right now - My Time, My Planet, My Home!"
"It won't work," Leer replied dryly, "Quanjis can't guide themselves, only others."

"Fine, I'll guide you to my bed. I've got a king-size mattress with clean sheets and I'll take the couch. Now can I put my hand up?" Blue pleaded.

"Same old Blue," Leer smiled, "nice try, but I've been searching for a Quanji for over twenty-five years now. If you're mine, then you already know where I'm going, intuitively. If not, you're either not my Quanji or you're not a very good one. No offense."

Blue moved in on top of Leer's toes and bent in low so his nose pressed down on Leer's nose as he whispered gruffly, "Well it doesn't take a Quanji to know that you don't want to spend the rest of your life as a balding Italian with horrible taste in clothing, too much jewelry and a homicidal girlfriend."

"Actually, this is a pretty nice watch," Leer replied as he thrusted his wrist up between their two noses forcing Blue back enough that he was able to step out from under Blue's feet. "Besides, it says it's dinner time and judging by the hole in your stomach, you gotta be pretty hungry!"

"Very funny, but you know, you are right. Perhaps it is you who is the Quanji, you who can see the destination," Blue laughed as he looked in his pocket for money. "Holy shit!" he exclaimed as he pulled out a billfold stacked with bills bearing the number 100 and the face of a man he had never seen before. Inscribed upon a scroll graphic within the design of the bill are the words "Together We Stand, One People, One Homeland" He held the bill up for Leer to see saying, "Maybe you're not Italian."

"This could get very interesting," Leer mused as he turned toward the crowd which was considerably smaller now, roughly three hundred feet away. "Max," he yelled, "Come over here, and tell the rest of the guys we'll meet up later." I have an idea, he whispered to Blue. "We need to get some understanding about who we are and what's going on around here, so we might as well use my homicidal girlfriend."

"Max," Leer grinned as he put his arm around her, "Tommy here gets the impression that you don't like him. I don't know if it's the hole you shot in his guts that's mixing him all up or if he's just a little dazed from hunger. So, why don't you buy us all a little dinner. You see, while I was dying a short time ago, a thought came to me, an epiphany, a new direction."

Max scowled at Victor then ranted," A new direction? An epiphany?

Dinner with Tommy? Have you lost your mind? What do you think my dad is going to say about this?" Max barely caught her breath, "and DYING? Victor, you weren't dying, you were dead. Your skin was already cold. I felt it with my own hands! Now, you come back from the dead AND you suddenly want to play nicey-nice with Tommy Levito? You expect me to accept that? AND you want me to buy you guys dinner? I ought to plug both of you right now! Max reached down for her gun but Leer's hand was already between her legs, where she kept her weapon. He had the piece, barrel to her crotch. She tensed up and reached out for his throat with her blade, as she did, she noticed that Victor's other hand was holding his own gun to her temple. Her eyes rolled silently skyward in resignation. She dropped her arms and her mouth turned to a pout.

"Max, c'mon now, I know it's hard to accept that I'm standing here, alive, in front of you, without a scar on me after the final beating of my life, but isn't it easier to accept than an early grave for yourself? Besides, I wouldn't want to waste such a lovely girl over a little misunderstanding." Leer said as calmly as he thought Victor could.

Max reluctantly softened and with quiet sarcasm replied, "Misunderstanding? Is that what you call simultaneous resurrections - a misunderstanding?"

"It's OK, relax," said Victor as he lowered his gun and gently placed her gun back into the holster between her legs. "C'mon, let's eat." Mickey's Diner in Rat Town is about as true to the definition of a greasy spoon railway car diner as any diner could be in this or any universe, parallel or otherwise. So, it came as no surprise to Leer that the first words out of Max's mouth were, "Victor, I keep telling you that stuff is going to kill you!" when he ordered the blue plate special - double cheeseburger with bacon, fried onions and mushrooms, devoid of vegetation and splattered with two heaping tablespoons of mayo, served with a fat garlic dill pickle and a combo basket of fries, onion rings and fried cheese curds on the side. This was a real shocker to Blue, who had always known John to be a vegetarian. His confusion nearly caused him to blurt out something that would have exposed them as someone other than who they claimed to be, but he held his tongue. Instead, he set out to find clues upon his plate as to why his order was referred to as chicken fried steak. As he did so, Max confessed that she always got "wicked hungry" after she plugged somebody because it tended to rattle her nerves a bit, but that this time she was going to have to be excused, forgiven, or just plain tolerated, for proceeding to devour two full-sized racks of ribs because the guy she just plugged had only seconds earlier asked her to pass the salt.

In the silence that followed, Victor quietly urged Max to refrain from mentioning death by cheeseburger ever again reminding her that he had just risen from the dead. Saying something to the effect of "Hey Max, just lay off about the cheeseburger, I've already been beaten to death and I think I can safely say that I'd rather die of a heart attack."

"Pounded" Tommy listlessly added - Max and Victor looked at him with surprise.

"Flattened" he added, oblivious to the stares now coming from Max and Victor.

"Look," Victor interjected "it's bad enough you beat me to death, you gotta insult me?"

"What?" Tommy snapped out of his trance "huh, no, not you, the meat, it's flat, pulverized, I mean I can't even recognize it, sirloin, round steak, flank steak, eh, whatever, it's actually pretty tasty!" Blue ate with conviction while Leer attempted surreptitiously get a handle on Rat Town by playing on Max's obvious need for attention.
"So, Max, enlighten me, how are we going to make Tommy Boy here work with us?" Max stared dumbfoundedly at Victor, then Tommy, then Victor, trying to work out the "work with us" concept for herself much less for Tommy. "Let's put it this way, what if you were me and you wanted to stop the fighting, get over it, move on - what would you do?" Leer asked.

Max gave Victor a look that told him that he had never asked her for her opinion about anything, so why, now, when she would obviously not share his views on the situation, would he bother to ask for her opinion and said, "Victor, you have never asked for my opinion on anything so why on Salta would you ask me now, when I obviously do not share your views on this whole situation."

Victor calmly replied, "Because Max, I just had my head kicked in and I'm not thinking clearly."

Max's expression turned from troubled to downright sour, "Bast yourself, Victor," Max sneered then crossed her arms and frowned into a sullen silence. Tommy and Victor were speechless, mostly because Leer and Blue didn't know what "Bast yourself" meant, but it wasn't too hard to imagine.

It was now clear to Leer that Victor was a real pain in the neck in general and that it was going to be difficult if not impossible to be himself and Victor at the same time. One thing he knew for certain, there was a reason he and Blue appeared where they did, when they did, and he was going to figure it out. "Listen Max," he said as soothingly as he thought Victor's character would allow, "I know I've been difficult to deal with in the past," Max lifted her eyes toward him, "but I promise I'm going to handle things a little differently now."

A smile warmed its way across Max's face as Victor's face flattened itself into what was left of his blue plate special and squeaked out a "what the fffff" doubling over to grab his balls where Max's steel-tipped heal was firmly lodged.

"Thought I'd better get that in before you changed your mind," she quipped as she withdrew her boot returning her foot to its rightful place below the table, harmlessly crossed over the ankle of her other leg.

Leer reluctantly choked a half-hearted "I guess I had it coming."

Leer had handled Max perfectly, by giving her what she always wanted from Victor, a chance to be heard about anything, without fear that he might retaliate if she said anything he didn't want to hear. It was like the starting gun at the Preakness had just been fired. The sheer power of what burst forth from Max's mouth, a hundred thoroughbreds could not compete. Before it ended, a dozen plates and twice as many pitchers of coffee found their way to that booth at the far end of Mickey's Diner only to be scraped clean or drained dry by the vociferous Max, Tommy and Victor, who were uncharacteristically though thoroughly attentive to her every word.

Before the night gave way to the dawn, Blue and Leer had the answers to every single question they had asked, however surreptitiously, and knew everything they needed to know to survive for at least a short time in this new world, named Salta.

"Well, I guess it's time to go home," Tommy yawned as he patted his healed but bloated belly.

Nearly everything they needed to know.

Blue looked at Leer as both of them inwardly faced the realization that they had no idea where home was.

Just then Max said, "Well we're not taking you home with us Tommy," then she gave a menacing glance at Victor as she continued, "I realize that you guys are planning to stop fighting, and believe it or not, I think you're right, after all who wants to die, especially twice, but I'm not going to bring you to my house, Levito.

"Well how 'bout droppin' me off at my place then," Tommy chimed in without missing a beat. Max looked deeply into Tommy's eyes, Blue's eyes looked back at her.

Max suddenly felt remarkably self-conscious as if Tommy was looking inside of her mind - reading her thoughts - thoughts of him, not only being in her house, but in her bed, so she said, "ummm."

The trio looked at one another in silence until the silence became timeless.

"Tommy! What the Bast!?" a big, bald, muscular biker shouted from the entrance to Mickey's diner. He stomped his way across the diner. Blue got to his feet, not sure if he should run or prepare to fight. Before he could run, the biker was on him.

10 VINNY

A good head taller and fifty pounds heavier than Tommy, the biker wrapped his arms around him and began to sob. "I thought I lost you, I heard you were dead, they told me that bitch Maxi-Pad blew a hole in your stomach," he continued as he gently released his grip cautiously backing up as he let go to look at Tommy's stomach. As he did so, he saw Max and Victor. "YOU!!!" He hollered and instantly lunged at Max. Blue quickly caught hold of his arms barely keeping him off Max who cried, "Tommy's okay, I swear, Vinny, he's fine." She reached for her gun and felt Victor's hand already on it - she turned to him as he said, "Max and I were just apologizing to Tommy, Vinny."

"Oh, my Bastin' Farbunkle, you have got to be shittin' me, Tommy," Vinny turned on Tommy, gripping his shirt into a ball nearly lifting him off the ground with one hand.

"Sorry Vinny," Tommy said quietly, " let me explain."

"Tommy," Vinny said as he loosened his grip, "there is no way in varst that you are goin' t' be able to explain why you are sittin' at a table in Farb Damn Mickey's Diner with these two assholes!"

"Gimme a lift home, Vinny, and I'll try to do my best."
The two of them left the diner, Blue awkwardly trying to say goodbye to his friend Leer while completely aware that whoever Vinny was, he hated Max and Victor, while apparently loving Tommy.

The ride home on Vinny's bike would certainly qualify as one of the most amazing motorcycle experiences of Blue's life if it weren't for one thing - Blue wasn't at all sure that this actually qualified as his life. After all, he wasn't really Blue, and he wasn't the real Tommy either.

Regardless, the ride was a trip!

The bike was a monster. It made any Harley that Blue had ever seen look like a child's toy motorcycle. It wasn't only the biggest damn bike he had ever seen, it was also remarkably well appointed and comfortable, even for two big guys like Vinny and Tommy. In fact, the thing seemed to know him. Vinny was still shaking his head in disbelief at Tommy's choice of dinner mates as he approached the bike and said one word, "T-bone."

It was all Blue could do to keep his composure as the bike altered its appearance instantly before his eyes, sprouting a second seat automatically, in accordance with the single command from Vinny. The seat wasn't just another pad that popped out of some hidden compartment behind Vinny's seat. It was a full-sized seat, nearly identical to Vinny's, that seemed to grow from the back of Vinny's seat, unfolding like a stop-motion or time-lapsed photographic sequence of the opening of an exotic, blossoming flower, adding a good three feet to the total length of the bike. Vinny climbed on and Blue quickly followed, careful not to hesitate, figuring that he must be T-bone and that this was not his first time as passenger on the "VinnCycle." The bike confirmed his supposition as it wrapped itself around his form, presenting him with custom fitted armrests, seemingly sculpted to the exact contour of his forearms. Just as he felt the urge to shift his weight, the bike repositioned the seat, bringing his body into a position of absolute comfort, creating a feeling of weightlessness.

"Let's ride!" Vinny howled.

Suddenly, a voice like an amplified evangelist with a tracheotomy echoed, "Let's ride," and the bike shot forth with a burst of speed unlike anything Blue had ever felt. Oddly, he didn't really "feel" a thing. He simply recognized that they were moving forward with tremendous speed. In fact, he was so comfortable that he felt as though he could fall to sleep right then and there.

"JumpJuice time!" he heard Vinny whisper as he felt a short burst of effervescence sparkle across his face. Instantly he sensed everything around him as if it was passing through some sort of amplifier. It was as if even his sense of feeling was getting louder. It was as if his senses weren't functioning, no, it was as if they were functioning but so quickly that he was unable to detect their origin before an even greater sensation would take over. No, it was like his brain was functioning so quickly that his senses didn't have time to feel or hear or smell. No, it wasn't that either, it was simply that he could do nothing but laugh and drool. Then Blue heard a voice that seemed to come from inside his own head.

"That's my T-bone! Settle in little bro, it's jump time for the VinnCycle."

In the time it took for Blue to realize that Vinny was actually Tommy's brother his own body seemed as though it had melted away completely. The VinnCycle had transformed again. Blue couldn't feel himself being repositioned at all, but he was hyper-aware that his body was stretched out like Superman when flying at top speed. Almost directly below him and slightly ahead, he could see Vinny. It was as though he was riding piggy-back on Vinny, but they weren't actually touching each other. Vinny seemed to be steering them with his hands alone. The technology in this cycle was beyond anything that Blue could have imagined possible, even in a so-called parallel universe.

Vinny and Tommy blazed their way down the expressway, darting in-between other vehicles. Vehicles that were already going way faster than anything Tommy had ever seen driving on the highway. It was like the autobahn to the third power, yet he felt no fear. It was as if nothing could stop them, every turn, orchestrated perfectly by the slightest movement of Vinny's powerful hands. Road signs streaked by so quickly that Blue couldn't believe he was able to read them. They seemed to be in English and everything was similar enough to his own reality to present a plethora of burger joints and pizza parlors punctuated by what Blue reasoned had to be churches.

The churches were massive buildings. Every one of them had a large eye framed in two triangles rotated at a ninety-degree angle to one another.

Each citadel had the eye logo with a different phrase such as Farb Sees, Farb Lives, Farb Reigns, Farb Hears or Farb Knows, flashing into Blue's subconscious between doses of neon pepperoni and LED double cheeseburgers. By the time the journey came to an end, Blue had only one question on his mind. Who in God's name is Farb?

He was so delirious from the ride, the JumpJuice or both that he forgot himself, blew his cover and blurted out, "Who is Farb anyway?" as he stumbled to the ground in his disoriented state.

He quickly regained his senses as the ominous form of Vinny loomed over him and in a single effort lifted him handily from the ground as if he were tissue paper.

Vinny's giant frame masked a gentleness that Blue instantly detected, as Vinny lowered Tommy gracefully to a position where he could regain his footing saying, "Little bro, you must've really been shaken up by that trashy little Max. You've never cared about Farb, the Council or anything spiritual, period. Next thing I know, you're going to tell me you saw the light or something. I'm not leaving your side tonight. Now, let's get you inside where you can rest."

It took Blue all of about two seconds to realize that he had just dodged a major bullet on the God thing. Shaking off the ride, he turned his attention to the house to which Vinny had just seemingly time-warped him. It took half of two seconds to re-evaluate his position on "crime don't pay." Partially regaining his balance, he slowly slumped his way toward the front door.

"Bastin' farbunkle, Tommy," Vinny laughed, "you really are messed up. You never use your front door. If I didn't know better, I'd say you aren't Tommy Levito!"

Blue laughed an exhausted sort of chuckle, "Look Vinny, I can't remember half the things I should, damn near didn't recognize you, had trouble figuring out what went down with Alonso and company, so do me a favor, help me get back in the swing of things. I just feel way too... different, ya' know?"

Tommy looked at Vinny. The two men stood just outside a side door that Vinny had meandered over to while Tommy was explaining his dilemma. The next thing Blue knew, Vinny had him by the back of the neck. Suddenly, Vinny held Tommy's face about six inches from a narrow mirror on the door. "Welcome home, Tommy," said the door, as it slid open.

"I guess your house knows it's you, eh Bro?" Vinny smiled and breathed a heavy, satisfied sigh, "Ah the T-bone shack - I love hangin' out at your place, man. Hey, I know you're tired but we gotta hit at least one round, whaddya' say?"

Blue had no idea what Vinny meant, however, he figured it couldn't be worse than what he had experienced over the most recent twenty-four hours of his and Tommy's combined life, so he said "sure."

"Yes," exclaimed Vinny, as he quickly disappeared behind a pillar. Blue wasn't sure whether he was supposed to follow Vinny or not, but he didn't want to appear timid in the eyes of his brand new big brother. So, he followed Vinny around the pillar. What he saw there was beyond his comprehension.

Imagine total blackness.

Now, imagine total blackness again because whatever blackness you just imagined is not as black as the blackness that Blue was now looking at. Blue let his jaw drop open because the only thing that wasn't black was really busy doing something else and would never notice that Tommy was behaving as if he had never seen this room before, even though it was in his own house, because Tommy was Blue, who was now closing his jaw because Vinny, the unblack, was approaching, beaming, "you gotta hit this shit before we start!"

Tommy, of course, had to hit that shit but Blue was pretty damn sure, by the look on Vinny's face that the shit in question was going to mess with his mind at least as much as the JumpJuice did and probably more. "You go first, Vinny, it's your shit man!" he managed as he tried to focus on anything at all in the room around him. There was absolutely nothing, other than the entryway through which they had come. Blue eyed it longingly.

"My shit?!, Funny Tommy, but varst, you don't have to ask me twice," Vinny laughed as he sparked up a bowl. "kmphff - kmphff- kmphff.. Phaaaaahh," he breathed as he handed Tommy a gorgeous little glass pipe, crystallized little buds still slightly glowing, while milky white smoke swirled its way around a small chamber, midway through the pipe, "you finish 'er off."

Blue hadn't smoked cannabis in about ten years, mostly because he had been holding down a corporate design gig, working for a guy who made it his business to know everything he could about his employees' personal lives in case he ever had to come up with a reason to fire them. Blue had pretty much said his farewells to his job the moment he and Leer boarded the star cruiser in what used to be his living room. But the boss wasn't the reason he hadn't "hit this shit" yet. He remembered how pot made him feel... he loved to smoke pot. He loved it so much that he had decided that he couldn't smoke it anymore. He knew that didn't make much sense, nor did he have the time to explain it. Add to that the fact that Vinny would be about the last person Blue would care to explain it to and... the crystalline particles crackled with blue flame as the tiny purple hairs were engulfed with the glow as Tommy inhaled, filling the chamber with even more swirling white smoke until he deftly released his index finger from the carburetor, allowing the pipe to release, filling his lungs with smoke from its cache. The room fell into complete darkness as the fire extinguished.

Blue's host body was a seasoned veteran of this ritual and Tommy held the vaporous prize in his lungs long enough for Vinny's hand to materialize from the infinite blackness, landing upon Tommy's shoulder to squeeze him affectionately as Vinny whispered softly into his ear, " there ain't a soul alive who can make love to the crystal princess like T-bone...But now, little brother, it's time to die!"

As if on cue, Blue felt himself falling into a seat which seemed to sweep him off his feet, up into the eternal blackness. The seat transformed to fit his body, just like the one on the VinnCycle. The moment he began to feel comfortable, a console appeared in front of him. As he became aware of it, the console became more complete. In fact, it became familiar. He had drawn something like this before when he had been contracted to do some work on a film. It was Sci-Fi, a Star Wars type deal, with all of the major special effects being produced by Industrial

Light Magic. For some stupid reason, the production company thought that ILM was going to actually create the spaceships, weapons and fancy gadgets for twelve million dollars, only to find out that the twelve million was really only going to cover what it would take to make all of those things look like they were actually doing something. By the time this memory told itself to Tommy's brain, Blue began to notice stars all around him. He looked out to see that he was in a ship of his own creation. It was mind blowing. Something he had drawn for a movie was here, in some sort of thoroughly realistic holographic game in his house, within a parallel universe. Suddenly, he was hit. The stars around him bouncing and twirling everywhere as if he and his ship were inside of a giant snow globe being shaken up by a very naughty little giant. The ship quickly righted itself and Blue felt as though he was perfectly stationary. The stars lay still around him. Just off to his left, in his peripheral vision, blue could see movement. Something rising into view, quickly yet silently.

It was Vinny, in a one-person spacecraft, a fighter of some kind, unlike anything Blue had ever seen in any movie or game. Blue could see right in to Vinny who was laughing his ass off. Vinny motioned to his mouth from inside of his cockpit, signaling to Tommy that he wanted to talk. Instinctively, Blue reached up to find that he was wearing a helmet. His fingers glided upward along its surface until he felt a small button just above his ear. He pressed it, releasing a small earphone/microphone combination unit which lowered automatically into place. Still laughing, Vinny asked, "What in Farb's name is that?"

"Something I dreamed up a while ago," Blue countered, "keeps me focused!"

"Great, you're going to need it, little bro, I've plugged us in for the Gamma Run. "Z" and the boys are going to be jumping in. My guess is somewhere near Omegalux," Vinny continued," so I'm going to need some serious back-up on this, it's T-Bone Time!"

Blue had no idea what to expect but he didn't care. He was floating in the middle of outer space, in a ship that he designed, and it was real, or virtually real. Plus, he was about as high as he could ever remember being.

Blue was far too excited by the thrill of being inside his own creation to even consider who Z might be or what he and Vinny were about to be up against. He wanted to see what his baby could do.

"Vinny," he called through his headset, "hang on for a second, I gotta try something." Blue grabbed the joystick in front of him and eased it back slightly. The nose of the craft rose slightly, noiselessly, effortlessly and exactly how he had envisioned it would. As Blue maneuvered, he realized that his ship, although cool in his mind, futuristic even, seemed a bit old school compared to Vinny's which was sleeker and frankly, cooler. Still, Blue was in his element. Blue could see very clearly what his fighter was capable of and that, he figured, would be good enough for any space battle. Regardless, he wanted to give it a little test. Instantly, he slammed the stick forward and to the right, breaking into an incredible dive. He didn't feel a thing. The craft cradled him completely, making his every move effortless, responding to his slightest touch. Suddenly, he ripped the stick straight back, burying his left foot into the floor, just like popping the clutch on his '65 Mustang convertible. Except that the Mustang couldn't instantly reverse its direction without losing speed. The fighter did just that. All without sending Blue's balls up into his throat. Without the slightest difficulty, Blue stopped the fighter in exactly the same spot from where he had begun and hovered there grinning.

"What in Farb's name? - How in the Bastin' Farbunkle? - Tommy, that was bastin' amazing!" Vinny shouted, causing Blue's ears to ring, but it was cool, in fact, nothing could be cooler, thought Blue.

"Thank you God-Farb or whoever the Fuck-Bast you are!" Blue silently prayed for the first time in twenty-some years. As he let out a barely audible but deeply meaningful, "whoa."

"Farb-Damn-it Tommy, let's go kick some ass!" Vinny laughed as he turned his craft and raced off through the stars.
Vinny shot off so quickly that Blue wasn't sure he'd be able to catch up, and how do you find a guy in the middle of space. Blue intuitively leaned into the gentle banking of his craft as he pivoted seventy-five degrees to the right, punching the thrusters without even glancing at his console. In less than a heartbeat, Blue was deftly maneuvering his craft into position over Vinny's right wing. Together, they bobbed and weaved

their way through an asteroid belt, strewn with the wreckage of less fortunate travelers.

"Freshies, " laughed Vinny as he expertly dodged a chunk of fighter by slinking to the left. As he did so, he realized that the chunk was sure to nail Tommy head-on. He spun his head around so quickly that it felt as though it might snap right off. However, he had no time to think about that right now. His mind was far too busy trying to muster up the resources to comprehend the images his eyes were feeding his brain. Indeed, the chunk was slamming into the nose of Tommy's craft with untold force and speed. However, instead of exploding, caving in or otherwise smashing to bits, Tommy's craft seemed to roll effortlessly over the debris. Seemingly effortless movements rarely are but often look so when performed by a practiced, well-disciplined individual. In this case though, practice and discipline were in short supply. Fortunately, Blue was flying with a boatload, rather a shipload, of intuition. As the creator of this fighter, he knew everything it was capable of. Recognizing that there was no way out of the collision, he acted quickly and instinctively to maneuver the craft in such a way as to allow the collision while softening its effect. Blue engaged the fore and aft thrusters simultaneously, directing the angle of their bursts, while pivoting the wing section, catapulting the fighter ass over elbow as Frank used to say. Then, just as quickly, Blue reversed the maneuver, righting the fighter just in time to rotate forty-five degrees to the right to avoid a smaller yet equally inconvenient chunk of "Freshie" fighter, which luckily for Vinny, had a second earlier, only narrowly grazed the surface of his fighter's right wing.

With ice cold delivery, masking his racing heartbeat, Blue said, "Yeah, it's as though they've never seen an asteroid belt before."

A single, deeply meaningful word escaped Vinny's lips, "whoa!"
As they finally cleared the asteroid belt, Tommy calmly said. "Hey Vinny, it appears as though that ass we're supposed to kick just showed up."
Vinny quickly signaled Tommy back into the belt.

"I can't believe that Z jumped in early," Vinny said," must be desperate for more Gear Points, trying to surprise us just out of the belt. If we had been any slower his plan would have worked," he continued as he tucked in behind the largest asteroid at the end of the belt.

"A desperate foe is only half a challenge," Tommy replied.

Vinny burst out laughing, "Tommy!?! Did you really just call Z half a challenge, this is priceless. A whole different fighter, complete with funky helmet and dinosaur-style joystick action, flying skill like I've never witnessed before - and now you dismiss Z, the highest ranked pilot in the system, as half a challenge. If I wasn't worried you'd dump your whole status, I'd send you out there alone, you cocky son of my mother!"

Blue wasn't too sure just how good Tommy was supposed to be, so he assumed it would be best to let Vinny lead. Still, he wasn't about to miss out on this chance to fly, fight and win in a ship that he designed in a game that kicked ass on anything he had ever played. If the opportunity presented itself, he was going blast Z and the other two fighters he brought with him out of space, straight to "Game Over." "I hear ya, Vinny - I got your back - but if I get the chance, I'll assume you wouldn't mind if I make Z wait a little longer for those points would ya?"

Vinny chuckled, "stop Bastin' with me bro, Varst NO! We want to keep that bastard Z from getting ANY more points than he already has. Farb knows he's got enough to spare."

"Hello Boys!" A new voice invaded Blue's head. "Took me awhile to figure out your new frequency, Tommy. I just think it's my job to let you know, it's not the fighter that wins the battle, it's the pilot. But judging by that heap you're flying, I don't think I have to worry about either."

"You must be slippin' Z," Vinny teased, "Tommy's frequency was pretty easy to detect, only took me a second or two."

"We'll see who's slipping, Vinny, as soon as you and your baby brother come out from under mama's apron to play with the big boys," Z chided as he and his team, Stew and Stan, who were laughing like cartoon hyenas, staked out positions on the other side of the asteroid belt. Vinny directed Tommy to the right with his eyes, then swung his ship around to the left side of the asteroid they were hiding behind.

Stew was so busy wiping the tears of laughter from his eyes that he missed a perfect opportunity to blast Vinny who emerged from behind the asteroid, directly in front of him.

Both pilots unloaded their weapons at the same time, but Vinny was quicker on his shields leaving a stunned and slightly disabled Stew with tears of a different nature. Vinny quickly turned his attention to Z who was slightly above him and to his right. Knowing he couldn't get his guns trained in on Z in time, Vinny put full power to his shields just in time to survive a blast that rocked his ship enough to leave him prey to Stan, who was hovering just in front of him, so close that Vinny could see him grinning, "See ya later V...," Stan's taunting was cut short by sudden death as his ship was cut in two from below by Tommy's advancing fighter.

Z unloaded zenon rays from guns positioned on both wings that would have sliced directly through Tommy's wings if he hadn't rolled between the beams just in time.

Z still had position on Vinny, however, Vinny was trained in on Stew who was mostly disabled but still a minor threat. Vinny could take him out, but he'd be demolished by Z if he diverted too much power away from his shields. He thought about Tommy's comment behind the asteroid and took a chance, "now," Vinny calmly said as he unloaded upon Stew, blasting him to pieces.

"Now it's your turn," Z said as he blasted Vinny's ship in half, "like I said, it's all about the pilot!" He laughed with confidence as he turned his ship up to find Tommy hovering just above him.

"Sometimes it's both," Tommy said as a projection device robotically retracted itself back into his ship. Z turned a disbelieving eye to his right as Vinny's ship cruised into view. Both Tommy and Vinny unloaded everything they had into Z who had activated his shields a bit too late.

His ship rocked then exploded as a barely audible yet deeply meaningful "whoa" escaped his lips.

Tommy turned to Vinny and said, "that felt good."

"Damn Tommy," Vinny hooted," you must've met up with Farb the Almighty himself, drank from the Cup of the Sacred Seven and been imbued with the gift by the Council, all at once! I just can't explain it any other way! You're back from the dead, dining with your mortal enemy and trouncing Z all in one night. Before I wake up and discover that I'm dreaming all of this shit, there's one more thing we have GOT to do.

"Now, you know that Z is gonna try to jump back into our run here, but since you terminated him, we can block him out," Vinny explained, "unless you want to let him back in, so you can kick his ass all over again?"

"No, Vinny, let's block the bastard out and do whatever you want to do. What have you got in mind?" Tommy asked, hoping they could just fly on and blast something. He was still nervous about saying something that would give away the fact that he wasn't Tommy after all.

"I'm pretty sure you know what I've got in mind, Tommy," Vinny laughed.

Blue wasn't sure how to handle the situation. The way he saw it, he could play it two ways... Option 1 would go something like: "Well Vinny, I'm just not my normal self today and you're going to have to give me a little more to go on." or Option 2... "Oh, varst yeah Vinny, I'm feelin' lucky, you got a plan?" Blue proceeded with option 2.

"Well, as a matter of fact I do, little bro," Vinny explained. "First, enter Violet 17 into your frequency field for the comline. I don't want to hear from Z while we're trying this at all. Even though you fleeced him, he can still jump in on the audio feed. It won't do him a damn bit of good if he can't find us and I just baked the scramble for Violet 17 two days ago.

"Agreed," said Tommy as he changed the signal.

Instantly, the conversation continued, "Now don't freak out, but we're going after the OmegaLux Crystal" Vinny said cautiously, waiting for the outburst from Tommy.
The silence hung in the air, or lack of air, void of space for some time. Vinny was worried that Tommy was assessing his status, weighing the

option to pursue the crystal when, in actuality, Blue had no clue what it was.

He supposed that it had to be a big deal and that Tommy would normally have a reaction to Vinny's proposition, but he wasn't sure what to say, or what not to say, so he said nothing.

Vinny had a headful of counterpoints to arguments that just plain didn't happen. Both men hovered in nearly empty space, in absolute silence a few seconds longer until Vinny said," Tommy? You alright?"

nothing.

"Tommy?"

Blue figured he'd better say something so his mouth started moving even though his brain was having a heck of a time trying to formulate relevant sentences, so it sounded a little like,"umm, ah, w-w, ah uh I, yeah, well, no, I mean, shit Vinny, I don't have any idea if I'm alright! I don't know how I survived tonight, how I got here, how I ended up in this awesome fighter, why I can fly this damn thing like I was born in it or if I even have a chance in this world or any other of getting that Bastin' crystal. BUT, Farb or no Farb, I plan to find out, because I feel lucky. So, just point me in the right direction, tell me what to do and I will go along with the plan, okay?"

"Okay?" Vinny cackled, "Okay? Bastin' Farbunkle, Okay? Varst yeah it's Okay! I've been trying to get you to go after that damn crystal for as long as I can remember and you're always like,"I'm not riskin' the few Gear Points I've got, goin' after some myth!" So, how in Farb's name could I NOT be okay with you tellin' me that you actually WANT to go, AND that you're feeling lucky!?...YOU, Tommy, "I don't believe in luck" Levito. Especially on a night where you return from the dead then hand the best pilot in the system his own ASS on a PLATTER!? Damn it Tommy, we gotta quit talkin' and get over to OmegaLux before we both wake up and find out that none of this actually happened. Follow me." Vinny said as he swung his craft around one hundred and eighty degrees and hit his thrusters hard.

He shot off quickly but Tommy was over his right wing before he could say, "Just stick with m..."

"I'm right here," Tommy said as he pulled alongside.

"Remember, Z lost it on level five, so we should be able to make it through level three without too much difficulty, maybe even four, if your luck holds out. I'll take the lead unless it begins to look like I'm holdin' you back," Vinny instructed.

"Got it" Tommy said, feeling so excited that he just wanted to let Vinny know how incredibly awesome the night had been so far. He knew he couldn't, so he just relaxed into his cockpit a little more and smiled to himself, at peace, moving faster than he had ever imagined possible, on a world far from home in a virtual space more real than anything he had ever felt before.

Vinny gave the order to disengage thrusters and both ships slowed to a drift. Looming in front of them was OmegaLux, half asteroid - half space station. It begged you to approach while shouting "I WILL EAT YOU ALIVE."

An orchestra of searchlights cut through space in all directions radiating from a multitude of axes surrounding OmegaLux. Countless fighters swarmed the perimeter of the complex. "I've just cloaked both of us and fed you a diagram of our approach. I've only mapped as far as access point 07. that's how Z got in. He traded me this approach plan for five Gear Points and a pint of McMahon's Stout. The points I can do without but right now I wish I had the stout." Vinny lamented as he surveyed the situation. "Just look at all of those "omies"! What could possess anyone to be so into a game that they would actually take a real oath to protect something that exists only in the game, if it even exists!? I mean, for all we know, the developers at Omnifab could just be jackin' everyone around, saying there's a crystal when there isn't one, just hyping the game. I mean Z only made it to level five and that Cromwell character on FighterChat claims he made it to level eight but that could just be bullshit, or worse - dude could be just a plant, some OmegaLux crony, an omie, just spouting off, making us all think that the crystal's real and that finding it is going to make any difference whatsoever. Like finding it is going to give you the ability to see Farb. Varst! With all the bastin' hype about it, whoever did find it might as well BE Farb. Damn it

Tommy, don't you have anything to say about this?!"

"Actually Vinny, I've got a really good feeling about this. Like I said, I have no idea why anything is going down like it is, but I think we're going to get that bastin' crystal. Besides, I doubt we can sit out here cloaked all night, so let's at least kick a little omie ass just for fun." Blue was really feeling something powerful coming over him, as if the game itself was some sort of a conduit, helping him to merge with the life of Tommy, energizing and integrating his being into this new world.

"That's true T-bone talkin' there my bro, let's hit it, access point 07 ASAP and spare no omies on our way!" Vinny cooed as he dropped the cloak and engaged his thrusters. Vinny and Tommy unleashed a hailstorm of short bursts peppered with a smattering of droid mines that carved a tunnel a half-mile wide through the swarm of omies. It was easy enough to navigate their way through said tunnel and to their delight the tunnel became self-widening. It seems that if you kill an outrageous number of omies in a very short period of time the rest of them become incredibly nervous. Omies, after all, have health and life levels like any other player in OmegaWars. Tommy and Vinny surrounded an unfortunate straggler and together brought his health and life levels down to a combined total of zero. Both men quickly realized that this meant that the path between their ships and access point 07 was now utterly clear.

"Let's go!" Vinny hooted and motioned toward the access point with a jolt of his head, but Tommy pulled the nose of his fighter up and backed away in the opposite direction. "What in Farb's name are you doing?" Vinny screeched, his face squinched up like someone had just force fed him a mouthful of sour gummy worms.

"Hang on," Tommy quietly replied, so quietly that Vinny got the sense that there must be some trouble but there was no sign of it. Vinny reluctantly backed up in the direction of Tommy, his eyes still glued to access point 07, yearning to hit his thrusters, aching to fly his fighter into the apparently vacant shaft leading directly into the heart of the OmegaLux complex. "Look around." Vinny heard Tommy whisper.

Nothing, not a single omie where moments before there was a swarm.

"Follow me," Tommy said as he barrel-rolled his fighter directly toward a rocky projection a quarter-mile off the access point.

Vinny fell in behind whispering in return, "This is weird."

Tommy snugged his craft up against the rocky wall and Vinny followed suit. Instantly, Tommy's projection arm deployed and floated out, like debris. It projected an exact duplicate of the rocky surface over the two fighters, masking them from view. "Why are..." Vinny started, stopping with his jaw dangling in disbelief as a mercilessly black mega fighter emerged from the very access point he was so eager to enter seconds earlier.

Inside the mammoth battleship a single light source illuminated what seemed to be a bridge or large cockpit of some kind. Although the light was dim, a single, recognizable figure was framed within its glow.

"Z," Vinny whispered in dismay, "damn, the single best free source fighter pilot in the system is an omie, even worse a suit jockey? That Bastin' Pudsucker set me up, set US up, Varst! Beyond that, he knows our codes as well as nearly all of the F-source jocks from the J-Quarter. He knows that none of us are registered and is totally capable of identifying us and shutting us down. Actually," Vinny took a deep breath, "this is our only chance. He can't shut us down from within the game, but he sure as shit isn't going to let us log in again. We've got to get that crystal tonight. I damn near flew right into him. Tommy, how did you know?" Vinny asked incredulously.

"I didn't," Tommy replied, "it was just a hunch. And since most of my hunches seem to be coming true, we'd better get moving soon. Z knows that I've got a decoy cloak, he'll spot us in no time. Let's see if we can fool him one more time. Get ready to make a break for access point 07. I'm pretty sure that they expected to waste us by now, so Z probably doesn't have any back-up in that shaft."

With that, Tommy sent the projection droid off in the direction of the megafighter where it projected exact copies of Tommy and Vinny's crafts spaced perfectly on either side of the megafighter. The decoys taunted Z as the droid sent out a decoy message from Vinny, "Hello Z." In less than a second the megafighter opened up on the tiny ships with all of her firepower, phasers, droid mines, torpedoes even pulse arrays upon the tiny ships. There should have been a perfectly splendid pair of explosions. Instead there was a rather meaningless scattering of firepower as the artillery passed right through the decoys. A frustrated and robust eruption of outrage hung pointlessly in the dispassionate void of space. "Reverse all Full and pursue," Z bellowed as a handful of omies scrambled to turn the large warbird around.

By that time, Tommy and Vinny were rocketing down the shaft toward level three at breakneck speed, laughing. "Man-o-man, Tommy, that was perfect," Vinny roared, "From now on, you lead! I am officially naming you my sensei whether you want to be or not. Y'know, I always just sort of tolerated Z, now I can officially hate his guts, full-on!"

"Do not hate, my brother, rather look with pity on he who is last in the alphabet," Tommy replied, barely maintaining his composure, then bursting out uncontrollably with laughter.
The warbird was fast, so Tommy and Vinny quickly reigned in the laughter. "We've got to get rid of Z, Vinny," Tommy said.

"I don't have anything that can do that, Tommy," Vinny admitted.

"Oh, I do," Tommy quickly replied, "but we can't let him know it's coming," he added. "He'll be wise to decoys so we have to lure him in and force him into our trap. He'll try to outsmart us and that will be his undoing. But we can't stop to fight him now. We need to keep going as fast as we can. Follow me," Tommy said as he engaged his thrusters and flew straight up smashing through the top of the shaft narrowly averting total self-destruction by clearing the way with a rapid-fire burst of phasor blasts, as if emanating from a Gatling gun, followed by a well-timed torpedo. He neatly maneuvered his fighter through the hole into what appeared to be a giant arena. "Unbelievable!," he said, "this is exactly what we need. It's just too soon. Well, sort of. He released a small craft from the front of his fighter. It hovered in the middle of the arena then disappeared toward the seats.

The seats were pods. The pods encircled the stage. Tommy looked around. All the pods were empty. "My gut tells me that these pods are going to start filling up very quickly and that we are going to be the main event!"

"I'm not sure I like that idea," Vinny responded.

"No Vinny, that's good, we WANT to be the main event," Tommy quickly reassured him. "By now, Z has discovered our little detour. Take a look at the diagram he traded with you," he urged.

"Okay, I'm looking," Vinny responded.

"Z should be on his way here, coming up through Sector G, Shaft 07A. It's the only one that looks big enough for that megafighter. I need to check something out," Tommy continued, "so I need you to lure Z up here. Follow shaft 07C. It leads to Level 4. On the way, you'll pass shaft07A. Make sure that Z sees you. Pass his position and then double back like you are afraid to continue. Try to draw his fire but stay back. Try to make him think "KILL." Make him follow you.

Vinny laughed, "Z is always thinking kill."

"Ha, right, well that's good," Tommy agreed, "now when you reach the arena, I'll be waiting, but I want you to drop straight down and out of sight, behind the pods, right down there." Tommy focused a laser beam from the front of his craft several rows below their position.

"Tommy, where the Varst did you get that awesome laser beam thing? Vinny exclaimed.

"Never mind, just be there. Now go get that asshole Z!" Tommy ordered.

"OOH! T-bone's a' sizzlin', you got it little bro," Vinny laughed, turning his fighter, singing, "gonna get you... get you sucka," Blue had never heard the song before, but he liked it.

Vinny flew off, down shaft 07C. He sped past shaft 07B as well as an illuminated doorway inside of which he caught a glimpse of hundreds of omies. They looked like kids on their way to a rock concert. At least as much as a bunch of omies can look like kids on their way to a rock concert. The difference between this group, and that comprised of kids going to a rock concert is that there were hardly any girls and instead of excitedly pushing and trampling one another to get to the show they just sort of annoyingly budged their way forward while self-consciously checking to see if they were coming off as remotely passionate or, Farb forbid, emotional. Vinny hardly had time to process that thought before he saw it.

Shaft 07A was substantially larger than shaft 07B and Z's warbird filled it neatly. Vinny hovered in front of then shot past the shaft. He quickly slowed his craft and turned a quick 180 back to shaft 07A to taunt Z further. He didn't have to work at it. Z was already thinking "KILL." He had brought the megafighter up fast already closing in to within a quarter mile of Vinny who had just returned to the junction of shaft 07C and 07A. Instantly, he was fired upon. Fortunately, Vinny's fight or flight instinct was gravitating more toward flight causing him to hit his thrusters as soon as he saw the warbird. The monstrous fighter had to slow momentarily to make the turn from shaft 07A to 07C. This gave Vinny enough of a start to widen the distance between his fighter and Z's ship, but not for very long. The massive craft quickly closed in on Vinny. "They're right on my ass," Vinny shouted, his urgency drilling into Tommy's headset.

"Keep coming Vinny, and don't forget to drop down to where I told you to. Now quickly switch your frequency back to what we had before. I want Z to hear us." Tommy instructed.

"What?!" Vinny replied with shock.

"Just do it!" Tommy snapped.

Vinny reset the frequency then yelled, "He's going to blast me, Tommy!"

"Oh good, there you are boys," Z smarmed his way into the conversation, "I was afraid I wouldn't get a chance to say good-bye."

"Wouldn't have bothered me any," Vinny quipped.

"Oh Vincent, I will miss you, good-bye, " Z taunted as he fired off all phasors and torpedoes.

At the same moment, Vinny piloted his craft into a full dive. He had reached the end of the shaft at the precise moment he needed to survive.

The phasor blasts and torpedoes from Z's megafighter sailed harmlessly over Vinny's fighter, his dive was so extreme and unexpected that Z had no time to react. "Well I guess you really do miss me Z," he laughed.

Two phasor blasts from Tommy's fighter exploded the torpedoes still trying to find their way to Vinny's fighter. "Hello Z," Tommy said blithely.

"Ah, Tommy, I believe I owe you," Z replied. "I must admit, the two of you have been rather lucky but we all know that luck runs out for everyone eventually, and for you the time is now. I may as well dispose of you before I obliterate your sibling. Going to be hard watching your brother die twice in one day, isn't it Vinny?" Z tried cunningly to provoke a response from Vinny who had managed to slink his craft in behind a row of pods which, just as Tommy had predicted, were now full of omies.

"I wouldn't be worried about Vinny right now if I were you, Z. I have all of my phasors trained on you and your shields are probably down, "Tommy said as he unloaded upon the megafighter.

With a wave of his hand in a very definite yet relaxed sweeping upward motion, Z cloaked his ship in its shields. The blasts rocked the ship ever so slightly and caused minimal damage.

"I have eliminated every fighter who has quested for the crystal. Some have made it this far, but none have made it beyond." Z announced to Tommy and Vinny, but also to the hundreds upon hundreds of omies who had assembled in the pods to see yet another free-source fighter eliminated. For it was only the free source fighters who ever made it to face Z. Subscription fighters never even made it past the omies. "I must say, I was a little surprised by your performance at the asteroid belt and your little trick outside the complex, but your projector is gone, and I will not be fooled again. Z continued, "You have a very interesting fighter. I haven't seen that design before and I have seen them all. I have been a developer with Omnilab since before I met Vinny, working my way up from the fighters on border patrol to the X-treme Combat Workshop Crew to the OmegaForce Fighter Squad to this, my own, custom-designed, eminently powerful "Z-Bird."" A resounding cheer rose up from the pods. The omies were soiling themselves with excitement, drooling with anticipation, panting with technical lust and adoration for the one known only as Z, who still stood in the glow of the bridge lights, arms raised, palms lifted upward, drawing the applause out of the very souls of the devotees.

"Now that you're done patting yourself on the back and all of your little omies have slathered you with their nauseating affection, I'd like to introduce you to what I call the blessed trinity," Tommy chuckled, "It's only fitting since you seem to enjoy being the center of attention."

Three concentric rings emanated from the front of his craft, widening on their way toward the warbird. The rings surrounded the megafighter and began rotating in a gyroscopic motion, increasing exponentially in speed, glowing with greater intensity as the warbird began to spin inside the center of the gyroscope. Z was thrown off balance but managed to make his way to his seat. The entire crew buckled in and attempted to fight the motion with thrusters, stabilizers, everything they had.

"All stop," Z commanded authoritatively. The crew disengaged all power and the Z-Bird continued to tumble over and over itself within the gyroscopic field created by the rings. A less robust ship would have been torn apart, but the Z-Bird managed to hold together as the motion of the rings slowed to a halt. The rings disappeared completely. As soon as they did, two torpedoes launched from Tommy's ship erupting into the body of the megafighter sending pieces of the giant warbird hurtling off in the direction of the pods.

"Damn you're annoying," Z shouted as he slung his chair up under the main com panel and began cranking on joysticks, flicking levers, pressing buttons and rolling trackballs with the dexterity of a master. In an instant, his ship righted itself and swung toward Tommy's fighter. "Game OVER Levito, Goodbye," Z snarled. A brilliant, wide horizontal beam of white light shot from the front of the warbird. It blasted Tommy's craft with such intensity that his fighter completely exploded, disintegrating into a shower of sparks. Z howled, "I love this job!" As Z celebrated, Vinny's entire craft shook, even in his position behind the pods. With the sound of Tommy's exploding craft still ringing in his ears, the sound that went unnoticed was a "POP" as Vinny's own fighter shook slightly more, as if it had been hit from above. Instinctively, Vinny looked upward toward the sound and there he saw Tommy, in a different craft, with a finger to his lips. Blue pantomimed Vinny's next move, his right hand representing Vinny's fighter, his left the giant warbird. Vinny acknowledged the plan by nodding his head.

Suddenly Z's voice broke the silence, "I'm coming for you now Vinny," he teased.

Vinny programmed the last move in his craft's sequence, then transferred to the Ship Blue had docked to his. He released the lock between the ships and responded, "No, Z, I'm coming for you," as his ship cruised out from behind the pods, arching upwards in a tight barrel roll toward the megafighter, phasors blasting, this one's for Tom...," before Vinny could finish his dedication, his fighter was blasted from the air, quickly and decisively by Z's awesome warbird.

The omie crowd burst into cheers of "Game Over, Game Over, Game Over." One of the omies on the warbird bridge turned to his captain, "Commander Z, won't the Levitos just tell their friends that you're a commander with OmegaLux now that you have eliminated them from the game?"

"Of course they will. However, that is of no significance. You see, I know all of the access codes as well as the usernames, passwords, Gear Point totals, frequencies even the favorite maneuvers of Vinny Levito's little group of free source fighters," Z bragged. "They'd have to start all over, and guys like that never do. I just wish I didn't have to blow up that little fighter that Tommy managed to slip into the game. That thing had some nice features, especially the gyro rings. I'll have a talk with the boys in development, they never should have let that one in, still they can probably grab the code, so all is not lost. I'm going to mount a few of those handy little projector devices on this baby before the next time we head out. But enough about that, all of you have earned a health 100 credit as well as a plus life 3 bonus from tonight's little festivities. I'd say it's time for a cold one."

From within the safety of their secret craft, Tommy and Vinny could still hear Z. He was so sure he had wasted the two of them that he never bothered to disengage from their frequency. Z's gloating was so nauseating to Tommy that he placed his fingers down his throat like he was going to vomit as he turned the communication system off ensuring that he and Vinny would no longer have to endure Z or the continued cries of "Game Over" from the omie crowd as they reveled in the kill.

Tommy and Vinny drifted out of the arena in the small, inconspicuous garbage craft that Tommy had released earlier. His plan had worked.

Z was so pleased with himself when he disintegrated the projection unit that he convinced himself that Tommy was without any means of diversion or deception. Z never even noticed the small craft which floated harmlessly by during the battle. It resembled the worker robots which drift regularly around the OmegaLux complex. On its side it had the words Keep it Clean, bookended by the Farb Sees logo. it was shaped like the love child of a New York City dumpster and a late 1960's model of a VW bus, but smaller. Though tiny, it sat two comfortably and more importantly, it flew extremely well. Completely loaded with four phasor banks, two rocket launchers and a Quar X module, it was every free source fighter pilot's dream. Particularly when you factor in the finest point of all. It was on its way to level 4, completely undetected by anyone or anything in the complex.

This was the exact thought which crossed Vinny's mind as he beamed with pride, "Z just got himself T-Boned!"

Tommy grinned equally wide as he responded in a hushed but clearly excited voice, "and I would say that the game is FAR from OVER!" Tommy touched the Comm panel, bringing up a holographic model of the inside of the OmegaLux complex.

"Oh, this just keeps getting better and better Tommy! I get the feeling that I'm going to find out that you really did die and that by some odd coincidence, I died with you and this is Heavana. If it is, so be it, Praise Farb and Hallelujah! I am going to savor this moment in Heavana and the first thing I will do in Heavana is to find that damn crystal! I will hold it in my hands, unleashing whatever amazing power it may hold. I will be all merciful and understanding because I am now in Heavana. I have no enemies, no one to protect or be protected from. I will forgive all who have wronged me and you including that bastard Z, that bastin' little prick, Victor, even that little bitch Max. Then, my dear brother, I'm going to find momma. I will throw my arms around her, give her a big kiss and ask her if we can go bake some of those delicious "Momma's Crack Cookies," you remember those, doncha? Varst, of course you do, it wasn't that long ago - Tommy?!?"

Blue felt like shit that he wasn't really Vinny's brother but there wasn't a thing he could do about that. "It's been too long, and I hate to say it, but this isn't Heavana," Tommy said softly and regretfully, " but we are going to get that crystal."

Vinny smiled with understanding as Tommy continued, "Look here," he said as he pointed out a large duct work system dead ahead of the little craft. "We'll follow that system right past level four and drop in mid-way on level five," he continued as he pointed out the spot on the holographic diagram. "With any luck that message you broadcasted to the other free source fighters during the fight in the arena will draw in some help. At least enough to distract the omies, Z and the rest of Omnifab long enough for us to gain some ground. This is where we are headed," Tommy indicated on the model, "This looks like the place where nearly every passage converges. Nothing appears to be there. Either everything goes out from there, or comes in from there and I aim to find out which."

Just as Tommy finished saying these words, a large warbird, nearly the size of Z's emerged from another shaft and hovered between the small craft and the vent they were headed for.

"Not good," Vinny moaned softly as the large warbird hung menacingly between the Levitos and their chosen path. Tommy calmly maneuvered their craft directly toward the warbird. "Are you insane?" Vinny whispered.

Tommy raised one eyebrow and the corner of his mouth as if to say maybe, then banked the tiny craft slightly, deploying a large robotic arm which reached out toward the warbird. Vinny thought for sure that they were toast. The crew of that warbird would see the little craft coming at them with its little robotic arm and fry it without warning. Then, through a small observation window he saw the answer. Tommy was guiding the arm toward a small piece of debris floating aimlessly in the shaft. Tommy grabbed the debris with the robotic arm and disposed of it in the rear of the craft which opened like a dumpster to receive the load. Vinny heard a synthesized female voice say, "debris contained - area clear," as Tommy guided the small craft around the large warbird, directly toward the duct work vent, out of sight of the warbird. Using the same robotic arm, Tommy melted four contact points on the vent and removed it. He slid the craft inside the duct work and resealed the vent from the inside.

"Beezle, Tommy, bastin' beezle!" Vinny cooed as the small craft eased its way down the duct work of level 4. They reached level 5 without incident.

Tommy maneuvered the robotic arm into position to melt the contact points on the vent to level 5. Just as he melted the final point, a blast erupted outside of the duct work. Tommy held the vent in place as he maintained the position of the craft. I don't think they're after us," he said to Vinny, "but I want to get a look at what's happening out there. You hold the craft steady and I'll keep the vent in position."

Tommy managed to keep the vent right in position, while adjusting the camera on the arm to get a view of the area just beyond the vent. What they saw was incredible. Three ships, most likely free source fighters, were in an all-out battle with the warbird they had steered around just moments earlier. By the looks of things, the warbird was losing. All of the ships were fighting in the central area where the passages converged, the very spot that Tommy had pointed out on the holographic model.

The free source fighters encircled the warbird, firing a ceaseless and beautifully orchestrated series of phasor blasts and torpedo attacks. The warbird rolled a little to one side then launched a powerful blast from the center of its nose, striking one of the fighters and disintegrating it instantly. Vinny had one hand on the steering and one hand busily searching frequencies when they heard, "We lost Jeffers, keep up the pattern and stay away from the nose." Vinny leaned over as close as he could to Tommy and whispered, "Sounds like Kowalski."

Tommy nodded. Just then, a huge explosion rocked the area and the entire warbird disintegrated. "Oh yeah!," the cry went up from the free source fighters. Immediately, another explosion shook the place hard. One of the two remaining free source fighters just shattered to bits.

"Ah, Kowalski, you recognize a friendly voice." Z drawled as the Z-Bird loomed into view.

"Friend?" Kowalski gritted his teeth, "more like traitor!"

"Now if you're not going to say anything nice, don't say anything at all," Z oozed with sarcasm, "Perhaps I should put that another way, have a nice day, Kowalski," Z punctuated his rapport with a searing blast that eliminated the last of the free source trio who only moments earlier seemed to be on their way to the final prize.

"Game Over, Game Over, Game Over," the omie cry went up throughout the complex as the event was broadcast system-wide.

Wherever Z went, broadcast followed.

One thing that could be said for Omnifab, they fostered loyalty like no other organization. With the millions of fighters, free source and subscription, one would imagine that Z's status as exterminator within the OmegaLux complex would be common knowledge within the game. It wasn't. Most fighters who made it to Z would do just as he imagined, give up the game, refusing to go up against a system which afforded them no chance. Those who chose to fight or tried to expose Z by getting back into the game were often ridiculed, humiliated or painted as conspiracy theorists by a marketing machine that made other product line corporations look like amateurs.

Inside of Omnifab, omies shared stories of all of the victories, but outside, never, and if things became too transparent to free source fighters or the rarest of subscribers, Z would be eliminated publicly in battle and simply move on to another free source core.

He had been X, Flash, Flint and his own favorite, Fuse.

To Z, every victory was sweet. Another opportunity to bask in his own superiority. He may as well have been Farb himself for all the power he had. Today, however, was a special thrill. Five free source fighters eliminated including a core leader, Vinny Levito. Z gracefully banked the Z-Bird into a full 180 degree turn and cruised off in the direction from whence he came.

"Bastard," Tommy and Vinny said simultaneously as Z left the area.

"Bring us out," Tommy said as he removed the vent. They quickly worked to replace the vent then turned the small craft toward the center of the area. "Let's do a little clean up and look around, Vinny," Tommy said calmly. Within moments, they found a small chunk of debris from Kowalski's vehicle and placed it in the dumpster. "Debris contained-additional debris detected," the voice said. Several minutes passed, Tommy and Vinny continued collecting debris until at last the voice said, "Debris contained - area clear."

At that point, Tommy pressed a small blue button on the comm panel. Instantly, both men were surrounded by their own personal cockpit. "Keep her steady," Tommy said as he looked over at Vinny, who now had full control of the vehicle.

"What are you up to?" asked Vinny with what could only be described as fear in his eyes.

"I'm going out," Tommy responded.

"What in Farb's name do you mean by going out?" Vinny asked incredulously.

"Out there," Tommy motioned upward with his head.

"No!," Vinny shouted, you can't, you'll die! The game will end, you will lose everything. Everyone knows, you can only exist within your craft or within a marked zone, outside your craft. This is NOT a marked zone!"

"We don't have any more time, I must go," Tommy urged, "Z is too powerful, we won't get back into the game anyway."

"Look Tommy, we came this far to look for the crystal and it's nowhere in sight. We have to keep looking until we find it. It's hidden somewhere within this complex," Vinny pleaded.

"Vinny, you gotta trust me. It's like everything else I've been able to do, I don't know how or why but I'm pretty sure that this is the ONLY way to get the OmegaLux Crystal. Now just keep her steady and let me go, please!"

Tommy sprung a hatch just above his head and pushed off with his feet like he was diving into deep water as his body left the craft.

Vinny watched from below as Tommy lifted out of the craft.

Tommy began to move as if swimming through the air, more of a breaststroke than a crawl. To his surprise, he moved much faster than swimming. He pulled with his arms and kicked like a frog with his legs. On his third such effort, as he brought his hands forward and kicked, a single point of light appeared above his head.

Vinny thought for sure that this was an opening through which a weapon would appear to blast his little brother from the game. In fact, he was amazed that Tommy still showed up in the game at all. After all, he was clearly outside of the craft now, and definitely not in a marked zone.

Tommy was blissful. Blue knew that he was doing the right thing, like he was in control of his most lucid yet fantastic dream. For a moment, thoughts of the giant peanut, the yeti and Glurp skittered across his mind but he quickly made them dissolve. This was his world now and he knew it. Blue had no idea what to expect next, he only felt certain that whatever was about to happen, had to happen, so he just kept going. As he raised his arms above his head to reach forward for another stroke, a giant white dome began to take shape overhead.

The dome quickly became a globe, encircling Tommy, Vinny and the small craft, isolating them from the rest of the complex. Tommy reached even farther forward, directly toward the center point from which the light originated. Vinny saw Tommy as he almost touched the point of origin as the light became unbearably bright, then suddenly, darkness.

Vinny was sitting in total darkness all alone in a pitch-black room. He was no longer within the game. He was no longer sitting in his craft or even in his gaming chair. He was on Tommy's game room floor, in total darkness without Tommy.

Blue placed his hands around the precise area of origin of the point of light. Although the light was blinding, he looked straight into it. He felt neither heat nor cold. There was nothing solid to the point of light, yet he held it between his palms. Intuitively he rolled it in his palms and as he did facets began to appear and dance between his open cupped hands. The facets solidified into a crystal. Blue was standing in the center of the globe. He stood upon nothing, yet felt remarkably secure. Around him stood seven figures dressed in white. An ethereal voice spoke a single word, "Welcome." Blue said nothing. He simply smiled.

Tommy sat directly across from Vinny in the total darkness of his game room. He let out the slightest laugh as he realized where he was.

"Tommy? Is that you?" Vinny almost whispered.

"Yeah, it's me." Tommy answered, the laugh still warming its way through his response.

"What the Varst just happened?" Vinny gasped. "Did you get to see the crystal? Did Z blast you, or did you just fry in space? I mean, I didn't even get fired upon and I ended up back here before you did, what in Farb's name is going on?"

Tommy opened up his cupped hands, the OmegaLux Crystal illuminated the whole room as if he had just thrown the switch on a thousand searchlights, he rolled it up to his fingertips and it calmed to a gentle glow.

Tommy smiled across the room at Vinny and said, "Game Over."

 "Bastin" Farbunkle, Tommy, you got it," Vinny shouted," BEEZLE little bro" it's REAL!

"This whole thing has been completely unreal." Max was now alone with Victor and had a few things to say without Tommy around. "First, Victor Alonso and Tommy Levito, both dead. Then, Victor Alonso and Tommy Levito UNDEAD!" Totally alive, back from the dead, the hole in Levito's gut, which I PUT THERE is GONE, magically healed. Add to this freakish occurrence the fact that suddenly Victor and Tommy are no longer trying to kill each other but instead decide to be friends and have a bite to eat together, ON MY DIME!"

"NOW THIS!"

"No lights, and apparently no power in the entire Bastin' house! I gotta say, Victor, I think I caught a bullet right after I plugged Tommy and this whole thing is my little piece of VARST! Not that I don't have it coming, but I never guessed it would be like this. I think I'd be happier with the flames, in servitude to the Queen of Despair, Elistay herself!" Max complained.

"Maybe you're right Max," Victor responded, "you might be dead, 'cause I'm guessin' the whole point of Varst is that you aren't happy...forever!"

"Cute Victor, you're a real mental mechanic, always have an answer," Max teased. "Well why don't you use that tool box you park on your neck to get the damn power on?!"

"Actually Max, it's a pretty nice night out, waddya-say we take a little walk first," Leer smoothly positioned, taking Max completely off-guard as he slid his arm around her.

"Maybe I was wrong, and I haven't been such a bad girl after all," Max cooed as she let her head fall to Victor's shoulder while they turned from the house and strode into the moonlight.

11 MAX

Max and Victor walked close together, quietly, down a winding path toward the falls. The moon was full and lit their way through the park, but it was the sound of the rushing water which brought them straight to the falls. They stared in silence at the water that danced and sparkled in the moonlight. Leer marveled within himself how profoundly the beauty of parallel worlds made him long for and appreciate his own. Something about Max reminded him so strongly of Catherine Kent that he had a hard time resisting the urge to speak to her as if she really knew him and vice versa. The fact that Max knew Victor so well was helpful but only slightly since Leer did not. Still, he knew that Max would be his best guide on his journey through this world and it didn't hurt one bit that she was as pretty as he remembered Catherine to be.

"You know, Max," he said, "I meant what I said. I'd really like to know what you think I should do next."

"Well Victor," Max warmly smiled, "That's a little like asking all of that water down there if it would like to go back up those falls. It would be a vast of a lot of work, and in the end, what would it matter? It would all come falling right back down again, now wouldn't it?"

"I suppose it would," Victor shrugged, "but let's just imagine that it wouldn't. What if you could change just five things? You would tell me what you wanted, and I would do it, and those things wouldn't go back to the way they were, and they wouldn't be taken away from you, modified, watered down, substituted or forgotten." Leer could see the anticipation in Max's eyes, so Victor continued, "There's got to be a few things you'd do differently," he smiled knowingly. It was obvious that she could think of considerably more than just a few things that she would like to see changed.

Max laughed, "All right Victor, I'll play along, what're my options? Are we talking about us, shit with my daddy, the bastin' pigs or just how many times we go out for sushi in a given week?"

"Whatever you want, Max, no matter how big, no matter how small. I just want to know what you would change," Victor replied sincerely.

Max recognized that he meant it and that made her grow silent. She sighed, and her eyes took on an almost wistful appearance as she inhaled deeply. "Y'know Victor, it's kinda' funny but I think you may have started a change I never would have admitted to wanting. I am just plain tired of the Alonso vs. Levito wars. How long can people keep killing each other over the same shit anyway? I mean the moment I blasted Tommy in the gut I thought, now why the Bast did I do that? Usually I don't waste anybody unless they're going to waste me. It's hard to explain." She thought for a little while as Victor just held her hand, then she looked very seriously into his eyes and said, "But you know as well as I do that my father isn't going to let ANY of the shit that happened tonight rest. Thanks be to Farb that we've got a whole week before he gets back so we can figure out the bastin' story about tonight. I think he'll forgive you for coming back from the dead, but dinner with Tommy Levito?   Good Luck!"

Leer knew he was facing a big problem when it came to Max's father. He had to get information from Max without looking entirely clueless, so he decided to leverage the fact that just hours ago, Victor was dead.

"Max," Victor confided, "I don't even know what to think about tonight myself much less what I'm going to tell anyone else about it. I mean, how often does a person rise from the dead out of the back of an ambulance bound for the morgue. Nobody seemed to really be grieving my loss, either. Even you looked like you were being horribly inconvenienced by my resurrection."

Max's face dropped open, she paused, then answered Victor's implication thoughtfully, "Victor, you can be very hard to live with. You're stubborn, opinionated, bossy, arrogant and not the least bit interested in anything that doesn't fit in a box that says, "What Victor Wants." There were plenty of people there tonight who would have loved for those ambulance doors to remain closed. Some of them probably even considered blowing the damn ambulance up, just to make sure! And I must admit, I was beginning to let ideas of what life would be like without you, creep into my head. But something has changed," Max looked deeper into Victor's eyes, "you're different." Max said softly, making Leer feel unmasked, exposed. Max continued, "But I'm not talking about that whole rising from the dead thing."

"What?" Victor blurted in response, "What do you mean?"

"Sorry baby, daddy doesn't really give a shit about you," Max sneered, "What he will care about is what happened before your fight with Tommy Levito. He's going to want to know what happened to a whole load of JumpJuice, and that means everything. How'd it go missing, or more like, how did someone manage to steal our whole delivery without a fight and where the Varst is Bobby? I mean Bobby could handle a half-dozen of Tommy's guys five out of six times and at least three of them the other one time out of six, so who in Farb's name got the drop on him? I guess it's time to ask your new best friend where he put our boy. If he does have him, that means he's got the Juice! He sure did get upset when you tried to pin him down on it before. Bet you don't want that to happen again."

"No, you're right Max. I want to know, but I'm not dying to find out!" Victor joked.

Max laughed with true appreciation. She was beginning to forget what an asshole Victor could be. Leer could sense that Max was opening up to Victor and realized that he had a limited time to get the answers he needed before morning.

"So what other part of everything do I need to come up with." Victor asked, "I don't know who has the JumpJuice and my guess is that Tommy doesn't either, and I don't think that's the answer he's after." Victor paused.

110

"What?" Max sensed something in Victor, something significant. She asked gently,
"Are you scared Victor?" Leer remained quiet, "I can't believe this, Victor Alonso scared of Sal Lorenzo!"

"It's not that!" Victor snapped back.

Leer knew he had to maintain some consistency in his behavior or risk the collision of this and several other parallel words, better to stick with newfound sensitivity than outright fear.

"I just want you to tell me what YOU want. Not what you think I want. Not what you think Sal wants or what Tommy wants. Tell me Max, what do you want? Victor sat down on the grass, leaving Max standing over him, the moon high above her as she pulled the baseball cap from her head, whipping her long, black hair free. She looked so familiar to Leer.

"I remember," he said without thinking.

Leer stopped himself from saying anything more that might incriminate him. He was remembering a time with Catherine Kent when she was Mona, a time that only he knew about but planned to share with Blue, when he was John, before he went back to being Leer, but he never got the time.

One of the things that is truly hard to grasp about alternate realities and parallel universes is that they are NOT the same thing yet they both exist, and one can become the other, while the other can't unless it is a mistake or a miracle, which many mistakes are.

Mona was not a mistake but mistaking Max for Mona and talking about a past which wasn't hers would have been just the kind of mistake that would have ruined all the progress that Leer was making with Max. But Leer did stop himself and that left a silence which hung in the air perilously.

"You remember what?" Max asked with an expectation fueled by the faraway look she noticed in Victor's eyes though it had been fleeting.

"What?," Leer mumbled.

"Yes, Victor," Max urged, "What do you remember?"

Leer couldn't think of a single thing he could make up that would fit. He was completely at a loss, so he said, "Nothing."

"C'mon Victor, you were going to say something," Max cooed.

Leer had spent over twenty-five years away from the Earth on which he knew Blue, but he had spent more than that away from Mona, and even more away from Catherine. He would have loved to talk about the feeling he remembered, but he knew he couldn't do that with Max. But he had to talk to Max about something and it had to make sense at this time, on this planet - with this woman! He decided to take a chance, "It's something I can't describe. I mean, it's how I felt," he sighed deeply, "I..."

"Victor," Max cut in, "it's okay, you never can express your feelings. So," Max beamed, "I am going to help you out." She sat down next to him on the grass. She walked her hands toward him, so her face was inches from his," Now Victor, tell me, were you remembering something about me, about us, or about the JumpJuice? And it better not be about the JumpJuice," she winked.

Leer was relieved to be past the initial blunder but feared the direction in which the conversation was going. There was only one hope in which he had any chance of survival, "Us," he said and leaned directly into her lips. Leer kissed Max for a very long time, after which he slowly withdrew. Max remained weighted in Victor's direction with her eyes closed and her lips soft. She slowly opened her eyes, gently biting her lower lip as if to check on the reality of the kiss and whispered, "You were saying?"

Before she could ask again, he held her, pulling her close while laying her gently back upon the soft grass and kissed her.

The kiss was powerful. It ended the conversation and started the night.

Most people would feel at least a little bit self-conscious about having sex in the middle of a grassy knoll just a few paces away from a touristy waterfall in a public park. However, when one of you happens to run the town and the other is your sizzling hot babe, and both of you are packin' heat, or at least have it close enough to your writhing, naked bodies, you pretty much throw modesty over the precipice like water on the rocks.

Afterward, Victor and Max laid back on the grass and looked at the stars. They lay there in silence for a long time until Max broke the silence, "Do you think we'll ever live like other people do?"

Now this is a very difficult question to answer when you ARE an "other people." So, Leer answered in the only way he could, "What other people do you mean?"

Max sighed, "Victor, haven't you ever tried to imagine what you would be doing if you didn't run Rat Town for my father - What it would be like if there was no such thing as JumpJuice?"

The urge to laugh out loud swelled within Leer, an urge he knew he needed to contain. Leer had learned a lot of things from travelling, how to survive, how to build, how to fight and to hide, but of all the lessons Leer had learned, the one that proved time and time again to serve him best was that of cultivating the ability to recognize when it was time to just shut up and listen, and generally that lesson served him best when in the company of a woman.

Max was ready to talk.

She had been holding on to a treasure trove of feelings for a very long time. Most of them concerned him, well rather, Victor, what he did to her, how he did it, what he said to her and how he said it, when, where, in front of whom and more. Leer had effectively not only unlocked the door to Max's heart, he had opened a gateway to Victor's past. He was granted admission and given the guided tour. He discovered that he was, for lack of a better description, a macho, arrogant, reckless, self-centered control freak, addicted to JumpJuice, film scores and board games and played well with the other boys when it came to sports and games of chance. He was a man's man, a short, stocky, balding man's man; cocky, forceful, omnipotent and fearless before all, except Max.

The two times that he confided anything to Max were enough to keep her by his side.

A mother's death can be a devastating experience for anyone and it was for Victor. But what disturbed him most is that nobody killed her. He didn't have anyone to blame; no one against whom to seek and have his revenge. She simply died.

When his brother died, he killed Jason "the Shark" by holding onto his long, beautiful, curly hair with both hands and suffocating him in a vat of freshly made hummus. When he was finished, he toasted his brother with "the Shark's" own wine while dipping pita wedges into the hummus. One of his "boys" thought he saw a tear in Victor's eye and said, "Hey boss, what's the matter, you look upset." Without hesitation, Victor smiled and, winking in Max's direction said," Of course I'm upset, I hate when there's hair in my food!"

Everyone laughed.

Victor, to ease his sorrow over the loss of his brother and to overcome the feeling that killing "the Shark" did nothing to alleviate that sadness, the boys because they thought that shit was funny, and Max, to get over the fact that she had to go home and sleep with Victor.

Victor didn't laugh when his mother died. He cried. He cried on Max's shoulder. He cried on Max's breast. He cried on Max's belly. He cried on Max's lap. Then he got ridiculously high on JumpJuice and drank. He did that for about a week. Then he threw up for two days. The following morning, he woke up, brushed his teeth, dressed, and said only one thing to Max before he left. It was the first thing he ever confided to her. "One day," he said, "I am going to love someone as much as my mother loved me." Then he walked out of the house. She did not follow him.

Leer listened with keen interest to everything that Max told him, attempting to judge where she was headed with the whole monologue, while recognizing that he was supposed to be all of these things she told him he was with the exception that now he was changed, transformed by death and resurrection into what Leer hoped he could present as a new and better Victor; all without raising the suspicion of those who lived, worked, fought and loved within Victor's world.

Max told Leer about Victor's gang, though she complained about personalities and clothing styles, he got the point that they were pretty tight and that any one of them would have loved to be his friend. He had made it clear in ways both subtle and not so, that he neither wanted nor needed friends. They were loyal, mostly stupid, but loyal, and since the death of Victor's sister, the only "family" he had, except for a nephew. The nephew, according to Victor, was too young to be good for anything. This evaluation was based upon the circumstances that the boy was home when Victor's sister was killed and couldn't or didn't do anything to stop it.

The story goes that these guys were going to "invite" Victor's sister out for a little party. The boy said that he had heard a bunch of laughing coming from upstairs, so he went upstairs, calling for his mother. Victor's sister then shushed him and sent him away and went back to laughing. About twenty minutes later the boy heard his mother saying "no." Then louder, "NO." Then louder, "Just get the BAST OUT OF HERE!" - Then the boy heard a loud crash followed by a thud and three different voices saying, "bast," "Damn!" and "BAST!" respectively and footsteps running out of the house. He went upstairs and found his mother, Victor's sister, Gloria, dead. Her head was bloody and a shattered vase lay upon the floor beside her body. The boy told the police who had been visiting his mother.

The following morning, the three visitors were on the front page of the local newspaper, dead. They had each been stuffed into a fifty-gallon drum full of water, their legs sticking up like flowers from a vase.

That was the way Victor dealt with loss, swift and mighty vengeance.

Max continued in great detail to further illustrate that she had feelings for Victor that ran deeper than he had ever before been willing to recognize. Leer understood this and was more than willing to listen to every detail. He had already decided that Victor would from this day forward be committed to Max in a way he had never been, and that Max was going to help him on his path through this life. Every bit of information that Max could provide about Victor would be of immense value to Leer, so when Max paused and looked at him as if she had been carrying on or boring him in some way he said, "please, Max, continue."

"Do you remember what you told me about you and Gloria, when you were young?" Max asked without waiting for a response before she reminded him of it. Victor's sister Gloria was at the very center of the second thing that he had ever shared with Max in confidence...

"When I was young, very young, before I had ever met any kids from outside of the family, not brothers, sisters, cousins, nothin' y'know, I stuttered," he told Max. "Horrible, serious stuttering!" When he told her, Max thought Victor was going to cry right then and there in front of her, his expression showing a profound sadness intensified by self-loathing at his own weakness. He continued, "uncontrollable, ridiculous, fitful and embarrassing stuttering, the kind you could never live down if it was ever heard outside of the family, so disgraceful that no Alonso dared speak of it. It was like trying to get a sentence out of a bag of microwave popcorn, the same bastin' syllable repeated, over and over again, slowly, painfully at first, then popping out faster and faster' til my whole body shook and finally I nearly choked on it, my face exhausted I let that same stupid syllable flop slowly out of my sagging lips and flaccid tongue, giving up, hiding away whatever thought I had that seemed so important at the time; turning away from whomever I was trying to talk to - sensing their relief that they wouldn't have to try to understand me or even pretend to care. Because none of them did, not anyone, no one cared about me at all, except Gloria and, of course my mother, but she was too busy nursing my brother or makin' dinner or ironing, for Farb's sake, who needs that many pressed shirts, ever! But Gloria, Gloria was different. Gloria loved me, not because she had to or anything, just because she did. She didn't run away from any challenge, ever. I think she stuck it out with me half the time just to prove that she could. No, really, I think she actually cared."

"Gloria used to sit down and start talking to this stupid little stuffed dog she called "Puddles" Then she would try to get me to talk to Puddles. Most of the time she'd tell me to just say hi to Puddles. So, I would say...H-h-h-h-h-hi P-p-p-p-p-p-up-p-p-up-pu... I sounded like an old-time car starting up, so Gloria would start doing it too. Then she'd pretend that Puddles was driving the car, scooting around on his ass all over the place, in the living room, across the dining room table and then we'd laugh, and she'd crash him into me and we'd roll around on the ground laughing." Victor laughed to himself, remembering the faraway, innocent joy, but checked himself as he realized that Max had just learned a secret that no Alonso had ever shared. He brushed it away casually saying, "Before I knew it, I was a Farb-damn, silver tongued orator with a precocious penchant for prose, pleasantly performing poetic palpitations in perpetuity, primarily if not purely for personal pleasure!"

Although Max sensed that Victor felt that he had gone too far, allowing her to learn something that no one outside of the Alonso family had ever known, he seemed to somehow be relieved, as if some monstrously burdensome feeling of guilt had been suddenly and completely lifted from his shoulders; and that her silent acceptance of him and his humble beginnings was somehow a sign, a blessing of forgiveness and compassion from Farb himself. Every once in a while, Max felt as though her very being, her energy, her soul, was somehow directly connected to Farb, to his divine will, or even something more basic, pure truth. This was just such an occasion. She spent several days thinking about it. Mostly because Victor, who gracefully bowed his way backwards out of the house on the heels of his homespun alliteration, did not return for several days. He just disappeared. Max figured that he had run off to his man cave, but he hadn't. His boys had checked for him there a couple of times during his disappearance, but he was nowhere to be found.

"Where did you go, Victor?" Max asked as she closed the lid on her treasure trove of the past so suddenly that it took Leer off-guard.

"I really can't remember," Leer said, almost without thinking, but it was the right answer for Victor, the old Victor.
The fact that Victor could only come up with a response as lame as the admission that he didn't remember something of great importance to Max was not a surprise to her, but it was offensive considering that Max was trying to really take Victor at his word that he wanted to hear what was important to her. But she had put herself out there and now he had hurt her. "That figures," Max snapped, "I tell you that I've stuck with you for two reasons and you can't even remember one of them!" She folded her arms across her chest, hardened her expression, and locked her chin into the, "I am never looking at another thing in my life again" position.

Leer was struck by how deeply this affected him. He wanted so badly to be able to remember anything about her, but he could only remember the past he had with Catherine. One extremely odd thing about this moment though, was that he had seen this exact expression on Catherine's face, Max may as well have been Catherine in this moment, her body language, even her breathing and the way she held both of her hands under her upper arms when she crossed them was exactly the same, and that meant that he was in trouble. "I'm sorry,' he said, knowing full well that he would get nowhere with a simple apology. Max remained unmoved. Leer was not a mind reader, but he didn't need to be to recognize that Max was silently fuming. He was just about to say something equally generic and meaningless when something unpredictable, almost magical and absolutely vital occurred.

He remembered something.

Unconscionably, inexplicably and conveniently, Leer remembered a moment from Victor's life. Unconscionably, because it wasn't just any memory, it was precisely the memory he would have been remembering if he truly was Victor. Inexplicably, because he wasn't Victor and conveniently, because it was the memory that Max needed to hear to feel that there was any reason at all to continue living with Victor. She was so confused over Victor, Tommy, wrong, right, Farb or Farblessness, that she was about to snap. That one slip into old Victor made all of the feelings of desperation return in force.

"I went to sit with your mother," Leer said. Slowly, Max lifted her eyes to him. As her eyes met his he could see tears welling up within them, and beyond the tears, everything else. He saw her nervousness within that moment - felt that she was struggling with an uneasy attraction mingled with a fearful hope, toward and about Victor. He saw a scared little girl who couldn't understand why her mother was taken from her, why her mother could spend hours at a time staring into space, as if her mind was elsewhere on some fantastic voyage - only to return to a chaotic, confused and thoroughly uncomfortable state - Then, moments later, behave as though not a thing was wrong with the world, the doctors were doing their best with her and surely she would be leaving the hospital any day but MY how her Max had grown, why only yesterday she was skipping off to her first day of school. "But everything changes, by Farb, doesn't it Max?" her mother would say, nearly every day for years at a time, until the day that Max decided to stop putting herself through it. Leer saw all of this in a single moment, a moment which seemed to hang in the air like smoke after fireworks. Then Max fell into his chest and sobbed, hugging him like he was the only sure thing, the only thing that was real in the entire universe. Like she needed to hold him in order to survive, so close and so tightly, like she would never let him go. They held one another like that for so long that their breath became one breath, their hearts beating a single beat.

12 ICE CREAM

"Single?" the girl behind the counter asked Blue.

"Who me?' Tommy responded dimwittedly.

"Just don't even tell me you're going to start down that road. sugar, I meant the cone. Single or double scoop. Actually, you're a pretty tall order yourself, so, how 'bout a triple?" the girl continued, obviously flirtatious but in no mood to hear the same old puns for what Blue quickly guessed had occurred far too often.

Tommy was supposed to be something of an ice cream freak, according to Vinny, who had made it clear, several times, during their ride over to Jen and Barry's Ice Cream Parlor that they were on a mission to complete the ultimate JumpJuice rush. Blue had decided to go along with whatever Vinny wanted to do for a couple of days, if he could live through it. That would give him time to figure out who he was and what he could do with the OmegaLux Crystal, if anything. Blue was a little concerned that he may not be able to keep pace with Vinny's JumpJuice schedule, but the ice cream was definitely going to be a welcome tonic for the dry mouth he was experiencing. So, Blue went for the double.

"Better make it a triple!," Vinny laughed and slapped Tommy on the back. Blue smiled reluctantly in the girl's direction and she eagerly heaped three large scoops of "Funky Monkey" onto a chocolate dipped sugar cone.

The cone went down surprisingly easily. In fact, it was so delicious and consumable that Blue was finding it easier and easier to assume the person of Tommy. He was far more comfortable being someone completely different from himself than he had ever thought he could be. He was thinking that he was either like Tommy on several levels or that people are like one another, in general, on a far more basic and essential level than he had ever imagined.

"I just love to watch you eat that shit, Tommy," Vinny beamed, " it does my heart good to see my little brother so happy. I mean, you seem to be really happy, and you haven't mentioned Victor Alonso or Sal Lorenzo the entire time we have been hangin' together."

Blue turned white.

He wasn't sure what to say. He really liked Vinny. He wanted a friend, maybe even better, a brother, but this was weird. If he exposed himself, Vinny could never be expected to understand. If he told Vinny and Vinny understood, Vinny would realize that his brother really was dead. So Blue said, "I just don't even want to think about those guys."

"Yeah, Tommy, I can tell," Vinny apologized, I didn't mean to ruin your buzz man!"

Tommy responded," What the Varst, let's get another bastin' cone and forget about it!"
Blue was pretty sure that another ice cream cone wouldn't solve any issues he was having in getting caught up on who he was supposed to be, but he knew damn well it wouldn't hurt. As he slowly licked the second cone, strawberry for one scoop and a flavor he decided to try solely based upon its name, "Crazy Rabbit," for the second scoop, he attempted to begin his quest for understanding by saying, "Vinny, I have absolutely no idea what I'm going to do. I mean, I damn near died for Farb's sake!" Blue was getting used to the idea that nearly everyone he had met so far referred to Farb as God. He hadn't seen any evidence of any other religion at all. He figured it was still early, but he may as well

go with the flow and at least speak like everyone else around him. Blue was already on his own spiritual journey before Leer jumped out of the page and into his life again. So much had already happened since then that it seemed like a lifetime ago, and not just a different lifetime. In Blue's mind, the whole issue of religion was purely an issue of semantics, either the same story with different characters or the same message revealed through a different story. There was something about this Farb thing though, that made him feel uneasy. From what he could see, it was the only religion. Not only was it the only religion, but everyone seemed to practice it, or at least made references to Farb. He figured there had to be a healthy share of Farbnostics out there somewhere, but he'd play along for now, after all, how he fit into the religious construct of this parallel world was not of the utmost importance.

"Or is it? Dunn-Dun-Dunn!" Vinny joked, snapping Blue out of his secret musings.

Blue was completely baffled because it seemed like Vinny was reading his mind. "What did you say?" Tommy asked in complete self-conscious bewilderment.

"Man Tommy, where were you just then? Did you hear anything I said? I was just joking. You know, like, A day without Victor Alonso and Sal Lorenzo isn't a bad thing, it's not the end of the world! Or is it? Dunn-Dun-Dunn!" Vinny tried again.

Tommy didn't respond very well this time either, but he did manage a half-assed laugh. Blue was too busy thinking, "what world is this anyway?" But he managed a reply of, "I think I could do with a week of not seeing anyone I normally have to deal with!"

"That's an awesome idea," Vinny exclaimed, "Let's hit the Shadowlands, visit the Leocrites - remember how you used to want to be a Leocrite?"

"Vaguely," Tommy groaned.

"Aw, Bullshit, Tommy!" it was all you ever talked about before you got into the JumpJuice business." Vinny chided.

"Yeah, well that was a while ago," Blue guessed out loud.

"Too long, "Vinny confirmed, pulling Tommy up out of his seat at Jen and Barry's, grinning from ear to ear, "and with any luck, you'll forget all about the JumpJuice business after a week in the Shadowlands!"
As Vinny pulled Tommy up to leave Jen and Barry's, ready for a chance to get away from it all, Blue was thinking that this would be just the right thing, even though he had no idea what the Shadowlands were. That's when Vinny walked straight into a brick wall. Actually, it was a well-built, motionless, statue of a man who stood directly between Vinny and the exit doors. When Vinny bumped into him, he remained expressionless, he did not budge.

"Excuse me, " Vinny said politely and gracefully stepped around the man, still pulling Tommy along by the shoulder. Instantly, another two statues appeared from behind the man, blocking the exit of Jen and Barry's Ice Cream Shop, passive aggression in the flesh. The danger was palpable. The men, both larger than the first stood motionless yet resolute. A couple of weeks earlier, Vinny would have known his next move, a quick right with the base of his hand into the face of the guy on the left, sending the cartilage of his nose up into his brain, excruciating pain, or death likely, giving Tommy the opportunity to perform a leaping kick right over Vinny's own outstretched body, to the throat of the other statue, breaking the windpipe, possibly severing the jugular or both, again pain or death. The third guy would be easy, unsure as to which one of them to go for, he would suffer the wrath of both, death. Today, however, things were different. Tommy was different, and Vinny was smart enough to choose another path. "Hello Gentlemen," he smiled as he let go of Tommy's shoulder with a gentle stroke, as if to say keep calm. Blue was not a fighter, so Tommy had no trouble at all following that path.

The fearsome duo swung open like an iron gate and a man no larger than a grade-schooler emerged from between them, smiling and popping whole peanuts into his mouth. He smiled sardonically, "Well, what do we have here? The walking dead and the next of kin! You know, I always get a kick out of zombie movies. Those damn things move so slowly, yet they always manage to catch up with everyone who runs and hides from them. And the only way to kill them for good is to cut their heads off or to blast them to bits. Well, I am not running, nor am I hiding. So, what'll it be? Taking off the heads? or Blasting to bits?

Blue hadn't met Sal Lorenzo yet, but it wasn't too hard to figure out that this must be him. This process of identification took him long enough to leave him seemingly speechless, prompting Sal to continue, "What's this? Max never told me that she blasted a hole in your gut AND cut your little tongue out, she's a good girl that Maxie!"

"I'm just a little stunned," Blue countered, making Sal laugh, looking to his minions for the obligatory chorus, but Blue silenced the laughter with a deadpan, "I just had no idea you liked ice cream, and look, you've brought your own peanuts, business must not be so good."

Vinny winced in mock pain and followed with a brilliant idea of his own. "If that's the case," he smiled as he smoothly fell backward onto a stool at the counter, " let me buy you and your "friends" an ice cream"

The "friends" looked to Sal with indignation but to their surprise he accepted with a grace that said two things. I can play this game as well as anybody and I am not going to kill you today. "Why Vincent, how very diplomatic of you," he accepted as he stepped up and ordered a fudge sundae with extra peanuts, " and three chocolate dipped cones, rolled in nuts for my associates." He turned to Tommy and Vinny and whispered, "gotta keep their gun hands free."

"Excuse me, Mr. Lorenzo," interjected the largest of the associates, a big black man, with a smooth deep voice, who bashfully added, "I'm allergic to nuts."

Vinny and Tommy laughed so hard that it was infectious. Sal began to laugh, as did his associates, one by one, including Duane, the allergic one.

"Make one of those without nuts," Sal added as Vinny held a fifty coin aloft, tears in his eyes, smiling and breathless.

The server took the fifty and Tommy quickly pulled Vinny up and toward the door saying, "Enjoy your ice cream gentlemen"

"Tommy," Sal replied in an ominous tone," You and I need to talk. And

Soon. And Vinny," he softened, "thanks for the ice cream"

Without hesitation, Tommy and Vinny left Jen and Barry's, destined for the Shadowlands.

13 ALL MIXED UP

"Where do you think Sal is right now?" Leer asked Max, knowing that an eventual meeting was unavoidable.

"He's probably still in Cleveland," Max smiled. "You know how he loves Cleveland, besides, he's got a lot of business to look after there, if you know what I mean?"

"Well, not exactly, I mean, what could possibly be going on in Cleveland?" Victor laughed.

"Very funny, Victor," Max replied, you know full well that Cleveland is probably the biggest city for JumpJuice on Salta, well, maybe Belfast is bigger, but Cleveland is at least second. Anyway, you're just yankin' my chain, aren't you?"

Leer realized that he had made a stupid mistake. It's hard to remain on your toes at all times when it comes to alternate time lines and parallel worlds. Just because beef is beef doesn't mean that Cleveland is Cleveland and Belfast may not even be in Ireland. Actually, there may not even be an Ireland, St. Patrick's Day, leprechauns or even Guinness, perish the thought.

"Oh, I get it," Max continued, "You're still upset about the last time we hit Cleveland and I left you handcuffed to the bed for a whole morning while Zeek hammered the roulette wheel for 30k." Max teased him, her expression triumphant as she climbed into Victor's lap and reached past his head to the backrest of the mind-blowing chair he found himself sitting in. It was like a Porsche and a luxury recliner built into one. Max eased her face closer to his by grinding into his lap, arching her back and leaning in, her triumph turning to a pout as she said, but you had it coming to you, didn't you Vic?"

If Leer had truly been Victor, he would have recognized this routine and known what to expect. As it was though, he was inwardly praying that he would survive.

"You had to drag me to every strip club, fantasy gift shop and pleasure palace on the strip, while you and the boys ogled and stuffed every G-string and plastic rack in Cleveland!" Max hula-ed her hips and ground down harder onto Leer so the only thing between them was the denim of his trousers and what little she was calling underwear these days. She bent her elbows, snapping in on him like a steel trap closing on a defenseless animal, her breasts tight against his chest, her mouth breathing his exhalations. "I thought I made you forget about all those girls Vic," she punctuated with a little more grind, then reached for a remote on the end table adjacent to the chair. "Looks like I'm going to have to try a little harder," she grinned and ground just a little more, pressing a button on the remote and the chair sprang to life. The arms opened forward at the front and speakers rose from within, gliding into place. Music enveloped them as Max danced upon Leer's denim. He still wasn't sure where Cleveland was, but for now, he didn't care.

****

Blue was beginning to become accustomed to living as Tommy in this new world and Leer was truly enjoying being with Catherine, Mona, Max. Confusing? Yes because neither Blue nor Leer intended to remain in this alternate reality except that they had no way of knowing what they should be doing to get out. Imagine, for a moment what it would be like to have none of the normal indicators we so easily take for granted at your disposal. For example, take away the identity of anyone with whom you are speaking, remove the location and context and see how you feel about the sureness of your footing.

"That was unbelievable, how smooth can you get. I thought I was going to die!"

"You thought you were going to die, what about me? I was just going along with you. You're the one who started off crazy, crazy good. You really got right on top of things the way you took control right from the beginning. I mean, I normally get a little nervous about what might happen even if I just hear Sal's name, but you took all those fears away. I was able to stand up and deliver, or in this case sit down!"

"Well, no one can resist that creamy goodness, I could guzzle down buckets of the stuff. With or without nuts."

"Farb, I feel like I'm sixteen all over again."

"Yeah, I know what you mean, I haven't felt like this in a very long time, maybe ever! Now that you mention it, you even look different. I can't quite put my finger on it, but somehow you've changed."

"I guess resurrection has its price."

"Funny, you know I mean in a good way, there's something about you that just isn't the same, but I'm getting used to it."

"Maybe I should get myself killed every day."

"Please don't say that, I don't want to lose you again."

This entire conversation took place at the exact same time between two distinct sets of individuals, Tommy and Vinny and Victor and Max. If you really think about it, you can well imagine who said what but this illustrates the flexibility, transmutableness and interconnectedness of our existence. It also exposes its fragility because both Max and Vinny have lost the very people with whom they think they are talking, loving and enjoying companionship.

****

Blue didn't know what to say to Vinny. The fact was that Tommy, the real Tommy, had already been lost to Vinny without his knowledge and Blue was beginning to wish that Vinny really was his big brother. There was a warmth to Vinny that, despite his brawn, spoke of a gentleness and kindness which few exemplify, unless you happen to be threatening someone close to him, then my friend, you had better watch out! But Tommy was his brother and Blue, by virtue of being Tommy, had a guardian angel. As long as Vinny thought he was Tommy, no one could touch him without Vinny jumping in with all his might to defend his little brother. Still, Blue felt as though he had done something to hurt Vinny, as if taking over his brother's lifeless body was somehow his own doing. It wasn't. Logically he knew that and comforted himself with that rationale whenever the waves of shame began to wash over him. Besides, there wasn't anything rational about popping up in someone's dead brother's body. All of this thinking and feeling shame took time. It left Tommy looking a little like a stunned deer, caught in the headlights of Vinny's heartfelt sentimentality.

"Hey Tommy, it's okay man." Vinny said as he laughed, "Ground control to Major Tom"

Blue snapped back to what he now knew as reality and laughed hard from Tommy's drop-jawed open mouth. Vinny thought that Tommy was laughing at his clever comment, but Blue was nearly in tears as he laughed, both out of relief at the opportunity to laugh in spite of the awkwardness he was feeling over the circumstances and the realization that Bowie existed simultaneously across two disparate parallel universes.

****

"Let's dance," Max cooed into Victor's ear as she slinked her way off of Victor's satisfied flesh.

The chair pulsing Bowie's familiar back beat into his spine causing his satisfied smile to widen into an ecstatic grin. "I thought we just did," Victor said as he rose to his feet and took Max into his arms, twirling her as the two of them sang together, "under the moonlight, the serious moonlight," it was the perfect night for getting to know each other. They danced for several songs until Max turned away, excusing herself with a kiss.

Leer fell back into the chair, the songs of Leonard Cohen now gracing the speakers of this magnificently comfortable sound system. Leer had once met Leonard Cohen in a world where a megalomaniac dictator had gained control over all civilization after a bloody war which lasted for decades, nearly eliminating Cohen's entire culture. None of his songs were the same but the voice and the style were unmistakable, unlike Bowie who seemed to be the exact same guy across multiple worlds.

When Leer met Cohen, it was the only time he ever divulged his secret of traveling between parallel worlds. He wanted to let Leonard know that in another world, terrible things happened to his people, but they were able to overcome the hardship of war and persecution. Leonard Cohen didn't seem to be the least bit surprised by any of it. He simply replied, "We all have our parts to play in life, mine, here, is to remind my people of who we are, who we have been and who we can be. Another time and place requires a different song."

Leer thought of these words as he continued to enjoy the post orgasm bliss that temporarily took his mind off the less than pleasant realities of this latest "mission." For Leer, it has always been about the mission. His path has been defined by what was needed by that which he refers to as "All That Is." Rarely did Leer find himself in a place of ease, physically, that is. His life was constantly in flux, always active and far more adventurous than it would seem possible for one man. Emotionally and spiritually, Leer was quite a different man. He was at peace. He had managed to achieve a connection with all that existed around him. His mind and spirit were one at all times and nothing external to himself could shake that foundation, nothing with the possible exception of Catherine Kent.

Max called to him from within her bedroom, "Victor, daddy's back in town and he wants you at the clubhouse ASAP. It's a text message so I can't tell what he's thinking but it's got something to do with Tommy. Listen to this, "Tell Victor to get to the clubhouse ASAP-What the Varst happened with you and Levito? Never mind," she continued reading," just get there, Now! Sal." Doesn't sound too good, we'd better hurry. "Max warned Victor, shifting back to her old frame of mind the moment the daddy bell rang.
Leer completely ignored the urgency of the message from Sal. He had no reason to feel the same way about it as Max did, all he could think about was her voice. It even sounded like Catherine's voice. Leer didn't need any stronger indicator that he was on the right path. His sense of calm deepened. "Everything's going to be just fine," he said as he entered the bedroom, walked directly to Max and kissed her. She felt warm, safe and remarkably like she did when she had fantasized about being with Tommy. She was now thoroughly confused, and loving it. "Besides, Sal's after the Juice, right?" Victor continued, "and we're trying a little different approach with Tommy. Sal might not like it right

away, but I think it will work."

Max felt more than just a little self-conscious and guilty that she had just been thinking about Tommy again when Victor said his name on the heels of kissing her. But, he couldn't have known, she was certain of that. Still, it had made her feel slightly deceptive, unfaithful and sexy all at once. It turned her on so much, in fact, that she forgot all about Sal and kissed Victor passionately, grinding into him, feeling him firmly against the place where she holsters her weapon. "You seem to have a knack for resurrection, Victor," Max moaned into his ear as she pulled him down on top of herself in the dark. As she did, her mobile phone buzzed another text from her father. Victor took the cell from her and held it tight against her, sending the vibration to the very spot still pulsing from their love-making. "Oh Victor, that is so wrong," she nearly giggled, throwing the phone over her shoulder and wrapping her legs around him.

****

"It was just orgasmic. I mean, I can't really describe the feeling any more clearly except that in addition to the feeling of supreme satisfaction there was an airy sort of bliss that ran through my entire being. When I held it, it seemed soft at first, like it was going to slip through my fingers, then it got so hard that I couldn't believe it was doing that, right in my hands!" Blue told Vinny all about the moment he first held the OmegaLux Crystal. It was good to get away from everyone who might want a piece of Tommy Levito and chill with Vinny. Blue found that Vinny was just about the coolest cat he had ever met and now he was his brother.

They had decided to get to the Shadowlands without hesitation after the brief encounter with Sal Lorenzo and the boys. The ride was quick, scenic and highly unusual for the Levito brothers. Tommy asked Vinny if he could ride WITHOUT any JumpJuice. This was not a new idea for Vinny who rarely used the stuff unless he was with Tommy, but his assumption was that Tommy ALWAYS wanted JumpJuice. When Blue asked Vinny if he could refrain from blasting him with the stuff while on their ride to the Shadowlands, Vinny outright hugged him breathless right there, the moment he asked and said, "Oh brother, you don't know how long I have been waiting for you to ask me that! You don't need the shit all the time."

Blue was relieved. He needed time to think clearly about all that was happening to him. There was a lot to learn about being Tommy and much to discover about this new world. Also, the dreams had started again.

14 SHADOWLANDS

Blue's dreams came on more strongly the moment he and Vinny got to the Shadowlands. They started as daydreams or visions, Blue couldn't tell which. As they entered the mountains encircling the valley, which gave the Shadowlands their name, Blue saw their peaks catch fire, the blaze, smokeless and uniform as if every flame was the perfect flame. Just as suddenly as the flames had engulfed the mountainous ridge, they disappeared with a flash and from the very places along the ridge from which the fires had issued forth there was light, strange, uneven, spectral light which wavered in intensity though constant and continuous from mountaintop to sky above. An overwhelming feeling of importance accompanied the vision. So strong was the feeling of significance that Blue asked Vinny to take him somewhere. " Vinny, let's go up as high as we can, I want to look out."

"Yeah, Tommy, there's nothing like the view of the Shadowlands from up here, I know just the spot," Vinny proudly exclaimed into the communicator on the VinnCycle.

"No Vinny, sorry, I want to look the other way," Blue quickly requested, "I can't shake this feeling that there's something I'm supposed to see out there!"

"No problem Tommy, we've got all the time in the world. You know I have deep connections with the Leocrites, especially Sansaa!" Vinny was feeling completely at ease and happy, confident that this trip was just what Tommy needed but he had far more personal reasons to be making the journey. He and Sansaa had been lovers for years when she told him that she was going to join the Leocrites. At first it was hard for him to understand. He took it as a judgment against him rather than a necessary, personal step toward her own growth. Her path did include him but was not glued to him. Vinny had become more accustomed to looking at things from a slightly different perspective in recent years and had grown to appreciate the relationship he shared with Sansaa. "Besides," he continued," I've become accustomed to looking at things from a slightly different perspective lately, I'd really like to check out the view from the "other side"!"

When they reached a place where they could survey the vista, their backs to the valley and the rest of the world before them, Blue found a spot to sit. He had recently started practicing yoga before he wound up in Tommy's body, so he wanted to assume the lotus position. Fortunately, Tommy's body was in no shape to perform such tricks, and it's just as well. Seeing Tommy in the lotus position probably would have been just a little too inconsistent for Vinny to ignore. Even so, Vinny gave Blue a quizzical look when he saw Tommy's body, cross-legged, back erect, gazing out at nature, peaceful and serene. "Come here, Vinny," Blue quickly said, before he had to field any questions form Vinny. "What do you see out there?"

Vinny turned to examine the view. He was blown away. It was beautiful beyond his imagination. He had never come this way before and among his friends, he was the only person who seemed to be truly interested in the Shadowlands. "I see land and water for as far as my eyes can see. A beautiful large river, the lake, more mountains, endless beauty. It was a great idea to check out this side, Tommy!"

"Do you see anything else?" Blue asked expectantly.

"What do you mean?" Vinny urged.

How about beams of light. Anything like that?' Tommy continued.

"No," Vinny laughed,"whatd'ya mean, like the hand of Farb or something?"

"Well, sort of, but not really," Tommy answered, "you see, I DO see beams of light, all around us out there, there are giant beacons of light, heading up to the sky right now."

"Tommy, I don't see them. Now that doesn't mean they aren't there, but I can't see them. I wonder if this has anything to do with the crystal?" Vinny said, trying to let Tommy know that he believed him. "I think we should run this by Sansaa."

Blue agreed and Tommy and Vinny hopped back on board the VinnCycle.

The ride down to the Shadowlands was quick. Vinny was psyched up, not only to see Sansaa again but also to be bringing Tommy along. Tommy and Sansaa knew one another from before, but they hadn't seen one another since Sansaa had left Vinny. Sansaa had been with Vinny when the brothers would party, but rarely joined in, and never with the JumpJuice. She preferred smoking. The tobacco was more like pot than cigarette tobacco but rarely came in anything but pure, high-grade varieties, nothing dirty or dry and nobody wasted your time with shake. No one bothered. With JumpJuice on the market, pot was basically legal, really cheap and packed a buzz that would kick ass like Diesel or Gravity back on Earth. However, since Sansaa had joined the community of the Shadowlands, beginning her journey to become a Leocrite, she had abandoned all such activity, seeking pure mindfulness, enlightenment and a totally different form of euphoria.

Upon their arrival, both men were immediately greeted by more than a dozen men and women, among them stood Sansaa. She did not lead nor was she subservient to any around her. They all seemed equally excited at the prospect of guests and most acted as though they knew Vinny, some addressing him by name while others nodded or smiled with friendliness. Vinny smiled in return, bowed his head and made his way to Sansaa whom he kissed rather passionately to Blue's surprise. Even more surprising was the reaction of the others who smiled even more widely, some of them laughing while all applauded as if they were witness to a momentous act. Blue was particularly impressed by the scene because he knew that none of the residents of the Shadowlands had been told of their impending arrival, yet they were clearly waiting as if anticipating his arrival with Vinny. After a long kiss, Vinny stepped back from Sansaa and motioned toward Tommy, presenting him to

Sansaa and the group.

"I am very pleased to be joined by my brother." Of course, you know him already Sansaa, but he is a stranger to the rest of you" Vinny suddenly stopped as Sansaa lifted her hand as if to ask for his silence, as an older man, eyes sparkling, smiling a nearly toothless smile stepped forward.

"Have you brought it with you?" He said kindly, "the crystal, Tommy? Sorry, of course you have." He corrected himself, nearly laughing at his own behavior. "You may need to stay a little longer than you had planned. Excuse me once again, you don't really have time, do you, no, of course you don't, many worlds to explore, people to be, habits to break both yours and others. Still. I am sure you are not in such a hurry that you couldn't do with a cold drink or perhaps a bit of ice cream?" The old man turned and walked toward a small hut made of rocks, branches, mud and something that looked a little like glass but different. As he did, without looking back, he gently urged the men to follow him with the flick of a couple of fingers, over his shoulder.

Blue reached his hand down into his pocket to feel for the crystal. It was there and as he touched it, the warmth flowed through it and up into his arm. He was worried at how much the old man seemed to know.

"Don't be Blue, Tommy," the old man said as they walked closer behind him, "You and Vinny will have a most enjoyable visit and no harm will come to either of you.
"I am Mojahdii," the old man introduced himself as Tommy, Vinny, Sansaa and the rest of the people who greeted the brothers filed into the hut. It was just like a scene from Harry Potter, Blue thought as he noticed that all of them fit comfortably into what appeared from the outside to be a rather small hut. As he thought this an incredibly strong flash of knowing passed through him, an understanding, or at least that's what he thought it was. Blue wasn't really raised a Christian because you couldn't call growing up with Frank as being raised, it was more like being bullied through childhood, but Frank claimed that he was a Christian, so Blue was automatically one as well. On one occasion where Blue had to attend a funeral for some family member who was going to leave Frank some money, even though he had never met Frank, Blue sat through a reading about Jesus Christ performing a

miracle where he multiplied a few loaves of bread and some fish so that an entire crowd was fully satisfied. It had stuck in Blue's mind that the story was another myth, tall tale or outright fabrication, but now, in this moment he knew exactly what had happened on that day. It wasn't one thing, it was a few. First, Jesus was a hypnotist. He had the ability to hypnotize very large numbers of people with seemingly little or no effort. Second, there was more food than originally reported because Jesus had already asked those in attendance who had brought food to begin sharing before any of the apostles had a chance to see where the food was coming from and when they actually saw what they thought was the food that was available, it didn't look like much and the reason they couldn't get a proper reading on that situation is that Jesus kept them looking in other directions, constantly diverting their attention and distorting their perception through careful and mindful manipulation. Third, a large number of people in attendance weren't very hungry to begin with. All of this occurred to Blue in the moment it took for Mojahdii to introduce himself and to smile, gesturing to a pillow at Blue's feet, indicating that he should sit. "We are all very pleased to have the opportunity to share a wondrous gift. There are those of us who have studied the symbols of the ancients, while others have explored the mysteries and magic of the elements, still others have trained both mind and body to transcend what is perceived by most to be the normal, physical limitations of our species. But today, we are joined by this young man who, without knowing how or why, has accomplished what none of us could have done."

Several of the men and women assembled looked on with crestfallen expressions, while many others beamed with a radiant glow of expectation, a few of them began to weep. Sansaa looked at Vinny and glowed with joy as she hugged him. Vinny and Sansaa then turned their attention to Tommy. Vinny whispered softly to Sansaa, "I think he means the OmegaLux Crystal."

Mojahdii, though far across the room, said,"Ahh, Vinny, you are only partially correct." The rest of the people who had gathered in the room had not heard what Vinny had whispered and wondered at Mojahdii's comment. "Vincent believes that I am talking about the fact that Tommy here has secured the OmegaLux Crystal!" The group gasped in unison. Some leaned slightly away from Tommy while others inched closer. One particularly attractive woman rose to her feet and left the hut. As she did, a very energetic young man with red curly hair bounced across the empty space from which she had risen and slid in next to Tommy, smiling and surveying him closely, trying to imagine where the crystal might be.

"Hi Tommy, I'm Targent," he said, the words popping briskly from his mouth like sparks as he quickly slid his hands under his own rear end, palms down, flat against the ground in a gesture that said that he wanted to be as close to Tommy as possible but he wasn't going to touch him or the crystal because he, though extremely excited and undeniably friendly, knew how to respect people, their privacy and their possessions.

"And Vincent," Mojahdii went on to add, "you are correct, Tommy does have the crystal, only it is NOT the OmegaLux Crystal. It is Shedavah." Judging by the reaction of the people in the room, Blue knew that he was now more than just your average tourist, out for a little R and R in the Shadowlands, in the eyes of all assembled. Most looked on him with adoration and wonder while a few seemed downright pissed. Targent giggled and bounced on his hands like a little monkey.

"Shedavah, at last my friends," Mojahdii addressed the gathering, brimming with love, happiness and hope. "Here, among us, ours but not ours, solid, physical, while anything but!" he looked with calm upon Blue as he said, "Welcome Tommy. I apologize for the suddenness of our devout attention to you and the crystal. It is presumptuous of me to announce your discovery and perhaps more than a little rude to assume that you might want to share a glimpse of Shedavah with those assembled here but I assure you, there is no better place and no more supportive an environment in which to reveal the treasure you now hold."

Tommy rose to his feet but did not present the crystal. He walked to his brother Vinny and laid a hand on his shoulder. Vinny reached his hand up to squeeze Tommy's, acknowledging the gesture of kinship yet oblivious to the motive. As Vinny's hand touched Tommy's, he pulled his brother up from the floor in a single sweeping movement as effortlessly as lifting a feather. Tommy had always been strong, but Vinny was stronger, until now. Both men looked at one another in surprise, then began to laugh. Mojahdii, Sansaa and a few of the others laughed with the brothers out of sheer amazement and excitement at the unexpected display of power. The rest of the group just sat in awe, silent and waiting.

"I didn't discover Shedavah, we did," Tommy smiled as he held Vinny firmly around the shoulders. I don't know anything about Shedavah or why you all want it so much, but I do know that the OmegaLux Crystal was well protected, cleverly hidden and cost many fighters their lives, even if it was just a game. Those who searched for it had a bond, they were joined in a quest and they were betrayed by one of their own. The crystal was nothing but an imaginary prize in a virtual environment within a game. I felt an indescribable sense of knowing. Each new thing that I had to know came to me as I needed it. I had a great teammate in the mission and I got lucky."

"That was not luck, but you are right about your brother, you could not have asked for a better partner in your quest than Vincent. In the brief time that I have had the pleasure of his company, I have grown to appreciate his gentle strength and humility, a rare trait in a man who possesses such physical strength." Mojahdii continued, "Might we all get an opportunity to see the crystal?"

Tommy smiled as he reached into his pocket. He felt the crystal instantly warm in his hands. As he lifted it from his pocket, it began to glow becoming more and more brilliant as he held it higher. When he had reached the full length of his arms, Shedavah glowed so brightly that few could look upon it any longer and suddenly it vanished.
Tommy was absolutely stunned as he felt the weight of the crystal evaporate with its light. The men and women who had assembled in the hut of Mojahdii were speechless, fainting, crying and looking on in disbelief, their faces contorted with mental anguish, their bodies rolling up into little balls or writhing in the agony of despair. Mojahdii stood close to Tommy, smiling, almost laughing as he said, "Shedavah, it truly is, nothing could be more certain, and you have certainly made the right choice to visit us at this time, Thomas Azure Levito. We can all be grateful to your brother, Vincent for guiding you to us at this critical time. There is nothing that occurs without purpose just as surely as there is nothing that lives without love." The old man's eyes telling Blue, once again, that he knew his true identity perhaps even better than he knew himself.

"But it's gone!" Targent cried out in desperation.

"No, Targent, not gone," Mojahdii consoled the young follower, "simply not visible."

"What do you mean, not visible, when is it going to be visible, I mean we have all been waiting for so long..." Targent began to rant.

"Calm yourself, Targent, I assure you, as long as Tommy is with us, the crystalline form of Shedavah is close at hand, or have you forgotten that Shedavah is always with us, in us, around and through us and that the crystal is only a physical manifestation of the power of Shedavah, made visible only so that our all too simple eyes and minds would be capable of sensing it's wonder?" Mojahdii was clearly repeating something he had been teaching to all assembled for a number of years, "and Targent, you have only been seeking the crystal through meditation and visualization for a little over a year. Many of your brothers and sisters assembled here have been waiting for the crystal to be revealed for far longer than you, so to all of you I say, please, continue your practice and as you do, focus your energy in a positive, supportive channel directly to Tommy. He needs all of us for the journey which lies ahead.
One by one the men and women who had gathered within the hut of Mojahdii began filing out into the evening air. It was a warm evening with the slightest breeze, just cool enough to make it the perfect night to soothe the disappointment they were all feeling. Even though Mojahdii acted as if they hadn't a care in the world that the crystal had mysteriously vanished, the people were inconsolable. They had been trying to accomplish the very thing that Tommy had accomplished though they looked for the crystal in very different ways. The people of the Shadowlands were many, so these few who had assembled in the hut of Mojahdii were a privileged group, chosen by Mojahdii himself to witness the very event which was now causing them such anguish.

"They will survive," Mojahdii intimated to Tommy as the last of the group left the hut. "They will soon come to understand that by helping you with their thoughts, intentions and meditation, they will be a part of what must be, facilitators of the new way, conductors for the great passage." Mojahdii smiled as Blue sat silently listening, acutely interested yet patient. "I realize that you were not looking for Shedavah, Blue, but now that you have it, you must learn to use it." Mojahdii paused, looking deeper into Blue, his eyes telling Blue that it would be proper to ask his next question while letting him know that he did not have to. Blue remained silent. "You are truly the right man for the job, Blue. It was good of you to come so far, you must have great faith in your friend John Tanner. Leer has done well to bring you this far, but even he cannot give you what you need to move forward, but I imagine he has already told you as much." Blue heaved a sigh of disbelief and relief with the same breath, Mojahdii would clearly be able to tell him whether he was a Quanji or not. "No, I cannot, Blue," Mojahdii said as he placed a hand on Blue's shoulder, "I am not permitted. Only you can discover whether or not you are Quanji. What I can do is help you to discover the answer, and yes, I will also explain what I mean when I say that you have Shedavah. There is someone coming who will help you first. You may have noticed that she left the hut when I revealed that you were in possession of the crystal. Do not misinterpret her silence for unhappiness, nor her humility for ignorance. She did not need to see the crystal to know that you had Shedavah just as she has no need for speech to teach what you must learn."

At this very moment she entered the hut. She was more beautiful than Blue was able to appreciate at first glance. She entered with a slight bow and held a small bundle of freshly picked herbs, leaves, grasses and flowers in her outstretched hands, seemingly from nowhere, Mojahdii produced a uniquely carved wooden tray upon which she set the plants. Blue had only one thought in his mind as he looked at her but he could never tell you what it was, in fact, he was pretty sure that he was able to think of nothing. He did this for several minutes while she slowly fanned the plants out on the board, arranging them very carefully, then looked directly into his eyes.

As Blue became immobilized Mojahdii said softly, "Tommy this is Anna Marie, Anna Marie, this is Tommy." Anna Marie smiled at Tommy then took his hand in hers. In his palm she placed the single blossom of a flower. It was the most brilliant blue flower he had ever seen. Anna Marie gently curled his fingertips around the blossom and held his hand between both of hers as she bowed sweetly to him, then slowly opened his curled fingers and the flower was gone.

15 DUMB LOVE

It was impulsive and she felt like she shouldn't be doing it but she did it anyway. She didn't care about anyone else, she was drawn to him. She allowed herself to dwell on every inch of his body, her sense of smell awakened in a way she associated only with childhood memories, as if noticing something so essential was reserved for that part of life, but her attraction to him seemed to amplify her ability to discern the nuance of his scent. It was basic, almost animal and in a way both surprisingly and indescribably pure. She thought that she would be in trouble for her behavior. Then she thought again, reasoning that, in fact, she was not a child and that she was entitled to this. Time, alone with a man, feeling warmth, passion and security. "Bast him!" she blurted out.

"Bast who?" he asked calmly.

"I'm sick of jumping up and running to his side like a little obedient dog every time my father calls," Max was a whirl of emotion, rationalization and determination all vying for control of her actions. Leer had guessed it was a Sal reference even before he asked but for a moment he thought she might be talking about Tommy. Leer is an amazingly good judge of character and even better at recognizing the clues which people place around to incriminate themselves through body language, facial expression and tone of voice, so it was easy for him to recognize that Max was attracted to Tommy both physically and out of a rebellious streak toward her father which she buried under the violence she perpetrated on his behalf. So it was of no surprise to Leer when the very next thing Max said to him was, "We'd better get going, Victor, or my dad's going to kill you!"

Leer knew that Max was terrified of her father and could guess why. He was undoubtedly the "Boss" whether it was mob, gangs, freedom fighters, unions, foundations or something like the Illuminati didn't matter, Sal was the top dog in the big hotel. He was Brando in real life, or at least this real life and Leer was smart enough to respect that but aware enough of the bigger picture to not give it much credence. So when Max began to rush him out the door, he responded with just enough energy to keep her from panicking that her father was going to kill the man she found herself falling for in a way she had never expected to. "C'mon Victor, I'd better drive, no time for your usual cruise down Market Street to remind the "little people" that Victor is watching." Max said as she brushed by him and gave his ass a little pat just to let him know that she was still feeling good about the way things had been playing out between them.

Victor probably wouldn't have liked that very much but Leer found it endearing. "I'm all worn out," he replied quickly, "so I think I might catch a nap on the way. After all, if I'm going to get killed again, I want to look well rested."

It was just the right sort of reply to put Max at ease and it gave Leer a great way out of driving. Max would normally have to compete with Victor over whose reason made more sense or which vehicle was better suited to the time of day or the weather conditions, but Leer had no way of knowing these things so he didn't pursue them, besides, he had no idea where they were going. When they got to the garage, Leer paused. He had never seen anything quite like it and he had seen a lot. There were three rows of cars with enough room in between each car and spacing in between the rows to accommodate a brisk deployment of any number of them. Max walked her way toward a sleek black coupe that tucked itself down inside a little corner at the end of the furthest row saying, you do not want to drive me, I am far too fast and will be extremely upset with you if you scratch my ridiculously lustrous finish in any way at all. She ran her fingers over its profile with the same sort of stroking attention she had paid to Victor moments earlier.

"On second thought, I think I'll keep me eyes open, I want to watch how you make this baby follow your every command," Victor flirted and Max responded with a kiss which she blew across the roof of the car like she was sending it directly across the lustrous finish, directly to Victor's lips. As they entered the vehicle from either side, they kissed one another passionately across the center console, the stick shift in Max's hand ready to drive. And there was no mistaking, she was going to drive it hard.

Max fired up the roadster and launched it from its little nook at the end of the line, shooting past the row of similarly awesome vehicles in Victor's collection. Anybody, even Leer, would be impressed with this line-up of automobiles. He was having the slightest feeling of satisfaction creep over him that he owned all these kick-ass cars until he reminded himself that he had more than likely earned them through criminal if not unsavory means. Ahead of them a door was opening slowly, too slowly he thought for it to open fast enough for them not to crash into it. Suddenly the surface upon which they were driving nearly dropped out from under them and became a ramp, much like those found on large military transport planes. With the drop of the floor and the continued opening of the door, they cleared it just in time, hitting the street at a good eighty miles an hour, if not faster. The dashboard displayed the number 83 but there was no way to know for certain at this point what 83 represented. It could be miles per hour, kilometers per hour or mushrooms per minute, if there even were minutes in the land of JumpJuice, Farb and money, or mushrooms for that matter. "Nice driving!" he said uncontrollably, after all, it was pretty impressive considering the last place he lived no one ever drove anywhere, man or woman, and the place before that, women spent most of their days weaving, baking and pumping out babies. He had forgotten that Victor was ordinarily more likely to complain than compliment.

Fortunately, Max was already getting used to the new Victor. "I think I should let daddy kill you after all, you're so much more agreeable after you've risen from the dead," she joked as she whipped the car around a hairpin turn then slipped nicely in between two large trucks a bus and a van.

"I'd be okay with that Max, as long as I got to do everything we've been doing all over again. Now that would be worth dying for, "Leer knew that Max wanted to hear that Victor felt that way about her and he wasn't sure if Victor actually ever did, but the truth of the matter is that he did. Leer was really enjoying himself with Max. He knew that Blue would be working to discover a way back home whether he turned out to be a Quanji or not but that didn't mean that he couldn't at least enjoy himself a little during the process.

Leer had been in and out of various lives too many times to let conventional morality cloud his judgment when it came to personal pleasure. In fact, he had become so good at allowing himself to experience personal pleasure that he practically exuded optimism which, although she could not define it for herself, was precisely the reason that Max found herself falling for him. As she sped toward her father's clubhouse, she did so with far more confidence than she had in a very long time, feeling that no matter what happened, it was going to be okay as long as she was with Victor. Normally she would have been dreading the meeting, arming herself mentally and emotionally against both Victor and her father. Tonight was different. Tonight, she and Victor were going to see Sal together.

"Don't worry about Sal, Max," Leer said soothingly as he reclined as deeply as he could in the passenger seat of the sporty little coupe that raced its way across the glittering highway at 90 something. "He'll forget all about us being late once we discuss the shipment. How he'll feel about the whole Tommy Levito issue is still a variable, but either way, I think it's safe to assume that any tardiness on our part won't factor too heavily into the equation."

Max felt like Victor could see inside of her very soul, like it was supposed to be when someone really cared for you and this made her nervous in an entirely different way. She decided stop thinking and focus on driving. The coupe shot up to 120, getting them to Sal's in no time.

Leer sat up and surveyed the situation. He quickly opened his door and leaped to the other side, springing over the hood with one hand as if he were a gymnast on a vaulting horse. Before Max knew what was happening, Victor had opened her door and was holding his hand out to her like a gentleman would treat a lady in some fairy tale from her childhood. She reached up and placed her hand in his allowing him to gently guide her up from her seat, in a single motion he took the keys from her other hand and closed the door to the coupe. As he did so, he gestured in the direction of the clubhouse and said, "After you, Max."

145

Although Leer truly is a gentleman, he did not behave in this fashion without purpose. The clubhouse was quite large, with a number of paths leading to a number of different entrances. By allowing Max to lead slightly, he was able to judge which entrance they would normally enter through.

Unaware of any of this, Max nearly curtsied as she walked past Victor saying in her best, flirting, princess-like voice, " Why Victor, a lady could get used to such treatment, I hope these little surprises keep coming." then she turned toward the back of the building, walking directly toward a stone-lined path which seemed to flow over the hillside, leading directly to a lower level patio where the large goon with a peanut allergy stood guard.

Chapter 13 Dumb Love Smart Comebacks4

"Hello, Ms. Lorenzo, Mr. Alonso," the large man with the peanut allergy said as he opened the door for them.

"Hey there, Cedric," Max quickly and energetically responded as she breezed by him, light as a feather. the tall, burly man smiled in a way that told Leer that this type of greeting was uncommon from Max.

"Thank you, Cedric," Leer said with a smile as he stopped in the opened doorway and turning toward Cedric asking,"and how are you doing today?"

With equal if not greater surprise in his eyes, Cedric responded, "I am fine sir, and you?"

"Just marvelous, for a dead man," Leer responded, knowing full well that Cedric had that very thought on his mind. When he could see that his casual manner had loosened the stone guard he asked," and how is Sal doing today?"

"Mr. Lorenzo is not pleased," the guard replied.

"Pity." Leer responded,"Let's see what can be done about that, any ideas?"

Leer could see by the look in the Cedric's face that it was not his place to have ideas so he reached a hand up to his shoulder and patted it saying,"Don't worry about it, Cedric, leave it to me." The look on Cedric's face was one of relief mixed with confusion. This sort of behavior from Victor was almost certainly unusual but Leer was in the mood to shake things up a bit and playing with Sal's goons seemed to be the perfect place to start. Leer continued through the doorway catching up with Max who was waiting outside an elevator door.

The clubhouse was architecturally average, leading Leer to surmise that Sal was either disinterested, ignorant or both. The other possibility was that Sal wanted to headquarter in an unassuming location so as to not draw attention to himself. He would later learn that Sal had no qualms about being the center of attention and that it was indeed that Sal was clueless when it came to matters of good taste in anything, which would more than explain his fascination with Cleveland. When the elevator arrived, Max entered first and pressed the LL2 button. Nothing happened. In fact, the light didn't even go on. Max stood looking at Leer as if waiting for him to do something. "Well?" she said.

"Very." he replied.

"Funny," she responded. "Oh, I get it," she continued,"you WANT to piss off daddy. You know damn well he's just sitting down there waiting for us. Cedric has already let him know we're on our way. Varst, I wouldn't be surprised if he's watching the damn monitors himself. Fine, I'll do it." Max lifted and waved her hand high in the corner of the elevator car. As she did, a small device projected from the side of the car. It was a retinal scan device which deployed at a level appropriate to her height. She positioned her eye in the right spot with a nervous hesitation. A second later she groaned and scrunched her face up, placing her hand over her eyes and forehead as if she suddenly got a headache. "You know I hate that feeling, Victor, why did you make me do it?"

"Just wanted to be sure you are who you say you are my dear, after all, you've been acting a little strange lately. Better to not take any unnecessary chances, what with the missing shipment and all." Leer responded, quickly diffusing the situation.

"Ha! I don't know what has gotten into you, Victor, but I really like it. You just better be careful when you talk to Sal, I doubt he's in the mood for comedy." Max warned.

147

Who said I was joking?" Leer responded, smiling and nudging Max gently.

"Right then," Max surrendered, "it's your funeral."
Max walked out of the elevator past two burly goons who didn't look particularly happy to see her or Victor. She headed toward an archway which led to a larger room, in which presumably she would find Sal. Leer was just a couple of steps behind her when a large chunk of the floor above him came crashing down directly on his face, at least that's what it felt like. Still it felt enough like a fist for Leer to realize that he was going to receive a beating at the hands of the goons. In the fraction of a moment that it took him to come to this realization, he reacted. With the weight of his body pulling him toward the floor in the direction of goon number two, he was an easy target for the club hand of goon number two who took it upon himself to deliver a more powerful blow than goon number one. As he bared down upon Victor's face with everything he had he was suddenly assisted, guided forward by an unexpected aide, Leer himself, who quickly caught the hand of his assailant, wrapping his own hands around the hand of the goon and leaning his entire body into the blow, thereby rolling himself up and over the back of the stunned behemoth. Before goon number two could understand what had just happened, Leer delivered a backward kick directly into the back of the knee of his would-be assailant, snapping it hard, forcing the giant to his knees. Attacker number one was already stepping into his second punch with a good line on Victor's face when Leer dropped down, folding at the knees, arching his back fully as he echoed the catch of the fist from a slightly different angle, turning goon one toward goon two while forcing his own right forearm up over the left of number one. As he did this he channeled his bodyweight directly into the twist, using his elbow to push down upon the back of the elbow of his assailant's left jab. This served two purposes, he broke goon one's arm and landed him directly on top of goon two. Both men lay groaning on the floor as Leer spun on his heels to face the sound of applause which suddenly rang from the archway.

Sal Lorenzo stood smiling and clapping before him with a stunned Max by his side. She turned toward Sal and snapped, "Daddy!," a look of consternation and disapproval, tempered by the understanding that the attack was over moved across her face as she continued, "Why in Farb's name would you do such a thing?"

"I didn't," he chuckled, "they did," he smiled, motioning to the wounded men on the floor.

"Hello Sal," Leer said, more than just a little disdainfully as he ripped his own shirt off his back and worked to fashion a sling for the arm of goon one who was clearly under orders and knowing that the fight was over was ready to assume his rightful place in the chain of command, which by all indications was , Sal, Victor, Max, then everybody else. "I don't think this was about being a little late," Victor continued as he skillfully pulled the leg of number two in just the right way to noticeably ease his painful grimace.

"You are absolutely correct Victor, do forgive me but I couldn't stop myself from indulging in a little test of your testicles!" Sal jauntily responded, "You see, I was a little worried that perhaps you were weakened by the whole death thing and that was why you didn't kill Tommy Levito a second time when you had the opportunity. Now that I know that you can still handle yourself with a certain measure of skill, I can only conclude that you have a good reason to leave Levito alive despite the fact that he is now in possession of MY JumpJuice!"

Leer was feeling exceedingly confident at this point. He had bested two formidable opponents quite handily. He had a great deal of respect for Victor's body after it performed so well. Leer had the experience of fighting in a great many different bodies but there was no way of knowing what the body you were in could do until you actually had to use it. Leer was pretty sure that he could kill Sal without too much trouble if he had to, whether Sal was armed or not, though he had no intention of doing so. Instead, he simply responded. "Tommy Levito doesn't have your JumpJuice."

16 ANNA MARIE

"Magic, it had to be some kind of magic. How else could it have just disappeared. Am I right? Is this all about some sort of magic," he thought to himself for a moment then continued," no, magic is too childish, too much of an illusion. This disappearance was no illusion. It simply vanished, there and then gone, no mirrors, no puffs of smoke, no beautiful woman to distract attention. Wait, what about you, he said pointing to her, it all happened shortly after you left the room!" Blue was not really implying that Anna Marie had anything at all to do with the disappearance of the crystal but he was so overcome with nervousness at her presence. A nervousness compounded by her silence. Still, it only took Blue a few moments with her to recognize that she did speak. Her reaction to his compliment, however shrouded in paranoiac hypothesis could have been recognized by a teenage boy half-way through a tweet delivered via Droid urgently attempting to LOL over OMG knows WTF, and Blue was instantly calmed by her blush and a smile that told him that she liked to hear him say that he found her beautiful, the true difference between magic and illusion.

Without a word, and despite his carrying on, she told him of the energy which flows between us all. Through a poetic dance of movement, she told the story, the small items she gleaned from the earth, characters in her silent play. Her hands like the wind which, over time, moves deserts and whips up the waves of the sea stirred in Blue a feeling both past and present, understanding, expectant and ultimately peaceful.

"Azure and Blue, together so quickly." Blue heard a voice whisper. He looked around to see that, as he had expected, Mojahdii had left him alone with Anna Marie. But she could not have spoken. He looked deeply into Anna Marie's eyes. She returned his gaze, "I didn't need to." Blue heard the voice more clearly now.

"Are you speaking to me telepathically?" Blue asked Anna Marie. This time her smile masqueraded a sadness both palpable and painful to Blue. Exasperated, he slumped forward, his eyes closed, his head in his hands.

"Trying too hard again with the ladies, eh Blue? Allow me!" a voice said closely into his ear as he felt a hand pull his shoulder back and there he was, Glurp, sliding in between Blue and Anna Marie.

"NO!," barked Blue who swatted at the air like he was surrounded by a thousand bees, each one mercilessly diving for his flesh. But there were no bees and there was no Glurp, only Anna Marie who sat, smiling peacefully, gently tying together the flowers and plants she had brought into the hut of Mojahdii.

She calmly reached out and took Blue's hand, gently opening it. Into his open palm, she placed the bundled offering with a warm expression which told him that he had been through enough for one day and that he should take her gift with him to ponder at a later time.

He wanted to kiss her, to thank her for the gift, to thank her for everything, but he realized that he had not received everything yet. How far he had to go, he did not know but of one thing he was certain, Anna Marie was going to help him get there. As he closed his hand around the bundle his sense of calm returned. Anna Marie took his other hand and led him through the hut and out into the night air.

17 TARGENT

"Wow! You two are a couple already. I knew it. I told myself, Targent, you might as well give up on pretty miss Anna Marie, the moment I saw you, Tommy. But that don't mean we can't be friends, you and me, heck all the more reason, we're sweet on the same girl. Don't worry though, I know you two are goin' steady, so I won't get in the way." Targent spewed at Anna Marie and Tommy who released one another's hands as Targent spoke.

"We, ah, well I, uh, We aren't a couple," Tommy answered hesitantly, eying Anna Marie to gauge her reaction as he said it. She smiled at him in a way that let him know that she understood everything about the way he was feeling. He had no doubt that she could see inside his heart, right down to his soul. "I think we can all be friends, Targent," Tommy added "as a matter of fact, friend, I could use your help right now. What do I do next, have you seen Vinny, any idea what happened to Mojahdii and just who is he, some kind of teacher or leader, is this a cult, a commune, a co-op, rehab or just a nice place to hang out and look at mountains?"

With this, Anna Marie gently took the shoulder of each man and turned them away from her in the direction of the river. "I think she's telling both of us we need a bath! Targent laughed and patted Tommy on the shoulder. He turned to look over his shoulder to see Anna Marie bounding away gracefully, her long hair blowing in the breeze as she waved happily at the new friends.

A few steps from the river, Targent stopped and began to take off his clothes. Blue thought he was joking around until he began striding freely and confidently to the water's edge. The river was not very wide and Targent was now standing directly across from two women who were washing a large bowl and a pitcher, both of which appeared to be handmade from clay. They were brightly colored yet slightly rough looking and the women cradled them carefully as they cleaned them. "Those are very beautiful," Targent remarked.

The women looked up from their work and said "Thank you, Targent" without the slightest surprise or shock at his nakedness.

"Did you make those today?" he asked as he stepped into the water.

"Yesterday," they said in unison. The older one asked, "who's your friend?"

"That's Tommy," Targent replied.

"Well of course it is," the older one continued, "he's the only new guy here. Hey Tommy," she called out, "why don't you take off your clothes and have a little swim, maybe we can help you find the crystal!"

Blue could tell that this was going to be an interesting visit to the Shadowlands. Still, the water looked inviting and it seemed like people in the Shadowlands had no trouble at all with nudity. Blue carefully placed his bundle on a nearby rock, took of his clothes and walked into the water. The women watched him walk the entire way into the water. He felt as though they were paying a little closer attention to him than they had to Targent. They whispered to one another, giggling slightly, then ran from the water's edge.

"What do you have for soap?" Blue asked half-jokingly.

To his surprise, Targent disappeared under the water for what seemed like minutes. When he popped back up again, he was holding a stone, about the size of a baseball. he tossed it to Tommy. "Go ahead, "he urged, pantomiming the action of lathering up his armpit, then he laughed and splashed like a little boy.

Blue tried using the stone like soap. To his great surprise, it lathered as well as any soap he had ever used.

"You can stay in my hut until you get your own," Targent offered eagerly. Blue had no idea what he was going to do while in the Shadowlands but it seemed like everyone else did. He really just wanted to avoid whatever Tommy was mixed up in but now he had become the central figure in a much bigger story. Too many people were interested in him for the Shadowlands to be any kind of retreat for him. Still, he wanted to kick back with Vinny. He wondered how much of a commitment his new brother was going to make to spending time together when he had Sansaa to entertain and delight him, and what about Anna Marie? Even though he had just met her, he felt as though she was essential to his well-being on this surprising new world. Blue had very little desire to spend the night in Targent's hut but he didn't know what else to do. "So, are you ready to go?" Targent urged.

Blue was about to acquiesce when Vinny showed up at the river. "Tommy, what's with the whole "free in the breeze" look you got goin' there, this isn't a nudist colony!"

Blue looked over at Targent who just stood there, naked and smiling, not even acknowledging that he did anything at all. Vinny's eyes followed Blue's, "Oh, I get it...Targent. You can't do what Targent does. He doesn't seem to have much of an understanding of what we might consider to be social norms, next time, you'd better ask me. At least nobody saw you, some of the people here are really reserved when it comes to certain things, nudity would definitely fall into the category of certain things. Anyway, you should come with me now, I need your help setting up the tent."

With those words, Targent slunked his shoulders and hung his head. He walked slowly out of the water and stood motionless, dripping on his clothes. Blue, noticing his sadness attempted to comfort him. "I want to get some time with my brother, Targent, but I really like your soap stone, thanks a lot!" Targent looked up with a smile and put his hands on his hips, proud that he could help Tommy. Blue could see as he looked at Targent how nobody would really care whether he was naked or not. It was more like looking at a unique, living creature than a man. It was quite different looking at Targent naked than looking at Tommy naked. "So, I guess I'll see you tomorrow," Tommy said as both he and Targent put their clothes back on. Targent turned on his heels and sort of skipped away saying goodbye to Tommy, apparently content with being the provider of good soap.

"Just be glad the first thing Targent did with you was go swimming, it could have been a lot worse. Think long and hard before you try eating anything that he may suggest and as many times as he may tell you otherwise, the people of the Shadowlands do not relieve themselves wherever they feel like it then build little villages from the result." Vinny warned Blue as the two men walked in the opposite direction of Tommy's new friend.

18 TENT TIME

"Tommy, I really had no idea what you were onto when you got the crystal. Sansaa has been telling me a little bit more about Shedavah. I had never really paid much attention to it. I mean, I figured it was just the spiritual stuff she was into but had nothing to do with me, but damn it Tommy, the crystal! First, my team had tried, over and over again to get the crystal and you get it the first time you go after it, pulling it out of thin air, then I bring you here and it turns out to be something supernatural that they have all been waiting for. Then, you pull the bastin' thing out of your pocket to show everybody and it turns into the light of Farb then disappears, what the Varst was that!" Vinny started talking so fast that Blue just listened. "Bastin' Farbunkle, Tommy, the crystal is almost like Farb to these people. Sansaa said that they believe that Shedavah is Farb and the crystal is Shedavah and that you are Shedavah. Oh and guess who else is Shedavah, three guesses and the first two don't count, that's right, me! Yep, every Farb-damned one of us is Shedavah, to a degree. You just happen to be right up there with Farb and Mojahdii right now. Of course, Sansaa keeps saying it isn't like that, none of us is better than the other, we all have our own part to play and we are all important in our own ways. Beezle, Tommy, you're it. All I know is, this isn't going to be the place to get away from it all. I'm really sorry about this, little bro'."

Blue was happy that all of Vinny's excitement led to an apology because he really didn't want Vinny to be pissed off or hurt about the whole crystal thing. Still, Blue was starting to feel like he had a fair idea of what had to happen next, he only hoped he could pull it off. He had to discover whether he was Quanji or not, restore the crystal to the people of the Shadowlands and get Leer and himself back to Earth, America, and apple pie. "I know you were trying to help, Vinny," he said, "but I had no idea the crystal was Shedavah either. We've got to stay here until we figure out why I ended up with the crystal. What I want to know now is, where do I sleep?"

"You and me, a nice big tent and nothin' but stars bro'." Vinny smiled as he patted Blue on the back. "I would have set it up myself but the whole thing is in one big bundle and I just didn't feel like moving it out of the shed all by myself. Besides, I think I just saved you from a night in the stinky hut. Targent is one of those incense guys, you'd be lucky if you were able to breathe in there let alone sleep!"

"Thanks Vinny," Tommy responded as the two men rounded the corner of the shed. Inside they found a large bundled tent, lifting it was clearly the work of two men with large supports and a thick, canvas-like fabric all tied together. Vinny positioned himself at one end and indicated to Tommy that he should take the other side. Together they lifted the large load and made their way out of the shed.

There was a large hill with an open field at its summit about a half of a mile away. There was a rather nasty little obstacle between the field and the shed, a dried-up riverbed ran through the projected path and there was no way around it. The land just dropped off, down into the dried-up bed and then rose straight up the other side. "There's an area over here that is just a little more gradual," said Vinny, "we should make our descent there."

The two of them walked another fifty yards or so and reached the spot, the load was getting heavier but was manageable. Vinny walked ahead, with the bundle on his right shoulder while Tommy had the rear, the bundle on the same shoulder. Vinny hoisted the bundle up into both hands, slightly over his head, and Tommy followed his lead. They began inching their way down carefully. All was going smoothly until Vinny's footing suddenly went out from under him as the ground just crumbled. The action of the fall made his hands fly up, launching his end of the bundle up in the air. He lost control and fell backward, his head hitting the ground where his feet had been a moment earlier, his end of the bundle speeding its way back down toward his face.

Inches from his nose, the bundle froze in mid-air. In the split-second it took Vinny to fall, Tommy reacted, quickly changing his grip, he reached out and held onto a pole, tied toward the outside of the bundle. One hand reached out toward the center of the bundle while the other firmly held his end. No one should have been able to do that, it was superhuman. Tommy remained standing in that position, smiling, long enough for Vinny to move out from below the weighty hazard, then he eased the bundle to the ground.

"Beezle, bro, you are bastin' amazing!" Vinny said, totally relieved that his face was still in one piece. The rest of the walk was uneventful. Tommy's speed in assembling the tent structure was no less astounding and he and Vinny were resting peacefully moments later. "You know, Sansaa said that you would get the crystal back soon, and I gotta say, I believe it. With what I saw tonight, I believe you could do just about anything" Vinny oozed with pride over his brother's newfound powers.

"Yeah, Vinny, something wild definitely happened on the night I came back, I just have to try to learn what it's all about. I'm glad you're here to help me." Tommy said as he stretched out completely on his sleeping back.

Me too, Tommy, me too," Vinny answered as he extinguished the lantern they had between them, "Goodnight little brother."

"Goodnight Vinny"
Blue had dreams, wild dreams incredible dreams; Glurp didn't show up in any of them. He dreamt all night in extreme detail. He saw things he had never seen and travelled to places he had never been and everything was full of light. When he awoke he was all alone in the tent but the smell of coffee hung so close he could taste it. Sunlight streamed into the tent and bathed his face. When his eyes had adjusted, he could see the burly silhouette of Vinny sitting with what appeared to be two women and a lanky bouncing monkey. As he peeked his head out from the tent he could see more clearly that the women were Sansaa and Anna Marie and the monkey was Targent.

"Good morning sunshine," Vinny laughed as he leaned toward Tommy his extended hand offering a piping hot cup of coffee. "We've been waiting for you to rise from the sleep of the dead, but I guess that you've been there done that!"

Blue laughed as he took the coffee from Vinny, "You're right, and I could have kept sleeping and avoided this whole Shedavah situation entirely!" Blue looked around the table to see that no one but he realized he was joking. "Seriously though," he quickly added, "I'm very happy to be alive but I feel terrible about losing Shedavah." Anna Marie shook her head and calmly smiled, placing a hand on his knee as he sat next to her. Targent stopped jumping and Sansaa stood up to walk around Vinny and sit closer to Tommy.

"You haven't lost Shedavah, Tommy. You have transformed Shedavah." Sansaa smiled warmly, letting Blue know that there was no reason to be concerned that he was guilty of any wrong-doing.

Targent climbed down from the rock he was perched on and sat at the table. Although he had been in the Shadowlands and was learning about Shedavah, he knew nothing of the transformation. His silly antics came to a halt as he learned of it. He was eager to know more and Blue noticed a difference in his eyes, focused and hungry.

Sansaa continued, "I am not the one to teach you," her eyes falling upon Anna Marie, "but now is the time for you to learn how to summon to energy of Shedavah, guide it, radiate it as only you, the discoverer of the crystal can. Mojahdii has been training all of us to find the crystal, or so we were led to believe, but a few of us have always known that we would not be capable. The discoverer is not only important in bringing the crystal into its physical form but also in transforming it, conducting it into its next phase, for Shedavah is a living thing, a developing state of being, existing in the physical, mental, emotional, spiritual and energetic states simultaneously across many worlds, confined by none yet inextricably linked to all. Even Mojahdii himself does not know what lies beyond the oneness of Shedavah though he has been to other worlds. Even Mojahdii could not conduct the energy of Shedavah in the manner in which it must be done because he was not the discoverer, only the preparer, "Koshvallah." "Onjadiavaan" is the only one capable of fulfilling the connection of Shedavah to our world. The discoverer, "Onjadiavaan," is you Tommy."

Vinny grabbed onto his own face as if checking to see that it was firmly attached to his head, squeezing his thumb and fingers into his eye sockets like the pressure would somehow enable him to comprehend what he had just heard. His large hand slid further down his face pulling his mouth down, opening it slightly releasing a small, "uh." Quietly, as if holding back the urge to shout out WHAT IN THE BASTIN' FARBUNKLE ARE YOU TALKIN' ABOUT he said, "Sansaa, I'm sorry but are you saying that my brother is some sort of holy man or something?"

Seeing the difficulty Vinny was having processing the information Sansaa tried to deliver the message in a slightly different fashion. "No Vinny, Tommy is neither holy or unholy." Vinny eased back in his chair a bit. "You see, truthfully, Shedavah is neither holy or unholy. Shedavah simply is, through all that is, in all that is." Vinny's face looked as though someone had opened a little door in the top of his head and dropped about a dozen ice cubes inside. Tommy on the other hand sat and looked at Sansaa as if nothing could have made more sense. Blue was thinking of the words "all that is," remembering them from the starcruiser.

Tommy got up from his chair and stood behind Vinny, placing his hands on his shoulders to comfort him in some way, "Well, I guess that explains everything, doesn't it?" He circled the table until he was looking back across it directly at Sansaa and leaning forward asked, "well, if it's all up to me, why did Mojahdii make all of you waste your time looking for the crystal?"

During this entire conversation, Anna Marie had been silently arranging small stones on the table. Everyone was so interested in the words that were shared that even Sansaa had not noticed what Anna Marie was creating. Anna Marie stopped, reached her arms straight out, palms down, then opened them upward and outward, inviting all to look at her creation. There, on the table was a perfect circle , concentric rings of stones surrounding a single stone in the center. She pointed to the center stone and then to Tommy. Then with her other hand she traced the rings of the concentric circles and motioned similarly to everyone else at the table.

Sansaa said, "We are all here to help you." She looked to Vinny to gauge his reaction. Tears were welling up in the big man's eyes as if he had just experienced a revelation. He stood up to his full height and gave Tommy the bear-hug of his life. Targent bounced up and down as if he had just been released from a cage and Sansaa and Anna Marie smiled with satisfaction.

When Vinny had set him down, Tommy spoke, "Well, this should be a rather interesting day, I think I might want another cup of coffee!" Everyone laughed.

19 BEGINNING

"Where do we start," Tommy asked as Vinny poured him a second cup of coffee.

Anna Marie picked up the stone from the center of the circle and placed it in the middle of the table, then she scooped all of the remaining stones into the bag she had taken them from, leaving only the stone representing Tommy sitting all by itself at the center of the table. She then reached back into the bag and pulled out another stone which she held to her breast and paused, indicating that the stone she now held represented herself. She placed that stone next to his stone and smiled. Sansaa stood up and walking over to Vinny and said, "I have never been told quite so eloquently that it was time for me to leave." Vinny smiled in agreement but Targent lingered. He looked longingly at Tommy and Anna Marie as if he needed to stay with them, not quite understanding the exclusivity of Anna Marie's gesture. Vinny reached out his strong right hand and with little effort pulled Targent gently backward, away with the table, down the path which led to the commons. Targent quickly realized that he had no choice but to accompany them and turned to join them voluntarily. He followed behind them, meandering slightly as they went, like a little red wagon being drawn on a rope behind a bicycle; whenever they stopped he continued past, always turning back toward them as if tethered. Eventually, the three of them reached the commons.

Nearly everyone who lived within the Shadowlands had gathered in the commons. It was an area the size of a large arena bordered almost entirely by a rise in elevation varying in height around the perimeter, as if some large meteor had punched a hole in the ground, a crater filled with wild grasses and lush ground cover like Creeping Charlie and clover but different, beautiful and soft. All at once, the eyes of every person assembled there turned to greet the trio, expectantly. They were clearly waiting for Tommy, nearly half of them quickly returned to their conversations but to Vinny's great surprise, the other half continued to stare. Not only did they stare but they seemed genuinely enthusiastic to greet him! He knew many of them, but now that he was the brother of "Onjadiavaan," he had become something of a celebrity. Vinny kind of liked that. He didn't really have to do anything like conduct the energy of the universe through a crystal, but he was looked upon with a certain measure of admiration, after all, he had brought "Onjadiavaan" to them. Beginning with his arrival in the commons, Vinny had a story to tell. The first time he told it, it wasn't really that well done. He left a few details out that really made the story. Even the second and third time were lackluster compared to the fourth and fifth but eventually he became one of the greatest storytellers ever to visit the Shadowlands. And why not, for he was telling one of the greatest stories ever told, the story of "Onjadiavaan and the OmegaLux Crystal - Shedavah."

Blue was feeling pretty confident that something incredible was happening to him that fell somewhere in the category of "Beyond Known Abilities." Whether the "Onjadiavaan and the OmegaLux Crystal - Shedavah" story was the proper explanation for all of the occurrences of late, had yet to be proven within his normally skeptical mind. However, he had been trying to open up to the supernatural, to extend his awareness and willingness to accept and to embrace possibilities no matter how unlikely they seemed. The hard part to him was the bit about channeling all of the energy, serving as a conduit between worlds across undefinable, possibly infinite spaces in realms he had no idea even existed. So when Anna Marie pulled a pad of watercolor paper, some tubes of watercolor paint, several brushes and a small mixing palette from her bag and set it before him on the table he was not only relieved but felt empowered; excited even. When she looked at him with eyes that said, these are for you and I'd like for you to use them, the radio button next to the category of "Known Abilities" was instantly clicked, on the "manage profile" page of his mind. This was how he had begun to think about things because it all seemed too much like virtual reality, like he was caught in an elaborate game. He was having trouble reconciling the fact that the symbol of great energy, oneness and spiritual enlightenment was delivered to him from within a video game. Granted, it was the single most spectacular video game he had ever played with the most believable interface ever conceived, but if the fight with Z could be as convincing as it was, and the crystal materialized from within the game, then why couldn't all of this still be part of a much larger game. Blue began to doubt his grasp on reality until he touched the paper, slightly textured, absorbent, thick enough to not be flimsy thin enough that he was happy that it was on a block so it would not curl. He touched it for a while, then did the same with the brushes, moistening the finer ones with his lips and tongue, surveying the fineness of their tips. The gentle touch of Anna Marie's hand upon his arm sealed the deal that this was real.

She looked at him with great seriousness and determination in her eyes, pointing to him, then to the paper. She made a gesture like she was holding a brush and sweeping it across the paper. Blue's eyes followed her hands as they came together like praying hands which she gracefully turned and slid under her cheek as if laying her head upon a pillow. Then, with her head, still tilted sideways, her eyes closed, she peeked one eye open and pointed gently with both forefingers directly at Blue's head. Closing her eyes again fully she motioned toward her own head whisking her fingers around her head as if little puffs of thought, dreams were floating out of her mind. Balling her hands around the very puffs she had articulated with her fingers, she seemed to capture them, pulling them down toward the table, dumping them out upon the pad of paper as she opened her eyes to see if Tommy had understood her pantomime.

"You want me to paint my dreams?" he asked. She smiled in response. "All of them?" he continued. She shrugged in response as if to say that it was up to him how much he painted. "Are you going to stay with me?" he asked. She shook her head no as she rose from the table and turned to leave. As she did, he asked. "How do you know I can paint? I might need your help." Anna Marie turned back toward him and shook her finger in mock disapproval as she turned away again, smiling... "Oh, I should have guessed, you know a lot about me. Please, do me a favor, when I get to the point where I know as much about myself as you know about me, will you let me know?" Blue said half-jokingly. Anna Marie smiled and curtsied, then turning like a ballerina, she left Blue to paint his dreams.

20 PAINT IT BLUE

Blue was pretty excited to get the chance to paint as a means of expressing himself in this strange new world. He didn't really care if Tommy was a painter or not. After all, Tommy couldn't do half the stuff Tommy did since Blue was Tommy. What surprised Blue most however, was what came out when he just let the painting happen. He was able to travel right back to one of those places he had been in his dreams. After finishing his first painting, he was so inspired that he quickly started another. His first depicted the "Light Wizards." From what he can surmise, they conduct energy through their hands. What that means, he planned to explore further with Anna Marie but at the moment, he needed clean water.

The next, a detail of the "Light Wizards Dream 1" painting showing Tommy "conducting." At least Blue is pretty sure it's him or Tommy or Onjadiavaan. He really wishes Anna Marie could just TELL him what's going on. Truthfully though, he knows, by virtue of the changes he has already undergone, that the discovery is his alone to make. Anna Marie and the others can only help him to find the way.

Blue worked quickly to create a painting called "Cosmic Dancer" before Anna Marie came back. He was pretty sure that she was the "woman" in his dreams who always seemed to be wearing a tutu. It really wasn't a tutu and she wasn't really a woman, at least that's how Blue evaluated the dream. He was trying to understand the dream more deeply by painting them without judgment, without evaluating each brushstroke as he normally did, without measuring every aspect of the content for its appropriateness or potency. He had the idea to make a potato print, something he hadn't done on a painting in a long time, but he was afraid he would be unable to do it since he needed rubber cement or another type of resist to achieve the look he desired. When he looked in the bag he saw three things that surprised him, there was a jar that looked just like a rubber cement jar labelled "Water Resist," a very sharp little knife, just like his exacto knife that he loved to use for carving fine details in things like rubber stamps and potatoes, and a potato. Blue decided to stop being surprised that Anna Marie knew him better than he knew himself. He did wonder, though if it was appropriate to ask a woman from another world for her hand in marriage. Slowly, the thought that it might not be such a good thing to be married to someone who knows him better than he knows himself began to crawl its way across his brain. It settled into the crevices between the fleshy, bumpy, tube-like bits even while his hand created a beautiful representation of the light wizard most likely to be Anna Marie.

Blue had just set aside "Cosmic Dancer" to allow it to dry and was picking up "Light Wizards" when Anna Marie walked silently up behind him. She placed a hand on his shoulder, very gently so she wouldn't startle him. He was so completely absorbed in his thoughts that he barely acknowledged her. She slid gracefully into the empty seat beside him, joining him in the search for meaning within the painting.

"I think this represents me." He said, pointing to the character on the right half of the paper. " I think that I am channeling some kind of energy that is more than just light. I tried to paint it with power but didn't want it to seem destructive. I'm not sure why the floating figures are in there, it's like they're not awake, like they're part of the dream but not really important. The other two, I think, are you and Sansaa, he pointed out the remaining two figures respectively. The figure he saw as Anna Marie was on the lower left and Sansaa was the largest figure in the painting, pictured in the upper left." He smiled at Anna Marie, he felt good that she was going to be able to help him channel the energy of Shedavah. As his eyes met hers he noticed that she was not smiling. She wasn't frowning, but she did seem to be concerned.

Anna Marie pointed to the wizard in the painting which Blue showed her was the one he thought had been her and shook her head, indicating that it was not. Anna Marie was not saddened by this thought at all but she could see that it was important for Blue to feel that he was putting this together for himself; she could also see that he was attracted to her. Anna Marie was accustomed to having men find her attractive. She was also accustomed to having each of them leap to the determination that he would prove to be her savior, the poor mute would at last find love in the arms of her rescuer. Blue didn't strike Anna Marie in quite the same way but it was clear that he had a thing for her.

She had been "in training" for her relationship with Blue for as long as she could remember. Her parents were both killed when a police chase forced her father's car off the road, into a cement abutment, causing her premature birth. The first person on the scene of the crash was a woman by the name of Julianna. before any public service vehicles arrived, before police or firefighters, Julianna delivered the baby before her mother Marie perished from the fatal wounds received in the accident. When authorities did arrive, Julianna and the baby were gone. Knowing full-well that she could never keep the baby if anyone found out, Julianna left her home, her job and her few close friends, saying only that she needed to try something new. When Julianna arrived in the Shadowlands, Mojahdii was sitting all alone on a bicycle. Behind it was a small cart. He bid them welcome and asked Julianna to place all of her belongings in the cart while he held the baby. After she had packed up the cart, he gave her the baby and indicated that she sit on the small wooden bench style seat at the very front of the cart. Already there was a soft blanket in which to wrap the newborn. After a short ride down a winding path, Mojahdii stopped the bicycle, got off and began to unload all of the belongings into a small, neat hut. He said goodnight and told Julianna that he would have to spend one half of one hour with the baby each day until it was time for her to go. That daily visit became the training which would prepare Anna Marie for her work with Onjadiavaan. Both women still reside in that same little hut.

Chapter 14 Continued 5 Anna Marie Returns cont

Anna Marie reached out for Blue's hand, she turned it over within her own and gently pulled his fingers open so his palm was open to the sky. He half expected a flower to appear, but there was nothing, just an empty palm. She gently brushed the open palm with the backs of her fingertips in a sweeping motion and guided her hand to the sky, as she did she echoed the motion with her other hand so she was fully extended as if showing Blue all there was above him. He followed the motion upward and his thoughts followed his eyes. Anna Marie was telling him that his hands had the power to open up and free the energy, not hers. She leaned in close to him and smiled, letting him know that it was absolutely fine with her. As she did, she stretched across him to look at the other painting. Blue reached for it and quickly slid it toward the end of the table attempting to hide it but she caught his arm. This made two feelings well up within him instantly, shame and admiration. He was ashamed because the dancer he had painted, which he had convinced himself was Anna Marie probably wasn't and he was struck with admiration for her because she had stopped him from hiding the painting, not by slamming her hand down on the paper it was painted on, as so many unaware individuals might, but by stopping his arm, allowing him to control the paper so it did not get damaged in any way. The odd thing about Blue was that he loved mixing up all sorts of media that weren't necessarily compatible but he loathed when someone dented his drawing or watercolor paper by mishandling it. Overwhelmed by the feeling of assurance this conveyed to him, he presented Anna Marie with "Cosmic Dancer."

She absolutely beamed. Immediately she sprang into the air as if she had been launched like and arrow from the string of a bow. She landed on the other side of the table, balancing perfectly on the very tips of her toes, as slowly, gracefully she bent the single supporting leg, her trailing leg, fully extended at first, sliding smoothly along as she drew it forward etching an unbelievably straight and even line in the sandy dirt using the very tip of the longest toe of her other foot. Her arms were both slightly raised above her head, her hands reaching, backward at first, then slowly, steadily forward as she stepped into the lunge. She was the Cosmic Dancer!

Blue watched as Anna Marie danced, his mind slipping in and out of a dream state, a timeless euphoria where sight, sound, memory and perception swirled together like the marbled ingredients of a most deliciously decadent dessert. Images flashed through his mind, feeling so real but for the moment intangible. Anna Marie could see that Blue was "traveling" as she would later define it to him. She continued to dance around him, allowing him to ride along upon her movement. Blue recognized that Anna Marie was working with him, in this very moment, she was his guide, while at the same time his instructor, she wanted something from him. So he began, once again, to paint. At the precise moment that he felt as if he could produce an image which might capture the energy of the moment, the sweeping curve of the brush, the liquidity of the fluid medium responding to his direction while he responded to the direction of a source he could not define, he looked up and Anna Marie was gone, leaving him with his inspiration.

The moment Blue had finished the energy painting, Anna Marie was there. He half-suspected that she was sitting behind a bush the whole time, just waiting for him to clean his brushes. She hadn't been, she was just that in tune with him. It was an ability she had developed over the years, an ability she could exercise with just about everybody. She just happened to be even better at it with Blue. She leaned in close, directly over the painting and began swirling her arms around like the action she saw depicted in the brushstrokes, her smile was joyful and at the same time purposeful as if she was creating happiness with her movement and intent. Blue, placing the clean brushes on the table before him, sat and watched Anna Marie. He became immediately caught up in her dance, his head and shoulders swaying back and forth as if she was a snake charmer and he the snake. But this was not a dance of control. He wasn't forced into any particular sort of movement, no count to follow, no mark to hit, no choreography, no right, no wrong, pure happiness.

His eyes were closed. He felt extremely peaceful while at the same time excited. Then Blue heard a sound he thought he would never hear, laughter. Laughter coming from someone other than himself. The only other person there was Anna Marie. He opened his eyes to see if Sansaa had returned or maybe another woman from the village. He knew before he saw her that this laugh had to be Anna Marie's, so sweet, and lush. Yes, he thought to himself, lush. Blue had never heard of laughter being described as lush before and he wasn't sure why he was so focused on the concept at the moment, but he was and not without due cause. If you were asked to define a person's laugh, you may start with adjectives like loud, shrill, echoing, mighty, mousy, nasally, maybe even pleasant, joyous, jubilant or intoxicating, but none of those would describe Anna Marie's laugh. It surrounded Blue in a bubble of pleasure, then filled that bubble completely with happiness that was palpable, soaking him with perfect rain and warming him with blissful sunshine, lush. Blue was so overwhelmed with the sound of her laugh that he completely failed to recognize that he was no longer sitting at the table.

He was, in fact, sitting in the exact spot in the hut belonging to Mojahdii where he had been sitting with Anna Marie shortly after they were introduced to one another. Anna Marie sat directly across from him laying out the small bundle of freshly picked herbs, leaves and grasses as well as the flower, in precisely the same design that she had laid them out in before, this time Blue noticed and recognized the design. It was the same shape as the energy, represented by swirling lines orbiting a bright, seemingly empty center. Anna Marie smiled at Tommy then took his hand in hers. In his palm she placed the single blossom of a flower. It was still the most brilliant blue flower he had ever seen. Anna Marie gently curled his fingertips around the blossom and held his hand between both of hers as she bowed sweetly to him, then slowly opened his curled fingers and the flower was gone. She smiled again, then winked and closed his hand again. Slowly, she opened his fingers once again, inside were two identical brilliant blue blossoms. A rush of pure energy shivered its way through Blue's entire body as he saw the blossoms reflected in his painting.

21 BAD MOON RISIN'

Many people believed that the face in the moon over Salta was the face of Farb himself, keeping a watchful eye over them as they slept. Despite mountains of scientific evidence to the contrary, the ultra-devout clung to the notion with the intensity of a free-climbers crimp. For Leer, always mindful of the mission, each story, every individual perspective was a clue. As he surveyed the landscape he didn't see the planet, the ground, the water, the trees, fields or mountains, he saw memories, parallels to memories, doorways to new sections in the labyrinth of "All That Is."

That feeling of having been somewhere before is a very hard thing to shake when it hits you. It is particularly hard to shake if you had actually been there before, and not just in the respect that you happen to be standing in the exact same spot where you stood a year ago or the last time you were in town, but the actual fact of existing within the exact same moment as you already had. This is the precise feeling that Leer now was busy experiencing without letting anyone else in the room know it. Fortunately, two of the people in the room were absorbed in their wounds, though remarkably less than one might have imagined given the severity of the injuries they had received at the hands of Victor. Max was in the process of stifling the urge to go for round three with Victor after seeing him move so flawlessly, not only managing Sal's goons but handling Sal himself by barely acknowledging the attack Sal had ordered upon him. Sal was quiet, pensive and absolutely glued to Victor's facial expressions and body language. He was waiting for Victor to explain what he meant when he said that Tommy Levito didn't have the missing JumpJuice. Leer returned Sal's piercing gaze. Instantly, he remembered what was going to happen next.

"Excuse me," Victor said politely as he quickly moved to the far side of the room. There, a full set of armor was displayed complete with a full-length shield. He deftly removed the shield from its mount in the display and just as nimbly changed direction back toward a large double glass door. Victor opened the door with his right hand as he raised the shield with his left at the precise moment that a projectile, the approximate size and weight of a large shotput ricocheted off of the shield. Immediately, he lunged back inside the room, slamming the doors closed as he dove for the floor yelling, "DOWN," just as an explosion rocked the clubhouse, blowing the glass from the doors and separating them from their hinges. The curtains, the rug and a chair near to the doors were on fire. Sal was surprisingly quick to his feet and was extinguishing the flames before they had a chance to spread.

After the smoke had cleared a bit, Max, Sal and Victor surveyed the damage to the outside of the doorway and the face of the building below. The tiny balcony had been blown off except where the supports were strongest, two points where the balcony attached to the outer wall, now clinging to what remained of the narrow floor, the shattered remnants of the guardrail. The facade of the building was blackened and the grounds had a hole the size of an inverted VW Beetle carved out from the blast.

"How did you know?" Max asked Victor as she held him by the hand. Sal's eyes, taking it all in, belied an uneasiness. Max noticed, though it would be hard to determine the exact motivation, the blast or the intimacy.

Leer knew far more than he was going to share anytime in the immediate future. "I had a source, but that's not what's important right now. Sal, it was one of our own," Victor said as he turned back into the room. "It's Bobby." Leer paused to get a good look at Sal's reaction, nothing. "But I don't think he's in on this alone. Obviously, he didn't take the shipment without help, but that's not what I mean. Someone else, a little smarter, maybe not much, but at least a little, came up with the plan." Leer noticed a little twitch in the corner of Sal's lips as he said this, then he finished with, "but don't worry Sal, I'll find him. Then, I'm going to show you what I do to guys who double-cross me. Leave it to me Sal, I'll handle it, I promise." Victor's eyes were focused directly on Sal's as he said this.

"I know you will, Victor," Sal responded, then quickly dismissed both of them saying, "let me know if you need anything from me, anything. And Victor, don't let my little Maxie distract you too much, we've got another shipment rolling out tomorrow, remember." Reaching into his pocket, Sal retrieved a small handful of peanuts." Let's not lose two of them." With a single flick he tossed two nuts from their shell, into the air and caught them in his mouth as he approached the door. He did not look back.

Leer knew what to expect, because he had already experienced what was to come. The difficulty with a situation like his was being able to recognize how much of an influence to have on achieving certain favorable outcomes. If he became too assertive, he might tip the scales in either direction, ending up with a different result than that which he knew would occur. His memory of the future was limited to a couple of weeks at best, after all, it had been nearly thirty years since he had said what he was about to tell Max, "Bobby's dead."

"What?" Max replied looking bewildered, "but you just told my father that he is the guy who took the shipment!"

"Exactly," he continued, "it isn't going to take Sal more than five minutes to find Bobby and have him snuffed." Leer knew far more than he was able to tell Max at the moment but he felt confident that letting her in on this much foresight would be harmless especially when he came up with a pretty solid fabrication as to how he knew that Bobby was a goner. "You know, Max, it doesn't take Sal long to get to anybody. He wasn't after Bobby until I said that he did it, now that I have, Bobby is history." Max nodded her head slightly, it was at times like this that she really hated being Sal's daughter. She wondered if she would have been able to live a life free from violence had she been born into a different family, was the stress and guilt from this way of living the cause of her mother's condition, would she end up the same way? "Everything is going to work out fine, Max," Victor said gently as he reached an arm around her.

At that very moment, the two goons who had been on the floor, unwilling to move, unsure of their own condition, got to their feet, brushed off the debris that had landed on them during the explosion and simultaneously realized that whatever Victor had done to them was healed by his own hands. The broken arm and snapped knee were apparently none the worse for wear and because they were already down on the floor for the explosion, they managed to escape any injuries that may have occurred from the blast. After looking themselves over in disbelief, they surveyed one another. They started laughing , hugging each other and patting each other on the back. Feeling slightly uncomfortable when they realized they were behaving like happy children, they quickly chiseled their own features back into place. Uncomfortably they approached Victor, each of them extending a hand for a shake. Victor shook each of their hands as both men apologized for attacking him. Victor simply smiled. As they headed toward the door through which Sal had departed, the larger of the two goons turned back slightly and said, "thanks Victor."

Leer knew that Victor was used to being called Mr. Alonso by all but a select few. The fact that goon number two felt it acceptable to address him by his first name meant that he recognized something different in Victor and, judging by the trashing he just received at Victor's hands, it wasn't weakness. Leer was perfectly fine with the idea of people recognizing that Victor was different, it would be only natural for him to have changed on some level. In fact, he was planning on leveraging the event in order to instigate the change that he knew was possible. Stepping into the body of someone else in the middle of what could basically be labelled a drug war might normally cause one to want to hide, to blend in, to go along with whatever might be happening without drawing too much attention to one's self. However, Leer had no intention of blending in. He was not afraid of changing things in Victor's life. He planned on it. The moment he remembered tomorrow, he knew what he had to do today. He absolutely believed in change because he had already seen it for himself. His challenge was to foster that change without destroying that which was meant to remain the same. Leer continued getting little memory flashes throughout the rest of the day, each one bringing him closer to the truth. He had his work cut out for him. Leer needed to convince Max that she must die. Very soon and very violently. He just wasn't sure when he would break it to her.

"What do we do now Victor." Max asked, bringing Leer's focus back to present day. "If Bobby's dead, meaning daddy got to him, what about the shipment?"

"The shipment is gone, Max." Victor responded. "Let's just do what Sal told us to do. Let's handle tomorrows shipment, make sure it goes without a hitch. It's time to get the boys together."

Max was a little surprised at this. She had imagined that Victor was going to dramatically alter things, possibly including the cancellation or at the very least the postponement of the shipment. Maybe she hadn't made herself clear enough to him about the fact that she was hoping that things would change, that the fighting and killing would stop and that the JumpJuice was at the center of it all. Max checked herself, giving Victor the benefit of the doubt, she thought about the fight at the clubhouse. He had been attacked, yet he only disabled the goons. Sal nearly accused him of being responsible for the theft or loss of the shipment going so far as to question his ability to manage the operation, his capacity to fight for that which belonged to him. Instead of reacting with anger or self-righteousness, Victor chose preservation and diplomacy, letting Sal know where he stood without getting into a pissing match like the men in her life had become accustomed to. As she granted Victor this moment of understanding she allowed herself to trust in him. "Alright, Victor, I'll get the guys together, how soon?" she asked as she pulled her phone out, a smile crossing her face as she remembered that which made them late for Sal in the first place.

"Now," he responded as he walked toward the hole to the outside world, its edges still slightly smoldering from the blast.

If you've ever had trouble figuring out whether or not you are in your own body, in your own time, in the body of someone else in a time other than your own or in the body of another but remembering a time when you were in that other body but it was about to happen, you have some idea of what it must have been like to be Leer about five seconds from now. Max was walking a few steps ahead of Victor toward a plain gray door on an equally plain gray wall. They were in the lowest level of a parking ramp which must have been thirty levels deep. This is exactly what was messing with his mind. The gray door and wall were too common. They were in Sal's garage, which was part parking garage and part fortress. Leer had a nagging feeling of nervousness, an unpreparedness which was troubling him because he couldn't remember how many times he walked through that door before all Varst broke loose. The most important clue was nothing more than a moment of hesitation by Max as she approached the door. Leer knew that if Max paused, he had to be ready to fight. For the moment, however, he could relax, Max stepped swiftly to the door and flung it open, passing through so quickly that Leer had to step it up a bit to catch the door before it closed itself. Max was on a mission. She may have been losing interest in the violence coursing through the system in which she found herself but she absolutely loved telling a bunch of hard-ass guys what to do.

"All right, all right, let's have everybody out here right now," she announced as she entered a massive warehouse after proving her way through a series of sophisticated security devices, establishing her identity and alerting those inside to her arrival. "Where's Aldo?" she asked sharply as she surveyed the men who approached as rapidly as a bunch of guys can without looking like they're running to mama. "I need Aldo out here now!" she exclaimed but no one seemed to pay any attention to what she was saying. They had all stopped dead in their tracks. Victor had slid his way right up behind her, so close and so quickly that his breath on her neck triggered her defenses. Instinctively she pivoted, driving her elbow into Victor's gut, following through in a single motion with a jab to his face, moving so quickly that she had no time to recognize his features. Fortunately, this was of no concern to Victor, he simply collapsed his stomach in on itself absorbing what little blow there was as his body bended in anticipation of the elbow. Her jab was effortlessly diverted into a body lead followed by a quick torque turn from Victor and then they were dancing. The moment she realized what was happening, Max burst out laughing.

"May I lead?" Victor asked.

"By all means," Max returned as Victor bowed slightly toward her, signaling the end of the dance, her slight curtsy turning the spotlight over to Victor.

Leer turned toward the men who were frozen in shock at what had just occurred. Max was actually giggling at this point. The men just stared.

These were some serious bad-asses, they carried weapons, knew how to fight, enjoyed JumpJuice and drinking and thought that the only dance of any value at all was a lap dance. Victor looked directly at each one of them in turn then said, "This shipment will not be taken from us. This shipment will go through. I have every confidence that you will deliver the Juice on-time and in full. However, if any one of you causes this operation to fail, I will personally teach you the dance of the dead."

There were roughly a dozen men looking directly back at Leer when he warned them that they had better not mess up the shipment. Half of them were his solid crew and the other half were like the migrant farm workers of JumpJuice trafficking, picking up the odd delivery here and there, often buying their own supply from their cut of the run, then selling that for a hefty profit, making the whole cycle very profitable. In other words, every single one of these men had a stake in the success of the shipment so none of them gave Victor a moments grief over his little pep talk. Max was noticeably tickled by the whole thing, the dancing especially, and her expression of amused satisfaction did not go unnoticed by the boys, Andy, Gavin, Manny and Franco the Fiorelli twins, and Marv and Aldo. Now the Fiorelli twins were always risking their own lives by hinting at a three-way with Max but today they took it one step further.

The thing about the twins was that they seemed to think with a single brain. Their unity of purpose combined with uncanny skills in observation, reinforced by superior physical prowess made them practically irresistible to women and unstoppable to men. They were also a little bit psycho. They enjoyed composing little duets a Capella and impromptu for a myriad of occasions, this would be one of them. "Max, oh Max, when you dance like that with Victor," Manny began. "You make me wish that I could paint a picture," Franco followed as they strutted toward the pair, Franco still singing, "so c'mon girl, let's get together and make art," Manny jumped right in with, "you can even bring your boy along and he can do the h-h-hard part," the Fiorelli twins laughing through their own improvised beat box while performing a perfectly synchronized pelvic thrust dance move that left very little to the imagination.

"Not a bad idea," Victor promptly replied as he took Max by the hand and spun her toward the door they entered by, "only you're not invited," he continued. Without looking back he announced to the ceiling, "and Aldo, I want tracers on every single unit that goes out, no exceptions, no excuses."

That night, Victor and Max made tacos, margaritas and music together. Actually they didn't do any of those things. The tacos were essentially the same thing as tacos but in this time at this place they go by the name "flappers" and margaritas are called "zosh," so you order a "zosh rocks" if you like your margaritas with ice and a "zoshee" if you like them frozen, otherwise, you will end up with a "naked zosh." Music is music both on Salta and in the place which Leer calls home, but they didn't pick up any instruments or crank up the karaoke, they made love. Leer was developing a fondness for Victor's body. It wasn't as beautiful as the one he called self but it handled quite nicely.

"Gavin just called," Max said as she slinked her way toward a relaxing Victor, "he said everything's in place for tomorrow, even Aldo's bit. You must've frightened them with your dancing." She sat across his lap, leaned in close and kissed him. She slowly withdrew as if she intended to stand right back up again but Victor's teeth would not let her. He had her lower lip firmly gripped between them, stopping her. "Ouch!," she gasped as he let go, not intending to harm her, only to keep her close. Which was the precise result, in fact, she liked it, so she kissed him hard right back. The kissing and biting went on for some time as in some animalistic mating ritual, until Leer reached up and stopped it all by holding her chin, tightly between his thumb and fingers, so she would listen to him.

"Listen Max," he said, "I've got a feeling that all Varst is going to break loose in the next few days, not exactly sure how or when, just a feeling." She remained quiet but looked directly into his eyes as he continued," I am telling you, so you can be ready for whatever happens." Still silent, Max grew with concern. "Tomorrow's run will be my last." Before she could speak he answered her next question, "I'm putting an end to all of this for both of us. You want it to end and I just want out."

At this point Max was really confused. She had been secretly waiting for the day that Victor would stop the JumpJuice traffic, the fighting with Tommy Levito and his gang and the general reign of fear over the people of Rat Town. She had even told him that she was hoping for an end to it all, but hearing that Victor was going to quit, cold turkey was almost too good to be true. Too good to be true because Sal would never let it be true. It was Sal who made sure the shipments happened and it was Sal who reigned supreme and profited most from the sale of JumpJuice. Max knew that if Victor tried to quit, Victor would die.

"Don't worry about Sal, "Victor said, knowing what Max would be thinking, "He can always find someone else, like the Fiorelli twins, and he'll leave me alone because I'll be with you. But I really want to clear up this whole thing with Tommy and that's where it's going to get messy."

Max was completely stunned. It sounded to her like Victor was planning to leave it all behind and start a new life, the kind that only happened to other people. She had spent so much time trying to shield herself from disappointment, protecting herself by being tough, disguising her own desires behind her father's ambition, that she found it difficult to acknowledge that she might actually be on the verge of getting what she wanted; love.

"Early! Too Bastin' Early. Farb didn't make the sun rise when he did so we could all get up before it does!" Gavin was the complainer of the group, but he was also the one most likely to die for you if you needed someone to do that. He also liked to make sure that everyone did as they were expected to do, especially if it was something that he didn't want to do himself but also had to. So he continued, "did all of you boys and girl," he smarmily eyed Max, "remember to swallow those pills Aldo made up for ya? Because we don't want to lose any one of our precious family. It's a big world out there and you know how it is these days, you just can't trust anybody, especially strangers."

"Nobody's stranger than you, Gav," Marv joked as he threw what looked like a bazooka in pistol form about thirty feet into the air, arcing perfectly down into Gavin's waiting hand. Gavin caught the gun by the grip and stashed it over his shoulder in a neat little holster on his back.

"All right you guys," Max bellowed so everyone in the warehouse could hear, "This shipment is going to make each and every one of us some snark, I don't want mine going to Levito, Palmeri, Kaspar, any of 'em, and if that little worm Masterson gets anywhere near this shit I will personally beat the bastin' farbunkle out of whoever is responsible, so keep your damn eyes open. Now, before we head out, Victor wants you all to gather around this little mark he has put on the floor, right here," she indicates the spot with the tip of her boot. The men move slowly toward the spot. "C'mon, c'mon, we haven't got all day, gentlemen, let's move!" They hustle just a bit and in a few seconds all of the men are gathered around the spot, including Aldo who is holding a small piece of paper up to Max indicating that he had received his "invitation" and did indeed show for the event. Max acknowledged his arrival, "Thank you all for coming, now step back from the mark just a bit, Heads Up!" she said just in time to move the men far enough back to not be hit by the falling body which made a heavy, dull thud upon the floor in the precise location of the mark. Max winced and opened one eye in the direction of the floor as if to summarize the ickiness of the situation. The men began to murmur amongst themselves.

Victor's voice echoed from across the warehouse. "Yep, that's Bobby! Found him on my doorstep this morning with a little note from Sal. Two words gentlemen, "Not Again!. That's what the note said and that's all I have to say to you, now let's get this job done." He began to turn from the group but caught sight of a concerned expression on Max's face. As he looked around Leer could see that the men were waiting for something. Max's eyes drifted toward the nearby pillar upon which the familiar "Farb Sees" icon was painted. He was happy that Max was on his side because even though he had lived this day nearly thirty years earlier, he could not remember every detail of it. To miss the prayer would be just the type of thing to raise suspicion or inspire mutiny. Turning on his heels, as if the whole thing was planned Victor said, "Abe, you were Bobby's closest friend, why don't you say a few words."

Leer's play was perfect. Almost certainly, Abe knew something about the missing shipment. Whether he was in on it or not, Leer did not recall, but putting him in the spotlight would do two things. Primarily, it would let Abe know that Victor was watching him, secondly it would let all of the others know that a similar fate would befall them if they interfered with the success of the shipment.

Abe began, his head bowed low, his voice nervous," for as much as it has pleased almighty Farb to take the spirit of our dear departed friend and colleague, Bobby, uhh," he paused as all eyes were upon him, not one of the others wishing to be in his place, at once all of their eyes dropped as if deep in prayer, he continued, "uhh, we, um, ask that you take him into your divine presence. We ask this in your name." Abe stopped and began to turn away. Several of the men cleared their throats and Franco gave him a little elbow. Realizing his mistake, he continued, "Almighty Farb, we also ask that you watch over the work we do here today and deliver us and the shipment we carry, safely to its destination. In your name, all things happen, by your will may all things be done."

With that, the group dispersed, each man bowing in turn to the painted image then grabbing guns, knives, grenades, lasers, a couple of swords here and there, rocket launchers the occasional taser and several rifles.

22 DREAM IMAGES

Blue continued painting the images he had seen in his dreams, only sharing them with Anna Marie. This painting captures the essence of a dream that had started when Blue was not yet Tommy but continued after he had become Tommy. Its meaning would be the focus of a discussion, not only with Anna Marie but Mojahdii, and Sansaa as well as a few of the other more advanced inhabitants of the Shadowlands, people who welcomed Tommy and challenged Blue.

Tommy was welcomed by all who lived within the Shadowlands. He was Onjadiavaan. He had brought the crystal to them. Some were concerned that the crystal vanished the moment he showed it, but most clung to the notion that somehow this was what must be. Most of them clung because they believed everything that Mojahdii said, others felt that surely the crystal had not vanished, it was simply lurking around in some in between world waiting for Onjadiavaan to pluck it back into existence and then it would light everything up all over again and all would be good. Still others were confident in their understanding of Shedavah and preferred to continue with their meditations and life activities exactly as they had done before the arrival of Shedavah and Onjadiavaan, these were the ones Blue liked best because they treated him like a normal person. He was among them as anyone else was, loved the same, treated the same, greeted the same, the same. There were, however, several others who considered themselves to be quite advanced, even illuminated. They were so convinced that they were illuminated that they had to be sure that any light in the darkness, ray of hope, blessed event or inspirational occurrence must be tested, scrutinized and verified as legitimate. Unfortunately for Blue, they, like Sansaa, Anna Marie and Mojahdii were aware that he was not only Tommy Levito, but that he was Blue. Onjadiavaan was said to be capable of great things and despite the illuminateds enlightenment, a few key members among them found it particularly hard to stomach that a stranger from another world should be chosen to deliver theirs. Blue had been fortunate that he was alone for most of his encounters with the "illuminati." He wouldn't have known how to handle quips like "How do you like our world? Tommy" and "Hey, why so Blue?" if he had been with Vinny. As it was, he just smiled. He didn't ask to be Onjadiavaan and he still wasn't sure that he was. what he was sure of was that he didn't want Vinny to know that he wasn't really Tommy. If Vinny was going to find out, he wanted to be the one to tell Vinny. He just had to find the right moment. Each day in the Shadowlands seemed to bring that moment closer.

"Hey Tommy, why so blue?" Blue heard a voice behind him saying softly, followed by a strong hand upon his shoulder. It was Vinny. Blue had nearly turned in disgust but managed just the right amount of patience, finding Vinny looking at him with concern.

"Oh, hey Vinny" Tommy responded, "it's the dreams I've been having. I have been painting what I see and sharing them with Anna Marie, but now I feel like I'm going to have to defend them to the others and I don't know what to say."

"Ahh, don't worry about it little bro! You're the one who grabbed the crystal when no one else could. You're the guy they've all been waiting for and they're just jealous. Sansaa told me that nobody, not even Mojahdii, knows what you are capable of. If anybody gives you a hard time, just look at 'em and tell 'em you're going to melt their insides out, very slowly, over time if they don't stop bothering you NOW! Make sure you point your finger right at their bellies and keep it there when you tell them. When they shut up, put your finger away."

"Thanks Vinny," Tommy said laughing, "I'm really not interested in scaring anybody."

"I know bro, just kidding," Vinny added," when you gotta meet these "special people" anyway?"

"This afternoon in Mojahdii's hut," Tommy said, happy to be with Vinny.

"I'd come with 'ya but Sansaa says it just for the "special people," Vinny said, slightly disgusted.

"I know," Tommy said," I don't even want to be there but they're supposed to be important in some way. Tell you what, why don't you help me over there this afternoon, I can show you the paintings before any of them get to see them."

"Isn't that against the rules," Vinny asked like a little kid.

"Bast the rules, "Tommy quickly answered, "you're my bro!"
"What in Varst is that thing you're eating now?" Vinny asked Tommy as the two of them enjoyed their first meal alone together since they arrived at the Shadowlands. "I think it's bleeding!"
Vinny peered in closer as Tommy took another bite which he chewed with relish.

"It's a vegetable," Tommy answered, sucking down the juice which seemed to burst forth from it as he chewed. "I have absolutely no idea what it is, but the girl who gave it to me really seemed proud of it. That, or she wanted me to have a whole bunch of babies with her and she was convinced that this vegetable would be that magic love potion to win me over." He laughed to himself and added, "She was pretty cute."

"Did you just say, cute?" Vinny asked with a look that bordered between dismay and disgust. "And, if that's a vegetable, that means that you have no meat in your lunch!" He went on, becoming even more animated, "Tommy, I don't think I should have brought you here. The expectations, the constant attention and the sudden changes all seem so...Sudden! And Weird!" Vinny continued to look concerned.

"I know Vinny," Tommy said compassionately, "there are many things that are quite different about me since I died, almost died, rose from the dead, checked out then quickly checked back in, whatever the Bast happened, who knows?" He thought for a moment, "I don't know what to say to you except, thanks for being here for me. I gotta believe that it's all related, the dying, but not really, finding the crystal and the dreams, I just need to figure it all out and I really think that the people here will be able to help me do that; and I have you to thank for bringing me here." Blue wanted to tell Vinny what he knew of the truth but everything was beginning to confuse him a bit so he decided to wait. "You know, Vinny, it's not just about me anymore, and if we believe what Mojahdii and Sansaa have to say about it, it's not just about this world, so whether I just eat vegetables or not seems like small potatoes." He laughed at his own pun and so did Vinny. "But hey," he continued, "it's time to show you my paintings."

When they got to the tent Blue pulled the cover from the paintings with care, "I really appreciate you not peeking at any of these, Vinny, but I feel like I need to show them to you now." As he said this he pulled one of the light wizard paintings from the stack. Vinny's jaw dropped as he fell a little backward, finding a spot to sit down rather than collapsing outright.

"You painted THAT?!" Vinny said in utter disbelief. "I was expecting to see some crappy, scribbled, messy, ugly, awful thing that I'd have to pretend I liked, but that is BEEZLE, Tommy, Bastin' Beezle! I don't know what in Varst it is, but it's Beezle!" Vinny must have said Beezle about a hundred times before Blue managed to show him the half-a-dozen paintings he had done so far. "Bastin Farbunkle, Tommy, what ever happened to you turned you into a damn genius, you could make some serious snark just selling those bastin' things. The next time you get that crystal to show up, let me hold it. I want to hold it, I want to rub it, I want to get into a bathtub and soak with it." Vinny was beside himself with excitement over the paintings Tommy had done. He had no idea that Blue was an amazing artist before he ever became Tommy but even Blue was unable to separate the inspiration which poured forth from within and the talent he had before the transformation.

"We'd better get these over to the meeting, Vinny," he said, not sure how to handle Vinny's enthusiasm. "Can you take the one on canvas while I carry these watercolors?" he asked, hoping to get moving without too much more discussion regarding his abilities as an artist.

"I would be honored," Vinny said, in all sincerity as he helped Tommy out of the tent with the art in hand.

The two brothers from different worlds walked together toward the hut of Mojahdii. As they got closer to the hut Vinny stopped suddenly, "Hey Tommy, what are you going to do about JumpJuice?" It was a legitimate question which Blue was hoping to get an answer to within his dreams or from the people helping him. He wondered what Leer was doing at the moment and whether or not he was able to break free from the dirty business they both seemed to be mixed up in.

23 VICTOR LEER

Leer was barreling down the freeway with a convoy of six of the most bad-ass rigs imaginable. The military of a small nation would have a hard time taking her. The convoy boasted an arsenal complete with rocket launchers, a sonic cannon, smoke screen capabilities, remotely guided drone air support (courtesy of Aldo) and a missile deployment vehicle capable of delivering its payload in any direction while on the move. The JumpJuice was allocated throughout the convoy in storage units specifically designed to separate from the larger vehicle, becoming mobile drones in their own right. Even if the entire convoy was assaulted and immobilized, these drones would have the capability to continue and would do so in separate directions, thereby increasing the probability that at least one major delivery would succeed. This was precisely the system in place when the other shipment was taken. One-third of the men involved with this delivery had been involved in the hijacked delivery. Not a single one of them could tell you how it was accomplished. Each and every one of them swears that they were asleep for the whole thing. Quite suddenly, and apparently ubiquitously, the members of the delivery team were put to sleep. Not a single vehicle was destroyed. No guns were fired. Many of the men believed it was the hand of Farb that snatched the shipment from them. In fact, only seven men were missing and of those who remained only a dozen were willing to return to run this shipment, and half of them were Victors gang. The same thing was simply not going to happen again. If it did, the remaining men would almost certainly find a new line of work, possibly even devoting themselves to the service of Farb. However, that was no reason to rule out the possibility of a conventional attack, therefor all preparations had been made and the finest team had been assembled.

The convoy continued down a stretch of highway that had all of the attributes of an ideal ambush location. The highway lay in plain sight of two small bluffs which lined either side of the road. It would provide attackers perfect high ground as well as reinforced cover behind a variety of natural rock outcroppings. The men became increasingly nervous in this particular stretch of the route. Leer did not. While Blue was exploring his dreams for insight regarding his place in this world, Leer was exploring the other side of dreams, memory. Although Leer had actually been in this very spot at precisely this moment nearly thirty years ago, it all seemed like a dream. He remembered how he felt when he reacted to things that had not yet been said. "Victor, why don't we deploy a couple of units up, behind those outcroppings, Banyan Pass is no place to get caught with your guard down," Franco urged as a nervous sweat broke out upon his forehead.

"Our guard is not down, Franco. We are all ready. Besides, this place is far too obvious." Victor smiled calmly and Franco seemed to be genuinely relieved. "I have an idea that I would like to share with all of you," Victor announced to all of the men in his vehicle, roughly a dozen. "I need a moment alone to figure out a few details but I'll be back right away. Do not be concerned about an attack, but DO keep an eye out for one." Victor walked toward the back of the vehicle. It was a little like an armored RV, well-appointed and fairly comfortable for a portable arsenal.

After several minutes alone in a small room at the back of the vehicle, Victor returned. "We're going to blow ourselves up!" he laughed as he quickly looked around the vehicle to catch the individual reactions. There was only one person who did not look in his direction at this announcement. It was Abe.

Most of the guys were trying to read Victor's expression to determine whether he was joking or not while a few simply laughed without even considering that he might be serious. Abe kept looking at his feet. He was moving them slowly under himself as he sat on one of the benches which lined either side of the vehicle where all of the bullet-proof vests, head gear, firearms and explosives were centered.

If you had been Abe at that moment and had any sense of humor or timing whatsoever, it would have been precisely the moment to act, but you aren't Abe and he didn't.

Instead he sat, cowering from his own thoughts in the middle of the most visible area of the vehicle and attempted to hide there. No one but Abe and Leer knew what he was thinking at that moment and because Leer did know, he said this, "We're all going to die."

The men were really beginning to wonder about Victor at this point. He gave a quick glance in Abe's direction to ascertain whether Abe was paying attention or not and determining that he was, continued, "you see, gentlemen, I believe we are going to be ambushed but not quite yet and the only way we can avoid a fight, which I much rather would, is to make sure it never happens, so," he walks over toward Abe and sits right down next to him. Then, he drops a helmet from the wall above his head onto the floor and props his feet up on it. "Let's all relax a minute, shall we, I have a plan I'd like to share with you."

The men walk toward him but do not sit down. "Sit down, put your feet up," he says jovially as he grabs Abe by the leg and yanks his foot up alongside his own, placing it on the helmet.

The men get the point and sit around him. Now there are two on either side of him and Abe and the rest, sitting directly across from them on the other side. "Alright, now the first thing we have to do is take a deep breath." He breathes in deeply and the men do too as Victor smiles at all of them, particularly Abe, who returns an uneasy and half-hearted grin.

"Next," Victor somersaults forward from the bench, grabbing both of Abe's feet as he spins back toward him in a single motion, "we grab Abe." He motions with his head to Marv, who is seated directly on Abe's right side. Reacting quickly, Marv is able to stop Abe from reaching for his gun and also thwarts his attempt to move from his seat. Victor's empty seat is quickly filled by Samuel, a very large man who, had this been Earth, would most certainly have been characterized as Native

American. He quickly held Abe down while skillfully laying the brutally sharp point of his knife to the trembling man's throat.

"Let me have that, will ya' Samuel?" Victor asked in his most polite voice, his eyes resting on the knife. Samuel flipped the knife so quickly that it was nearly imperceptible to the eye and handed the knife to Victor, the tip balanced between his forefinger and thumb. "Nice touch," Victor chuckled as he pointed to the shallow crimson slice left by the blade on the neck of Abe. Taking the knife from Samuel he immediately sliced at the feet of Abe, artfully carving his boots from his feet in seconds. He pulled them off quickly and just as quickly drove the blade to its full length threw both feet, binding them together in a single motion. Without hesitation he reached inside of one of the boots removing its cargo of explosive putty and shoved it into the screaming mouth of the impaled Abe. "Tie him," he said to the men who held him, "we'll deal with him later," he continued as he threw on a helmet and barked the command of, "Stop" into its microphone. Immediately the convoy came to a halt.

Victor threw open the armored door just beyond the writhing form of Abe. He tossed out the boots and fired at them, exploding them with a single shot as he closed the door to shield himself from the blast. He quickly instructed the men to grab every explosive device they had in the vehicle for a rendezvous in two minutes, outside. He opened the door, smoke still hanging in the air, areas of earth still on fire, his vehicle blackened from the explosion. Leer ran to the front of the convoy. As he ran he called all of the men to action, instructing them all to meet outside the vehicles, and fast. In less than a minute they were all outside, every one of them loaded with hand-held explosives. Victor quickly planted an explosive under one of the vehicles, directly in front of the men assembled closest to him. "Like this," he said, "everywhere." Then he turned to Max, "You and I are going to release the drones, I'll take the front half." He smiled as he ran to the first vehicle in the line. Without hesitation, Max dove into the closest vehicle and headed for the drone deployment station. It was simply a matter of typing in an access code and pressing a button and the drone was launched. Victor and Max repeated the routine in each of the vehicles and within minutes, the drones were off.

"What do we do now?" Franco asked Victor as all of the men had emptied their arms of explosives.

Sure enough, he was right. Hobbling, but on his feet, only moments after Victor called it, Abe appeared in the doorway of the large transport vehicle. He fell his way out of it, wrists bound together, barely managing to scramble fifty feet away before Victor gave the order to, "FIRE!" All Varst broke loose as the convoy erupted in a series of blasts. It was really quite beautiful the way they fired off, one by one as the men shot them to life, one would start the other in a rhythmic daisy chain of blasts. None of the explosions were powerful enough to destroy the vehicles but they sure gave the appearance of a major attack. If someone had been planning an ambush, and Leer knew that they had, they would hear the explosions and investigate, only to find the convoy decimated and empty.

As the last of the explosions fired off a low rumble seemed to be coming nearer to the men of the convoy. They looked around suspiciously only to discover Victor smiling and moving slowly closer toward the source of the rumbling. Less than thirty feet from him the ground opened up as a large claw burst from the ground, seeming to eat the very dirt it had just pulled its way through. The points of the claw arched up again then turned down and spiked right into the surface, each lodging itself into the ground by about a foot of dirt. This created a sort of archway, inviting them to enter, which Victor was only too happy to oblige. He turned to the others, "Hurry along now, our ride is here!" then he walked through the archway, down into the darkness. As the last man followed him down the claw jumped back into action, scraping and digging in an apparently random pattern, effectively sealing itself back inside of the ground, leaving no obvious evidence of what had just transpired.

Abe, looking up from his painful, face-down, shrapnel encrusted landing did his best to understand all that had just occurred. He heard the sound of engines roaring their way toward him. He pulled himself up from the ground and tumbled in the direction of the new arrivals. These must be the people he had nearly martyred himself for, the people who would have remembered that he had sacrificed himself for their cause and in so doing avenged the death of his friend Bobby. At least he had tried, at least he could tell them what had happened. Abe was beginning to feel relieved that he did not go through with the suicide bomb detonation. He felt somehow stronger, more confident now that he was a fighter, wounded in battle. He walked toward the approaching vehicles, through the smoke and dirt of the explosion and as he did one last explosion burst forth, sending shrapnel toward the new arrivals. They caught sight of Abe moving slowly toward them through the smoke and quickly shot him in the head. His mouth still stuffed with explosives, his face burst apart, dropping his headless body to the ground, his sacrifice complete.

The subterranean escape route which Leer had planned worked brilliantly. Within minutes the team was reassembled in an underground garage stocked with bikes, decked out rides much like the VinnCycle. "Two to a bike, quick as you please, destination and route maps are already loaded into your navcom panels and we've got Aldo ready to talk us through individually as we get near enough for air to ground links with our drones, right Aldo?" Victor said as he instructed the team like an orchestra conductor, first pairing the men then pointing them to their bikes.

"Right Victor," Aldo confirmed so everyone could hear within their headsets." You're all going to see a red light flash on your navcom as you near your drone. Use the panel to navigate closer and when the light turns blue, I'll guide you through the rest. Feel free to listen in as I guide the others so I can keep repetition to a minimum. We've got six drones and three times as many teams, so we should be able to round them up quickly." Aldo continued, "Those of you who aren't driving, I don't want you to be tempted to jump on your phones to tell anybody about what's going on right now. Whoever was waiting, thinks we've been hit and is probably wondering who did it. I want the mystery to endure. Those of you who are driving, well, I don't have time to quote statistics, but using a phone while driving significantly increases the likelihood of an accident and we can't afford any losses."

Victor spoke to the team as he straddled his ride, "Oh, hey everybody, about Abe, for those who didn't know, he was planning on blowing us up, his boots were full of explosives. Someone set us up and I'm pretty sure I know who it was. We are going to deliver this shipment, but not today. Let's get to the drones and link up. After that, I will fill you in on the rest of my plan, now let's move out!"

Leer felt bad about driving the large knife through Abe's feet but knew
that he had to do what Victor would have done. Actually, Victor
probably would have just shot him in the head right away. Leer had a
pretty good idea that Abe was dead by now, but at least he didn't have
to pull the trigger. He wasn't really against the idea of killing people
when he felt that his own life was in danger but in this case there was
even greater reason to get rid of Abe. He sent the team a clear message
that he would handle the business that needed to be handled and he
was relying on them to be there for him when he needed it.

"How did you know?" Max asked Victor as she leaned in close against
his back. "Those sources again?"

"No, Max," Victor laughed, "I could just tell that Abe was an asshole and
too stupid to do anything on his own."
The cycles fanned out in all directions except for that from which they
came. The terrain was varied but mostly ridable. The cycles were built to
handle smooth and rough terrain, they had what Vinny referred to as
the 'dillo pillow, on the VinnCycle. If you felt like you were getting into
some rough territory, where you might spill or even drive right off a cliff,
by engaging the 'dillo pillow, you could effectively seal yourself inside a
lightweight armor capable of withstanding just about anything. As you
might imagine, the 'dillo pillow is great for getaways, no matter who's
chasing you.

After just a short time in pursuit of the drones, the first red indicator
light flashed on the navcom panel of the Fiorelli twins' cycle. Franco
quickly turned the bike in the direction of the signal and nearly drove
directly into the rock face. Recovering quickly, he attempted to quickly
shoot out around it to the left. Unfortunately, he lost track of the drone.
"Bastin' Farbunkle!, I lost it," he cried out, upset that he was no longer
the first to have a drone within range.

"Never mind the panel," Manny cried out as he slapped Franco on the
back and pointed to the sky beyond the outcropping. There, but distant,
a drone was cruising through the sky in the opposite direction from
them. "C'mon bro, gimme some squeelie!" Manny hooted in Franco's
ear. Franco popped the clutch and hit the throttle, burning a stripe into
the road leaving an acrid cloud to drift across a nearby field, bursting
with Cunja Berries, the very fruit from which the prized JumpJuice is

made. the berries grew abundantly with very little maintenance. The difficulty was in the harvest and the processing. It kept most people from even considering producing it for income and it was illegal. Or at least, theoretically it was illegal. The government, having outlawed JumpJuice at a time when the fruit was used for more practical purposes due to rivalling interests championed by powerful lobbyists, continues to struggle with the issue of JumpJuice legalization sporadically. As it stands, however, the machine that has sprung up from the illegal status, distribution and consumption of the commodity hums along with such force that no one, politician, lawyer or cleric dares to place a foot in its path, regardless of how obvious the flaws in the status quo may be.

Franco and Manny sped their way toward the sighted drone. Victor and Max got a blip on their navcom screen. The drone appeared to be within a couple of miles as the crow flies but there was no way to get a visual. In front of them rose a large grassy hill and perched upon the hill was a cluster of the most majestic trees Leer had seen since he was in the Redwood National Park, home to some of the tallest trees on any of the worlds he had visited. These would rate a close second. "Beezle Victor!, Max gasped as she gawked at the immense and beautiful old wonders. "How old do you think those trees are Victor?" she asked like a child filled with awe.

"Somewhere in the neighborhood of five to seven hundred years old, maybe more, I would guess," Victor responded. Suddenly a wave of that feeling of a distinct memory came over Leer, only this memory was not about the future. However, it was about this very place eight hundred and twenty-seven years earlier. As he sped around the first tree, he saw himself as a young woman. He was planting that particular tree. Leer was really wishing that he could share that memory with Max. In another life perhaps.

As Victor and Max cleared the grove of gargantuan trees they immediately caught sight of the drone. It was cruising down low in a valley that seemed to have been formed by a gigantic celestial ice cream scooper. The growth of grass on the ground was so smooth that Leer just punched it, right over the side of the crest and into the valley making a direct line to intercept the drone. He was closing so fast that he barely had time to notify Aldo before they were closing on it.

"Thanks for the warning," Aldo said sarcastically as Max gave the call that they were close. "I just got a call from the Fiorelli twins so let me talk you both through at the same time. You might as well all listen up," Aldo said as his voice needled its way into the headset of every member of the team. When you get within range, that's when you get the lock signal from the red lights, three fast bursts which will cycle over and over as long as you are within range of a connection, you're going to hit the yellow triangle on the lower left of the navcom panel. When the whole screen goes green, the riders need to complete the engagement process by entering their birthdates into the keypad between their legs, that means all of you who are on the backs of the bikes. When this step is complete, state your name clearly. Your voiceprint will be recognized and the drone will lock onto a remote guidance mechanism on your cycle. When you reach your destination, simply say the words, Drone - Destination. I trust there will be no problems but if you should find that you are having trouble, I can help to establish a lock between your cycle and any drone so long as you have maneuvered yourself into range." Aldo added with just the right inflection to be clear that the success of this part of the mission was undeniably attributable to his technological superiority. "However, I have no idea what your destination is, so the very next screen you will see after you have established contact with and control over your drone will be a map indicating the position of Victor's cycle versus that of your own. Victor, if you would be so kind as to say a few words to ensure that everyone can hear you." Aldo requested impatiently.

"Let's get to the drones quickly gentleman, we are seconds from ours and time is of the essence," Victor said, eager to wrap this phase of the operation up as expeditiously as possible.

"Right," Aldo broke in, "you heard the man, now one more thing, the drones are very responsive so try to restrain from any wild driving while you're out there today. I've seen most of you on the road and, I personally want my full share and nothing less. I will not be very happy if a drone crashes because one of you jack-asses decided it was time to show off!"

Aldo was not the most loved of the team but he was indispensable in all matters technological so he was generally forgiven for being a complete dipshit, still no one was going to buy him a beer when this thing was all over. Actually, Victor was planning on buying him a beer when this thing was all over so he said, "Thanks Aldo, and remind me to buy you a beer when this thing is all over, the rest of you, listen up. Max and I are linked in three, two, one, we have a connection. The moment you are locked in you'll see my location. I'm not waiting around for any of you so make it quick. Fiorelli's I have you on my screen, nice work."

"Hey Victor, how about beers for us, or better yet just a little extra snark?" Franco said half-joking in response to the acknowledgement.

"Sure, Franco," Victor laughed, "and while I'm at it, I think I'll give you my house, cars, first born and my own personal invitation to a one hour discussion face to face with Farb himself. And for the rest of you, lifetime JumpJuice and a pension that's just plain Beezle! Now let's keep it moving, I've got Samuel and Nick locked in, just a few more and I'll let you all in on where we're headed."

"I thought we were deliverin' the Juice to the Sin Shack," Samuel questioned, looking for a little clarification as to just how dramatically the plan had changed.

"Apparently, Samuel, so does someone else," Victor quickly replied. "Gavin and Marv are now linked, so let's get down to it. Those of you who didn't link to a drone, meet us at the location that appears on your navcom panel in a few minutes...All of you who are the VR link for your drone, enter your birth dates followed by the three digit number you see flashing in the upper left hand corner of the numeric keypad you used for the link now." Victor gave them a few seconds to do so, Max gave him a little rub on the back when her code was entered. "What you see now that all of your codes have successfully been entered is the exact location where we are all meeting. I will see you all there in less than thirty."

Max leaned in close to Victor as the cycle hummed its way toward the location. She felt good to be with Victor now but she was troubled by what was happening with the shipment. She felt a little out of the loop, like something secret was going on that Victor somehow knew about and she didn't. Max had become used to being a heartbeat away from the head of the operation, her father, and although it was sometimes uncomfortable, she felt more powerful. Her heart was torn between her feelings for Victor and her need for security which she always associated with her father. She worried that she was just passing one dependency over to another so she hugged Victor tighter to fight off the fear that one day he would be gone and she would be left alone.

"We're here," Victor said calmly into his head set, quietly but with enough of a nod to his head to get Max looking in the right direction.

"Drone - Destination," she said, without hesitation and the craft automatically hovered to a stop just a short distance from their cycle. Within five minutes all of the team along with all of their drones had arrived at the site.

"Okay, let's move." Victor ordered. 'I want Gavin, Samuel, Marv and Franco up in the cabs." Four large diggers were lined along the edge of the work site. The whole area was under construction.
"Max, I want you and Manny heading up the unload. The rest of you, let's get the Juice out of the drones and into the digger shovels. Split up and take a drone, I will meet you at each drone to open them and Nick, I want you to wait. I need you at your cycle and will meet you there as soon as I get the drones open, Now go!" Victor was firm but not upset. If anything, Leer was excited, he loved danger and while there was no sign of it now, the shipment was still in danger.

Everyone hurried to their tasks and within minutes Victor was at the cycle with Nick. "I'll drive," he said as he jumped on the bike and Nick took the back seat. "We're going for the trucks." At the far end of the site stood two large dump trucks. Nick and Victor reached the trucks quickly and were heading over to the diggers in no time. The team had worked quickly and nearly all of the Juice was in the shovels by the time they arrived with the trucks. "Dump 'em," Victor ordered, then quickly added, "GENTLY!"

Gavin, Samuel, Marv and Franco skillfully maneuvered the payload of each shovel into the dump trucks. The shipment was once again mobile.

"Gavin, Samuel, Marv and Franco," Victor called out, "stay in the cabs. I need you to bury the drones. Manny and Nick, jump into the dozers and help dispose of the drones. Max, Drive the dump truck Nick brought over. The rest of you, on the bikes. Let's head out. We'll be back tomorrow for you guys," he said to the drone disposal crew, and before anyone could ask any questions, he sped off. As he drove the dump truck away he ordered into the headset, very clearly and with conviction," REMEMBER, absolutely NO contact with anyone outside the team until I say okay."

Less than an hour later Leer pulled his rig into a tunnel, high up the side of a fairly large mountain just north of the construction site. As the rest of the vehicles drove into the tunnel behind him they slowed to a stop. "We're staying here tonight," Victor announced. "Make yourselves comfortable and stay in the tunnel. Fred and Dominic, take the north side entrance of the tunnel and set some flairs. Keep them inside the tunnel. We don't want anyone driving into us but we don't want to be visible outside of the tunnel. Gino and Todd, you guys have the south side. Okay boys, our engines are overheated, let's pop the hoods and give 'em a rest. That's our story and we're stickin' to it."

The tunnel turned out to be the perfect place to spend the night. Very few cars came through from either direction and those that did gave the crew a wide berth. Thunderstorms pummeled their way across the whole region but the team stayed dry under the shelter of the long tunnel.

Franco and the rest of the team who stayed behind to bury the drones spent the night in the work site trailer. It was reasonably comfortable though a bit noisy as the forceful rainstorm pounded the roof, the metal shell reverberating like an old Stratocaster through a daisy chain of distortion, reverb, and flanger effects pedals which was music to some and pure annoyance to others. They seemed to be far more interested in the card games they had going than what was happening outside. That is until the reverb turned into a clanging sort of drumbeat. In unison, every one of them stopped talking, some stopped breathing, and all pulled their guns and knives as they quietly created a makeshift barrier behind which they hid, eyes trained on the door, weapons ready.

Samuel's best friend in the world, Garldiparn, a short man with no hair and a tattoo of a old-time train which ran the length of his torso, spiraling steam from his chest to his navel, approached the door. he answered it nonchalantly," Ah, yeah, whatchu want?" Three large men stood in the doorway with rain pelting them from above, having a hard time even looking at Garldiparn. "Well, c'mon in, you'll catch your death out there," he said, grinning from ear to ear, smoking a big fat cigar of some homegrown hand-rolled that stunk up the air and sent clouds toward the visitors faces. "You guys shouldn't be out here, nobody supposed to be on the site at night, but hey, I get super lonely, ya know, I got cards, you guys play cards? "Course you do, c'mon, I got a table back here somewhere," Garldiparn rambled as he walked back toward the team.

"Oh no, ah, never mind," the largest of the men said in the nicest voice he could muster. "We're just looking for some friends of ours, thought they might have stopped here. We'll just be moving on."

"Okay boys, you suit yourself. Hey, do you think your friends are lost?" he continued, the men looked unsure of what to say. "Because if they are lost then they are definitely on the north road, it's been washed out all day, "bout twenty minutes north of here, damn broke. Everyone who drives past here been goin' on the southwest pass road, only way out of here, but if your friends are stuck? North road for sure, maybe dead, who knows, so sorry to hear 'bout your friends. You close? I got some good friends, real close..."

"Yeah, thanks pal," the big guy cut in, "We'll be going, we really have to find our friends," he said turning away, pushing the other two out the door. "That guy wasn't about to stop talking, let's get the Varst outta here. My guess is that they're well past here now, beyond the southwest pass, they sure as Varst aren't about to take the Juice up into the mountains when the road is washed out." The other two men nodded in agreement as all three got into their cars and sped off in the direction of the southwest pass trailing a motorcade of another ten cars, identical to theirs, behind them, on a mission, after the Juice.

"Okay, gentlemen, they have departed, you may all come out now. I believe they have been properly misled and are currently in pursuit of nobody on a road to nowhere," Garldiparn said as he rubbed his hands together eagerly, "I believe I was just about to increase my wager if memory serves!" The rest of the team burst out laughing as they emerged from behind the wall of boxes, site maps and safety gear to congratulate "Gardi" on his brilliant performance.

Early the next morning Victor sent enough of the team to pick up those that stayed at the site, keeping the others with the trucks to guard the Juice. It wasn't long before the whole team was assembled within the tunnel and ready to move the juice to the delivery location. "I'm going to call daddy to let him know we're still delivering," Max said, assuming that the threat was over and that Sal needed to be informed.

"No Max," Victor answered firmly, several of the team listened attentively to his explanation as to why Max was not permitted to call her father. It had never happened before, for two reasons. The first being that Sal was the boss and as the boss was entitled to know everything that ever happened and it was just assumed that Max was going to be the one to tell him. The second was that Max usually got extremely pissed off if she didn't get her way when it came to anything that had to do with her father unless it was Sal himself who said no. Even though Victor was in charge of the team, everyone knew that Max was along to remind Victor just where he fit in and that, just as quickly as guys like Bobby and Abe, he could be replaced. However, something had changed dramatically between Victor and Max, even the least observant of the team could recognize that. Still, they were prepared for a battle. "I don't think we're in danger anymore, Victor and you know that Sal is going to want to know what is going on with the shipment," Max said in the most reasonable voice she could muster up.

"I have absolutely no doubt that Sal is acutely interested in the whereabouts of the shipment, Max," Victor began, "but I don't think that now is the proper time to fill him in." Leer knew something that no one else on the team knew and he could not tell any of them. In order to gain not only Max's acceptance but also that of the entire team he was going to have to be very convincing that what they did know warranted the stealthy completion of the mission. He continued, "Look, we nearly got our asses blown off yesterday, first from inside and certainly, had we continued on our course, from the outside. We all know that Bobby was one of our own, then Abe. Now I'm not saying that any one of you is involved in this betrayal, however, someone out there is still waiting for us to show ourselves, knowing full well that we are under armed and under protected. With any luck they'll still be looking for the drones. So, Max, any communication with others has to be under only the most secure connections. That is why I had Aldo set up the delivery protocols the way he did. We MUST remain below the radar for the duration of our journey. When the job is done, I will personally dial the number to Sal for you." Victor looked at everyone on the team with an expression of sincerity and need unlike anything they had ever seen from him. In that moment, for each individual in the team, Victor transformed from boss to leader.

Max walked slowly to him and sliding up his chest, wrapped her arms around him and kissed him saying, "I'm with you , just tell me where to go."

The rest of the team let out a collective "WOOT!" followed by a good minute of laughter, relieving themselves of the awkward nervousness they were experiencing at such an unusual feeling of excitement, loyalty and enthusiasm, emotions that few of them felt very often and certainly rarely with respect to Victor. Leer had won them over even more quickly than he had imagined he could. If his plan succeeded he would be certain that he was on the right path with regard to the even larger, universal mission.

"Okay then, it's time I let you all in on my little secret... I'm going to kill about, um, well, I'd say about, a little over half of you," he smiled a wicked but comical smile, "and we are going to lose the shipment." The entire team was silent at first but quickly figured out that he had to be joking so they started laughing all over again. "Yes, that's right, we're going to lose lives and the Juice and head back home, beaten and empty-handed. Max, it has been a real pleasure, but I'm afraid you have to die first," Victor said as he bowed to her. "Now let's get moving. I want you all to follow me to my little hideaway beneath the sea." He walked over to the big lead truck and climbed up, "C'mon Max, ride with me. Nick, drive the other truck, and Samuel, ride shotgun. The rest of you, hop on the bikes and let's move out."

A few minutes into the drive, Victor cued to Max to remove her headset by pointing to hers as he removed his. She got it right away and with their headsets off he could speak freely. "I know it sounds like a crazy plan Max," Victor said calmly, "but I have reason to believe that I have to handle it this way and I want to be sure I have your full support."

Max was noticeably undecided. To anyone other than Leer she may have appeared to be upset by the change of plans or the restriction against calling her father but he knew better. He knew better for several reasons, not the least of which is because he could remember her telling him what she was about to say, thirty years ago. "I don't know Victor," she said reluctantly, "I mean, you do, it's just," she hesitated as if she was trying to pick her words like poorly formed parts from a far too quickly moving assembly-line conveyor belt, "I can't seem to, I mean, I don't know why, but I absolutely do think" she paused again, "sorry, I know, you're right." She continued, "Something is absolutely wrong about this whole thing. I felt really weird the moment we woke up, something inside of me, telling me to watch out, telling me to be careful, that I was going to be betrayed by someone close to me." Max looked directly at Victor, her eyes searching him for any reaction. Leer felt her eyes and turned his from the road to meet her gaze. He knew that he was not whom she thought he was and certainly that was a betrayal of sorts. He also knew that it was not the betrayal of which she spoke. He looked back to the road as she continued, "The moment you pulled those boots from Abe I thought, that's it, it's him, it's Abe! but the feeling hasn't left me. Her eyes, still drilling little holes into the side of his head, rather than taking the less destructive route through his ear hole to his brain, returned only feelings of trust, warmth and an ease she hadn't felt with another person in a very long time, not since her mother knew the difference between a dog and a Life Quality Care Specialist. "I know it's not you," Max said to Victor, her voice growing fainter," so it must be," her voice a strained whisper, "my father." Her forearms slunked into her lap and her shoulders drooped forward. Leer said nothing. Max looked over at Victor, realizing that by his silence he was acknowledging her fear, she fell backward in her seat and putting her hands to her head gasped, "oh, daddy, you really are an asshole!"

The next twenty minutes of driving was fairly silent with only the sound of the road to fill up the emptiness Max was feeling. Leer let Max sit with her realization, each moment of silence filling her mind with another example of why her father should not be trusted to do anything but look out for himself, like the day he told her that he had decided to enroll her in an immersion school for the fighting arts and that her previous three years of rigorous dance instruction was a perfect base upon which to build the skills she would learn to master at the school. Then there was the year of her eleventh birthday when he invited the guests and told her that it would be better than if she had chosen, that the guests he chose were better sorts of people, only to discover that he had invited well over a hundred guests of which only six were children, two of whom she did not even know. In fact, he had not even purchased a cake, nor did he have any intention of sharing that cake with her mother whom he promised they would visit to celebrate his little girl's birthday. Anything that he had gotten for her would somehow serve him. Her education with a major focus on the history of war and the essentials of business, her diet, highly nutritional, healthy, athletic, her cars, motorcycles, boats, all fast and well armored and even her clothes, attractive enough so her looks were admired but functional, militaristic and no-nonsense as if to say "you can look but don't touch, or that hand of yours, I'm going to snap the arm it's attached to in half, like a little twig."

Her eyes had welled up with tears and her spirit had been crushed. She knew that it was unfair to blame Victor for any of this but he just sat there, driving. Driving her father's JumpJuice in a big dump truck out in the middle of nowhere. She began to think of how he was just like her father, that they were going to be stuck in this life, just as it always had been, on Sal's terms, doing Sal's dirty work. She turned to him filled with hopelessness. "Here we are," Victor said with a gentle smile as he turned the dump truck down a tree-lined road toward a lovely little cottage. Max wiped the tears from her eyes as she began to notice just how beautiful the land around the cottage truly was. She had been so deep in thought that she hadn't noticed the landscape through which they had been driving.

"What is this place?" she asked breathlessly as Victor pulled the truck into a large, rustic and slightly weathered barn.

Victor turned toward her as the vehicle came to a stop, reached into his left breast pocket and pulled out a set of keys which he held out to her with a smile and said, "home."

24 HOME

We can go home if you want to," Vinny said as he and Blue were kicking back in the tent without a care in the world. "I mean, you don't have to try to get the crystal back right away. Varst, they've been after it for centuries according to Sansaa," Vinny laughed hard, " then you come along and find it without even looking for it. Still, you've got other stuff to do, and the Shadowlands, Sansaa, that's all my idea. I mean, I'd understand if you don't want to hang around any longer."

"Things getting a little too serious with Sansaa for ya, are they Vinny, got you a little scared," Blue dove right in, where any other guy would have been wise to keep clear of. Vinny pulled himself forward in his lounge chair, preparing to rise, struggling internally, trying to find the right words and deciding how to handle the "scared" label. "Don't worry bro', you two are meant for each other. You're just having trouble dealing with the fact that you're gonna have to do it her way." Vinny gave Tommy a look that was half "deer in the headlights" and half "raging bull," which is hard to describe but unmistakable. "Besides, I want to stay. Bastin' farbunkle Vinny, this place feels just as much like home as any other. Varst bro', I've got you, a nice place to stay," Blue gestures toward the spacious interior of the tent, and Anna Marie. I know I'm supposed to be Onjadiavaan but I'll tell you Vinny, it's Anna Marie who's truly magical."

"Vinny fell back into his lounge chair and let all of the awkwardness, pent-up emotions and swelling feelings within, puff out, exhaling like a whistle on an old-time steam locomotive, uttering a single word as he threw his hands up in the air, "Women!"

Tommy reached into a small cooler, which Sansaa had brought over to the tent when she delivered the most remarkable meal Blue could remember enjoying in years, to retrieve two ice cold beers which he held high in the air between himself and Vinny, "to Women!"

His timing did not go unappreciated and he and Vinny laughed for a solid hour at the unpredictability that was their past few days together. Blue thought about how close he had become to Vinny and Sansaa, Mojahdii and even Targent, but mostly Anna Marie. Despite the awareness that he had some sort of higher purpose to perform and that he was only a vehicle or messenger of sorts, an element of a more universal whole, he thought about just staying put, suspending any sort of quest for the crystal and spending the rest of his days on this world, with Anna Marie.

At that very moment a long convoy of large black automobiles arrived in the Shadowlands.
There's nothing really intimidating about a single long, black car pulling up to your home, or the place you had just been considering calling your home, but a convoy of a dozen limousines simultaneously crunching to a halt, side by side in perfect formation on a dry dirt road does instill a sense that something meaningful, at least to someone, is going on. Normally, Tommy's reaction to such an arrival would be something along the lines of grabbing a gun, jumping into a fast car or calling his gang together giving the directive to engage the enemy. Vinny, though not directly involved in the JumpJuice trade, would nevertheless jump to his feet to protect Tommy. Instead, they both sat there, continuing to enjoy their beers while sporting matching looks of astonishment, curiosity and boyish appreciation of the truly remarkable parking job that had just been executed by the visitors. As the dust settled and blew off toward the northern fields, all twelve driver-side doors swung open and a driver, one for each car, each wearing a chauffeur's cap, stepped out. Precisely two seconds later, all twelve passenger-side doors swung open and a man with a rifle, one for each car, each wearing sunglasses, stepped out and steadied his rifle on the top of the door frame. This made both Blue and Vinny laugh. The whole thing was just a little too perfect and each of them were just a little too relaxed to acknowledge

any sort of a threat. Five seconds later the rear, back, passenger-side door opened on the far-right vehicle in the line which was, in the view of Tommy and Vinny, the car on the far left. A man got out of the car wearing sunglasses and holding a briefcase. He took one step to the right of the door, placing his left, empty hand on the corner of the open door. He stood motionless, looking directly toward the tent.

Suddenly, Mojahdii was standing directly next to the man with the briefcase, also looking in the direction of the tent. "Hello." he said quietly, making the startled visitor drop the briefcase as he jumped a good foot and a half in the air. Mojahdii remained standing directly next to him, smiling.

When the man had landed, he stood silently for a moment. He was so completely taken off-guard by the sudden appearance of Mojahdii that he lost all sense of who he was or why he was standing where he was. He was completely dumbfounded. He had been in more fights, combat operations, brawls and contests of fighting skill than he could count and prided himself on his ability to face anyone. Even more than that, he prided himself on his ability to sense his opponents presence long before he would need to engage him. He had just been stripped of that by what looked to be an eighty year old man wearing a bedsheet.

"Welcome to the Shadowlands," Mojahdii said, knowing full well that he had just mortified the visitor, he continued, "how may an old man be of service?" Mojahdii had a way of knowing just what to say in every occasion and one of his specialties was using that wisdom to influence, if even by the most subtle of ways. He knew that this man would remember his humility at a moment he had displayed true mastery and hoped that it may serve the man well in the future. He continued, "My name is Mojahdii, May I ask yours."

The visitor had clearly not been asked his name in a very long time. In fact, as he reached for the briefcase to pick it back up, the man struggled to remember the last time someone had expressed any sort of personal interest in him at all. He drew a blank and said with the delivery of a teenage boy on his first day of high school, "Jason, Jason Marberry."

"Well, it is nice to meet you Jason," said Mojahdii, "may I ask what brings you all the way out here today?" Mojahdii had already noticed the variety of armaments tactically distributed throughout the vehicle.

"Sir, a shipment, belonging to our employer, has been stolen and we have reason to believe that the group who stole it have driven here in an effort to hide out. We mean you no harm and are only here to recover the stolen property."

"Mr. Marberry," Mojahdii answered kindly, "I can assure you that your shipment is not here. However, it is a long trip from the city and assuming by your vehicles that you did, in fact, travel from the city, I would not be a very good host were I not to offer you and your friends a meal. Please join us and feel free to have a look around while you're here. Should you find your shipment, you are free to leave with it after you eat." He laughed a little, softly, as if to himself, "If you find what is yours you can have what is yours..." he trailed off like a senile old man might, laughing and shaking his head back and forth.

The visitor was truly surprised by the invitation and was actually feeling quite hungry, so he leaned into the vehicle for support in making the decision. Inside, a bulkier man tried to act as though he had not been listening, keeping his eyes straight ahead. "Tevlin," the visitor said to the bulky passenger, "he's asking us to stay and eat, whaddya' think?" Tevlin shrugged. "Are you hungry?" he asked Tevlin. At this, Tevlin turned his head and looked from side to side as if to see if anyone was looking at him. He pressed his lips together into the slightest little frown and nodded. Jason stood back up and as he did caught sight of the rest of the row of cars. the whole team was now standing outside of their vehicles, peering over open doors and hoods to see what was going on. Jason turned to Mojahdii and held up his finger as if to ask for a minute. He leaned back into the vehicle and grabbed a headset. Putting it on he said, "no shipment, code yellow, Mess!"

Along the whole line the men exchanged large guns for small ones as they closed up the cars.

Mojahdii smiled at Jason and stepped out in front of the whole group, his arms open wide, then turned and walked down the path in the direction of the commons. Jason followed and the men fell in behind each one looking as stunned as the next that they were about to eat rather than fight.

Normally, curiosity gets the better of most people when presented with an unusual spectacle unfolding before them, so no one could have blamed Tommy and Vinny for leaving their tent and following Mojahdii and the visitors toward the commons, except that it didn't and they remained seated. In fact, neither one of them seemed to be the least bit motivated to leave the comfort of the lounge chairs and the ice cold beers. "That was weird," Vinny said to Tommy as he leaned all the way back in his lounge chair, his muscles bulging as he cradled the weight of his head then slowly relaxing as total ease spilled over them cascading down to his shoulders, then his chest, ribcage and abdomen which began to bounce slightly as a little laugh gripped his solar plexus. "Did you see that guy jump when Mojahdii crept up on him like that?"

Blue was just polishing off his second beer when he swallowed quickly to avoid spraying Vinny with LPS - laughing projectile spray. "Varst Vinny, I didn't even see Mojahdii over there until he popped out right next to the dude and all of a sudden he's like 'pip' hello, I'm standing right next to you. Sweet!"

"Whoever that dude works for - no more. Those other cats are going to rat him out as soon as they get back, he'll be lucky if he gets to drive." Vinny added.

"No, Vinny, he won't even get that, those guys can drive, maybe he'll get to ride shotgun, maybe, depends on who he working for." Tommy responded.

"My guess...Lorenzo. Those guys, those cars, they gotta be Sal's goons and they're after something." Vinny theorized.

"Or somebody," Tommy continued as Mojahdii approached the tent with a half-dozen goons, led by Jason. He looked calm but a little put out, as if what he was doing was necessary but unpleasant.

"Hello, Tommy, Vinny, several of our residents were talking about you around the tables this evening and this gentleman here, his name is Jason, well, he tells me that he knows you." Mojahdii explained diplomatically.

Vinny's muscles were no longer relaxed as he rose to his full height, slowly, menacingly, never taking his eyes off the new arrivals who packed in closer to Jason, each brandishing a different weapon. Blue had risen in unison with Vinny but placed a hand on Vinny's shoulder, gently pulling him back to one side. He calmly stepped one step closer to Jason and the rest of the goons. "Yes, we saw you arrive, nice driving!" Tommy said with a disarming smile.

"Mr. Levito," Jason said "we have never met, but my team and I are here on business for Sal Lorenzo. We had no idea that this was your place, I apologize for just showing up like this." He said, concerned that he had just brought his team into the mouth of the beast.

"Jason, right?" Blue said in an inquisitive and welcoming tone as he held out his hand, "Tommy," he said as he shook hands with the leader of the team. Vinny and the team members each took a step back and Mojahdii smiled and headed back toward the commons, confident that Blue could handle the rest. "Please come into the tent, there is a place for all of you to sit. There is no need for your firearms, you are free to look around for whatever you came for, assuming it is not me!" he laughed, lightening the tone of the conversation without revealing that, in fact, none of his men, those who would normally be armed to the teeth, were anywhere around. "So, tell me, what are you looking for?"

Jason looked around at the other men, then looked at Vinny who sat quietly, exuding a sort of energy that made it clear that no matter how heavily armed these guys were, he was pretty sure that he was going to be the last one standing if all Varst broke loose. Jason was still feeling the effects of the Mojahdii incident and doubt seemed to be his right-hand man. "I am not sure that I can tell you that, Mr. Levito." he looked at Tommy who gave him a look reminding him that he had just introduced himself by his first name, so he continued, "uh, Tommy. Would you mind if I took a minute to make a phone call?"

"Not at all," Tommy said, realizing that the evening was going to end up as anything but the relaxed dream it had started out as.

As Jason stepped out of the tent one of the goons said, "Hey Tommy, Vinny."

Blue looked at him and realized that he had no idea who he was. He was just about to answer with some comment citing his recent death and resurrection but Vinny said, "Hey Butcher. How the Varst is Martha?"

"Fat as a thumpin' prize-winner, 'bout to pop out a double I think. Sweet as ever." Butcher answered.

"Another double? What's that make it, five sets of twins now, Butcher?" Vinny laughed and Blue laughed along, relieved that Vinny was handling the conversation. "When did you hook up with the Lorenzo squad? I thought you gave up the Juice trade?"

"Did you not here me, Vincent? Another double!" Butcher blurted out as he started laughing at his own situation. In fact, everyone in the tent was laughing as Jason came back in, looking rather put out.

"I'm supposed to ask you to come with me." He said to Tommy. "To see Mr. Lorenzo"

The whole tent went quiet as Tommy and Vinny looked at each other and back to Jason.

"I think that would be a marvelous idea." Mojahdii said as he popped out from behind Jason, sending him straight up a couple of feet into the air. As he landed he lost his balance and fell backward across the cooler. Everyone laughed, including Jason, as Mojahdii reached out his withered old hand and helped him back up with a single pull as if Jason weighed nothing at all.

Blue was pretty certain that this was as much instruction as it was agreement on the part of Mojahdii, "I'm good, Vinny?" He looked to the big man who answered with a 'why not' expression.

"I just want to let Sansaa know..." Vinny said as Sansaa cut him off by appearing in the doorway to the tent, immediately adjacent to Mojahdii. She was holding up a small bag, presumably packed with all that the two would need for their journey. The visitors looked around at one another, unsure what to make of anything that was going on while

Tommy and Vinny just smiled and walked out of the tent. Vinny threw his arm around Blue's shoulders as the two of them made their way toward the VinnCycle.

It was already growing dark as Vinny and Tommy neared the cycle with the whole team now heading toward the cars. The sound of Mojahdii and Sansaa giggling to themselves drifted toward the men, they turned to look but Mojahdii and Sansaa were gone.

25 SAL

The ride to Sal's was interesting. Blue wasn't sure why he was wanted by Sal but he knew it had to do with JumpJuice. What he understood even less was why he had agreed to go, he just knew it was the right thing to do and sometimes knowledge must be allowed to exist without understanding. "but I just don't get it, Tommy. Why in Farb's name would you willingly leave an ice cold six to get on a bike in the middle of the night to go to Sal Bastin' Lorenzo's?, Vinny asked through the unparalleled clarity of the VinnCycles' comm system.

"It's the right thing to do Vinny, I know it, I feel it, I just can't explain it. It's like finding that crystal. Varst, it's like everything that's been happening since that crazy chic Max shot me," Tommy exclaimed only to be cut off by Vinny's all too valid retort...

"Crazy, you said it, that's what she is, Vinny continued as the convoy of limousines surrounded the Levitos on all sides." That's what all of this is, and now we're driving over to her bastin' father's house for what, so he can finish the job?"

Vinny had a point and Blue had no good answer to it so he sunk to emotional manipulation. "Mojahdii even said it was the right thing to do, Sansaa trusts his judgment, maybe we should too."

Vinny groaned a little but didn't say another word for the rest of the ride to Sal's.

When they reached Sal's it wasn't at all what Blue had expected. Sure it was a true example of how tastelessly wealth can be squandered on what the unrefined perceive as luxury and elegance from gaudy chandeliers and curtains to pointless collectible exotica, but he was welcomed graciously by the staff attending the estate, even the goons were polite and respectful, not forceful or intimidating. He and Vinny were escorted to a study, replete with the obligatory historical and exotic weaponry and books too numerous to have been read within a single lifetime, a distinction Blue was learning to view with a fresh perspective. "Tommy Levito," a voice echoed from the doorway behind them. Tommy and Vinny turned around fully, their backs now facing the ostentatiously adorned fireplace they had been staring at in mutual disbelief, to see Sal who now struck Blue as a cross between Hugh Hefner and Danny Devito, so much so that it was all he could do to contain his laughter. ."..AND the mighty and always enjoyable Vincent Levito," Sal continued as he walked toward them pulling peanuts from his bathrobe pocket, eating them and tossing the shells upon the floor as he did. Less than a foot and a half behind him a very well-appointed attendant swept every single shell up, just seconds after one would hit the floor into what appeared to be a dust pan fashioned from gold. " I am so pleased that you have agreed to visit. It seems that a matter of great importance to both of us must be dealt with immediately. I am sure that you will find it well worth the time and energy it took to make this short trip to my home. Like your father used to say, 'guys who raise bees don't complain about a few stings now and then, do they?'"

Blue had no idea what Tommy's father used to say about anything but Vinny sure did. "Never thought I'd be around to hear you quote my father again, Sal." Vinny said.

"Actually Vincent, I think of your father's words every day of my life. You might say that they are the very cornerstone of my dynasty. After all, if your father hadn't mercilessly butchered my father, then said those very words to him as he lay screaming in pain, I'm not entirely sure I would have been so driven to control Rat Town so completely. Oh, but you probably heard the story a different way, undoubtedly with a Levito spin. Regardless, our fathers who are most likely chained together in some fiery pit deep in the bowels of Varst taught me one thing. Never let anyone get the best of you. So you see, Vinny, your father did me a favor; and in some respects he did the old man a favor by pulling that trigger, the poor old crunge probably would have hung on in agony for hours, bleeding to death on the floor otherwise. But I didn't ask you here to reminisce about old times and I am afraid that my interests concern only your brother. So, make yourself at home," as Sal said this a beautiful woman carrying a tray of assorted nuts and a small ice bucket with three chilled bottles of beer entered the room. "Tommy and I will be in the next room and I assure you, I will return him to you, unharmed, quite shortly." Sal opened his arms toward Tommy as well as toward the other room, the doors of which opened automatically as he gestured toward them. Blue headed toward the open room with a quick glance over to Vinny as if to say that everything was fine, as he did Sal suddenly added, "Oh, I nearly forgot! Congratulations to both of you on your acquisition of the OmegaLux Crystal, no small achievement from what I understand of such things." Vinny and Tommy looked at one another, then back at Sal, then back at one another, then back at Sal and said with confused politeness,

"Thank you.”
"No, Tommy, thank you, for joining me on such short notice," Sal said as they entered the adjacent room and the large doors closed behind them. "Now, I'm not sure how much you share with your family about the business, and of course it isn't my place to tell you, but I want to be absolutely certain that you have never spoken of our relationship." Sal turned meaningfully toward Blue who answered so quickly that it nearly startled him.

"Of course not." Blue had no hesitation because he had no relationship with Sal and trying to figure out what Sal was driving at would have been an utter waste of time. As it turns out, this was precisely the right track to follow, saving both men considerable time as Sal had something urgent on his mind and mulling over the details of who Tommy might have said what to would only have served to infuriate him.

"Good.” He started, "I have several very important matters to discuss concerning our arrangements. First of all, I assume that you are aware of the missing shipment?" Blue, knowing that going with the flow is usually best in situations when dealing with an individual tied to an agenda, simply flipped his hand in the air as if the mere mention of it was repetitive enough to be monotonous. "Right," continued Sal, "are you then, also aware of the other missing shipment?" Blue raised both hands slightly, turned his palms upward and parted his arms wide, illustrating that he was sitting in Sal's house. This caused a little glimmer of a smile to cross Sal's face as he went on, "and I can assume since my men did not bring you back here dead that you had nothing to do with the disappearance of said shipment." The smile was mirrored back by Blue. "Oh, speaking of which, sorry to hear about Maxie's little outburst. Can't say I understand what went down that day but apparently neither you nor Victor were meant to die. Nicely done on the pummeling as well, heard you really kicked his ass!" Sal's smile grew a little wider. "Still, I told you not to kill him. I've spent a lot of time setting this whole Farb-damn operation up and I don't need you, Maxie or Victor Bastin' me around. Come to think of it, Maxie probably did the right thing to blast you, would've upset the balance to leave you alive if Victor was dead." Sal's smile grew into laughter. Blue crossed one leg over the other and leaned as far back as he could while still keeping his eyes on Sal. If he was going to listen to this shit, he was going to get comfortable. "Tommy, I gotta hand it to ya, you really have changed since you got shot. You know what they say 'What doesn't kill you, makes you healthy, wealthy and wise! So let's get down to the business of wealthy. I have no doubt that both shipments will be recovered. Nobody wipes their ass in Rat Town without McGoogle knowing about it and there isn't a breath that McGoogle takes that isn't first cleared through me. So you know what that means..."

"Yeah, sounds like you end up smellin' a whole lot of shit!," Blue couldn't help himself. He couldn't believe the set-up and if he didn't drop the punchline he'd not only regret it on this world, but just about any other. His own laughter was surprisingly overpowered by Sal's.

"Guess I stepped right into that one!" Sal was actually scoring bonus points with Blue at the moment. Nobody enjoyed beating a dead horse more than Blue. In fact, Blue liked to not only beat the dead horse but he would often crouch down real low, dig his shoulder right into the withers, forcing his upper arm under the animal and push with all of his might. With any luck, the horse would slide out into the road a little bit, just enough to get run over by a semi or bus and then he would wait. Blue would wait until the horse got nice and flat and then he'd roll it up like a rug. He'd take that rug and he'd throw it up over his shoulder and start walkin' down that road a piece 'til he came to a clearing in the otherwise elephant's eye high cornfield, a path, down through which he could see a farmhouse, with a clothesline. He would walk that rug over to the clothesline and he'd toss one end of it over the line so the whole rug would hang free in the air. Then Blue would walk up to the door of the farmhouse, introduce himself in a well-mannered yet confident tone and politely ask to borrow a broom. With that broom he would tirelessly beat the dust of the road from the rug, whistling to himself, usually a tune like 'Horse with no name' or 'Wild Horses'. Sometimes he would sing to himself, something along the lines of the theme song to a favorite TV show from his childhood called, 'Mr. Ed', often carrying on until he became hoarse.

"The point is, Tommy, that we're all going to get through this shit and I don't want to hear any talk about 'TOGETHER'!" Sal had reached his reason for the 'invitation' and it went against everything Blue was working to achieve. "I want you and Victor to keep the war alive. Nothing is better for business than competition, and right now, you two are the heavyweight champ, and the top contender for the title."

"Which one am I Sal?" Tommy asked as if it actually meant something to him.

"To me, Tommy, you're the Champ and always have been, to the rest of Rat Town, however, you are the top contender. The way they see it, Victor's my boy, you know that. He's been with Maxie long enough, the two of them shoulda been pumpin' out some babies by now. Guy's probably got somethin' wrong with his prick. Anyways, it's not like I give a rat's ass about grandkids. Family ties are the whole reason we can't let the truth out. You've been doing a real nice job of drivin' the numbers, Victor keeps thinking that he's callin' the shots but you and I both know, there hasn't been a single change in the price of Juice that we didn't personally instigate. Now that's why I've called you here, Tommy. Change is good and I want to be good, right now, in a big way. I'm after another ten an ounce, so you know what to do." Tommy nods even though Blue hasn't got a clue. "Good, after you drop your prices by five an ounce, Victor's going to have to follow. Make sure you cap it at fifty barrels, including exports, then cry dry. Victor's going to mirror that shit, but before he does, he's gonna want to squeeze for everything he can get and that's when he'll inflate the price, and he'll get it too. Then I'll tell him to dry up, if he doesn't do it on his own. The small timers are going to start selling their juice like crazy, probably in the neighborhood of twenty more per ounce. By then, we'll have our shipments back, we'll hit the streets at ten an ounce higher than we're getting now and it will be a bargain. We should be able to ride that wave for a few months with sales peaking just in time for Farb Fest." Sal laughed with self-satisfaction. Tommy joined in. Blue didn't know the particulars of the JumpJuice business but the supply and demand model Sal was just spinning seemed to make sense. More importantly, he discovered that Sal was actually an ally, which meant that Tommy had nothing to fear from Sal or Victor which was good news, even if he did have to keep it to himself.

That's exactly what Blue was thinking when he decided to take a chance, "So Sal," he started off matter-of-factly," where are the shipments? I realize that the one you're looking for now may actually be lost, missing or just out of your reach at the moment, but Sal, I can't believe that YOU don't know the whereabouts of missing shipment number one," he closed with a shower of praise, "it's simply incomprehensible that someone got the better of Sal Lorenzo, so where is it?"

Blue's training was paying off, he was reading people well, judging situations well and saying only what needed to be said but this time he really nailed it, Sal was really dying to brag about how smart he was and the only person he could have done that with, who really knew just how devious he had been, he had to dump dead on a doorstep. "With great power comes great responsibility," Sal said as he confessed his longing to share in the news of his triumph. Tommy hadn't been privy to any aspects of the Bobby story until this moment so the whole thing was really quite enthralling but what captivated him most was the pure selfishness and greed which fueled every iota of Sal's being. The man lived for nothing but the acquisition of wealth. Blue thought about how easily Sal could have blended in on Wall Street if only Earth was his home world, but Sal had Rat Town and Cleveland and several other major cities across the land, what he didn't have was compassion or scruples of any sort. "I would have liked to share my victory with Bobby, sort of, for an hour, maybe. Unfortunately, Victor was on to Bobby, so, I had to make a sacrifice. Well, anyways, I do know where the shipment is and YOU are going to find it. I will tell you just where and when to find it when the time comes. For now, I just have to tell you my favorite part of the story. Victor's team is really far too good to pull one over on, so I had to split them up. Only a few of his regular guys were on this shipment and they kinda hated him so it was easy to get them to go along with the plan, plus, they were weak-minded and horribly insecure, *my favorite thing about having a staff psychologist, profiling!* Naturally, they jumped at the chance for more money and more power!

"Bobby was a natural to run the operation, as a matter of fact, he would have been my first choice to take over for Victor if you actually had beaten him to death, or more correctly, if he hadn't gotten back up after you did. So, Bobby was every bit as good at getting the boys to hustle, load and arm the shipment efficiently as Victor and everything was in place. The convoy was set and the drones were loaded just in case anything went wrong, which was the plan, so the drones had to be disabled. Well, the only way to disable the drones is to disable Aldo because Aldo is fiercely loyal to Victor, as loyal as that bastin' collie on the TV, you know the one that barks for a minute and then the guy says, 'what did you say girl, Timmy fell into the well, but everything's okay, just a few scrapes, minor cuts and bruises', bark, bark, bark, 'what's that girl, he's hungry and we'd better get him some food or he'll pass out?' Dammit Tommy what's that Bastin' dog's name?!" Sal seemed genuinely distressed by the name of the TV dog escaping him and Blue started to laugh. There was no way in hell or varst for that matter that it could be the same damn dog.

"Lassie?" he said, almost inaudibly.

"LASSIE! Bastin' Farbunkle that's it, LASSIE, you see Tommy, that's why you're number one in my book. I could have recited the whole bastin' show and none of these mollywumps would even know what I was talking about. Could you believe that dog? Farb! She was amazing, and loyal. Loyal, that's my point, Aldo is, was and always will be loyal to Victor. He may seem like he's always complaining and making fun of everybody for being dumber than him but he loves that Victor. I think it had something to do with Victor kickin' the crap outta anybody who messed with Aldo when they were kids, leastwise anybody but you and Vinny, but you boys never seemed to go in for that bully shit. Not back then at least. Anyways, Aldo; so we had to deal with Aldo. You remember Theresa Sedgewig, right?" Tommy nods. "Turns out she's a chemist and Bobby just happened to be on her periodic table of elements to use the vernacular. So he pays her a little visit and gets a custom mixture that he slips into Aldo's coffee the night before the shipment. Tasteless, odorless, but absolutely debilitating for a period of about twenty-four hours. Theresa seems to enjoy mixing up little concoctions and her next one was the key to the whole plan, that and the fact that these days nobody seems capable of taking even the shortest drive in the summer without turning on the air conditioner. By introducing just the smallest amount of Theresa's magic potion into the system, Bobby was able to knock out everyone in the convoy, including the drivers. Aldo's replacement at base camp simply turned off the system and no drones were activated. Bobby, who pretended to be out, hid himself in a corner of the main transport vehicle where he steered the entire convoy with a remote Victor had Aldo dream up about a year ago in case a driver got taken out during an attack." Sal managed to inform Tommy through a mouthful of peanuts.

"Several key players, including Abe, who we just found dead at the scene of the other missing shipment, had also faked collapse thanks to nifty little pocket-size respirators from your friend and mine Sven Midderhaussen. The shipment was unloaded and transferred to helicopters then moved to a location not too terribly far from here. The truly ironic thing about this story is that less than a couple of minutes after the "sleepers" woke up they were attacked. They didn't even know what had happened, had no chance to check the drones and fought to protect a shipment that had already been taken. They lost three men in the fight but kicked the tar out of the MacKenzies who went away, seven down and empty-handed. After the battle, they checked the drones, Bobby acting just as surprised as anyone to find the shipment gone." Sal stood smirking with self-satisfaction.

"You leaked the route to the MacKenzies, didn't you," Tommy said dryly.

"And THAT is the other reason I love you Tommy! Sal laughed as he stepped in a freshly dropped pile of peanut shells. Looking around the room, he realized he had left a substantial trail. He pulled a small electronic device from his robe pocket. It looked like a golf ball but one half seemed to be mesh, like a microphone grille. He lifted a peanut to it, then cracked its shell. The moment he did so, the door to the room opened and the smartly dressed attendant entered with the broom and the golden dustpan. As the attendant swept up the shells, Sal threw his arm around Tommy and said, "Always good to have you over Tommy," he released Blue and headed toward a slightly darkened room across a large hallway," you'll be hearing from me shortly, be sure to tell Vincent to drive safely, so many people just don't see the motorcycles, such little regard for the lives of others, goodnight."

"What was that all about," Vinny said as he and Tommy left Sal's place.

"It's complicated and I need to ask you something, but I don't want to have this conversation on your bike." Blue said hoping it would be enough to hold off Vinny's curiosity.

"That's cool, bro, nothing's ever simple when Sal's involved." Vinny said understandingly.

The ride back from Sal's wasn't long enough for Blue, mostly because he couldn't figure out what he would say to Vinny when they got back. He had to tell him some of it but he wanted to tell him all of it. Telling him all of it would mean that he would have to tell him everything and he just wasn't ready to do that. The VinnCycle was a lot faster when it wasn't surrounded by a fleet of limos and they were back at the tent in no time. "Pull up a beer, sit down and tell me all about it," Vinny said as he tossed a beer from the cooler, still chilled, over to Tommy and grabbed another one for himself. It was late, but not late enough to seek refuge in bed. Blue was going to have to tell Vinny something, but he could not determine what to tell or where to begin. "Don't tell me you forgot already." Vinny teased, but that was just the inspiration Blue needed.

"Well, Vinny, that's just it, I have forgotten quite a bit." Vinny looked a little stunned and disappointed, "Not about my conversation with Sal," Tommy continued, "before that. Ever since I woke up in that ambulance, I've been trying to piece together my past." Blue was doing his best to be perfectly honest with Vinny without giving away the farm. "I'm not sure how much of this mess I've actually told you about already."

"Oh, that, no problem, nothing." Vinny laughed. "You never tell me anything little bro." Vinny leaned back and flexed his arms behind his head, settling right back into the state he was in before Sal's goons arrived. "Why should today be any different, we'll play it just like we always do, I go first. Well, I didn't hear anything breaking, so he didn't try to attack you, no shooting, no yelling and some laughing. I don't even have to guess to know that it's about JumpJuice. Those guys came here looking for something, didn't see it but found you. So they were looking for a lost shipment of Juice and thought you had something to do with it." Blue said nothing, which to Vinny was as close as he could get to saying yes, "Oh, I knew it, I'm on to something here, well paint my toenails and call me Madam Chandrala 'cause my third eye just opened and it's staring right at you little bro!" Both men started laughing as Vinny continued. "I am seeing Victor Alonso and Max Lorenzo, I am unclear how they fit in but my guess is that it's one of their shipments that has gone missing." Still, Blue said nothing. "I am on a roll!" Vinny applauded himself as he went for more, "So Sal called you in for a friendly reminder that he owns Rat Town and even though he doesn't know what to make of your resurrection, it doesn't change the fact that he will eliminate anyone who stands in his way."

Blue felt instantly relieved. Vinny's guesses were close enough to right to count as truth and he wouldn't have to divulge any secrets about his identity. "Did I say we had to talk?" Tommy laughed as he held his beer aloft in a salute to Vinny's skill.

"Actually, Tommy, you said you needed to ask me something." Vinny reminded him.

Blue did have a real question for Vinny, "Did Sansaa tell you how long my training is supposed to last?"

"Yeah, Tommy, she did, but it was one of those Sansaa answers, she said, 'for as long as it takes'.

26 ACTING LESSONS

"You can't be serious, how can this be?" Max asked, just trying to understand how Victor could have managed to find a place like this, let alone buy it without her ever knowing. She tried to rewind through the footage of her years with Victor, hoping to see a moment that he could have been gone from her, or more like it, a moment that she wasn't by his side, doing his bidding, a time when he could have driven out here, met with a realtor or the people who lived here and actually purchased this place. "We have been together every day for as long as I can remember," she concentrated, "wait a minute, no, it couldn't be. Victor, did you come here when you visited my mother? That's it, isn't it." Leer said nothing. The truth was that he had purchased the house fifteen years earlier but it is a very complicated story and he had no intention of telling it to her at the moment. "She really got to you. But that was ages ago. This is just too weird, good, but weird." Max was having a hard time understand all of the changes in Victor, even though they were very positive changes, they were all too sudden.

"It's going to get weirder," Victor said, "I'm sorry Max but there really is no other way. And don't let these guys know that this is our place. As far as they're concerned, it's a rental. I'll explain later, just go with me on this for now." Leer said with a smile, hoping that Max could trust the new Victor enough to be patient with the changes. Leer threw the headset on and gave the order to lock down both trucks inside the barn. "Let's make sure the Juice is safe. Get all of the bikes inside. Samuel, Nick, Marv and Gavin, get outside and hide any evidence of our arrival, clear all of the tracks from the barn to the main road and do it quickly. There's all the equipment you'll need on the other side of the shed, just past the well." Victor climbed out of the cab of the dump truck and hoisted himself onto its hood. He looked back toward the other truck and motioned toward the payload of each truck, "I want the rest of you to make sure that none of this Juice is leaking. Check every container even if you have to take them out and move them around a bit, I want every ounce accounted for." Leer jumped down from the truck and started toward the far door and Max followed close behind. He stopped and turned back and said enthusiastically, "Outside, there's a long narrow shed, mostly blue with a tin roof. When you're all finished inspecting the product, head over to the shed. We've got food and drink for everybody. After that, I want you all to get some rest. We've got a busy day tomorrow, breakfast at the break of dawn followed immediately by your acting lessons."

Nobody moved. Leer stood looking at his entire team, each one of them, including Max looking as though they were doubting Victor's sanity. "What are you waiting for?" Victor said with his usual forcefulness and then some, snapping the team out of their frozen state. They were still confused but there was no doubt that Victor meant business. Most of them had learned that when Victor raised his voice above his usual clear and undeniably audible level, to a notch just slightly higher, it was best to do what he had instructed. Possibly the most concrete example of this was an incident involving a guy named Ozzie Warburton.

It happened less than a year before the fight with Tommy Levito, the very man responsible for the incident, sort of. Ozzie was an all-around hand. He did alright with manual labor, packing and unpacking the Juice, helping to maintain the grounds and the equipment, but he also helped with the books. He was good enough with numbers to be useful when it came time for accounting. He just saw everything as work and as long as he had it and got paid, fine. However, he did seem to have an appreciation for how the numbers worked that went beyond a system of checks and balances. He paid attention to what the various operations around Rat Town were into, how they made their money, who they chose to work with, and who they did not. So, one day, Ozzie was going through some books and he pulled out a newspaper during a short break. In the paper was a story about the Carrullo Brothers Construction Company, who everybody knew was linked to the Levito family. As he read the story he started writing down a few numbers, some from the article, some from his brain and others from Victor's business. He discovered what he thought was a really useful bit of information which illustrated that Tommy was actually improving his control over Rat Town by developing partnerships with these other businesses like the Carrullo's. Ozzie approached Victor one afternoon as they were packing up a shipment, "Mr. Alonso, I beg your pardon, but I have been looking through our books and comparing them to what I know of the Levito operation and I think I have an important suggestion." Ozzie waited but there was no response, Victor kept talking to the men as they prepared the shipment but did not acknowledge Ozzie's presence. "Mr. Alonso, I'm afraid you didn't hear me, I said I think..." he paused in mid-sentence as Victor turned, facing him directly, "I think we ought to establish some relationships with other businesses, not associated with JumpJuice." Victor continued to look at Ozzie as he added, "It seems as though the Levito organization nets an additional twenty percent from investments into other business." Ozzie stood in expectant silence as he watched the expression change on Victor's face.

"I don't want to talk about other options, Warburton." Victor said in his usual tone.

"But we might be able to increase our revenue and expand our influence all at once," Ozzie tried again.

"I said, I am not interested in discussing this at the moment, " Victor said, his tone slightly louder indicating that he was, in fact, unwilling to listen to any suggestion no matter how good. Ozzie seemed prepared to go on but his friend Harvey Tweed, who was standing right next to him, grabbed him by the shoulder and pulled him away from Victor, telling him that Victor didn't like continuing conversation past the point when he has called to end it. Both Ozzie and Harvey got back to packing, leaving Victor to continue with the process of instructing the team and addressing the security of the shipment.

In an ironic turn of events the team wound up dropping the Juice shipment in a location directly across a narrow road from a new condominium expansion site, under construction by none other than the Carrullo Brothers. The site was empty except for a small team of men who appeared to be working to pour some concrete support columns. Victor was aware of the proximity of the Levito-partnered site, in fact, he enjoyed setting up shipments in unexpected places and in general this strategy worked well to ensure the safety of the shipment. Everything went off without a hitch. The buyers all received their Juice and the team members were getting back into the vehicles when Ozzie stopped and turned toward the work site across the street, pointing. "See Victor," he said, interrupting him as he was filling in Marv on a few revisions to the route back to base. "that site over there is a Carrullo site. The Levito organization is pulling in about half of the profits on that job because of the terms they have in place with the Carrullos."

Victor looked over at him and said, "Not right now Ozzie, let's keep it moving."

"But Victor," Ozzie returned, "it's not that big of a deal and we could set the whole thing up with some standard cookie cutter terms, easy as pie."

"Ozzie, get in the vehicle, now is not the time," Victor said, his voice turned up that one little notch higher, indicating that he had reached his limit and that it would be best for Ozzie to save his idea for later.

"Look," Ozzie continued, "everything they work on, every bit of snark that rolls in on a job gets split up with the Levito organization."

Victor looked at the men standing on either side of Ozzie and with his eyes and a subtle clenching of his fists, indicated that he wanted Ozzie held. He turned away from the vehicle so that Ozzie was behind his back, held by the men. Victor made a sweeping motion with his arm, indicating with his hand that he wanted them to follow him in the direction of the work site. He crossed the street and entered the work site through a break in the chain link fence. The men followed him, Ozzie practically being dragged at this point.

"Hey, Victor, it's okay, we can talk later, I-I just w-wanted to help, really," Ozzie flailed for pity.

At this point the workers caught site of Victor. Even though they were affiliated with the Levito organization, the Carrullo Brothers staff were not Juice-runners or fighters, they were workers, craftsmen, engineers and carpenters. The appearance of Victor and the other two men dragging Ozzie along, crying for mercy was not only unsettling, it was a little intimidating. One of the men, feeling tough, strong and capable actually had the audacity to yell out, "Hey, what's going on down there," standing on a raised platform, guiding the wet cement into the mold for the support column he continued, "this is a closed site."

Victor pulled a rather large weapon out from the inside of the left side of his vest. He aimed it directly at the shouting man's head then gave it a little wave, instructing the man to get down from the platform by means of the adjacent ladder. The man felt a little less strong, a little less tough but on one level he was far more intelligent than Ozzie, he did not need to be told more than once. He quickly, without argument, descended the ladder and left the site, closely following his workmates who had already determined that they had done enough work for the day.

Victor surveyed the site quickly as if looking for something he knew he would find. He was not disappointed. he walked over to a large spool of electrical wire and started to unwind it as he walked toward Ozzie. First, he bound Ozzie's hands together, who was crying pitifully, though he would receive none. Next, Victor, pulled the wire up and wrapped it around Ozzie's head, winding it around below his ears and across his face, pulling it firmly through his crying mouth capturing his tongue as he pulled the wire tight in several revolutions around Ozzie's head until he could barely breathe let alone sob. "That's better," Victor said as he looked into Ozzie's face, "now, maybe you'll listen to what I am telling you. When I say that I don't want to talk about something, I really don't want to talk about something, whether you think it's a good idea or not. Now, you have wasted my time and taken me off of my schedule." Finally, Victor bound his feet together as he continued walking toward the freshly poured column. He raised his voice so Ozzie could hear him as he walked away, "I prefer to be listened to the first time, I do not like being taken off of my schedule and I will ask for ideas when I want to hear them. By now he was on top of the ladder. He threw the wire over a pipe which connected the platform to some scaffolding which ran up the side of a completed wall to the structure. He then grabbed the rest of the wire leading toward Ozzie and began to pull, dragging his body, still kicking in an effort to break free, until it rested below him on the ground. Victor wrapped the wire which was slung on the opposite side of the pole and jumped over the side of the platform. As he descended toward the ground, Ozzie's body rose toward the platform. The two men began to laugh but quickly stopped as Victor glared at them and held the wire out toward them. They quickly rushed over to take the wire from him. As one of the men held on he was nearly pulled off his feet and almost lost grip of the wire, Victor quickly grabbed the wire with one hand, steadying it to allow the other man to help. "When I tell you to let go, let go," Victor said, "and not a moment sooner." Victor climbed back up the ladder to find himself looking down at the tearful, bloody face of Ozzie.

Victor reached over the side of the platform and maneuvered Ozzie's hanging body over the freshly poured but incomplete column. Ozzie looked up from eyes that knew they were going to die only to hear Victor say, "You know, Oz, I don't even think your idea is such a bad idea, but I just can't stomach someone who doesn't understand that there is a right and a wrong time for conversation. Sadly, once again, I don't have time to hear your side of the story but I will take the matter you have raised under consideration, in fact, the idea is firmly cemented in my brain!" Victor looked over the side of the platform to see the two men looking up at him, he turned on the cement loader which started gushing fresh cement out over the shoulders of the hanging Ozzie, filling up the mold around him. Victor held his arm out with a thumb in the air and with a large, emphatic, sweeping gesture turned the thumb down. The men released the wire, dropping Ozzie's writhing form completely into the fresh cement.

Someone being buried alive in wet cement is the sort of thing that just sticks in a person's mind, and news of that type of activity tends to travel quickly. It would be hard to prove who did it and it was not going to be proven by anyone within the Rat Town Police Department. So it became the stuff of legend. Victor had no problem with being the name attached to the legend even if it was followed with adjectives like brutal, unfeeling and maniacal, then capped off with the all too easily added monster, tyrant or asshole. In fact, he quite enjoyed it and it made him laugh as he relived the moment, the helplessness of Ozzie and his own complete disregard for the man's suffering which only served to further distance him from Victor as Victor was clearly the alpha male, not just the one who would survive but most certainly the one who would dominate.

The incident worked well for Victor as a message to all who worked for him, that he would not tolerate anyone who did not strictly follow his orders. It also sent a message to those who did not work for him that he was just plain scary. For several months following the live burial of Ozzie there was not a single missed payment or botched deal. People who had dealings with the Alonso organization were considerate, responsible and respectful of the organization as a whole and particularly of Victor himself.

Ironically, less than two weeks after the demise of Ozzie, Victor began forging agreements with a variety of businesses in various trades, widening his reach and generating some purely legal income. With frighteningly bad taste Victor would refer to the process of selection regarding new partner or acquisition decisions as "Ozzilating" and the establishment of an arrangement leading to a final contract as "Ozzification" as if in doing so he bolstered his own stature. Most everyone else found it disgusting, repulsive and horrible, except Sal who really seemed to admire the way Victor handled every aspect of the incident with Ozzie. In fact, Sal invited Victor over for dinner, without Max, shortly after the incident so they could sit around afterwards, get blasted on Juice and shots of liquor and discuss the various ways they had made the weaker people in the world suffer.
Needless to say, the shipment was checked, the tracks were hidden and everything was locked down tight in no time. The entire team found their bedrolls rather quickly and settled in for the night. Not a single one of them asked what Victor had meant about acting lessons even though the Victor they were all working with today was clearly not the same Victor who buried Ozzie Warburton alive.

Leer shocked the Varst out of everyone in the morning when six of the most beautiful people they had ever seen showed up for breakfast, four women and two men. There was a gentleman who was in his mid-fifties who arrived with them but no one seemed to pay much attention to him. He was the person Victor would tell them all to pay the most attention to, but for now they sat with their mouths open, the only sound a communal humming of open-mouthed breathing with occasional low-level groaning as if they had all spend the last week trudging through the desert without water then suddenly saw a fountain spouting the stuff freely just beyond their collective reach.

"You've come just in time," Franco started, "I was just about to go for a walk to a most splendid spot I discovered only just last night, the view is quite fabulous..." he was cut short.

Manny stepped in front of him and continued, "Though not quite so fabulous as the one I am surveying right now," he swaggered his way toward the women, careful to keep his eyes moving to each of them equally.

"Manny, Franco." Victor needed only to speak their names in a certain tone and they immediately stopped talking. Neither could resist the urge to pucker and wink with hideously nauseating self-love which filled the room with the odor of smarm, the stench of which lingers and makes all things that come near to it, wither. However, the women smiled, one even giggled and Franco was certain that the last girl his eyes fell upon blushed at his gaze. "We are joined today, gentlemen," Victor continued, his eyes falling directly upon the Fiorelli twins, by Dr. Stanislas Case. He and his team are going to help us. I want you to give Dr. Case your undivided attention as it is he who will most likely be responsible for saving each of your lives."
Stan Case was one of those rare educators who could instruct so engagingly that the student was seldom even aware that a valuable lesson was taking place. Humorously, unexpectedly, he prepared the team for a learning experience that would not only help them to carry out their mission, despite the fact that it had been altered, but also would give them insight into basic human behavior. Later, he would lead the team through a series of exercises which would illustrate the need for the lessons in the first place. Stan spoke for about an hour and a half and in that time not a single one of the team wanted to leave the room. Normally, this level of attentiveness could be traced to the feeling that Victor would kill, or worse, torture them if they even thought of leaving, but in this case things were different. A transformation seemed to be happening within the room, even to the Fiorelli twins who spent the first five minutes drooling over the women who had arrived but since were glued to Stan's every word and gesture. If he had stood up and marched them all out of the room and over a cliff the team

would certainly be dead. But he didn't. What Dr. Case did do was inspire them to learn and being inspired to learn is half the task.

Stan Case had been called to help the team nearly fifteen years before he actually arrived. Leer's plan had been devised long before that but it took him all of thirty years to prepare for what he was going to try to accomplish over the next week. If you try to understand how he could have already done it all thirty years before, the whole thing becomes far too difficult to process unless you are a Quanji or a Wuoshigah, which you probably aren't or you would be far too busy to read this book given the current state of things. Simply put, Leer knew that in order to pull off what he was about to attempt he would need to embody the qualities of both fearless and numinous leadership.

Leer had already begun to show signs that Victor was, in fact, becoming just the sort of leader to inspire loyalty. The way he handled the meeting at Sal's club house made an impression on Sal's goons which was quietly spreading below Sal's own radar. Victor's response to the discovery of the shoe bomb and his quick and decisive reaction to Abe's disruption illustrated his ability to handle the unexpected, while everything that followed right up to the present indicated that he had a plan to move in a new direction. For most of the team, any time they weren't being shot at and were being well fed was luxurious, so compared to some of the other guys they had worked for, Victor seemed pretty alright. Dr. Case had made a good initial impression and was about to assist in the process of establishing Victor as the sort of leader one could believe in, beginning with lesson one.

The team was split into four groups and each of those groups had a leader, chosen at random by drawing lots. Victor was not permitted to be in any of the groups because he had other assignments to perform as part of the group's education. Each person in each group was paired with one of the beautiful people. They were allowed to choose which beautiful person they wanted to be with as long as they had not already been chosen. It actually worked out quite well with the exception of the Fiorelli twins who couldn't make up their minds and Marv's inability to decide between the two beautiful men. Since they had already agreed to go with Max on her turn, they agreed to do the same with Marv. Samuel also chose to go with a male partner, he chose Vladimir and Nick went with Carlo. While one group was going into these "meetings" the others were playing games. One group was playing the "I am the Leader" game, another the "I'll tell you with my body game" and the third the "very first person I would kill" game. While all of the games were enlightening for players and instructors alike the one that was most critical to the success of the mission was the "meeting game."

The build-up to the meeting game was overtly sexual. Each couple or threesome would enter a room together and close the door. The room was dimly lit and soothing music played inside. As the team members were brought into the room, the beautiful person would ask the team member to take a seat, offer a drink and then sit directly across from the team member and begin a conversation. Each conversation started with a few getting to know you type questions such as "What do you like to do with your spare time?" - "Do you like animals?" - "What is your favorite color?"; and all of these questions were asked by the beautiful people while flirtatiously fondling certain items in the room or sprawling gorgeously across some innocent piece of furniture. In the course of less than five minutes each of the beautiful people had found out everything they could ever hope to want to know about the shipment and dismissed each team member with a dazzling smile and the promise of a special surprise as long as the team member kept their conversation secret and private.

Several hours later the team assembled in the shed, each member confident that he or she would be receiving the surprise. That fact of the matter is that they all did.
The team assembled, Victor and Dr. Case walked to the front of the room carrying a small stack of papers. The team looked at them with an almost annoyed sense of waiting. Following close behind, the beautiful people also walked to the front of the room and the team seemed truly interested, almost eager to see what happened next. The beautiful people spread smiles around like clowns throwing candy at a big parade. Each member of the team blindly imagined that the smiles were solely theirs to see, as if the beautiful people were sending reassurance that the surprise was soon to come. Even Max seemed to be entranced by the beautiful men who spent only five minutes alone in the room with her but asked her questions, smiled, flirted and showered her with individual attention. In her heart she knew that she shouldn't be feeling anything for them but she couldn't keep her eyes off of them while her mind told her that it was all okay because Victor brought them there in the first place. Surely he was aware of what they were doing, what they were saying, how they were making her feel. Suddenly she felt guilty, as

if she had betrayed a trust. She quickly asked Farb to forgive her, to make sure that Victor never found out what she had been feeling.

Farb must have been busy. The whole time she had been thinking about it, she had been staring at the beautiful men. During that time, Victor had left the front of the room and maneuvered himself into the seat directly next to Max. "They are truly beautiful, aren't they Max" Victor's voice spoke softly into her ear. She gasped and looked at him with a mixture of guilt and anger. He simply smiled saying, "Stan is about to go over the lesson, we should all listen to what he has to tell us." Somehow, his relaxed tone and his willingness to include himself as one who was about to learn something, made everything alright. He placed his hand upon her thigh and she reached down to hold it.

"Thank you all very much for your time today," Dr. Case began, "we have a lot of information here to evaluate but I'm not going to bore you all with that right now. What I will tell you is that we were testing you." The team began to look around at one another. Most of them were looking to see how the others were reacting. Were they just as mystified by what was happening or did they know something. A few of them thought they knew something and sat smugly. In fact, the only one who knew anything about what was really going on was Leer, and he was sitting with his eyes glued to Dr. Case. Following his example, the team turned their attention to Stan Case. When he determined that they had stopped looking around, that he now had their full attention he told them, "You ALL failed!"
"Don't worry about it, nearly everyone fails the first time," Dr. Case said sympathetically. The members of the team continued to look around at one another because they really didn't know that they were being tested in the first place. They all seemed to be searching the faces of one another for some sign of understanding or lack thereof signifying that there had been no clear indication that they were being tested in any way. Again, their eyes turned to Victor. Sensing their unrest, Leer stood up and did what Victor would normally do if he had called a meeting. He took control.

"We only have a couple of days to get this shipment where it needs to go. I have asked Dr. Case to help us get that done. Pay attention to what he has to say because it is very important." He looked toward Stan and nodded then sat back down.

"Okay everyone," Stan began, "as Victor has mentioned, I am here to help you. These people sitting before you," he gestures toward the beautiful people, "are also here to help you, and sadly for you, no, none of them will be spending any special one on one time with you." The beautiful people smiled toward the team, but the team just frowned and looked disappointed and bewildered. "These lovely people are my team. They help me to test and to instruct. The test we ran was a combination of role playing games and interactive personality assessments. The reason you failed is that each one of you divulged information about this mission to a member of my team which would certainly put the mission into jeopardy." Victor's team stopped looking around and looked to Dr. Case then to Victor, then back to Dr. Case, waiting to see what he would say next, judging whether Victor was upset or not. "This is all perfectly normal behavior," Stan Case continued, "we are here to teach you how to keep those normal tendencies in check as well as to develop the ability to role play convincingly. In order to perform the tasks necessary to complete this mission, several of you are going to have to become actors, and we," he gestures once again to the beautiful people, "are going to show you how." He paused for a moment, then held his hand out toward Leer who stood up and began to walk toward the front of the room again, "Victor has a very interesting plan which he would like to share with you all now, so I will let him tell you. It is a good plan and should work. If it doesn't, it means that we have failed him, my team and your team, and I for one have a very hard time accepting failure, particularly from myself!" Dr. Case looked at the group with sincerity and intensity. He had made a very strong impression on them from the time he had arrived and as he took his seat he transferred all of that energy to Leer who now stood before the team, no longer just a boss, Victor had become a leader with a plan.

27 THE PLAN

Planning was never really anything that he considered himself to be particularly good at, and following a plan imposed upon him by another person was always a challenge, to put it mildly, even if his life depended on it. So, faced with the choice whether to plan or be planned upon, Blue decided it was time to devise a plan of his own. Until now he was happy to go along with whatever Anna Marie, Mojahdii or Vinny might come up with on any given day, but that was before Sal made it patently obvious that Tommy was deep into some kind of arrangement with Sal which was not sustainable if Blue intended to peacefully fulfill his new role as Onjadiavaan.

Most of what was happening to Blue was just that; happening to Blue. He was not the master of his own destiny. He felt powerless to control the course of his own actions because he was in a foreign place, time and body. However, he felt fully at ease with his own feelings. Essentially, Blue was still himself, living in the corporeal form of Tommy on a planet which he discovered only recently was called Salta, he possessed all of his former talents and had acquired a few rather remarkable new ones. He decided to start with what he felt, rather than what he knew and that meant that he was going to have to get up very early in the morning, which he knew he hated whether he was Tommy or Blue, because he had to speak with Anna Marie as soon as possible. She had been teaching him, patiently helping him to develop a deeper understanding of Salta, Shedavah and that which binds all things together throughout space and time. Anna Marie was giving him the opportunity to discover his own abilities to explore, investigate and experience this new world in order to realize his place within it so that he might then be able to recognize his place outside of it. Blue was beginning to sense only a fraction of what that truly meant but he knew that he must learn. He knew that he had to be ready. There is only one Onjadiavaan and if Blue knew anything for sure it was that he was the one. What he didn't know was how to take a million flashes of a thousand different moments happening in a hundred-thousand different places at once, pull the energy from those moments into a neat little ball, small enough to fit into his hands and crystallize it. He had already done that but it was beginners luck and he had since lost the ball, the OmegaLux Crystal, Shedavah.

So the plan was simple. Wake up Anna Marie, nice and early in the morning and tell her that he needed to get Shedavah that day, and that he also needed to be able to unleash all of its power in order to get the worlds across space, time and anything else that was critical, to resonate, align, harmonize or otherwise blend smoothly, so he could avoid having to run JumpJuice for Sal, or end up in some crazy battle with Victor or Leer who was actually a very skilled fighter and would surely dominate him were it to come to that. He determined that he was going to need to be fairly well rested if he was to try to accomplish this over the next couple of days or so. He brushed his teeth, climbed into bed and asked All That Is for whatever help was available to a guy like him.

Blue was awakened earlier than he had planned to get up, not by an alarm clock, a rooster or the smell of fresh-made coffee, but by the gentle stroke of a hand upon his face. There above him stood Anna Marie. He was about to speak, to launch into a story about how he planned to wake her, but his vision cleared of sleep and he recognized that she had been crying. "What is it," he said as she gently pulled on him, clearly in a hurry to leave the tent. "Okay, Anna Marie, I'll follow you," Blue said softly as he stepped into his pants and shoes and slipped on a shirt with the speed of a fire fighter answering an alarm. He had trouble keeping up with her as she bounded down the path and made her way to the hut of Mojahdii. As they neared the hut, a crowd that had assembled around the outside parted to allow Anna Marie and Tommy access to the narrow doorway, made smaller by those assembled, all showing signs of fear, dread or grief. Whether Mojahdii was dead or dying, Blue could not yet determine but he knew it must be either. All eyes were upon him as he slid his way closer to the center of everyone's attention, to the very spot where he had first met Anna Marie. There, directly on the ground, lay Mojahdii, eyes closed in what the yogis might call rest or corpse pose, his feet several inches apart, legs outstretched, arms by his side, hands a few inches out from his waist, palms upward. Blue could tell that he was not dead but only by the subtle heat, slowly passing from his nostrils. No one said a word. Seconds later, the hulking form of Vinny was standing just behind Blue, his hand gently but firmly grasping Blue's shoulder in support. Sansaa raised her eyes to Vinny, through her tears a peaceful acceptance shone.

But Blue looked around at everyone within the hut; and for an instant could see right through its walls, outside to the multitudes already gathered and still on their way, and he did not feel acceptance. In that moment he saw both the living and the dead, those who had come before and those yet to be born. He saw great ribbons of light in varying intensities and sizes stretching for an eternity away from him while passing through him. As he turned his eyes toward Mojahdii he noticed equally strong bands of absolute lightlessness, beyond blackness, so dense yet so vacant that the weight of them was visible, palpable and at the same time forbidding, as if touching them would swallow the very life of the soul. The most ominous of these lightless bands passed directly through Mojahdii and precisely where it did all of the ribbons of light ceased. Though the light filled the hut and every soul assembled within, without and beyond, these same ribbons died at the very heart of Mojahdii. And then he saw it. Floating in the middle of what appeared to be miles of lightlessness, seemingly stretching deep into the very earth upon which Mojahdii lay, was the faintest of sparks, like a single fleck of glitter floating in an endless night. Without a word or a moment of hesitation Blue plunged both of his hands into the blackness, into the breast of Mojahdii.

A shriek of horror rose up from those assembled within the hut, confusion and fear gripped the crowd as Onjadiavaan vanished and Vinny's arm, still reaching forward as if clutching his brother for his very life turned black as pitch. The blackness crawled its way up his arm toward his shoulder then began to take over his chest and neck and for the first time in as long as anyone who had ever known him could remember, fear crept across Vinny's face.

Suddenly, light, the equal of which no living being had ever encountered filled the entire hut. It blazed its way through the very walls of the hut and drenched the valley with its glow. Then, just as suddenly, it was gone and Onjadiavaan stood before the crowd holding Shedavah in his hands. "Tommy!" cried Vinny, restored to his normal self but weeping as he reached out to hug his brother.

Mojahdii sat straight up into what the yogis would call the lotus position, looking as healthy as ever if not more so and said, smiling form ear to ear, "Onjadiavaan, thank you for delivering Shedavah to us all," and then he bowed his head in respect.

Blue smiled then held the crystal high for all to see and this time it did not vanish.
Everyone was rejoicing, hugging one another, crying and laughing. Targent was bouncing up and down with so much energy it was as if he got a direct charge out of Shedavah. In fact, many of the people who had gathered were noticing some pretty dramatic effects from what they were calling the "Glowburst" which, only moments earlier, Blue had released from the crystal. Many of the crowd had pushed in closer to tell Mojahdii how glad they were that he was alive. They tried desperately for an opportunity to shake Tommy's hand or even better, touch the crystal. Although it was of great value and power, Tommy held it out to each person who asked, freely and openly, Blue sensed that the crystal was now as much a part of him as his own beating heart. He did fear that someone would try to steal the crystal or try to destroy it, but not today. The people assembled here had come to pay their respects to Mojahdii. They were devoted and loyal followers who would not even consider attempting to take or damage Shedavah.

"Onjadiavaan," Blue heard a voice he thought he had heard before, pure, like song from a dream, coming from behind him. As he turned, before he could see who it was he realized who it must be. His heart soared with happiness even before he saw her because he knew that it would be Anna Marie.

"You're talking!" Blue said in a tone, not of surprise but of understanding, "I am so happy to hear your voice, absolutely beautiful and so gentle."

28 LEARNING

"I've been waiting to speak to you for as long as I can remember, Onjadiavaan," Anna Marie said to Blue in a voice full of love and adoration.

"I like it when you call me that, Anna Marie, but it may take some getting used to." Blue said quietly, knowing full well that she was one of less than a handful of people who knew who he truly was, so he whispered," I'd kinda like to hear you call me Blue."

"Okay Blue," she whispered back and he just about melted into the floor, "but I have to tell you something very important," Anna Marie continued to whisper, "No matter who you were before, you are Onjadiavaan, and that is more important than anything you could have imagined as Blue or Tommy. Nothing, not fame, not power, not wealth, not even the love of someone special," she paused and smiled, leaving no doubt that he had her love, "nothing can compare with what it is to be Onjadiavaan." Her eyes welled up as if the feelings inside of her were about to gush out and the only way that she could avoid bursting would be to tell him every exquisite detail of her vision of what it meant to be Onjadiavaan, as though the voiceless silence she had endured could only be fully cured by telling him everything she knew. She grabbed him by the arm and pulled him toward the door but they didn't make it more than a few feet before Mojahdii and his entourage of followers were standing before them, anxious to speak with Onjadiavaan.

Actually, Mojahdii could sense that Anna Marie was bursting and he would have gladly allowed them to leave were it not for the throng of high-level dignitaries crowding their way around him, committed to taking full advantage of the prospect of being one of the first to actually speak with Onjadiavaan, even though several of them had outright ignored Blue since he had arrived, judging him to be a fake or simply lucky. In light of his recent cure of Mojahdii and reclamation of Shedavah through the Glowburst, however, their skepticism regarding his validity was summarily abandoned. As they shoved forward in unison, Blue could see the discomfort in Mojahdii's eyes. That, coupled with his empathy for Anna Marie, filled him with a sudden desire to be far away from the crowd. He looked at Mojahdii who began to laugh and reached a hand toward Blue who reached his own hand toward Anna Marie who completed the circle with Mojahdii. Blue quickly concentrated on the hill at the top of the commons and just as quickly, they were there, far away from the crowd, walking toward Blue's favorite waterfall.

"I think I'll take the path back to my hut," Mojahdii smiled and continued, "I believe Anna Marie has a few things she would like to say to you Onjadiavaan." He began down the path toward his home then turned back toward the couple, "and Blue, thanks for getting me out of there, it was getting a bit crowded. Oh yes, also, nicely done with Shedavah, but just one more thing, that was the easy part. Come to my hut when things die down a bit." The old man walked away leaving the two younger lovers to walk, talk and enjoy the soothing sounds of the waterfall.

The walk was everything Blue had ever imagined true love to feel like, long stretches of simply walking hand in hand, feeling as though there was no reason to even consider what time of day it might be, interspersed with occasional stops along the way, to look at the beauty of nature or to stare into one another's eyes and then, to kiss. Kissing now, kissing Anna Marie, was not like kissing in college (Blue didn't really have any memorable comparisons to make before that time), nor was it like any kissing he had engaged in since college. He enjoyed kissing but if his mother had actually survived his birth, he would not have bothered to write to her about it, until now. In fact, Blue rarely thought of his mother unless he felt particularly thrilled with life, which regrettably did not happen very often. When he did think of her, it was usually coming from a feeling that he would like to have someone he knew, someone who he could be absolutely certain loved him, to share in the joy of the moment. He could truly say that this moment qualified as one he would have liked to tell his mother about. That thought flashed through his mind so quickly it made his own head spin. Actually, after another moment of quick thinking he narrowed the spinning down to euphoria which is the feeling that this kissing was generating far differently than kissing that had happened in the past.

There were long stretches of simply walking with Anna Marie and long stretches of listening to Anna Marie, actually, because she did have quite a lot on her mind that she simply had to let Blue know about, all of which filled her with a nearly orgasmic sort of enthusiasm. To be Onjadiavaan meant that he had the power to do amazing things. He had already become aware of a couple of them rather recently but Blue was having a little trouble resolving what he considered to be a classic chicken and egg situation. The situation had to do with the cure of Mojahdii and the retrieval of Shedavah from deep within a lightless void inside of Mojahdii himself. The chicken was Mojahdii and his illness, the egg was Shedavah, and Blue couldn't answer the question of which came first, Mojahdii's illness or the existence of a large crystalline energy source deep inside him. He was hoping that Mojahdii might explain that to him later during his visit to the old man's hut. If he had been able to process all of the information that Anna Marie was so willingly and passionately bestowing upon him, he may have been able to answer that question for himself. However, he got stuck on the part where she said that Onjadiavaan can fly.

The moment she said that he reached both arms around her, looked up, and before he could even bend his knees as if preparing to jump he and Anna Marie were already lifting off the ground. For Onjadiavaan, many of the things that he could do were more a matter of learning how to control them than to make them happen. Anna Marie fully intended to make a point of telling Blue all about it but for the moment, flying through a beautiful sky with the love of her life was all she was able or wanted to think about.
Blue thought about flying many times before. After all, he was a comic book illustrator, or at least a wannabe comic book illustrator. The point is, he knew just what at least three dozen different superheroes were capable of and was in the middle of doing what only a handful of them

could actually do. He was flying. He wasn't using any fancy machines, surfboards, glowing rings or flames to make him fly, he was just thinking about how he wanted to fly, where he wanted to fly, how fast and how high he wanted to fly and he was doing it all while holding on to the most wonderful girl he had ever been with so she could fly with him. In all the time that Blue had thought about flying, he never even considered what it would be like to land. He thought about mentioning that to Anna Marie as they neared the ground, but didn't. Instead, he thought about how smooth it would be to just step right down onto the ground and keep walking as if he was descending a staircase and had reached the bottom step, nice, easy and fluid. So that is exactly what he did. Remarkably, all went according to plan and he and Anna Marie continued their walk, Anna Marie giggling at the sheer thrill of it all, holding his hand and skipping along the path.

Suddenly, someone jumped down in front of them from the tree branch which hung just ahead of them along the path. "Hey, you two little lovebirds, and I DO MEAN BIRDS!" Targent laughed as he bounded toward them excitedly. "Amazing, absolutely amazing, you guys were just flying, whooeee! You have got to show me how you do that Tommy, I mean Onjadiavaan. Oh man, you are the real deal, you are Onjadiavaan, I knew it, it was just like I said, nobody believed me, but I knew it, Tommy, sorry, sorry, Onjadiavaan, Awesome!" Targent just blurted out every word, so fast he barely had any breath left.

"Hello Targent" Blue and Anna Marie responded.

"You, you, YOU," Targent stammered, pointing to Anna Marie, "You talked!"

"Yes, Targent," Anna Marie said sweetly, "I have found my voice," she added as she looked to Blue.

"We were just on our way back. Anna Marie was just filling me in on a few things, Targent," Blue said evenly in an effort to calm Targent down, "what brings you out here?"
"Who me, well I, um, so anyway, you and she and, well, Mojahdii. I mean I was just, well, I was, like standing there and looking at you guys and then, 'PffffffTttt', you're like gone... Just gone." Targent spits out clumsily as he begins to hop up and down. "And Then, then, I, well I,

then, y'know, then I, like, y'know, I uh I, well I know it must all be true. Y'know the whole thing, Tommy, that you're Onjadiavaan and that you have brought Shedavah to me, uh, I mean us, yes, us, Shedavah, and you're like totally Onjadiavaan which means that you can do amazing things like disappear and fly and run super-fast and hear things like a super-good-hearing animal and you can be here and there and heal people and grow things and stuff like that." Targent held himself in his own arms like he was holding in his bones for fear they might jump out and hug Tommy with enthusiasm and then he looked at his own feet and said," so I came out here to find you 'cause I know you like it out here... and here you are, and I got to see you fly and you were like going up and down and all over and like upside down and Anna, she was like hangin' on and like,'ahhhhh-ooohhhh-ahhhh', and you're like all shootin' through the sky and stuff, and I'm like, 'Ooh, I wanna fly, I wanna fly, I wanna fly', and then you're like back on the ground so I got scared and jumped in this tree. So you're probably done with flying now and totally all ti-i-i--i-i-rrrrrrr!"

Blue had taken Targent quickly by his shoulders and launched into the sky with him so fast it took his breath away. They rocketed straight up into the sky with ease then levelled out into a coast roughly half-a-mile up.

"Tired, hmm-mmn," Targent laughed sheepishly to himself in a tone that said 'I guess I was wrong as well as the next time I pull the poor me, I guess I missed out routine, I'd better be ready if they call my bluff!' He was dangling below Blue who had a firm hold of Targent from behind his back and around his chest. "Barfunkle, Tommy, this is awesome, I mean Onjadiavaan, totally Beezle."

Blue shot in low over the tree-line with him and landed smoothly on the path just meters away from where they started as a delighted Anna Marie laughed and clapped, applauding their return. Targent gave her a big hug then she reached out and took Blue's hand as the three of them walked together, back toward the village.
The walk back to the village didn't take very long especially with Targent running ahead every five minutes, scoping out who might be approaching them on the trail. As soon as he would see someone coming, he would run back to Blue and Anna Marie and throw his arm around them so whoever might see them would know that he was with

them, he was a friend of Onjadiavaan. One of the people they passed was a photographer who had set up her tripod to capture a beautiful scene along the path. When the trio reached her spot, Targent hovered over her, peeked over her shoulder to see how her shot was framed within the viewfinder, then tapped her repeatedly on the shoulder, then the other shoulder, then the head until she finally acknowledged his presence with a grumpy stare. He bounced up and down and ran over to Blue then pointed to him, then back to himself and repeated that motion a few times, his eyes sparkling with pride. "Can you take a picture of us together?" He asked the photographer who kindly explained that she was already taking a picture of the landscape which lay on the opposite side of the path in the distance. "It'll just take a second," Targent went on, "really, it's so nice out right now, and bright, so actually it'll take less time than that. Boyo, if you had a second long exposure in this light, Cripees, that would be a bad shot fer sure," he laughed then walked in real close to the photographer, "SO-o-o-o-o, it would actually be less than a second and then we would just leave you alone." Targent was relentless.

The photographer was really looking unhappy and turned her eyes toward Blue. She was about to explain why she didn't want to take the picture and was actually going to apologize to the entire trio even though it was really only Targent who seemed to think that the photo was a good idea, when she noticed that she was about to address Onjadiavaan. She nearly fell to her knees but caught herself, then straightening back up she scurried toward the camera saying, "I'm so sorry, I didn't know, I would be honored, may I please take your photo, Onjadiavaan?"

"You do not have to take the picture, please continue with your art," Blue quickly responded placing his arm around Anna Marie and turning toward the village by way of the path.

"Please Onjadiavaan," the woman called out, knowing that this would be the very first photo of Onjadiavaan since the recovery of Shedavah, "I would much rather have a photo of you." trying her best to not be so obviously fame smitten she motioned to the entire trio.

They agreed to stand for a portrait which actually turned out to be a beautiful shot with the trio framed by the flora which grew with such lushness all along the path.

The walk back to the village was quite brief from the photo spot and Targent wanted to run off and tell everyone where he had just been. Blue wanted to sit down in his tent and have a little something to eat and Anna Marie just wanted to be with him. When they arrived at the tent, it was difficult to find the entrance as it had been decorated lavishly with countless bouquets, handmade signs and other offerings all to honor Onjadiavaan.

"Tommy!" a booming voice burst from within the shrine of gifts. It was Vinny who was holding a cold beer out with one arm and knocking one back with the other. His head and eyes gestured toward his own beer, "Thought I'd help myself, since there's a big enough supply in there to last a lifetime," he said indicating the interior of the tent.

"Where's mine?" Anna Marie teased softly followed by the cutest little laugh which Vinny began to echo until...

"Hey!" Vinny nearly spit out the swig he took in mid-laugh, "you're talking!" Anna Marie just smiled at him. "Well Bastin' Farbunkle, by all means, one for the lady!"
"One might think that in an enlightened community, important, possibly life-changing events and the news of those events might be handled with care, discussed only when appropriate and only with others who understood the more comprehensive picture of what such news meant and what it might affect. Nothing could be further from the truth. The reason for this is simple, the enlightened tend to behave as if everyone is enlightened or at least aware that what the enlightened are enlightened about is ultimately true. However, it is not true that everyone is even the least bit interested in enlightenment. So, people who may not be the right people to trust with important news such as the recovery of Shedavah by Onjadiavaan end up having that news shared with them by naive, enlightened folk who by their faith in others expose the innocent to the wiles of the wicked. Ultimately, it is this very irony that maintains the balance of good and evil within the universe. Still, good people end up dead all of the time because of things just like this." Mojahdii said as he walked back and forth slowly, smiling warmly at Blue so as not to discourage him. "So, Onjadiavaan, you are now here with us so that you can deliver that which has been promised, and all of

us who have been waiting have great hopes in you. Nearly all who have waited think that since you have arrived, the stories that have been told of what has been and what is to come are certainly true. You have learned many of these stories already, nearly all in fact, while you prepared to reclaim Shedavah but I can imagine that it feels quite different now that you are actually Onjadiavaan." Mojahdii winked at Blue and continued pacing. "What most of the believers don't understand, Blue, is that you are Onjadiavaan only so long as you fulfill that which it is to be Onjadiavaan. "Mojahdii stopped pacing and turned to see Blue's reaction. Blue did not seem to be the least bit surprised by this information, in fact, he seemed to be relieved. "Perhaps you have already figured this out? or maybe you no longer wish to be Onjadiavaan," Mojahdii postulated with a half-smile, then waited for a response.

"I am Onjadiavaan," Blue responded," I do not know for how long any more than I know why, but I don't care. For some reason, my friend turned out to really be a character he made up in a comic book we were writing together, or was it the other way around." Blue paused, as if considering this question one more time might somehow, this time, wind up being answered, then he continued, "doesn't matter. We travelled through space and time, became a few different kinds of creatures, ended up in bodies that weren't even our own on a world that seems like the one I call home, though Farb knows why," he laughs at his own, internal joke about the nature of divinity, "then I find, lose and recover Shedavah. Now if that doesn't mean that I am meant to be Onjadiavaan as part of some greater plan, then I will just have to find out the hard way. There is only one thing that I know and that is that I know something. I can't explain it, hell, I don't even understand it, but I don't have to, so, please, Mojahdii, tell me what I need to know about being Onjadiavaan because I have a feeling that all Varst is gonna break loose any day now!"

Mojahdii laughed very softly to himself then looked at Blue calmly but with a seriousness that said that everything that was going on right now, for all of the people whom Blue had come to know and love, was absolutely critical and dependent upon his actions. "Onjadiavaan delivers Shedavah to all. You are absolutely right Blue, you are Onjadiavaan and only you can know what is right, what must be done at any given time. I can only tell you that your path will be difficult, you will be challenged. If the stories are true, by someone of this world, Salta, who is very powerful, by someone who travels through space and time and by one who is very close to you. If you fail, our world and many others like it will be plunged into great darkness and despair. If that is the case, then it is meant to be and it is no more a reflection on you than on me or Sansaa or Vinny, Anna Marie or Targent, or any of the people of the Shadowlands, Salta or the worlds beyond. You must do your best and that is all that is required of you. If your best is to go outside and sit on a rock for the next ten years, then you must go sit on that rock." Mojahdii smiled warmly and rubbed Blue on the shoulder then added, "I do want to give you one little bit of advice though. If you sense something unusual, such as seeing into someone else's mind, or feeling the change of weather, long before there is any sign of it, if it seems as though the animals, plants and trees, or you feel as though Salta herself is speaking to you, do not disregard a single element. You are Onjadiavaan and you are connected with 'All that is', perhaps more directly than any one of us has ever been. And Blue, enjoy the rush and let your light bring happiness to those around you."

It was true, Blue now seemed to possess an inner knowing which was so powerful and inexplicable given his usual M.O. which consisted of going along with the flow of just about everything with nearly everyone around him, with no definitive course of his own. Perhaps that is what made him most suited to become Onjadiavaan. What he was feeling now was a strong sense of purpose with absolutely nothing for a plan. As a matter of fact, he seemed particularly confident that not having a plan at this particular moment was the best possible plan he could have. What he knew was that it was time to leave the Shadowlands. What he told everyone was nothing. He just left. He didn't pack. He didn't say goodbye. He didn't kiss or hug anybody. He didn't shake hands with or leave a note for anybody. He simply left the Shadowlands in the middle of the afternoon, on foot with only the clothes upon his back. He didn't even bring Shedavah along. He put the crystal in the center of a small shrine just outside the back door of Mojahdii's hut then walked down the narrow footpath which wound its way along the fields which filled the valley floor until he reached the slope of the mountain range that formed the edge of the valley on the far north side. Then he leaped up into the air and glided to the top of a large outcropping of rock at the summit where he sat and waited for sunset.

29 PULP

His plan was to kill off at least half the people there. The other half would be so traumatized by the massacre that they would have little or no recollection of what had happened. Then he would return. He was going to need some back-up, someone to corroborate his account of the events which took the lives of so many, but he wasn't sure who he could trust. Or perhaps more to the point, who would give the best performance. Luckily for Leer, he had Dr. Case to help make that decision. With half of the team in hiding, pretending to be dead, including Max, and most of the other half useless to him, Victor would be alone with whoever he picked to join him as he faced a Sal whose reaction to the loss of another shipment, his star team and his daughter all at once could be downright murderous.

So Stan Case came up with a solution. He chose Samuel to be the remaining "sane" team member to return with Victor because Samuel had impeccable delivery. He could talk about anything in the same matter of fact way whether it be fact or fiction, joyful or depressing because that was what he did anyway. He is even-toned but not lifeless and that's just the type of guy they would need to convince Sal of everything that Victor was going to claim to have happened. Max had to stay behind because it was part of Victor's overall plan. The rest of them picked numbers out of a hat. Those who drew odd numbers would stay and die, those who drew even would go suddenly mad.
"Hey Samuel, "Leer called out across the yard out behind the shed that had now become the "actors training studio," a mixture of picnic tables

and assorted fitness stations, Samuel had just finished a couple hundred sit-ups on the incline bench and was still halfway upside down as he looked across at Victor, "I'll give you one quarter of my share of the profits if you can take me, two falls out of three," Leer wasn't about to count on acting or make-up to accomplish what he was after, a good, severe beating, something along the lines of that Victor had received at the hands of Tommy. In the process, he had to make damn sure to hang in there long enough to do the same to Samuel. Both men looking as though they were just barely clinging to life was tantamount to the success of the mission.

Samuel rolled all the way back so he was fully upside down and releasing his feet from the bars, flipped all the way back and was standing on his feet a second later. He turned toward Victor, smiling. he walked over slowly, wiping the sweat from his own face then flexing his arms forward and over his head as he leaned from side to side, stretching in preparation, still approaching Victor, his eyes glued to Victor who stood nearly a whole foot shorter than he. "When do we start?" Samuel asked.

"N..." Victor was unable to finish the word now because the moment he began to say it Samuel unloaded a full-fisted bashing to the center of Victor's face, the nose of which was almost certainly broken on contact. Victor stumbled backward, nearly hitting the dirt but catching himself just inches away from suffering his first fall. He was obviously caught by surprise and noticeably hurt by the punch but he began to laugh. "A quarter of my share is twice your share Samuel, so you're going to have to try a little harder than that."
Victor moved with unprecedented speed which stunned the members of the team who had assembled to witness the challenge, particularly those who were his crew, Manny and Franco Fiorelli, Gavin and Marv, even Max who had witnessed Victor's skillful fighting at Sal's clubhouse but thought she might have been a little biased since she had just spent the greater part of the morning making love to him. Now however, he was up against Samuel who was undeniably the mightiest as well as one of the swiftest fighters in the team and Max hadn't gotten so much as a lick of sexual attention from Victor since they reached the hideaway. They all marveled as Victor leaped to the side of Samuel who attempted to follow his crushing punch with another jab only to be thoroughly thrown off his feet by a flying clothesline headlock from Victor. Leer

knew he had to allow himself to be pummeled, but the point was to mess up Samuel in the process. Besides, he didn't much like the idea of losing any of his share regardless of how long he ended up staying on Salta. The first fall went to Victor. Samuel, though not physically scarred from being dropped was sufficiently enraged by the fact that Victor had gotten the drop on him so quickly that he completely ignored Victors offer of a hand up. Sulking stormily, Samuel rounded on Victor with a relentless series of roundhouse kicks. The first two missed wildly but the third was truly unusual, coming twice as fast around as the first two, catching Victor off-guard, caving in the side of his face, nearly breaking his jaw. Leer went down hard.

"Hey Victor," Samuel taunted as he towered over his fallen boss," you can spare yourself th' beatin' and just give up the quarter." He laughed a deep and gloating laugh which was suddenly cut short by an excruciating howl as Victor caved his knee backwards with a quick kick from the ground. As Samuel doubled over forward to clutch the knee in agony Victor bounded up directly into his face with an elbow pushed from below by the full force of his other arm and legs standing up directly into the blow sending Samuels head back fully. The big man tried to stay on his feet as he fell backward his nose gushing blood, both lips bleeding. Then Victor reached out and caught him, helping to steady him on his feet. Despite the assistance, Samuel lit into Victor with a series of punches. The two men stood toe to toe, bludgeoning one another with punches from the gut to the head, so quickly and forcibly that there was a shower of blood drenching the onlookers. Then everything stopped.

Both men stood teetering on their own feet, arms dropped to their sides from exhaustion. With one final jab of the base of his hand into the chin of Samuel, Victor put the big man down for the second and final fall. He had won the contest but collapsed directly upon his adversary, a pile of bloody pulp.

Max leaned in close to check to see if he was breathing. Leer pointed to a pocket on his shirt, there, slightly sticking out of it, was a bloody piece of paper. She removed the paper, unfolded it and began reading. The plan had begun.

30 MAX IS DEAD

Sal Lorenzo walked slowly toward the bank entrance, careful to take his time, letting everyone who cared to look, have the opportunity to recognize that it was he who had just emerged from the stretch limo, guarded by three large, hulking masses of muscle and fitted silk. Sal was especially well dressed because today he was going to dispose of a bank president on his way to the Opera. He didn't really like the Opera but he did enjoy removing high ranking executives from their lofty positions by virtue of his own power and wealth, the Opera was for Sophia, his sister, who lived for the nights that her baby brother Sal would treat her to the Opera. She was the kind of woman who could pull the goodness from a person and make it dance, making the world seem a slightly brighter place even if only for a short time. She never dwelled on the particulars of Sal's reality, it was a truth she could not let herself acknowledge, which is probably why she was capable of such optimism, such joy even when in the company of such evil. She continued to treat him like her little brother, cute, spunky and deserving of love. And Sal let her, and only her, call him Sally. Several of the bank employees who wouldn't even dare to call Mr. Lorenzo, Sal, saw him coming and began to talk amongst each other about the possible reason for his visit. He never came to the bank unless something bad was going to happen, so suddenly about fifteen bank employees needed to go to the bathroom.

When Sal was within a few yards of the entrance to the bank, a van screeched alongside the curb, directly in line with the entrance. Sal's bodyguards turned and drew their weapons with dazzling speed but did not unload into the van because Sal had raised his hand in a halting motion, curious to see what happened next. The side door to the van had already been flung open and a body was tumbling out, followed immediately by another body. Sal recognized the second body instantly, despite the badly beaten features of the face which seemed to slosh from one side of the head to the other as the body continued to roll toward Sal. The van sped off as quickly as it had arrived, leaving Victor and Samuel still rolling along the concrete, all eyes glued to them in an effort to determine whether or not they were even alive. Before the bodyguards had a chance to realize that they were being distracted, a beautiful woman, dressed exactly like Max, except for the substitution of some very feminine stiletto heels in lieu of Max's customary jack boots, stood a foot from Sal. His eyes turned to her as she reached between her partially exposed breasts to pull out a small scroll, tied in a red ribbon. In the same motion her stiletto heel lifted from the ground and came to rest, dead smack in the middle of Victor's chest who's barely breathing body had stopped rolling just a foot shy of Sal and the young, beautiful woman. She held the scroll out to Sal, in just the right spot so his eyes would see the scroll and Victor's pummeled face at the same time. He took the scroll from the woman as she stepped through, walking directly across Victor's chest as if he were a minor, inconvenient little bump in her path.

"Take her," Sal shouted. As his bodyguards raised their guns they were all simultaneously eliminated. One by some sort of long-range tazer, leaving him twitching on the pavement. Another was just down, whatever happened to him had happened too quickly for anyone to see. A shorter person, dressed in a very dark black suit from head to toe, was running away about twenty yards from the spot where his motionless body lay. The third was tumbling across the ground after having been hit by a speeding cycle which not only threw him head over heels but also managed to pick up the girl and speed away before Sal even had the thought to draw his own weapon.

He bent down to listen for Victor's breathing as he unrolled the scroll and read 'Thanks for the Juice-Keep it Coming-We Need More'.
As they lay there in the hospital, it became quite clear that it was going to be awhile before Victor or Samuel could talk. So Sal just waited. He sat staring at the Opera tickets. He thought about the fact that he was

going to have to get new ones to make it up to Sophia. He had no idea how to get Opera tickets. He never did anything like that. He had people to do that for him. As a matter of fact, Max had bought the original tickets for him and right now he had no idea where Max might be.

Sal Lorenzo was not what one would call a compassionate man. He was concerned about Victor and Samuel's health, but only insofar as it pertained to his own interests, namely the JumpJuice shipment. While Sal did wonder what might have become of Max, his apprehension over the whereabouts of the shipment overshadowed his concern for her. The feelers he had put out for information about the shipment and any evidence of a violent struggle for the payload revealed a trail to nowhere and the headless corpse of Abe who he never really liked anyway.

He was a busy man, Sal had places to go, he couldn't hang around waiting for a couple of guys to wake up and tell him his JumpJuice was taken from them. He had to find who took it, get it back and kill everyone involved. "Let me know when either of these guys so much as blinks an eye," he said to Gus, his sister's kid who needed a job so he could pitch in a little rent money every now and then since he had turned his mother's basement into his apartment ever since he graduated from the Rat Town Community College with a MicroSalta IT certification. "If they say anything, Gus, anything at all, write it down," Sal added, "better yet, record it." He tossed Gus a small hand-held device about the size of a small iPod.

"Miss a word of it and I will personally pull your mother's black dress out of the closet for her, got it fat boy?" Gus nodded his head violently as Sal left the hospital room, littering an otherwise pristine hallway with freshly shucked peanut shells.

Opening one eye slowly, then the other, Leer began to look around the room he was in. He was in a hospital, there was no mistaking the tiny holes repeated over and over in the ceiling tiles. He'd been in dozens of hospitals across half as many galaxies and at least a third of them had the same ceiling tiles. Gus was over in the corner using some medical shears he had found to open a candy bar wrapper. Leer didn't know Gus. He looked in the other direction to see Samuel, equally beaten, still unconscious and reclined fully upon his hospital bed. He was having trouble remembering who Samuel was. He decided to close his eyes and think about things for a minute before letting anyone know he had awakened.

Slowly his memory returned. He had planned to be badly beaten, it was his own idea. The guy in the bed next to him was the one who did it because Leer had told him to. No one else could know any of that information. What everyone else was going to hear about the beating was part of a much larger plan. A plan that involved a bunch of rookie actors, an incredibly valuable shipment of JumpJuice and a natural disaster which Leer had barely survived, roughly thirty years ago, that was going to occur in less than seventy-two hours. Leer only hoped that Samuel would remember what he was supposed to say when he woke up, otherwise Leer might not live to see the natural disaster he survived thirty years before.

Within about an hour, Samuel began waking up. It was a process. First, he opened his eyes, then he closed them again, hoping that the world he opened his eyes to was a dream. If it was, that would mean that the pain was also a dream. Neither was true. Samuel had noticed Gus in the room and had immediately summed him up as useless. He also decided to keep his mouth shut until he had time to get his bearings. Unfortunately, Gus had been in the process of investigating his own reflection to see if he had started growing nose hairs when Samuel awoke. As chance would have it, Gus caught site of Samuel's open eyes and decided that it was his job to get Samuel to do some talking.

"Hello there," Gus began," my name is Gus. Look, I know you probably don't feel much like talking but Sal said I was supposed to tell him anything that you say. If you don't say anything, then I can't tell him anything and I will probably get fired, even though Sal is my uncle. If you do say something then I have to record it so could you tell me first if you plan on saying anything? Oh, and I know your name is Samuel, so you don't have to tell me that if you don't wanna. Also, I know that you're one of the toughest guys so whoever got you must've been totally beezle. So, do you have anything to say?" Gus really just wanted Samuel to say anything so he could call Sal and go home.

Samuel opened his eyes again. He reached up his hand and motioned Gus over to himself with his index finger as if he needed Gus close enough to hear a whisper. Gus came in close, pulling the recorder from his pocket and holding it our toward Samuel's mouth. When Gus was close enough, Samuel grabbed him by the throat and squeezed, just hard enough to sink into the fat. He pulled Gus's ear to his mouth and said, "Go Bast Yourself, and get the Varst out of here before I pop you." Samuel fell back against his hospital bed pillow only after he watched the engorged wood tick nephew run from the room with the speed of a trained athlete, accidentally dropping the recording device as he ran, leaving it pointing in the direction of the two injured men who shared both a hospital room and a secret plan. Samuel didn't want to think about the plan. He wanted to think about what might happen were the plan to fail even less. He remained silent, his eyes involuntarily counting the rows of dots in the ceiling tiles until his brain told them that he didn't want to be doing that, as the eyes rested in one place, the dots began to advance toward him like cloned armies, magically recreating themselves until, "Hey Samuel," Victor's voice quietly pulled Samuel's eyes from the mesmerizing advance, "you okay?"

"Yeah Vic, you?" Samuel responded as both men leaned toward each other to get a visual.

"We have to tell Sal about what happened to the others," Victor continued as his eyes darted to the location of the recording device on the floor then returned to Samuel. "They really did a number on you, Sam, I don't even think your mother would recognize you," Leer added, letting Samuel know that the plan was active, the play had begun, the stage had been set and that everything he would do and say from this moment forward had to happen exactly as they had rehearsed or he and Victor would most likely wind up dead.

"They did a number on all of us, man, and I still can't figure out where the Varst they came from," Samuel responded, clearly understanding his role.

"Too bad you scared off the fat little bastard, we need to let Sal know what happening right away," Leer began, "and you'd better leave telling Sal about Max up to me," Victor warned, "Sal's not going to let this go unpunished and if anyone is responsible, it's me."

"But Victor," Samuel quickly replied, "you couldn't have done anything about it, none of us could, and you know just as well as I do that Max could kick the shit outta half the Farb-damn team, how those bastin' shitheads managed to get the best of her, the best of all of us, I'll never know, but I do know it wasn't your fault."

Just then, the door to the hospital room burst open, "what wasn't your fault, Victor?" Sal was standing in the open doorway. He clearly couldn't have been far away, and in fact he wasn't. One of his goons had seen Gus running down the hall, fleeing the room and intercepted him then quickly notified Sal who was occupying himself with one of the attendants, in a previously empty room doing Farb knows what with surgical tubing and a previously full canister of nitrous. "Tell me now, Victor." Sal demanded, looking strangely out of sorts and clearly in no shape to receive the kind of information Leer was about to lay on him.

"Max is dead." Victor said grimly, Leer knew that he had to drop the whole bomb at once or the plan would fail, "and the shipment is gone." Before Sal could say a word Victor added, "everyone was killed, only Sam and I, and a few others survived. And the Farb-damn, Bastin' shitheads who killed her only left us alive to tell you that they want more juice." Leer delivered the line through clenched teeth and knuckles that strained from the pressure of hands that gripped themselves into fists so strongly that the white bone of the knuckles popped out like polished marbles balanced in perfect rows upon blood-red rocks.

Sal looked to the men in the hospital beds with the stunned expression of a man who had just been told that he had only two weeks to live, then burst out laughing.
It only took a minute for Sal's laughter to turn to tears, but it was a truly agonizing sixty seconds, each one framing a more disturbed snapshot of Sal's seemingly instant descent into madness. It was as though every other part of his body was attached to Sal's face. As his eyes clamped shut, his brow tightened with the strain and the corners of his mouth pulled down as his teeth clenched in rage and despair, a barely audible groaning sobbed its way into the dead hospital air and hung with a sterile darkness. A single tear fell from Sal's eyes before his fingers pressed hard against the locked lids. His body tightened in around his weeping face until he crumpled to the floor, stricken by grief. He lay there sobbing, turning small circles like a fetus in a slow-motion whirlpool.

Suddenly, he stopped, sprang to his feet, leaped to Victor's bed and began pounding Victor's already badly beaten face. "Who the Varst did this?!! Sal hollered as he grabbed Victor around the throat and began choking him to death.

"He can't tell you anything if you kill him," a voice calmly said from the doorway. Dr. Sophia Kirby had seen just about everything imaginable that could happen in a hospital. She had been patching up goons for her brother Sal for decades. Most of the hospital was paid for by Sal. Most of a lot of things in Rat Town were paid for by Sal. Sophia preferred to turn a blind eye to the violence behind Sal's business, figuring that the good she could do because of Sal's investment in the hospital far outweighed any unsavory acts that Sal Lorenzo might actually commit himself. Still, she wasn't about to allow him to beat a patient to death right in front of her.

Sal turned to Sophia, his eyes full of hopeless rage tinged with startled disbelief as he felt the sting of the needle at the base of his neck.

31 SUPERMAN

Blue went up on a mountain and there he sat. He thought about a great many things. He began to picture the paintings he had created while working with Anna Marie, realizing how they had brought him to the place he now sat, or rather how the visions which had inspired the paintings had brought him to this place. Stylistically, the paintings varied, some were illustrative while others were more abstract, though all seemed to speak of an energy which moved through, into, between and around all things, people, places, beings and living things.

Some beings do not perceive light at all. In our human understanding, that would lead us to believe that they therefor do not perceive color. This is simply not true. Color, Blue has come to understand, is not simply a manifestation of light made visible by pigmentation, reflection or refraction. It is also a shade or hue of emotion, thought, breath, philosophy, imagination, blood-food or Sharshanii as the Gnolamaii call it, or any number of other essences, perceived, sensed or otherwise experienced by the multitude of species which inhabit the universe. Painting is one way for the humanoid form to attempt to illustrate the awesome richness of color.

Blue sat, reliving the events of the past few days, trying to understand how each occurrence was related to another, hoping to weave a sensible fabric of truth in which to wrap himself both for protection and reassurance. He had left Earth less than a month before but it seemed like years to him now, leaving behind a society that he had never really fully felt connected with, a humanity which at best, was evolving and developing and at worst killing itself and its home in a blind hunger for more, bigger, faster. He had come to a world, just as developed, technologically, if not more so, yet riddled with the same issues of inequality, violence and greed.

Blue walked to the edge of a large outcropping and threw himself over the side, free-falling, feeling the wind rush past him, watching the river rise to greet him with impossible speed as he ripped into the water sending a liquid plume, thirty feet into the air. Blue darted his way to the bottom of the deep blue river, zipping past curios undersea life, then just as quickly, he shot up out of the water. He rose higher and higher into the sky until he reached a place where he hovered and thought about his next move. How he could easily create for himself a great garden, high walls and an elaborate labyrinthine entrance, a fortress of solitude, just like Superman.

32 BACK ON EARTH

""Superman, Superman, wish I could fly like Superman..." the last known words of a local artist whose house just disappeared last night" CNN anchor Robyne Robinson spoke compassionately with a friend of the missing artist.

"Really, he was singing that Kinks tune, "Superman" as he walked that way, right there, toward his door, well, where his door used to be," Chris Beaker had been Blue's friend for about a year, ever since Blue rushed Chris and his finger to the emergency room, a finger he now stood pointing at the place where Blue's door used to be.

Shortly over a year before Blue's house mysteriously shattered into a thousand bits and disappeared, Beaker removed his own finger with the help of a very dependable radial arm saw and a totally distracting ex-wife who had just hit him in the back of the head with a J clamp from a distance of roughly thirty feet.

His head would have hurt a whole lot more if the finger didn't come off when it did.

Blue just happened to be passing through the building on his way from the liquor store to his car with twelve cold Surlys and enough ice to keep them cold long enough to serve his purposes when he heard the painful cries of the broken Beaker. Blue rushed toward Beaker's shop and bumped directly into ex-Mrs. Beaker who backed into him with the

260

force of a lineman, "and don't even tell me you can't take those kids an extra week after I put up with your fuckin' drinkin' for as long as I did," she wailed to the moaning carpenter, collapsed on his knees, fumbling for his finger through a torturous blur of blood, sawdust and tears.

"Oh!" she half giggled as she saw Blue, instantly fantasizing the various ways she could manipulate the attractive stranger but settling for a slow brush against his ass and thighs as he turned the box of beer away from her girth in an effort to pass through Beaker's doorway, intent on helping the poor wretch. Blue moved too quickly for the ex to even speak. He pulled his shoelace from his shoe and tied off the finger at its base, then found it's missing phalanges. "You okay?" he asked calmly, not expecting a response, pressing ice upon the wound with one hand while burying the finger in the ice with his other.

"We have been friends ever since," Beaker went on, but Robinson was already directing the camera toward an unusual sight just over Beaker's head.

The tree-top above him seemed to curve inward, as if a very large ball had been pressing up against it for an extended period of time. As the camera pulled back to envelop the shot it became clear that this was not the only tree affected in the area. In fact, the entire neighborhood looked as though the same ball had rested across all of the trees at once, pushing them down in unison and leaving a lasting concavity, interrupted by the homes which miraculously remained intact. Only Blue's house was missing; missing to the extent that nothing remained of it or any of its contents. The yard still held all of its special features, the gated archway which until yesterday abutted the south exterior wall, the stone path which encircled the foundation, even the umbrellaed table, with all four chairs remained undisturbed by the inexplicable disappearance of the three story house with finished basement.

"Police are baffled by the disappearance but assure us that every effort will be made to enlist the aid of the experts; once they have determined who the experts might be in a situation such as this." Robinson held her forearm to her brow as she raised her voice against the wind and dusty shrapnel of a landing helicopter. "It appears as though this is about to become a military operation," she continued "several uniformed soldiers have just been lowered into the space left by missing artists missing house. We are being directed to another area as military motorcycles, jeeps and trucks are arriving and surrounding the location." Robinson signaled the crew to cut then strode confidently toward the shiniest of the military vehicles, intent on getting the story which only became more interesting with the arrival of the nation's finest.

Beaker was no longer needed. If anything, he was given the distinct impression that he was actually in the way. As he walked toward his studio building, just a few blocks up the hill from Blue's place, a feint golden glint pierced through his confusion, his eyes pulling his addled brain closer to the source, what appeared to be a coin. He picked it up, examining it quickly. It really looked like gold. It was heavy for its size. It had the words Farb Sees inscribed upon it, as well as an icon which reminded him of the Star of David. He quickly pocketed the coin, uneasily looking around himself to be certain that no one had seen him pick it up. This had to be related to the disappearance of his friend but he'd be damned if he was going to put the only piece of evidence in the hands of the government.

As he continued up the hill he thought about Blue. His hand drifted to his other pocket. Inside was a small kaleidoscope. He was going to return it to Blue that morning. It was one of those kaleidoscopes that distort the real landscape through a series of lenses and mirrors. Beaker turned around to look at the spot where his friend's house had been. He marveled at the oddly shaped trees then lifted the kaleidoscope to his right eye.

Turning the lenses slowly, he stopped suddenly. "SHIT!" "Oh my fuckin' God," Beaker said to himself, half-laughing, half-crying, like a strung out mental patient. There, through the kaleidoscope, he saw the entire valley, the image created by the shape of the trees, the houses, the streets and the mirrors was the same image he held in his hand only moments before. Beaker was certain of one thing, whatever had taken his friend was extremely large and very intelligent. He was fairly certain of another, he was holding on to what might be the only example of extra-terrestrial currency ever discovered, and also, Farb frightened him.

"Well Blue, you finally got what you always talked about," Beaker said to himself as he pocketed the celestial currency, "Robyne Robinson's talkin' about you on CNN!"

33 TRUE BLUE

Blue had been thinking in complete isolation for several hours while watching the sun set on thirteen different worlds simultaneously. The vastness of "All That Is" was revealing itself to him through every atom of his being and he was absorbing it.

If Blue had been a doctor or a rocket scientist, someone accustomed to learning and problem-solving in a conventional sense, his mind would have exploded within the first hour.

But he wasn't, Blue was an artist.

His normal way of thinking about things wasn't what one might call normal to begin with, but he also had a taste for experimentation which opened his mind to possibilities most people write off as fantasy or experiences others may consider too unusual.

Just as the thirteenth sun set, a wave of energy passed through him causing the light of his own being to flare.

Scientists on Earth reported it as an isolated anomaly, stating that there was absolutely no record of a celestial body in that location and that the sudden burst of light coincided precisely with readings indicating a surge in gamma radiation, much like that experienced during a solar flare. When asked whether this sudden flare might be of any concern to the people of Earth they all concluded that the incident was singular and therefor almost certainly unlikely to happen again.

Conspiracy theorists quickly blamed the government and warned that the flare might instead be an explosion from one of the many secret tests the military were conducting to prepare for an imminent alien invasion.

Blue wasn't entirely sure what had happened as his body surged with energy unlike anything he had imagined, and he had just flown into space without any concern for breathing, let alone a destination or purpose.

He felt like an actual star and for all intents and purposes, that is what he had become. A small one but not without mass. In fact, small bits of space matter had begun to take up an orbit around him as he floated through space, all the while the cosmos kept pumping his mind full of revelations, relevancies and an unshakable knowledge that the universe is a creative life force, expanding endlessly in infinite directions and that he could go anywhere in it, at any time.

He had decided that it was no longer important to answer his earlier question of why was it him and not someone else. That really didn't matter anymore. He was chewing through the universal mind-dump like a bear at a buffet table. Blue was working on what he what going to do next when he could do anything in the entire universe and that's when it hit him.

It did matter that it was he who found the Omega Lux Crystal.

It mattered that it was he who became Onjadiavaan. At that time, in the presence of the people of the Shadowlands. It mattered that he was an artist and it mattered that he left Earth and became Tommy Levito on a planet known as Salta. It mattered that he found Anna Marie, saved Mojahdii and met Targent, Sansaa and Vinny. It mattered that he was Blue.

But he wasn't just Blue.

The truth that Blue had already been living, as a man who awoke in another man's body, was only a glimpse into the truth of the universe. So many inconceivable notions of his past were now not only conceivable but were only minor elements of a greater truth. And Blue knew how to use the truth. He understood the purpose of the truth. The truth exists to reinforce and protect what is right.

"The truth exists to reinforce and protect what is right." Blue thought to himself.

He knew that he had to become a beacon of truth in order to protect the people of Salta, but in all of his expansive understanding there was nothing to show him what exactly he was saving Salta from. It was clear to Blue that he was being tested and he had a pretty good idea by whom. If Farb was going to be revealed as "ALL THAT IS," Blue was going to be sorely disappointed.

34 MOMMA

"Farb-damnit, you're back!" Hollered Vinny as he saw Tommy approaching on the path to the village, the same path he had walked out of town on as he left Shedavah behind with Mojahdii.

Sansaa and Anna Marie were sitting with Vinny when Blue approached.

"I am sorry I took off like that," Tommy said as he gave his brother a hug. Vinny grinned and lifted Blue up in the air, "Oh look, I'm flying away," Vinny laughed as he held Tommy over his head like he was weightless. "Hey, wait, Tommy are you doing that?," Vinny asked, not sure of his own hold on Tommy.

"No, it's all you Vin! You drop me, you drop me, that simple." Blue laughed as Vinny eased him back to the ground. "I am so happy to be back," Tommy said as Anna Marie leapt in a single bound to land by his side. The force of her landing would have thrown her into Blue if she didn't have such incredible control of her body. She just looked right into his eyes, advancing toward him only with her lips which he hungrily accepted.

Vinny let out a customary, "Whoot, let me get you a beer!" as he reached for the cooler.

"Hold up for a second, will you Vin?" Blue asked, "I want to tell you something."

Tommy put his arm around his big brother and guided him into the tent he shared with Vinny. Blue had spent the entire return trip preparing to speak with Vinny. He had reasoned out exactly how to say everything to make his explanations to Vinny be the best they could be. What he said instead was, "I'm not Tommy."

Vinny looked at him with a completely blank expression.

Blue repeated, "I said, I am NOT Tommy!"

Vinny continued to look at Tommy, without the slightest change of expression.

"I am Blue, Vinny," Blue said, "My name is Blue."

Vinny laughed, "Of course it is." Vinny smiled, "But you're also Tommy."

At that instant Blue had a sudden flash of memory, but it wasn't his memory, it was Tommy's.

Blue experienced an actual memory of Tommy's as if it was his own and in that single instant he understood everything about his transition from Blue to Tommy, including the time spent as an extra-terrestrial, amphibious lifeform and a living, breathing emoji.

He could finally tell Vinny the truth without concern that he would get it wrong. It didn't hurt that Sansaa had prepped Vinny with a vague story of her own as to how Tommy could be both Blue and Vinny's little brother. And as it turned out, her explanation wasn't too terribly far off the mark. "What do you mean, Vinny?" Blue asked, looking for a way to link Vinny's expectations to the actual truth.

"Sansaa told me that she believed that you could live multiple lives in the same body and that you are still Tommy as much as you are Blue." Vinny went right ahead and cracked a couple of cold ones as he continued, "And as far as I can tell, you're mostly Tommy and if anything, Blue, if you're in there right now," Vinny pointed to Tommy's heart, "I want to thank you for bringing back my little brother. And I don't just mean from the dead. Since you showed up, Tommy has been just like he was when we were kids, before the JumpJuice." Vinny had a tear forming in his eye as he handed Blue a cold beer.

Tommy took a long drink and drained the bottle in a single go. "He looked directly into Vinny's eyes and said, "I remember us sitting at the kitchen table having grape juice for the first time. You were acting normal, but I was blasted outta my mind, jumping up and down and making crazy sounds with my tongue.

You got in trouble for saying I was acting like I was on JumpJuice.

Momma really laid into you, saying that I would NEVER do such a stupid thing like messing with JumpJuice. If she could see me now it would break her heart." Tommy held in a small laugh and continued, "Funny thing is, I can see her looking at me right now and she looks just as real as when she was alive." Blue went on to explain, "I can see whatever I want to see, whenever I want to see it. If I can consider it existing, I can experience it. And since I had all of the understanding of the universe dumped into my brain, I can consider quite a lot." Blue smiled and put a hand on Vinny's shoulder. "I can show you mom," Tommy said as he took his hand from Vinny's shoulder and pointed in front of him.

As he lowered his hand completely to the ground, their mother appeared before them. She appeared to be somewhat in shock. Blue flicked his arm and wrist up in a single motion and a wave of understanding flowed over Angelique Levito. Even though she had died before her boys were men, she recognized them.

"Hello Momma," they said in unison as she reached to hug them both. She was there, with her two sons and they could actually feel their mother in their arms.

"How is this happening?" She asked in dismay.

Blue smiled and held her hand and then she knew.

"Tommy," she said, and she kissed him on the cheek. "And my "not so little" little man, Vincent. You have both grown in to very handsome men." As she said this she began to fade away.

"I love you," the Levitos said in unison, and she was gone.

I guess she went blind after she died," Vinny laughed to himself through his tears, "She thinks we're handsome!"

Tommy put an arm around his big brother and laughed along as both men reached for another beer. Vinny turned and threw open the flap to the massive tent to find Sansaa and Anna Marie waiting outside, smiling and full of love. The women hugged and kissed their men passionately.

"Ahem," a high pitched little yelp sprung from a Targent dying for attention. Just as suddenly, Targent was lifted off the ground by an unseen force and gently nudged down the path in the direction of the village.

Without releasing Sansaa's lips from his own, Vinny held out his fist and Tommy responded with the bump that said, "Yeah, I did that!"

It was an evening of relaxing and enjoying one another's company like Blue had not experienced for as long as he could remember. He could now fully enjoy Vinny's company without fearing that he might be exposed as an imposter, because he wasn't.

He was at once Blue and Tommy, and the Onjadiavaan!

Tommy spent the night reliving some of Vinny's fondest memories of their childhood and Blue was able to remember the sensations because he had actually been there. He even called Vinny out on a few of the more precise details including the time Tommy was grounded for two weeks for breaking the cellar door when it was actually Vinny who tossed him onto the doors in the first place. The worst part was that, no matter what happened, his mother would never believe him when he told her that it was really Vinny's fault, because Vinny was the man of the house and wouldn't play silly games like his little brother would. Still, Vinny was the best big brother a kid could ever wish for. He showed Tommy how to do all of the things the older kids did and he always backed Tommy up, no matter what.

"Hey Vin," Tommy asked out of the blue, "Do you remember that time in second grade when Max Lorenzo came to our house to sell those cookies for her school?" Vinny nodded. "She said that I tricked her and didn't give her the money we owed her. You said that I did and that you saw it with your own eyes. She said that I switched it out and gave her a single instead of a ten and she held up a single. You called her a liar and accused her of trying to pull a fast one over on us. You practically tossed her out on the sidewalk while I just stood there and watched, holding the boxes of cookies," Tommy said as he scratched his head thinking of the best way to put it. "Well, I have to admit that I actually did switch out the money that day. I was trying to be slick and cool because I kinda' had a crush on Max back then. Guess it backfired 'cause she hated me ever since."

Vinny burst out laughing, "You really weren't even close to slick, Tommy. I knew you pulled the switch and I knew that Max saw the whole thing and caught you red-handed. I just wasn't about to stand for a Lorenzo calling a Levito a crook!"

35 WHAT HAPPENED

Sal Lorenzo was propped up in a hospital bed, his wrists and ankles bound to the frame by leather straps, his head balanced on a neck brace. His eyes opened slowly to the sight of two beaten men, also propped up in hospital beds, directly across from him.

"Sorry I had to shoot you Sally," Sophia said calmly as Sal awoke. "I also had to bind you on account of your temper." Sal began to squirm as he realized all she was saying. "But don't fight it hun," Dr. Kirby continued, "The neck-brace is for your own safety. Move that neck of yours the wrong way and the swelling from the shot could cause a momentary lapse of some vital blood-flow to your brain and you'd pass out. Now Victor here is finally able to speak without you beating him to death." She smiled in Victor's direction. Leer wasn't sure how well Victor knew Sophia until she stepped closer to him and kissed him on the forehead. "My niece's man, and you have to go beating on him."

"Max is dead," a drowsy Sal mumbled.

Sophia's eyes immediately grew sharp and angry as she looked to Victor for confirmation. Leer's eyes conveyed a deep sadness and Dr. Kirby sank to her knees and sobbed. No one spoke. The men all looked at Sophia whose head remained buried in her trembling hands. Then the men looked at one another.
Samuel broke the silence, "Max was a Bastin' Varst Beast right from the beginning of the attack. She saved my ass in the first minute when she

272

kicked me outta the way of mortar fire. Blew up one of them big-ass boulders up there on the edge of the pass."

"What the Varst are you sayin' Samuel?" Sal coughed as he tried to sit up. "You guys were ambushed in the pass?" His eyes turned to Victor. "Did they hit you IN the pass Victor?"

Leer knew that Sal knew where they were going to be hit. He also knew that it wasn't supposed to be in the pass. "Yeah Sal, they hit us in the pass." Victor shook his head. "Stupid, obvious place for an ambush and we were ready." Victor continued, "I had just said to everyone in the convoy to keep an eye out, weapons ready and then it hit. We were completely swallowed up by the ground and inside of the ground there were soldiers, trained, armed soldiers." Leer watched Sal look to Samuel. Sal was not going to be satisfied by one story. Victor said, "Samuel, why don't you tell Sal what happened to you?"

This is what Samuel had been training for the whole time since Victor rerouted the shipment. When the beautiful people sat with Samuel they learned everything they ever wanted to learn. Within a few hours of their training, he had become one of them. He could have convinced his own mother that he was someone else's kid.

"I don't want to," he said, like a little boy.

"You have to tell Mr. Lorenzo what happened," Leer urged.

Sam blurted like a five-year-old with a confession, "I jumped outta the truck as soon as we stopped. I had both arms full of everything I needed to blast a hole in anyone and then Max kicked me over." Samuel slowed down a bit and said, "as I fell, I saw the mortar blast a hole in the rock wall behind us, I realized that Max had saved my life and that I still had my arms full of stuff I could kill those bastards with. I rolled backwards and hit my feet with a rocket launcher on one arm and a one-armed Gatling gun on the other. I watched as Max sliced her way through a half-dozen guys on her way toward a group of roughly forty soldiers. I had maybe ten left directly in front of me, so I peeled off a few hundred shells in their general direction and spit against the blood as I tore through them like a barbed-wire drill."

Samuel paused for a moment, looked at Victor, looked back to Sal and continued in a barely-audible, raspy voice, "and that's when I saw her explode. I watched Max explode in front of me. It was like she was the bomb." Samuel's eyes were dripping tears as he looked at Sal and said, "That's when the boot hit me, and I went black."

Sophia had regained her feet while the men were talking and had taken a seat in the corner of the room. After hearing that Max had literally exploded, she got up and left the room.

"Where the Varst were you Victor?" Sal winced as he tried to right himself in the bed.

"I was busy killing everyone in my path as I tried to reach the driver's seat of whatever it was that came from underground and was about to eat the convoy." Victor began to raise his voice, "The deeper I went, the more soldiers came. I had no ammo left, so I continued with my fists. As the sheer number of men overwhelmed me I realized that we were in a vast tunnel and that the thing that was swallowing the convoy was just a part of a much larger system, and that system had an army."

"What about the Juice?" Sal asked, as Leer had expected he would. He had a good cry over the death of his daughter, but it was time to get back to business.

"We launched most it before they could close the tunnel on us." Victor confided, "I have no idea who survived, or how much Juice got through. Didn't anyone check in yet?"

"No," snapped Sal, "I have my men out looking for the shipment right now."

"What about Aldo, Sal," Victor questioned, "shouldn't Aldo be meeting up at the Sin Shack, tracking the shipment? He's our last line of defense!"

"No sign of Aldo either, Victor. No sign of any of them." Sal said as if he had no more energy to speak. He called out for Sophia and then for Gus. He tried to yell for them both but sounded more like a dying lamb. Sal tried to point to Victor's buzzer but his bound hand prevented his finger from pointing directly to it.

Leer knew what he wanted and that was to be out of the hospital. Leer could see that Sal wanted to leave so badly that he could think of nothing else. He began to fight against the constraints, then Victor said, "Easy Sal, I'll buzz for the Sophia."

Sal Lorenzo gave in and sank into the bed.

Sophia returned with Gus and kindly reminded Sal to behave himself as she removed him from his straps.

He stood from the bed and stepped toward Victor. Sophia gently laid a hand on his shoulder. "I think we can remove this now," she said as she undid the Velcro straps on his neck-brace as if releasing a dog that had finally settled down.

Sal continued toward Victor. He grasped the rails of Victor's hospital bed so tightly that his knuckles turned bright white. "I want you to get better, Victor. Then I want you to find my shipment. I will not believe that Max is dead until I see her with my own eyes. Find her and bring her to me. Dead or alive." He turned and walked toward the door, stopping as he reached for the doorknob. "And if you find out who did this, I want you to kill every last one of them. Do not fail me again." He left the room without closing the door behind him. The sound of peanut shells cracking mixed with footsteps trailed off down the hallway.

"I am sure you did all you could Victor," Dr. Sophia Kirby said as she ushered her son through the doorway and left the injured men in peace.

"I can't believe Max is gone either, Sam," Victor said when they were alone.

Sam picked up on the clue that they weren't free to say anything without being under the scrutiny of Sal Lorenzo, the man who built the hospital. "I gotta admit, I would sometimes hope that she'd take a bullet, just so she would shut up. Y'know, yellin' out what to do and how to do it."

If there had been an Oscar for heartfelt confession by a supporting actor on this or any other planet, Samuel had just earned it.

36 HEAVANA

"Get everything down below now," Max yelled, "and do it carefully, we can't leave a mark or a sign that any sort of payload was moved into the sub-chambers." Her voice both annoyed and rallied the men.

Every single one of them wanted her. Even the men who preferred men wanted her, some as lovers, others as friends or even rivals. She drew people into her sphere, without even trying. The team was working as just that, a team, and Max was leading them through the plan Victor had shared with her moments before leaving to fight with Samuel. "All right, all right, if you've finished your jobs, gather around me.

Everyone was there. They had quickly moved every last bit of JumpJuice below. They had removed any sign of moving through the house and the surrounding areas. They were all standing a few hundred yards from the end of the land that Victor had purchased without Max having any clue. That's because Leer had actually bought the land based on a feeling in his gut that happened 15 years before, as a result of something that had happened fifteen years before that.

"Move out," Max yelled as the trucks fell in behind one another as they sped off to a place that can only be described as Heavana.

"Well, leastwise, that's what they call it, for lack of a better word." The tour guide was round and short but moved like a man three times his size, commanding attention with grand gestures and a voice that sounded amplified, "Heavana, the ultimate communal living opportunity on Salta." He guided the team toward the entrance to a grand hotel, of sorts, set in a rural landscape with plenty of parking for the rigs the team had driven in on. "Now I am sure that you all wanted to get settled in as quickly as you can, but I've got you for the next hour or two because we want to make sure that you are going to be happy here." He turns back to face the group just as they reach a large set of double doors. "My name is Gordon, and I am going to be your guide and your admission advisor." If Victor hadn't taken the time to explain Heavana to his team, they would have all bailed at this exact moment. But Leer had a solid plan and the team had grown to trust Victor implicitly since his resurrection. Still, the team stared blankly at Gordon who brushed their disregard aside and continued with his welcome speech. "The first thing I need to know, however," he scolded, "Is whether or not you really want to be here, so you are going to have to convince me. Now all of you in favor of being here, raise your hand and say Heavana!"

Everyone in the team raised a hand while barely uttering, "Heavana."

"Well, you certainly aren't a very enthusiastic bunch," Gordon complained as he held his chin between his thumb and forefinger and searched the sky for what he was going to say next.

That's when Max remembered her training and began to act like a person who really wanted to be joining commune named Heavana. "I'm sorry Gordon," she said sweetly, in a voice the team had never heard before, "It's just that we have all been driving for quite some time and we are a little tired."

Some of the boys began to catch on and did their best to smile. Max motioned in their direction, "Also, it is true that we have been together for many years and the thought of joining a new community is making us a little nervous."

The entire team was slowly coming around to their training and began grunting in agreement.

Gordon perked up considerably and began again, "Welcome to Heavana, the ultimate communal living opportunity on Salta, where everyone is welcome to enjoy the most wonderful moments life has to offer." He turned to the group once again and smiled, "So who wants to be here, raise your hands and say Heavana!"

This time the entire group raised their hands and with a believable amount of enthusiasm shouted "Heavana."

Gordon set off on his monologue with all the zeal of an evangelical preacher, outlining the amenities while enumerating the responsibilities. He informed the group that they would no longer be needing any of their wallets, money, keys to vehicles, phones or personal records. They were, in effect, now in Heavana, and much like the real Heavana, they were no longer of this Salta. They would no longer have communications with anyone outside of Heavana and no one on Salta would ever know they were in Heavana.

Some of the group had already begun to think they might really like it here in Heavana while others were hoping that Victor's plan would come through quickly and that they could go back to the juice.

"Here we have our JumpJuice Bar," Gordon motioned to his left while the entire team stopped and looked left. "I can see that some of you are interested," he grinned sarcastically as he turned right and continued walking, "I'm afraid it'll have to wait until the end of the tour and after you have checked in fully, though I can assure you that it is completely legal and free to all who live within Heavana." A few more of the team started to think that Heavana might actually be the place for them after all. "Now down this hallway to the right of us you will find the fitness area. It is quite extensive, so I recommend touring it on your own. However, I can tell you what we have for you there while we work our way to the garden." Gordon continued as he led the group down an impressive hallway with numbered doors. "You will notice a great number of doors that we will be passing. These are dwellings for your fellow Heavanans. In fact, some of you may end up on this floor, depending on how you fill out your paperwork. I will be there along with my colleagues to help you with any questions should the need arise. So, as I was saying, we have facilities for every sport imaginable here in Heavana. We even have professional teams, should any of you wish to try out. Now I'd be very sure you are qualified before you try out, after all, team captains Michael Jordan and David Beckham are very serious about their sports."

The group, having assumed their roles completely by now, responded with the expected oohs and ahhs as Gordon continued to list off the features of the athletic area. By the time Gordon had reached his destination at the end of the long hallway he had convinced the entire team that this was going to be a fantastic place to chill while waiting for the rest of Victor's plan to unfold.

And that was before they saw the garden.

The hallway opened into a vast valley as large as any they had seen on Salta, except that this one was indoors. "I can see that you are marveling at the vastness of the valley, it's really quite breathtaking," Gordon mused, "And you may be thinking that surely it is the most astounding feature of Heavana, but I can assure you there are many more wonders to behold. But since I have only a limited amount of time with you I would encourage you to investigate all of the possibilities after we pass through the intake area, which is just this way," Gordon guided the group using his entire body as they made a sudden turn to the left and up.

It was a small and unexpected step up then forward through a very narrow corridor which burst open at the other end into a magnificent chamber with vaulted arches and large screen video displays, running a montage of images of cities, parks, wild lands with snow and resorts with sunny beaches. "Everything you are watching on these screens exists for you to enjoy in Heavana. No matter what you choose to do here, you are free to travel to and enjoy everything that Heavana has to offer. The only thing left for you to do is decide!" With a grand sweeping motion of his hand he indicated a row of chairs, neatly positioned and comfortably spaced at a long, curved table. There were seats for everyone for as far as you could see in either direction.

It was time for Max's first practiced line, "Well, I think I speak for all of us when I say, We would gladly sign up for any job to live in such a swell place, but are there jobs that are more for people like us?"

Gordon looked at her with alarm, "What do you mean, "people like you"?"

"Y'know," she sweetly responded, "roadies. I mean, you prolly don't have work for roadies here. Do you?"

"Well of course we do," Gordon eagerly responded. There is work for everyone here. Even if you decide you wanted to be an airline pilot, you could learn how to do that."

"Wait, there are airplanes in Heavana? I didn't think that was possible," Aldo said without thinking.

Gordon responded like it was the most normal question in the world. "Because you think that we are underground and therefore cannot possibly have airlines, am I correct?" Gordon continued without waiting for an answer, "Well, you are right and wrong. Firstly, you are correct that we are underground and secondly, you are completely wrong to think that there can be no airlines underground. Thirdly, we are not literally underground everywhere. Heavana exists in complete unison with Salta but exists completely outside of Salta at the same time even though we share the same planet. In fact, we have vast stretches of land open to the sky where only our airlines can fly. Some of Salta's finest beaches are the property of Heavana and can only be accessed by its residents. And the best part is that all of this now belongs to you, or more precisely to all of us. Please take your seats, fill out your forms, press the submit button at the end, after reading our terms and conditions thoroughly," he chuckled, "and join me over by the double doors behind you when you are finished."

"Hold on a second," Aldo once again questioned, "We just drove in here, no one stopped us. We all got out of our vehicles and all of us, well, except for me, are still carrying weapons and you haven't even noticed them or asked us why we are here? We could probably take this entire place for ourselves right now, just with the weapons we are carrying. What's up with that?" Aldo thought he was being smart, exposing the weaknesses of Heavana, when in reality he was actually putting the mission in danger with his momentary lapse in character he had gone through in Victor's hideout.

"Oh for Farb's sake, Mr. Anderson," Gordon explained as he pulled a small device from his pocket as Aldo gazed at him in surprise, "Mr. Alonso made all of the arrangements before you arrived, hmmmnn!"

Gordon paused as he looked more closely at the device. "Apparently, Mr. Alonso made the arrangements for all twelve of you to arrive fifteen years ago; funny!" Gordon giggled to himself until a hacking voice startled him.

"I ain't known Victor for more than 5 years, ain't no way he knowed I'd be here fifteen years ago," Spike Almary, rasped from behind Aldo.

"You are correct Norman."

"Spike! Everyone calls me Spike!" Spike Spat.

"Yes Mr. Almary, I mean Spike," Gordon responded, slightly rattled despite years of conditioning, "Mr. Alonso filled out the form as though he were filling it out today but fifteen years ago." Gordon beamed slightly as he surveyed the expressions on his new neighbors faces, then he continued, "You see, Mr. Alonso is one of the founding members of Heavana."

He waited and watched their expressions change just a bit before he continued, "And according to this form, in the section marked Recommendations and Referrals, in the space for years known, he has 20 years for Aldo Anderson, 17 years for Andy Reynolds, Gavin Ross, Manny and Franco Fiorelli and Marv Taylor, 5 years for Norman (Spike) Almary, Todd McFarland and Oslo Armijahni and 3 years for Frank Meyers and Lee Camp.

He also wrote in next to the lady's name, "All her life." Gordon raised his head for only a second to ensure that he had their attention and he did.

"So, you are all recommended by the founder of our great community, the only thing left is to sign on." He laughed to himself before continuing, "Oh, and Aldo, as far as not being prepared for you," He pointed to Aldo's shoulder. A small drone lifted up from Aldo's shoulder and locked a bright red beam of light between his eyes. The drones on every other shoulder in the group also rose up and locked on each specific target. Spike tried to swat his away.

"Oh please Spike, "You'll only provoke the poor thing, she's only doing her job." The drone bounced happily up and down in front of the confused Spike. "These little friends of yours will only be with you until you are signed in, then you are free to enjoy all that is Heavana."

Gordon again indicated the row of chairs where the stunned team could sign up to live in a place they'd never heard of for an indefinable amount of time before they could get rich from something they hid a short distance away.

Each of them walked to the chairs slowly as they considered the fact that this moment had been planned fifteen years earlier by Victor Alonso and right now each of them was weighing their trust, not only in Victor but in his whole plan. Each one of them slowly took a seat and began the admission process. Gordon skipped happily toward the double doors where he waited, admiring his own reflection within them.

Some went through the process faster than others and as each of them reached a certain point a small bucket appeared from inside the floor next to their seats.

Max and Aldo's buckets appeared at about the same time and they looked to the buckets, then to one another.

Max was the first to stand.

Aldo slowly rose to his feet as he watched Max reach between her legs for her favorite piece. She lifted it slowly and even more slowly, laid it in the bucket. Every member of the team noticed her movements and nervously looked back at the admission form as she continued by unbuckling her belt and holster, her blades and throwing stars were added to the bucket.

Aldo was transfixed as he watched Max shed her weaponry. His gaze was broken by his little drone who flew in front of his face then hovered by his sidearm.

Aldo got the point and shook off his gaze from Max and slowly pulled his sidearm from its holster.

Max was busy unloading a full arsenal from various parts of her clothing, but the only thing left after Aldo dropped his belt was a knife he kept strapped around his ankle. The happy drone flitted around his hands as he unsheathed the knife then worked to release his ankle straps. As he returned to his admission form the drone went back to his shoulder.

At this point, both Fiorelli twins stood up, turned to each other and laughed. "Should we do it Manny," asked Franco.

"Okay, Go Bro!" Manny replied and the two men quickly removed every weapon the other man had and placed them into the buckets.

Generally, Manny and Franco worked as a team and often in battle they would reach for one another's weapons rather than pulling one of their own. This technique had saved their lives on more than one occasion but it was quite impressive to see it all done at once.

Everyone else in the group fell in line and surrendered their weapons, then went back to filling out the admission form except for Lee Camp and Spike who leaned back on their chairs and saw each other's bewildered expressions.

Spike, who was four chairs away from Lee said, "Hey Lee, they want us to dump ALL of our weapons!"

Camp responded with equal frustration, "Nobody, not even the Farb-damn government has gotten me to drop all of my weapons."

Max leaned back on her chair, she was two away from Camp. "Now gentlemen, you remember what our teacher said," reminding them of their training she continued, "give to Farb what is rightfully his and when serving his will each gift is a blessing."

Lee Camp was kinda the "political criminal" of the group. He justified his every crime by explaining that the government had left him no choice when they decided to enact this or that law. "Well Spike, I hope the lady's right and this isn't just another layer of an oligarchical system where guys like us are used and abused."

As he said this he rose to his feet and disarmed himself. With a look of frustrated acceptance Spike did the same.

It didn't take long for the team to finish up the admission process once all of the arms were dumped. They assembled at the double doors where Gordon was standing. He had been primping himself the entire time the group was filling out their admission forms. He hadn't been the least bit interested in them until he saw all of their reflected eyes looking at his.

"Oh good, you have all finished. Please follow me through these doors and we'll be all finished." Gordon's voice seemed to get so thin it was impossible to hear then suddenly ballooned out until it was so far out that it was unrecognizable as speech.

They had been passing through a chamber that had taken all of the data they entered about themselves and matched it to their DNA. Using indicators collected while they filled out their forms, an algorithm was capable of determining who was who, how they felt and whether or not they could be trusted to do what they said they could do. It also determined where each of them would be most comfortable within the community. "I am so happy to welcome all of you to Heavana," were the first words they could all hear clearly from Gordon since they followed him through.

"This is where you get everything you need to begin a life with us, here in Heavana." He pointed across an expansive lobby with a check in desk which stretched around a turn and out of sight.

"If you're in no hurry, we have the JumpJuice bar to my left, your right, just around that turn, just past the column. I should let you know that you may begin consuming anything you'd like for as long as you'd like and there will never be a bill. You do not have to start working until you have settled into your residences and have your bearings. If you do not show up at your assigned workplace within two weeks of your arrival, a member of the Heavana staff will be assigned to bring you to work and train you in." Gordon smiled and continued, "No one in Heavana works more than twenty hours per week, the is no charge for health care and it is rarely needed as nearly all food is farm to table here. You can cook within your own residence at any time but there are also open table events all day and night long throughout Heavana. All of these events can be found with a simple app that is standard with every phone. You can pick up your phone when you pick up your clothes. They are available at most department store outlets as well as in unique shops all over Heavana. You are free to choose any clothing you want at any time." Gordon stopped as he realized that the whole shared living concept was far beyond what any of this group could imagine.

"Maybe it's time for you to see your new homes," Gordon smiled as he raised both of his arms in the air. A dozen people suddenly scurried into place, one for each member of the group. "These lovely people will be your guides. They will get you settled in and up to speed on your new life, here in Heavana!"

"See you around," Gordon chuckled as he walked directly to the JumpJuice Bar.

37 A TASTE OF BLUE

"Who do you see when you look at me?" Tommy asked Anna Marie.

"I see the Onjadiavaan," she answered without hesitation.

"I see Tommy asking weird questions," Vinny laughed, "who's right?"

Sansaa stood up and put a hand on Vinny's shoulder, "Let's go grab a few things from the village and leave these two alone for a minute," she smiled and Vinny got the hint right away.

As they left the tent Vinny turned back to them and said, "I see Tommy," then laughed his way out of the tent.

After Tommy knew that Vinny and Sansaa were out of earshot he asked Anna Marie again, "Who do you see when you look at me? I mean with your soul."

His question caught her off-guard but was the perfect one for him to ask.

From the moment Tommy began painting his dreams, Anna pictured him as a completely different person from Tommy. His build was different, his mannerisms were different, even his eyes were different. She told Mojahdii about it and he told her that she must be seeing his body as Blue, but this made her feel awkward because she felt closest to him when he looked like Blue.

When they flew together, he looked like Blue. When he pulled Shedavah from inside Mojahdii's belly he was Blue. "I see you as Blue, I think," she bit her lip as if tasting the thought, "and I think I like looking at Blue more than Tommy." She said as she held even tighter to Tommy.

Tommy reached up and took her hands from his shoulders as they rose to their feet. Using her hands as guides he turned her body to face away from him. She moved up onto point to make the movement a dance and as he let loose of one hand and turned her back toward himself with the other she saw that he had become Blue.

Anna Marie smiled and laughed as she danced along with every movement Blue initiated. He had become the dancer he had always dreamed he was when he was a young man and far better. One of the benefits of being Onjadiavaan is that you can pretty much do whatever you think you can and Blue was beginning to feel that in every fiberoptic fiber of his being. He was channeling energy at all times and could alter the degree at will.

They danced as if gravity had no sway over them.

Blue felt like he was dancing in a Disney movie and Anna Marie was the most beautiful princess of them all. Lovely little flowers bloomed, bursting forth from every footfall.

They had, in fact, created a carpet of fresh flowers on the floor of the tent. Their movements slowed as the scent of the flowers rose. Their movements grew closer and closer until they were wrapped in each other's arms, Blue's body passionately moving into Anna Marie's upon the bed of flowers.

"I like the way you took my clothes off," Anna Marie sighed as they lay upon the flowers, staring at the roof of the tent.

"I like the way you continued to dance, so in time with everything," Blue smiled, "You are truly beautiful."

Anna Marie threw one leg over Blue and rolled up on top of him and began kissing him. As she pulled up to look at him she realized that he had become Tommy.

"Oh Varst, I mean, sorry, I never, um," Targent blurted as he covered his eyes in the doorway of the tent.

"Step outside Targent," Tommy said sternly but calmly.

Targent backed out of the tent. He spun around and looked at his feet, then spun again and looked at the sky. He whistled, did a little beatbox and a few moves, then convulsed in bizarre laughter as he moved his hips like he was chopping ice with his penis, then stopped laughing abruptly and stood very still, self-consciously looking around until he saw two figures approaching from the village. "Hey, don't look!" He called out as he pointed over his shoulder at the tent entrance.

Vinny and Sansaa continued slowly toward the tent and stopped next to Targent. "Caught 'em naked didn't 'ya Targent," Vinny whispered as he winked.

Targent blushed. "You decent bro?" Vinny called out.

"Yep," Tommy responded. Vinny saw Tommy and Anna Marie lying next to one another on large reclining chairs with the cooler open next to Tommy as a cold one flew toward his own head. He reached up and caught it in stride.

"Thanks bro, don't mind if I do!" Vinny set down a bag filled with his favorite snacks and opened the beer.

Sansaa put down a bag she was carrying and dropped into a recliner next to Anna Marie who handed her a beer. Targent was sheepishly standing it the flaps of the tent.

"I bet you don't drink beer, do you Targent?" Tommy asked, knowing the answer before Targent shook his head. Blue knew a lot of things about a lot of people. "A little JJ Cola is more your speed, am I right, " Tommy said as he pulled a can from the cooler and tossed it to Targent who had to step fully inside the tent to catch it. "Have a seat," Tommy continued, "I am curious about your reason for coming here, do you mind sharing it with us?"

Targent hadn't been spoken to like that since he met Mojahdii.

Everyone assumed because he walked differently than most people and because he did peculiar things, that he was somehow different, and they were right, just not in the way they thought they were.

Blue recognized just how alike he and Targent truly were and knew how important feeling welcome truly is.

"Thanks Onjadiavaan," Targent said as he sat across from Tommy.

Vinny was about to laugh at the formality of Targent's response but recognized in Tommy's eyes that he was being the Onjadiavaan and at that moment quite intensely.

Targent didn't even notice Vinny.

Tommy just sat and waited. "I came here to meet you." Targent took a small sip on his JJ Cola, then he took a longer one. Tommy did not respond, Tommy waited. "You see, I knew you were the Onjadiavaan before everybody, well not everybody, there is Mojahdii and I would imagine Farb." Targent stopped talking when the tangent had gone into a much deeper thought than he had intended talking about. "What I mean to say the point is, is that, well, I pretty much knew you were the Onjadiavaan long before I ever saw you and I never even met you, so I figured I had to and so I travelled pretty far to find you here."

The only person in the tent who realized fully how deep this explanation went was Blue.

"That's remarkable, Targent," Tommy said with enthusiasm. "I had no idea I was going to become the Onjadiavaan but you did, and we ended up here together sharing beer and cola!"

Targent felt relieved and accepted and actually relaxed into his chair.

"Is there anything you wanted to ask?" Tommy was genuinely open to answering any question that Targent wanted answered.

"Why do you think it was you who got to be Onjadiavaan?" Targent blurted out then burped for punctuation. He tried to hide behind his can of cola but he had already said it and everyone could sense a deep jealousy behind his voice.

Tommy crossed one leg over the other and laying further back in his recliner said, "Because I didn't want it." He could see the anger growing in Targent as he continued, "I didn't even know the Omega Lux Crystal existed, let alone Shedavah which is the very reason I found it." Tommy smiled and added, "Any other questions?"

Targent practically exploded as he jumped out of his seat screaming, "You have no idea!" at the top of his lungs.

He began to beat himself in the face with his own fists as he ran out of the tent.

Both of the women sprang to their feet and moved to exit the tent.

"Hold up!" Tommy said quickly but quietly. He motioned toward their chairs and said, "please, sit back down."

They consented, but both of them turned and said in unison, "That was cruel."

Still, very quietly, Blue said, "He has to accept the fact that he would never have become Onjadiavaan because his desire for it made it unattainable. The cruelty would have been sheltering him from that lesson, prolonging his misguided vision of himself as Onjadiavaan."

Both women relaxed back into their chairs as Vinny said, "Tommy that was deep, Blue, Onja-Dog, whoever you are, I think I get it!"

"Of course, you do, Vinny, I think you'd make a great Onjadiavaan!" Blue laughed as he pulled a soft pretzel from one of the bags that Vinny brought back, watching Vinny's eyes follow it the whole way until he held it up with one hand and warmed it with the other, heat clearly coming directly from Blue's palm, but for only a moment. He placed it on a small wooden plate on a table just next to the cooler then reached into the cooler and pulled out a bottle of yellow mustard. Tommy squirted the mustard onto the plate then ground a small pile of fresh salt next to the mustard. He handed the plate to Vinny. "Just like that, right Vinny?"

Vinny smiled as he took the plate, "Just like that bro, just like that."

38 DR.KIRBY

Leer had shape-shifted so many times in his life he had become accustomed to it but there is no way of knowing how each new body reacts.

Victor's body had done remarkably well, so it was no surprise to Leer that Victor was already healing from the massive beating he got at the hands of Samuel, who unfortunately, hadn't been resurrected recently and was stuck with the body he was born with. Some of the energy Blue was channeling when he and Leer arrived on Salta must have lingered in Victor's body because he was ready to leave the hospital just hours after rolling up to the curb outside of the Opera.

"Samuel," Victor said as he climbed out of bed, "it's time to get outta here." Samuel did his best to move but was in terrible pain. "It's okay Sam," Victor reassured, "I'll get help."

Leer glanced quickly at Sam's chart and left the room but didn't go anywhere near a nurse or a doctor. He had been in more hospitals than most doctors and was a far better nurse than any. He had no trouble finding the medications he was looking for after a quick walk down the hall and an unceremonious picking of a rather inferior lock.

When he returned to the room, Samuel was watching the equivalent of the WWF, hurting himself as he yelled at the men on the screen to do moves that apparently neither one of them could do.

"Settle down Sam," Victor laughed, "your gonna hurt yourself more yellin' at them goons than if I beat you up all over again."

"I think I won that fight, Victor," Sam tried to smile but winced noticeably instead.

"Sure did Tiger," Leer smiled as he gave Sam a decent dose of morphine. It was only a minute before Sam was just a very heavy lump of hard to position flesh that Victor miraculously guided into a wheelchair.

"Sophia," Victor called out to Dr. Kirby as she looked through charts behind the nurse's station.

"Is there something I can help you with Mr. Alonso," a frightened nurse said from behind the desk. Leer forgot for a moment that nearly everyone in the hospital probably knew Victor. He was able to read the nurses name badge but figured Victor never would have given a damn about the nurse so he never would bother with her name.

"Um, no, uh, thank you, I see the Doctor," Victor answered clumsily as the nurse opened the small door to let him back to see Sophia Kirby.

"I am going to take Sam back to my place and let him sleep it off there," he confided, "Is there anyone left I can trust that you can call to pick us up?"

Sophia thought about it for a while and said, "Nope. But I'm finishing up here. You boys gave me a little overtime and I just have to make a note of that here." She said as she wrote a few notes in a folder and handed it to the nurse. "I'll take you home Victor, and empty your pockets, you know you don't have to steal from me to help out your boys. Farb knows I been patchin' you boys up enough for two lifetimes, but I gotta record where all my meds go, you hear me?"

Victor shamefully emptied his pockets of the morphine, some bandages, syringes and a small bottle of Phlagene, a medicinal version of JumpJuice that's like JumpJuice on steroids might be, if steroids existed on Salta, which they do, so it's just like that only better or worse, depending on whether or not you were counting on having a conversation with the person on Phlagene within the next day or so.

Sophia just smiled and walked to the medicine supply room where she wrote down what was in Victor's pockets and called out, "And how much did you hit him with before you dumped him into that chair?" "20," Victor called out as Sophia shook her head and kept writing.

"You boys are always the same, you can't do anything the right way, nothing normal. Gotta steal it or it isn't any fun," Dr. Kirby put the meds in a bag and handed them to Victor. "Sometimes, Victor, the proper channels are far better than you'd expect."

"I'm sorry, doc," Victor said like a little boy.

Sophia was a lovely lady, on Salta or any other planet, she's the kind of humanoid others like to be with, entirely genuine, caring and smart.

Leer felt terrible that he couldn't let her in on what was happening, especially with Max, but there was no safe way he could. It would put their entire plan at risk and may even endanger her if Sal got even an inkling that something suspicious was going on.

Sophia drove the men to Victor's house and helped Victor get Sam inside and laid out on a very large and comfortable couch. As she and Victor loaded up her vehicle with the wheelchair from the hospital Victor asked her a question. "How do you keep this up, Sophia?"

She looked at Victor and understood what he was asking her. It was a question Victor would never have asked in the past. She had heard that Victor was different after the resurrection, but this was something beyond what she was expecting. She knew that he was talking about Sal, the JumpJuice, the hospital, the Opera, the whole cycle of what her life had become in a family where great love and great violence sat in direct balance to one another and she said, "Until today, it was always Maxine." She sobbed uncontrollably into Victor's arms.

He held her in silence for a long time, then said, "Keep going Dr. Kirby, we need you."

She lifted her eyes to his and saw that he was sincere.

"It's going to get better," Victor continued, not taking his eyes off of Sophia's, "I promise."

"Thank you, Victor," she said quietly, got into her vehicle and drove away.

Victor's house was immense. Being with Max, Leer had only gotten a quick feel for the house and missed several rooms as he tried to learn more about Victor.

Sam was out on the couch for at least the next several hours so Victor was free to look around the house like a person who had never been there, which was nearly true. He had a great many refrigerators, TVs, game rooms, five of them, a couple swimming pools, steam room, sauna and an athletic facility that would serve a pro sports team.

And he had a tower.

Right up from the center of the house arose a great tower with a long, spiral staircase and, more conveniently, an elevator. Victor took the elevator to the top floor. It was a full restaurant with a bar but without the restaurant because there wasn't a wait staff, kitchen staff or even a bartender.

So, it was a dining room.

A dining room that looked like a restaurant that could seat about sixty, but tonight it was just Victor, who wasn't particularly hungry and wasn't entirely Victor.

Outside the dining room, through large automated sliding doors was a balcony, It surrounded the restaurant and provided a view of everything around Victor's house which was situated at the top of a hill. The only thing taller than the top of Victor's house was the next highest hill.
The house that sat on top of that hill belonged to Sal and you could see it from Victor's house. With binoculars, you could see inside it.

There was a telescope mounted on top of a small outlook on Sal's house, it was pointed toward Victor's house. Victor had a flagpole installed between his favorite place to sit on his balcony and Sal's telescope. He has flown a flag of Salta as well as the Alonso and Lorenzo family crests, from that pole ever since. Today Leer sat in that very same spot, looked to the sky, threw his hands in the air as he arched his back over the backrest of his chair, joined the fingers of his hands behind his head and said, "we need to talk."

39 JOHN

"Excuse me," Tommy said as he stood up, "I need to go somewhere for a bit, I'll be back soon." He didn't bother walking out of the tent, taking a running start or even looking up. He just disappeared.

"Hello Leer," Blue smiled as he appeared directly across from Leer, in another chair, hidden from Sal's telescope by the massive flags.

"Thanks for coming," said Leer as both men stood up, shook hands then hugged one another.

"Absolutely, how's it going being Victor?" Blue asked without really needing the reply.

"Good, you? Tommy, all that?" Leer responded.

"Good, yeah, me too." Blue said as he floated off the ground, just a little.

"So, you can fly now. And apparently teleport, and receive thought messages, what else can a Quanji do?" Leer asked Blue, still trying to understand why they ended up in the bodies they did.

"Well, John, I am not really sure." Blue wasn't sure of much and at the same time he felt connected to everything. It was no longer difficult for him to comprehend being Blue and Tommy at the same time, or even that he was being called Onjadiavaan by all of the people in the Shadowlands but he still had no answer about whether or not he was Leer's Quanji because a Quanji is a guide, destined to help another find true meaning and purpose.

Instead, Blue felt like he had found his own purpose.

He just wasn't sure what to do next, but everything that pulsed through him told him to just let it happen. "Dude, I don't know why, but I'm apparently a very important part of something much bigger and the people here call me Onjadiavaan."

Leer practically jumped higher than Blue was floating when he heard the news. "Onjadiavaan? Really? That's remarkable, do you have any idea what this means?" Leer continued, "You can do far more than any Quanji I have ever heard of if you are the Onjadiavaan. Did you learn about the cosmos, y'know, the big picture?"

Blue nodded.

"So, you got it all, the big mind dump!" Leer grinned as Blue nodded.

"And your brain didn't explode!" Leer laughed but Blue looked disappointed. "Why so Blue?"

John knew that Blue hated that joke long before Salta, he also knew it would snap him out of it.

Blue confessed, "I really wanted to be your Quanji and help you find your destiny."

John smiled and said, "We aren't home yet, who knows what the future holds? Oh wait, do you?"

Both men laughed, then Leer said, "Y'know Blue, I am getting a lot of memory flashes. I was here before." Leer was trying to focus but could only grab pieces of the memories. "Thirty years ago, I was here. I was Victor. I was alone, in a room, on a folding chair. I had just been beaten." Leer was sweating as the memories came. "Next, It's fifteen years later, that's fifteen years ago. I am still Victor, only now I am not alone. Four others are behind me. I am second to last to sign a document, as I sign, I am aware that the last space is empty, waiting for his signature, the last, most important signature of all, and then I feel his hand on my shoulder as I move away, and he takes the seat as I hand him the pen. I shake the hand of a beautiful woman who kisses my cheek and calls me silly."

"It sounds as though you are the one who can tell the future, have you tried to look ahead?" Blue was curious because he had started to see some visions that he felt almost certain were glimpses of the future.

"I am only getting little flashes, just bits and pieces, but you and I are there." Leer answers while pressing his forehead, hoping to squeeze out anything he can.

"Can you see anyone else?" Blue wonders as he experiences a vision of his own.

"I can see Max and a couple of women I can't recognize along with a few men, including Vinny, your brother, sorry, I mean Tommy's brother." Leer rarely confuses lives he travels through.

"Hey, it's not a problem," Blue explains, "Turns out Vinny is an amazing guy, he knows I'm the Onjadiavaan and Blue and Tommy all at the same time but he just acts like I'm his brother."

"Well, you aren't, and someday, soon I hope, you're gonna leave, and I'm leaving with you!" Leer adds, "it's only gonna be harder if get too attached!"

"Um, about that, there's someone else I am growing attached to," Blue confesses. "She helped me become Onjadiavaan through painting."

Leer looked at Blue and saw that he was gone. It was clear that, at this rate, Blue was going to have an extra travelling companion. He wasn't going anywhere without the girl. Leer, on the other hand, was busy denying to himself that he had any interest in Max, beyond the mission, so he wasn't exactly the one to judge. Still, he felt obliged to be the wiser, more seasoned space traveler and asked, "You know you can't take that girl with you back to Earth, don't you?"

"No, I don't" Blue said reflexively. As he thought about it more, it still didn't make sense to him. "I mean, that doesn't really make any sense. I can do things no ordinary human can do and I haven't even tried to do what I want to do yet. Well, except for one thing. No, strike that, I have done a couple of things I wanted to do right away. Even more reason to believe I can bring Anna Marie with me." Blue looked at Leer.

"Oh, so it's Anna Marie, then." Leer continued, "Well, in that case."

"Do you know Anna Marie?" Blue asked.

"Anna Marie, no, I don't think so." Leer laughed, "Besides, it doesn't matter, you can do anything you want. At this point it just looks like I'm along for the ride. However, I will need you to explain to me how you can be Blue and Tommy and stay both when it's time to head home."

This was the first time John had mentioned Earth as home and Blue felt that his friend was tired of being Leer.

"I can't really do that right now John, but I am going to get us home and do whatever I came here to do." Blue promised as he placed a reassuring hand on Leer's shoulder.

"Well, about that, Blue. I am in some pretty deep shit with Sal Lorenzo right now and I need your help." Leer shook his head and continued, "and there's Max to think about too. I mean, she's a dead ringer for Mona AND Catherine and I can't seem to resist her, even though I know she isn't either."

"Can I take a look?" Blue asked as his eyes fell on Leer's hands. His friend held them out and Blue held them firmly. "I can see everything as long as you remain open," Blue stated, "For example, I am now completely aware of your plan and it seems a little risky! How well did you train those people? And how in Salta did you plan this fifteen years ago?" Blue laughed through the rush of information coursing through his senses. "Never mind," he said, "I see it now." It took only minutes for Blue to see the entire picture of what Victor was going through with Sal as well as the years leading up to the plan. "I had no idea." Blue said to Leer after a long silence. "I had no way of knowing what I was doing back then, John. I never would have started drawing *Leer,* if I had known."

"I don't hold you responsible, Blue. I mean, I was the one doing the writing," John added, "I should have seen it coming. I knew she was stepping into that explosion and I didn't do a damn thing to stop it." John was doing his best to relate a story that happened to him over thirty years in the past but Blue had just experienced it in its entirety, in an instant. "I thought I was losing my mind, Blue. I had fallen in love with my own character, a woman I made up, based on a dream, and I was losing her. I tried everything I could think of, an alias, a case of mistaken identity, but no matter what I tried, the story kept unfolding and as it continued, the more inevitable it became." John looked at Blue with profound sadness. "I woke up in an airport I had never seen before, wearing Leer's clothes, his passport and a currency, at that time unfamiliar to me, in my pockets. I felt just like Leer. All of my senses were heightened, without suffering the blindness. From that day, I lived out the Leer story as I had imagined it, where both Catherine and Mona were dead." John looked for reassurance, "You saw it for yourself Blue, I never came back. You pulled me out of a world, I had created, where the woman of my dreams had died twice, then you brought me to this one, where I just killed her for a third time."

"Well, technically she's not dead and It's a pretty good plan, the more I think about it." Blue responded excitedly. John looked at him with cautious enthusiasm. "This might just be the answer to everything." Blue continued as he looked to the sky, "And let's talk about Heavana before we do anything else."

40 A NEW HOME

Max was the first one of the team to be admitted to Heavana. The written application had asked the customary questions regarding the applicant's willingness to observe and uphold the laws of the community.

While the terms and conditions included a clause whereby the team had signed away any rights they had to carry weapons, only a few had actually read that part.

The slight eruption that burst forth from Spike upon finding out that he wasn't getting his weapons back was quickly stifled by Max's perfect performance. "I hear you, Spike." She hollered as she stepped up into his face, "but you know who hears all and sees all," Max quickly continued with even more enthusiasm, "and we have made a commitment to Farb himself, that we will do his will." She reached into her pocket and pulled out a shiny red coin. "It's like it says on the money, He Sees, He Knows, In Farb We Trust." Max holds the coin right in front of Spike's face, grabs his hand and shoves the coin into his palm, "and you can take that to the bank!"

The person assigned to Max gently put a hand on her shoulder and said, "He won't be needing any of that here."

Both Max and Spike looked at her with disbelief. "I'm keeping it," Spike said, "I dunno what your talkin' about but I'm not givin' back a fifty."

Barbara, Max's admission agent, smiled at Spike like he was a little boy and said, "Oh you go right ahead and keep it, throw it away, eat it, I don't care and quite frankly neither should she. That money is of no use to any of you. We don't use it here." She smiled as they stared at her. "You're perfectly welcome to keep your currency as a souvenir, but it's absolutely worthless."

"Are you telling us that no one uses money here for anything?" Max asked, truly realizing it for the first time.

"That is correct," Barbara said definitively.

Max felt surprisingly liberated at the prospect. Not that she had ever wanted for money, but money certainly played a big role in her life, whether she wanted it to or not. "So what do we have to do next?" Max asked.

"Nothing," Barbara smiled. "You've already completed the Admission Form with all the information we need about you to get you started, living in our community." Barbara laughed a self-conscious laugh then said, "Well, I guess there is one more thing you have to do. You have to enter Heavana. Step through this door and you are officially a member of our community.

Max walked through the door and saw a circular garden ahead of her.

"Go ahead, Dear," Barbara said as Max continued toward the center of the garden, "Keep going 'til you get to the center," Barbara guided Max as the rest of the team were led by their agents. When they had all reached the center of the garden Barbara made an announcement.

"From here, we can bring each of you to your new home. We are here to help you settle in. You can ask us anything you'd like."

"How will we find each other" Aldo asked immediately.

"Well, we agents will show you everything you need to know about the communication system we use in Heavana. It's quite functional and very current. For example," she continued as she pulled the equivalent of a tablet phone from her pocket, "you are all listed as the most recent people in Heavana."

She turned the tablet in their direction so they could see the list of their names. "Each of you will have several of these, in your home to use freely," she points to the tablet, "so you can find each other right away." Barbara had welcomed thousands of people to Heavana and she could see that this group was ready to move on with their own agents. "So Welcome to Heavana, please go with your agents and enjoy your new home!"

The team split up and went with their respective guides. Max wondered how Victor and Sam were faring with Sal and how he took the news of her death, but more than that, she was missing Victor.

41 MEMORY

"How is it that you ended up being partially responsible for creating Heavana?" Blue asked incredulously, "And why didn't you tell me you already met Farb? Clearly, this isn't the first time you inhabited Victor's body. right?"

"That's just it Blue," John confessed, "I have no fucking idea!" He leaned in close to Blue even though no one was near them, "I can barely remember any of it and the parts I can all run together like a music video on Vh1."

Blue began to laugh but realized it was inappropriate. Even so, John stopped telling his story. "What?" John asked pointedly. "Seriously Blue, what's so damn funny?"

Blue apologized, "I'm sorry, John, it's just that, well, that's not really a thing anymore."

"Whaddya' mean it's not a thing? What's not a thing, Blue?" John continued, feeling slightly hurt and a bit left out, "music videos or Vh1?"

"Both really," Blue said, "I mean, they still exist, it's just a lot different than when they were first starting out. But I'm sorry, I know it's not funny that you can't fully remember life as Victor before."
"No Blue, it's worse than that," John lamented, "I can't remember full chunks of my life as Leer or as John!"

Blue did his best to keep a straight face when he responded, "I can't remember all of one life, let alone three. I mean, seriously John, I remember you really well but I don't remember a ton of specific things that we did together, no offense. I just figured it was age."

It's true that Blue didn't remember specific things that he and John did together very well, until his transformation. Once he changed and took Shedavah into space, he remembered every single detail of every single second of his life alone and with others. What he was seeing now, by holding John's hand, was everything John had lived as Leer, Victor and John, at least everything John opened himself up to reveal.

While Blue held his hand, John began to remember as well. "You're doing this, aren't you Blue?"

Blue smiled calmly.

John's face was a kaleidoscope of expressions as he remembered all the tiny details of the lives he had lived and lived inside. He remembered exactly how he became Leer. "I wished that I could follow her" he blurted out as the memory of the wish crossed his mind, then just as quickly his eyes went blank as the memories streamed through his brain.

Blue wanted to talk about Heavana but no longer needed to, the answers were all in John's past. The men sat for hours as the memories poured in and as they did, Blue and John began to think as one. They had spent hours reliving moments from the past then transitioned into planning for the future. They began to finish one another's sentences and didn't bother stopping to acknowledge the fact. They had become a single, immensely powerful source of creation.

42 BUY A GUN

Targent was bathing in the river, scrubbing himself and mumbling when an intense and uncontrollable shudder ran through him. He quickly jumped into his clothes and ran to Sansaa's tent. He barely stopped at the entrance as he bellowed, "It's me, Targent, I need to see Blue Tommy," he burst through the tent flaps, "Tommy, I mean Onjadiavaan, I'm sorry, I- I -I."

"He isn't here," Vinny said as he stood directly in front of the trembling Targent.

"W-W-Where – er -is he?" Targent mumbled as he tried to understand what drove him to rush into the tent in the first place.

"Out," Vinny replied. "He went out. Can I help you with something?" Vinny said with little to no enthusiasm.

"Um, well I, I mean," Targent tried to explain why he rushed into the tent. "You see, Vinny, I was washing myself in the river," he laughed shyly to himself, "y'know, the way I like to. I mean all of you think it's strange but where I'm from we all do it every day. I don't think there's really anything wrong with it, I mean it's just a bath," his eyes travelled up to Vinny's stare, "and like I was saying I was just there, minding my own business when I felt this strange feeling like I had to come here."

"Why was that?" Tommy said as he stepped through the entrance of the tent to a place directly behind the startled Targent who screeched and jumped a good three feet into the air.

Vinny burst out laughing.

Targent landed on all fours like a frightened cat, then curled up into a little ball, holding his knees as he rocked on his feet and said, "I don't know why I had to come here and find you and now you're here and I'm so sorry Onjadiavaan that I ever got jealous, that I ever thought I could be Onjadiavaan, I'm sorry, I'm sorry, I'm sorry."

"Stand up Targent," Tommy said kindly. "The reason you are here is because I called you here."

Targent stood up as he and Vinny looked at Tommy with the same bewildered expression. It was as much a "why me/why him" bewilderment as it was a "how the Varst?" bewilderment and neither of them could speak.

Blue looked at them with a calm strength that caused them to back toward a pair of unoccupied chairs within the tent where they reflexively sat down as Tommy stood in front of them.

"I need your help, Targent," Tommy said with a smile as he flipped a blue coin in Targent's direction. Targent caught the coin and stared at it as Tommy continued, "I want you to deliver a message."

The coin that Tommy flipped to Targent was a 1k Blue, which was equivalent to a week's pay for an average citizen of Rat Town.

Targent continued to look dumbfounded.

"I know you don't need any money Targent, and that you are happy here, but I am asking you to go into the city." Tommy explained, "I'd like you to buy something for me, will you do it?"

"Uh, uh, I mean, uh, of course Onjadiavaan, of course I will," Targent said with quiet obedience as he cautiously continued, "but why me? I mean, I'm absolutely horrible with people and I've never even been to Rat Town."

"Precisely. Good, I want you to buy a gun." Tommy said to a double drop-jaw from Vinny and Targent. "It's not just the gun I want, it's also the holster and belt." Neither Vinny nor Targent were moving at all, not eyes, not jaws, not even their tongues, as Blue continued, "and it's tailored for a woman. You can't miss it, the gun goes right here," he thrusts his hand as if holding a pistol directly down between his legs. With his other hand he holds his index finger up to press against his lips to silence Vinny who undoubtedly recognizes the description of the gun and knows it must be the one belonging to Max.

Anna Marie and Sansaa enter the tent to see Tommy with his hand between his legs pressing his finger to his lips while Vinny and Targent look on.

"Hello ladies," Blue smiles as he holds up his pistol fingers and blows across them, a stream of smoke from the end of his gun. Just because he could, he made the smoke real. He turned to the ladies and began to dance toward them as a glitter ball and laser lights suddenly burst forth with music none of them had ever heard playing at the perfect volume as he danced toward Anna Marie. Suddenly Tommy stopped in his tracks held up a single finger and everything paused. He had actually only paused the music and the lights but since everyone was still a little stunned, no one was moving, except Tommy who turned to Targent and asked, "Can I trust you?"

Targent looked at Tommy with eyes that said "I'm terrified so of course" and said, "What exactly am I being asked to be trusted about? Can I do it? Will I screw up? Probably, I don't know. I mean, Yes, you can trust me."

"Good," Blue quickly replied, "Now I'm going to drop you right outside the place, right in the alley. It's a little pawn shop. I know they have the gun right now, so don't waste any time. Oh and you might feel a little sick."

Targent was gone instantly.

Tommy restarted the music and the lights and the dancing toward Anna Marie.

"WAIT," she said, "What was that about a gun?"

Blue paused the music and the lights and looked at Anna Marie.

Blue eliminated the music and lights and answered Anna Marie, "There's something I have to do for a friend. It would take longer than I have to explain it," he said as he took one step closer to her before he drew her off her feet by sheer force of will and he held her and kissed her. "I have to go as soon as Targent gets that gun." Blue said as he stepped away from Anna Marie.

Suddenly Targent materialized directly next to Vinny who reached out and grabbed the surprised Targent as he lost all control of his legs.

Vinny placed him gently in a chair and took the gun and holster from the recent arrival's shaking hands.

"Sorry to leave him with you, but please take care of him," Blue said, "Coming along Vinny?" Blue asked as Vinny handed him the gun.

"Anywhere you're goin' bro."

And they were gone.

43 BEER

Leer had absolutely no trouble adjusting to two men popping up out of nowhere in his living room but Vinny was not expecting to materialize in the living room of Victor Alonso.

The feeling wasn't one of anger or hatred, it was more a feeling of intense nausea. Vinny felt like he was going to vomit all over Victor's house and he didn't really want to do that, yet at the same time he felt like Victor had it coming.

After all, it was because of Victor that his brother died. On the other hand, it was because of Victor that his brother came back to life as some sort of superhero. As he tried to sort out his inner conflict, his nausea amplified his discomfort.

"Sorry about that Vinny," Blue said as he helped Vinny find a nice place to sit and rest after the instant transport made his stomach feel like it was riding a roller coaster while the rest of him stayed put. "I needed to get here right away. We only have a short amount of time."

Tommy walked behind Victor who was sitting on his couch. Tommy still had Max's gun in his hand as he circled behind Victor. He placed the holster down on the back of the couch and held the gun in his hand. "As you probably noticed, Vinny, this is Max Lorenzo's gun," he held up the holster, "This holster gives it away, right?" Vinny nodded as Blue continued, "I needed Targent to get the gun for me so I could give it to

Victor here. It's all part of a plan and for that I need to introduce you to someone." He put the gun back into the holster and dropped it on the couch next to Victor, put a hand on each of Victor's shoulders and said, "This man has been missing from my life for twenty-five years. He was my friend on another world." As he said this, Victor became Leer, then Leer became John.

Vinny watched as his brother changed in front of him. Tommy changed his own appearance so that now, Vinny was looking at Blue and John.

"So where is Tommy now?" Vinny asked, doing his best to understand, while trying to keep his lunch where it had landed when he ate it.

"I am Tommy," Tommy replied as he immediately returned to the body his brother had become familiar with. "I am also Blue right now."

"Are you ever going to be just Tommy again?" Vinny asked, worried about the answer. He truly loved his brother but he didn't know if he wanted to have just Tommy back. He had grown very fond of the Tommy he had seen become the Onjadiavaan.

"That depends on you, Vinny." Blue responded.

"How can it possibly depend on me?" Vinny puzzled, "I mean, Tommy died, then you woke up in his body. Then it turns out you're some guy from another planet but you're in my brother's body. Then you discover the Omega Lux crystal, something everyone has been looking for, right after you take over my brother's body. Then you turn into the Onjadiavaan after you reveal Shedavah to a colony that has been searchin' for it just like everyone was searching for the Omega Lux crystal because they are the same thing."

"Yeah, I know, I was there." Tommy laughs as he puts his hand on his brother's shoulders and says, "I'm not going anywhere, bro."

Vinny looks at Tommy for a long time. He sees his brother smiling back at him but he feels someone much closer to him than his brother had been through the years of JumpJuice. He settles back in his chair, looks over at John, then back to Tommy and smiles, "okay bro, you can turn him back to Victor, then tell me whose ass we're going to kick."

"Well, I hope it isn't going to be mine," Victor said as he rose from his chair and extended a hand to Vinny. "I remember you as a very level-headed man Mr. Levito," Leer continued, "It's Sal Lorenzo we have to concern ourselves with."

Vinny accepted the handshake while trying to process what exactly Leer meant by his statement.

"You see, Vinny," Leer explained, "This is the third time I have been in Victor's body." Vinny let his hand drop loose, as if all motor control fell to the back of his brain as he tried to imagine what Leer was talking about. "The first time was when he was ten years old, I was twenty-five." Leer motioned toward the chair behind Vinny and the big man sat down.

"Beer?" Leer asked as he walked toward a row of taps on the other side of the chair.

"Make it a tall one," Tommy laughed as he sat next to his brother, "and another for me please."

Leer poured three tall beers from the center tap and placed them on a table in the center of the chairs. Leer raised his glass as if beginning a toast, said nothing, and drank. Vinny grabbed his beer and downed half of it in a single go. Tommy did the same.

"Ahhhhh, beer," Leer smiled, "it's the one thing all of my bodies have loved. Actually, I should clarify, it's the one thing all of my human bodies have loved. I was once a Fanderahl, a nasty creature with ten legs, completely allergic to beer," Leer revealed, "the damn thing was so allergic to beer that its legs would fall off its body if it came into contact with even the smallest amount of beer. I found out the hard way when I popped into the body of one of them on a planet called Parthnos about twenty years ago." Leer took another long drink of beer. "My head and body lay on the ground for days after some creep spat beer all over me at what I can only guess was some sort of Parthnothian frat party. They took my legs away and began hitting each other with them, leaving my head and body behind on what was, I must say, a very beautiful beach." Leer finished his beer. "Fortunately for me, the same

314

imbalance in my energetic essence that landed me in that horrible body, righted itself, drawing me back to my previous body, a young woman by the name of Theresa who was studying to become a shaman in all the wrong ways."

"John, your point?" Blue interjected.

"Right, sorry Blue." Leer laughed, "I'm just trying to give Vinny here an idea of how I ended up being Victor three times, but I guess that really doesn't matter as much as the fact that I did. So, I will continue. Sal Lorenzo is a threat to the well-being of this planet because he perpetuates a system that creates an illegal market for JumpJuice, just like what happens with marijuana on Earth."

Vinny burst out laughing. "You gotta be kidding me!"

"Vinny, you must see that Sal is a major threat, you know him," Victor urged.

"No, no, not that," Vinny continued laughing, "marijuana! Illegal?" Tears were rolling from Vinny's eyes at this point. "What kind of world would make marijuana illegal?"

"Well, it isn't illegal everywhere on Earth, but that wasn't really my main point." Leer tried to focus Vinny back on Sal.

"Stupid, just plain stupid." Vinny reached into his pocket and pulled out a case. He opened it and pulled out a perfectly rolled joint. "This stuff is the original and best JumpJuice, without all the fighting." He lit up the joint and took a huge hit then burst out coughing and laughing at the same time as he choked out the words, "marijuana illegal," the tears continued to stream from his eyes as he passed the joint to Tommy.

"Seriously though Vinny," Leer continued, "marijuana is controlled by large drug cartels, guys like Sal who manage the supply, the prices and the law enforcement agencies who are supposed to incarcerate them."

"Now that sounds a lot like Sal," Vinny admitted.

"Exactly," Victor leaned in close to Vinny, "Sal's control over Rat Town is well-known, but have you ever stopped to consider the question of why he is never stopped?"

"Because he owns everything except for Tommy and his boys," Vinny slapped his brother's thigh for emphasis, "and me of course."

"That's only what you know about," Leer explained, "Sal has a hand in the entire JumpJuice market on Salta and he has help, very powerful help, in maintaining the JumpJuice trade."

Vinny had never bothered to consider how people got their JumpJuice outside of Rat Town. He had always figured there was a Sal for every town. Since he wasn't a big user and his brother was the only competition for Victor in Rat Town, Vinny figured he knew everything he needed to know about JumpJuice.

"I've noticed that Salta has a worldwide government," Leer began, "and that there are cities all over Salta that belong to the government despite being spread across different continents. I've been able to get caught up on Salta history, thanks to the "Channel," which is remarkably similar to the "Wave" on Teslos, that godforsaken planet you pulled me out of when you finished drawing me, Blue." He smiled in Blue's direction, then noticed Vinny's expression. Leer turned to Blue and asked, "You haven't told Vincent that part yet, eh Blue?"

"And I don't want to hear it!" Vinny said quickly, "It's plenty to wrap my head around just trying to understand that Blue and Tommy are the same guy right now. Maybe later you can tell me, like after we kick Sal's ass all over Rat Town! And you can call me Vinny"

"Okay, Vinny, sure thing," Leer agreed, "we're going to kick Sal's ass, but it's not going to happen in Rat Town. We're going to Heavana. But first, we need to visit Farb."

Vinny burst out laughing. "Visit Farb!" Vinny continued to laugh like each breath made him laugh even more, "Hello Farb, do you have a moment? You see, we're having a little issue we'd like to discuss with you, if it's not asking too much," Vinny joked as he finished off his beer. As he placed his empty glass on the table he saw it fill itself with beer.

He looked at Tommy who smiled reassuringly. "Okay brother, that's a neat trick," Vinny gulped his beer to test that it really tasted like beer.

"Strange, isn't it?" Tommy asked.

Smiling at the flavor, Vinny continued, "but making beer out of thin air and getting to see Farb are two different things!"

"Not in this case," Leer interjected, "you see, Vinny, Blue - Tommy here has the power to meet Farb anytime he wants to." A quick glance from Vinny to Tommy confirmed what Leer was saying, "The important issue is reason and timing. We need to approach Farb with our plan at precisely the right moment and give him good reason to change up the power structure he has so carefully kept in place for decades."

Vinny wasn't much for politics but neither were most citizens of Salta, after all, they had one "God" and one government for as long as most of them could remember. Questioning the power structure was futile because there were no special interest groups of any might to speak of. Some groups practiced a different religion from the majority established "Farbism" because of localized differences dating back centuries within their specific culture or region, but all of Salta's religions saw Farb as the one true God. The Sacred Seven were the only representatives for the major land masses of Salta and those positions were earned by appointment not by vote, so citizens of Salta simply accepted their leaders with little to no reaction or interest.

"We need to get Farb to remove Sal from his position of power and that is why I founded Heavana fifteen years ago." Leer explained.

"I always thought that Heavana was a myth," Vinny smiled as he drained his beer again and watched it fill before him.

"A great majority of Saltans share that belief, Vinny," Leer observed, "and that is precisely why this power structure exists. We need to convince Farb that this no longer needs to be the case."

"How are we gonna do that?" Vinny inquired.

"We are going to expose the truth about Sal." Leer explained. "And we are going to need some help from Rat Town's own Sacred One, Madonna."

Vinny looked at Tommy, "Don't tell Sansaa, but I always wanted to meet Madonna."

Tommy smiled at Vinny, lifted his glass of beer, and toasted, "Me too brother, me too!"

44 RAT TV

"The Sacred Seven meet occasionally, in different locations. They prefer staying in places where they can enjoy themselves in any way they please and today's location is no exception. They are assembling at Rivers Begin, an exclusive resort just east of the Shadowlands." Jenny Land, a reporter from Rat TV has positioned herself at the main entrance, "All of the members of the Seven are here except for our own, Madonna, Sacred Leader of the Seventh Nation. Sources say that she is in a meeting with the Mayor of Rat Town, Marlon Podesta, trying to sew up some loose ends in a deal the city is attempting to push through to make JumpJuice trafficking laws more stringent across the nation. Critics argue that Rat Town's own laws governing the sales of JumpJuice are already too harsh and should be abolished, citing that JumpJuice was only criminalized after the "War that Made Nations" nearly seventy years ago, when the alcohol industry boomed."

Ms. Land is interrupted by a voice in her earpiece, she places the tips of her fingers on the earpiece to hear the voice more clearly, then continues, "We will be back with more coverage of the Sacred Seven in just a moment."

"Nuts," Sal Lorenzo snaps into the air as he hangs up his phone. A small woman enters through a door behind where Sal is sitting and replaces an empty bowl on the table next to him with a bowl full of nuts just as his hand reaches the former location of the bowl she had replaced. As she leaves the room an equally diminutive man briskly sweeps the shells that adorn the floor around Sal's chair. The small man remains beside Sal's chair and immediately removes each new shell as it hits the floor.

"Leave me," Sal barks as he waves the man from the room.

"We have received word that Sacred Leader Madonna has left Rat Town and is headed our way," Mike Branson, an intern with Rat TV, smiled his way through his instant replacement of Jenny Land after a rapid firing of Land, for reasons undisclosed. It would become clear to those who follow the media that Land's comment relating the criminalization of JumpJuice and the boom in alcohol sales was the reason for her termination.

Rivers Begin Security escorted Land from the premises, where she was left to walk home. Rivers Begin Security would be holding on to her phone to ensure that she hadn't caused a threat to security. She could have her phone back, unharmed, after submitting the proper paperwork.

Mike Branson saw none of this as he continued, "It is unclear as to what will be the topic of discussion at this meeting of the Sacred Seven but sources are hinting at a possible appearance by Farb himself." Mike Branson practically climaxed in his pants on national TV at the prospect of being so close to Farb.

Then he remembered he was reporting live and considered how his entire career could explode with an exclusive look at Farb. "We at Rat TV have been on the front lines of news reporting from the very beginning and tonight, we may just get our very first look at Farb. Back to you Katie."

"Nuts!" Sal yelled. A small woman arrived with a full bowl of nuts. She stared for a moment at a half bowl of nuts on the table next to Sal. The small woman turned and left the room.

Sal picked up his phone and made a call. "Meet me out front in two minutes."

45 R&R

As the rest of the team walked off in various directions, Spike stood right where he had been when informed that no one used money in Heavana and that his money, everything he had on him, and everything he was planning on earning from Victor's big job was worthless, now that he was stuck in Heavana. He was about to yell at the top of his lungs when a remarkably beautiful woman gently laid a hand on his shoulder and said, "Are you coming with me or are you just going to stand there, staring at that useless old coin?"

Spike was so busy looking for reasons to argue with the idea of entering Heavana that he had no idea who had been sent to welcome him. "My name is Evana," she smiled as she handed him a green coin, worth three times the value of the one he was holding, then she gave him another.

He smiled with glee as she continued to hand him coins. "I have a whole bag of these," Evana pointed out as she opened the bag she had slung across her shoulder. "Oh, and I have quite a few more bags that you can have if you decide you still want them after seeing your new home."

Evana took the bag from over her shoulder and handed it to Spike. She turned and walked away from him saying, "Follow me Spike, unless you want to make me lose my job."

Spike drooled.

He drooled over the coins, he drooled over Evana, he drooled over the thought that she was taking him home. He followed like an obedient puppy.

Max had reached her new home in minutes.

It was beautiful, not too big and not too small, with several rooms, a marvelous kitchen and beyond the living room, a dance studio. Max let out a sort of sighing sob as she reached the studio. There was a large wooden floor with mirrors on two walls, one with a barre and one without. The other two walls also had barres, except for a small area between them containing an ornate cabinet. Max walked lightly toward the cabinet, as if her steps might ruin the flawless dance floor. She opened the cabinet doors to find a state of the art stereo system which began playing immediately upon opening the cabinet. It was "The Lotus," one of her favorite ballets from childhood.

"Your shoes are in the drawers," Barbara said with a smile. "I have quite a lot to show you when you are ready."

Max opened the top drawer to find a pair of ballet slippers and tap shoes in her size. She sat in a small chair that accompanied the cabinet in the corner of the room, kicked off her boots and tried on the tap shoes. Max compulsively tried a few combinations then awkwardly stopped and looked at Barbara. "How long has it been?" Barbara asked pleasantly.

"More than twenty years I guess," Max replied with a shrug.

"Not bad," Barbara winked, "Your lessons start tomorrow, if you want 'em. Any time, just ring that buzzer over there by the water cooler."

Barbara performed a quick but nice pirouette then added, "Your instructor is Franco, he is incredibly handsome and kind. However, he is only the first of your instructors if you choose to pursue dance as an occupation here in Heavana."

"But I chose security as my occupation when I filled out the admission form." Max said in confusion.

Barbara laughed, "We have way more security professionals than we need here in Heavana. We also have a full supply of Martial Artists and Martial Arts teachers, so there goes your second choice. Our military is by appointment only, so that's not gonna happen for at least five years, which leaves us with your last choice, professional dancer."

"That was a joke," Max said as she took off the tap shoes, "I'm no dancer."

"Here in Heavana, you can become a dancer," Barbara responded, "We are very thorough in our assessment when placing new arrivals in positions that will benefit the community. I am sure there is a place for you in the entertainment corps, otherwise, that placement would not have been made."

"But what if I'm not good enough?" Max asked with the voice of a child.

Barbara looked at Max with eyes full of compassion and hope, "Don't be afraid to try to become the person you always wanted to be. People do it every day here in Heavana. No matter what you did in the outside world, Heavana is a place of new beginnings and endless possibilities. Now put those shoes away and let me show you something I am quite sure you are going to love."

Max returned the shoes to their drawer and reached for her boots. "I'm too old to become a professional dancer."

"Nonsense," Barbara quipped, "I didn't start until I was fifty and I have performed in hundreds of shows to audiences of all sizes. They didn't send just anyone to welcome you here my dear, they sent a professional dancer," she laughed as she glided gracefully ahead of Max, "come along."

Through a short hallway, Barbara led Max to her bathroom, a sparkling clean bathroom complete with a bidet, sink shower and a hot tub with room for more than one adult, adjustable jets and a tub-side wine bar with chocolates. Max looked at it in awe for far too long and began to feel a bit self-conscious. Barbara, being an excellent welcome host explained, "If you'd like to take a bath, I can wait." Max looked as though she was about to speak but Barbara silenced her with a finger to her own lips. "I am here for as long as you like, until you feel settled. I can wait in the other room until you've had a nice tub, then we can talk over a glass of wine. Sound good?"

Max answered by turning on the jets and taking off her clothes. Barbara turned and walked into the other room.

The rest of the team found themselves in similarly wonderful situations. And all of them, including Spike, relaxed.

46 RIVERS BEGIN

"She has arrived," Mike Branson began, "with a small entourage of attendants and no security guards to be seen, Madonna has just stepped out of her stretch Morrison, one of only ten made, her car alone is worth more than most homes in Rat Town. Her Excellency looks pleased as she makes her way inside." The cameras linger on the car as the driver closes the rear door and returns to his seat and drives away.

"Still no sign of Farb, but the team here at Rat TV are staying on-sight, we are your eye on the news, Katie…"

"Get me over there," Sal bellowed as he watched the arrival of Madonna from the comfort of his less-valuable limousine, "and do it fast."

Sal hated driving, so he always had a driver. He loved to blab about everything he was thinking to his driver. He had instructed his driver to never respond and never repeat. He killed his first driver for asking a question. His other limo ended up in a lake because he shot the poor guy while he was driving. Sal had enough time to climb out of the back seat before the limo made it all the way under the water. "I can't stand how they talk about her, like she's special or something. She's just like the rest of us, grew up on the streets and got Bastin' lucky. She's an old model for Farbssake!" Sal moved around uncomfortably in his seat, "She's not even that great looking, least I don't think so. You like her Phillipe?" Sal asked as he cracked another peanut.

Phillipe had been Sal's driver for ten years. He knew that the right response was no response. Phillipe had grown very accomplished at holding his head and shoulders firmly in place whenever he was asked anything by Sal. He didn't budge. He drove on.

"Of course you don't. You have taste, ain't that right Phillipe. You like pretty much the same stuff I like. I know that about you Phillipe. I've been paying attention. You have class." Sal dropped another shell to the floor of his Reynolds Legacy, opened its well-stocked mini-bar and poured himself a shot. Sal pressed a button and vintage lounge music filled the limo. He sat back as Phillipe drove the Legacy to Rivers Begin.

"I never thought I'd see the day when Victor Alonso would blow up a perfectly good handgun," Vinny laughed as he surveyed the remnants of the blast.

"I'm not Victor Alonso," Leer replied.

"How does that work," Vinny wondered, "I mean, Blue says he is Tommy and he knows everything about Tommy, I mean he is Tommy! But he is also my new friend and brother Blue. So who are you?"

"Well, it's different with Blue because he is the Onjadiavaan, with me and Victor, we go our separate ways, but with Blue and Tommy, I think they are always going to be one." Leer explained, "but before any of that, we need to bring down Sal. You've got to write the note, he knows my handwriting."

Vinny sat and wrote the note that Victor would deliver to Sal.

One of the advantages of living under the watchful eye of Sal was that Leer could watch a fair bit of activity at the Lorenzo home. He glanced up and noticed Sal's Legacy leaving in a hurry. "Vinny, we need to go." Leer urged the big man to finish up the note which was written beautifully in cursive, "nice, hand it over, we gotta fly."
They raced to the garage where Victor's cars were lined up based on rarity and speed.

He headed over to his Agastar Coupe and whistled. The gull-wing doors opened in unison and locked into place with precision. An urban myth about this model, the 300 SL, claims that a man was travelling at extremely high speed along the coastal highway when he completely missed a very vital turn, sending him and his coupe off of the side of the mountain. In his panic, he hit the switch to open the gull-wing doors which opened in unison and locked into place with precision. To his great surprise, the car began to glide through the air. As luck would have it, the road eventually made its way down to the base of the mountain where it continued across a small plain and into a valley. This is precisely where the man's Agastar Coupe eventually landed. He simply retracted the doors and continued on his way.

"Nice Agastar Victor," Vinny cooed as he stroked the passenger door, "Can I drive?" he ducked in toward the passenger seat laughing.

"Yes, that's an excellent idea," Leer answered quickly, grabbing the big man by his arm and pulling him out of the passenger side of the vehicle.

Leer slapped the keys into Vinny's hand and continued. "Get in and drive. Oh and put on the sunglasses in the visor there."
Vinny found a pair of sunglasses with large rounded lenses that obscured most of the upper half of his face. Leer laughed as Vinny checked himself out in the visor's mirror. "Victor's incognito glasses for driving around without being recognized. He wasn't the brightest bulb our Victor, Leer laughed. "Driving around in one of maybe five Agastar Coupes in Rat Town and thinks he can hide behind sunglasses."

Vinny looked at Leer. He looked like a big, buff bug.

"Okay, take those stupid glasses off, just drive so Sal can't get a look at you. He can't know that you, me and Tommy are working together."

"Oh yeah, that. Hold on a second," Vinny smiled as he put the sunglasses away then jabbed his fingers into his own face. Noticeable sounds of bones and flesh smashing together in uncommon ways filled the interior of the coupe for a good two minutes then silence. Vinny turned to look at Victor.

"Holy shit!" Leer gasped, "I can't even recognize you."

"I know, right? Sansaa taught me Khinsajutiso, the art of self-disguise. She said that it would help me cope with Tommy being the Onjadiavaan. Sort of like my own superpower." Vinny laughed to himself, "Silly woman, we have been lovers for years and she can't see how I am nothing but happy about Tommy becoming the Onjadiavaan." He turned to face forward, grabbed the wheel and smiled, "pretty cool though, huh? You didn't even recognize me."

"No, I did not, Vinny, you are absolutely right." Leer responded, knowing full well that Sansaa was a very considerate and wise woman without ever having the pleasure of meeting her. "Now show me how a Levito drives outta Rat Town, to Rivers Begin!"

Vinny lit the tires on the 300 SL and launched her toward the massive doors to Victor's garage. They opened so quickly that the burning coupe didn't even need to hesitate for a moment as she coughed out of the garage onto the absurdly long driveway leaving the drug lord's mansion.

Leer had been in many cars on many planets, driven by himself and by skilled drivers from around the universe, but Vinny put them all to shame the way he was driving this little Agastar Coupe 300 SL. His sheer mass made the car behave like the VinnCycle, hugging curves as he leaned his brawn into the road. Leer caught on early into the ride that it was going to be a participation sport, both men leaning with the car around turns, breathing with the thrum of the engine.

Vinny didn't even need to worry about Sal recognizing him because Phillipe would never risk the slightest bump, disturbing Sal's drink or causing him to drop a single peanut. Victor and Vinny arrived at Rivers Begin a good half-hour before Sal's Legacy made it to the red carpet.

Vinny couldn't resist seeing everything unfold so he stuck with Victor anyway.

As Sal got out of the limo, Victor approached him, holding Max's gun and a note.

"That's Max's gun," Sal said with an unusual display of emotion. He froze and looked at Victor. "How did you know I would be here. You were at your house," Sal slipped. He had never actually acknowledged that he was spying on Victor.

"I saw you leave in a hurry, Sal. It works both ways." Victor responded, "but we have a chance of getting this bastard." He held out the note to Sal.

"We're going to kill anyone who ever got near my Maxie, Victor. You and me, we are going to wipe them out. I am going to personally cut the cock off whoever made that Bastin' bomb that killed my Maxie." Sal was melting down. "Gimme that Bastin" note."

Leer handed Sal the note that he had dictated to Vinny. *I wanted to know if you might be interested in buying back some of your daughter's limbs. I have far more than I need and all you have left of your daughter is her gun, which I am kindly giving you for free. Farb Bless.*

Leer could see that Sal was ready to trigger.

"I think I can find this bastard, Sal." Victor said as he pulled the note from Sal's immobile fingers.

"Find him," Sal said as he numbly walked toward the entrance of Rivers Begin.

47 MADONNA

Victor and Vinny walked in with him as Mike Branson reported, "Sal Lorenzo and Victor Alonso have just appeared at Rivers Begin. To my knowledge, the Sacred Seven have never met with anyone outside of the seven during these retreats, unless it is Farb, himself."

Mike Branson was hoping that each new appearance might bring Farb but was missing the story of a lifetime. Sal, Victor, Tommy, Vinny and Madonna all under one roof at the same time, except that Tommy was Blue and Vinny looked like Sly Stallone who no one on this planet even knew about.
Madonna had secured a private room, away from the meeting room where she would join the other members of the Sacred Seven. She entered the hallway just in time to run into Sal who was walking like a man who knows he must keep moving to stay alive but beyond that has no real plan.

Madonna recognized Sal immediately and assumed the worst.

She assumed that everyone around her was out to kill her and Sal had shown up to gloat or kill her himself..

Madonna had been a real bitch to Sal. She had taken him for sixty percent of his earnings since becoming the Sacred Leader of the Seventh District. This made her the wealthiest of all the Sacred Leaders, who incidentally are the richest people on Salta other than Farb himself.

Madonna did what she does when she thinks people are out to kill her.

She struck first. The speed of it was so blinding that everyone was blinded, temporarily but effectively. Everyone except for Blue. He watched her walk between Vinny, Victor and Sal without them seeing her and he watched her watch him watch her.

"You're not blinded," Madonna said as she entered a private room a short way down the hall.

As she entered the room she looked behind her to see if she had been followed. Blue tapped her on the shoulder and she jumped into the air, a good three to four feet, easily. Madonna had seen a great many things on Salta, she was capable of extraordinary feats, but she could not figure out Blue. She couldn't sense him in any way. He could be right next to her and he had no energy reading as she had come to think about things. She was pretty sure that everything had an energy reading and that it could be detected. By her.

She was standing next to the man who had just proven her wrong, unintendedly, but truly, he had proven her wrong. Blue had no energy reading. Madonna hadn't felt frightened in centuries. Now, she was dealing with the unknown.

"Excuse me Your Excellency, I have come to ask a favor." Blue said with a smile.

He was Blue in physical form for the first time in public since he awoke in Tommy Levito's body.

"Who the Varst are you?" Madonna said in surprise. Then she yelled, "Angelo!" She yelled Angelo's name several times but each time it met with the same fate. It died. Her yelling, her shouting went nowhere. Blue simply caught the sound in the palm of his hand.

Madonna looked at him with curiosity. She had seen powers like that before, from Farb, but she wasn't expecting to see it from someone new.

"I just need a moment of your time before you meet with the Council," Blue said as he detected her powers. He knew that she could easily leave if she wanted to and he had no intention of making her feel as though he was trying to hold her there.

"Where did you come from?" she asked as she leaned on a nearby table.

"Earth" Blue responded, "same as you."

"But you're not famous on Earth are you Blue?" Madonna asked with a measure of superiority.

"Not yet," Blue responded with a smile. "I will be, but that's not really what's important." Blue looked intently at Madonna. His entire being flared up as if he was a campfire and she was a bellows.

She lifted up off the floor, Her hair rose up from curling around her shoulders as she hovered and continued to listen.

"Salta is in the perfect state for a revolutionary change on a planetary level and I need you to help me make it happen," Blue said as he rose up to look her in the eyes. "It's about Sal Lorenzo."

Madonna dropped to a standing position then into a chair. "Okay, I'm ready to listen. You have five minutes."

"My name is Blue. I know that you are Multi-Verse Madonna, but I just wanted to say that even though I didn't listen to anything you ever did after your first album, I totally think you are a superstar. At least where I come from you are. So, I thought that maybe I could ask a favor, as a fan?"

Madonna couldn't believe it. A rank amateur traveler had bested her, snuck up on her and exposed her.

"And why would I want to do anything for you?" Madonna questioned, "you make me feel uneasy."

"I am so sorry, I want to make a simple request," Blue stated. "Whatever Sal asks for, please tell him "NO"!"

"And what's in it for me?" Madonna asked calmly.

"Nothing." Blue responded.

Madonna looked at her fingernails and started picking at one of them with her thumbnail. She looked up to respond to Blue and he was gone.

Sal Lorenzo regained his vision and began searching for Madonna. He found her behind the first door he opened and walked into the room.

Madonna had moved beyond her irrational fear that everyone was coming to get her and faced Sal. She did not let her guard down, however, and stood within a force-field, protecting her from any harm. The field was invisible but its efficacy was battle proven.

"Lady Madonna," Sal began, "I have come to you with a heavy heart," He lifted Max's holster up over his head, "My daughter has died in your service. I ask that you help me control this situation." Sal slammed the gun to the floor, "these people must be stopped."

Madonna dropped the shield, "What people are you talking about?" she asked with valid concern, "And I am so sorry to hear about Max, she was a good one. Who is responsible for her death?"

"I," Sal froze. Madonna could sense his frustration.

"You don't know who killed you daughter? What about Levito, didn't she just blast a hole in his gut?" Madonna suspected Tommy because it made sense. The fact that Sal hadn't grabbed Levito immediately made her suspicious. "Do you have some reason to believe that Tommy isn't behind your shipments getting heisted?"

"I – I – I just don't think. I mean, I know it's not Tommy Levito," Sal stumbled through an explanation, "I've got eyes on Levito, he's got nothing to do with the missing shipments or Max."

Madonna had no reason to doubt that Sal had eyes on Tommy because it is exactly the type of thing that Sal does. He gets eyes on people when he wants eyes on people, but he hadn't called for it since Tommy first agreed to secretly work with him.

That was before Max blew a hole in his belly.

Sal remembered that Tommy did seem a bit odd the last time they met. He turned from Madonna, opened the door to the lobby and called out, "Hey Victor, get over here!" Victor moved to the room quickly. Sal whispered in Victor's ear to get eyes on Tommy immediately, closed the door and stepped back into the room. He picked up Max's gun. "I need an army. I need to send a message. No one gets our Juice, no one muscles in on our business and no one can take my Maxie away from me and live."

Madonna considered the fact that Blue had just been in the very same room only moments earlier asking for just one thing, that she deny Sal whatever it was he would ask for. As one of the Seven, Madonna had the power to use the military to do her bidding in her own district. Sal provided a healthy share of her income through the various arrangements they had agreed to. Supporting Sal meant supporting those arrangements and her own income. However, Blue had been impressive. He clearly had abilities and, after all, he had asked quite nicely.

On the other hand, Sal had just shown up with Max's gun in hand, moved by grief over her death and had no idea who could have killed her. Madonna could clearly sense that Sal was telling the truth about what he knew, yet she could get no read on Blue at all. There was a strong possibility in her mind that the stranger from earth had something to do with Max's demise.

Madonna looked long and deep into Sal's eyes, "Okay Sal, for Max, let me know where and when. You'll have your troops." She walked toward the door, "Now I've got a meeting with the other six about your JumpJuice business. So, I'm gonna go stick a knife in your back and tell 'em to crack down hard on the sellers, just in time for you to jack up JumpJuice and alcohol prices everywhere on Salta. Remember, if anyone ever connects us on this, I'm the one being manipulated here."

She smiled and winked at Sal, "Just be sure they think you hate me," and she walked out the door.

"Bastin' Farbunkle!" Sal hollered from within the room, "You can't do this to Sal Lorenzo, Sacred Seven or not, you hear me!" His cathartic outburst relieved him of the rage he indeed was feeling over repeatedly handing money that he had earned, over to a woman. It also worked to fool the media into reporting exactly what Madonna had hoped.

"Strong words were hurled at Sacred Leader Madonna, just moments ago by notorious JumpJuice King Sal Lorenzo," Mike Branson placed his fingertips to the headphone in his right ear as the station played a recording of Sal hollering at Madonna.

"We can only guess that the thing that Sacred Leader Madonna "can't do" to Mr. Lorenzo would be to make the laws more stringent when dealing with sellers of JumpJuice." Branson lowered his hands after making the obligatory hand gesture for quotation marks. "We at Rat TV are in negotiations with those representing the Sacred Seven to be able to bring our cameras in for this once in a lifetime opportunity."

Mike Branson then makes the unfortunate decision to try to conduct an interview with Sal Lorenzo. He rushes toward Sal with his microphone leaning out toward Sal and says, "Mr. Lorenzo, sir, were you talking with Sacred Leader Madonna about the new law regarding tougher punishment for sellers of JumpJuice?"

In a single motion Sal rips the microphone from Branson's hand and uses it like an ice pick to shatter the lenses of three different cameras aimed at the budding reporter's foolish maiden voyage into journalistic interviewing. "No Comment," Sal snickered as he left Rivers Begin with Victor and Sly Stallone walking beside him. He turned to Sly, "Who the Bast are you?"

Vinny wants to punch Sal and tell him who he was but Leer interjected at just the right time with just the right response. "He's my new driver Sal, it's Aldo's baby brother." Victor laughed, "Baby, sorry Geno, nobody calls Geno a baby, ain't that right Geno?"

Geno/Vinny lifted Victor/Leer off the floor by cradling his ribcage in his massive palms and pushing up.

"Okay, I get it, Geno," Sal chuckled, "Now set him down." Sal was very used to giving orders, even when he had no idea what the varst was going on. But something was happening to Sal, ever since he really began to accept that Max was dead, ever since he saw her gun. He was now a father with no child. He was now angry with himself for never valuing his daughter. He was not going to accept that it was his fault so he was now a man with a mission to pin the gross injustice of losing his daughter on anything he possibly could. "Victor, give him the keys, you're coming with me."

Leer nodded to Vinny.

"I have the keys Mr. Lorenzo," Geno said quietly, "I will drive Mr. Alonso's car home for him." Vinny turned toward the Harrison 37, "I'll park it in front and put the keys in the box Aldo made for you."

Victor and Sal climbed into the Legacy and Phillipe drove her out of Rivers Begin and into the night.

48 BROTHERLY LOVE

Blue suddenly materialized within inches of Vinny who had spent the previous two minutes hitting pressure points for bringing his face back to normal.

Blue had once again become Tommy, but Vinny had seemed to miss a few important pressure points, leaving his face somewhere in between Sly Stallone and Vinny Levito.

Blue burst out laughing.

"What?" Vinny cried, "What is it?"

Tommy pointed to Vinny's reflection in the window of the 300SL. Vinny yelped like a chihuahua when he saw himself.

He jumped up and down as though it would shake his face back into place.

It didn't.

In fact, it made his face seem as though it might never go back into place. He tried poking points he had learned from Sansaa but nothing worked. Tommy sat and laughed at every attempt.

Finally, Vinny could take it no more, "Why are you laughing at me Tommy? I'm your brother! Aren't you some kind of all-powerful guy who can fix this for me?"

Tommy laughed, "Oh, I'm your brother all right, but I think you are the one forgetting that." Tommy stood up as tall as he could, he was clearly imitating someone as he said, "Vinny, tell him he's just a baby and he can't hang around with you anymore, because you know, Vinny, you're my baby." Tommy dropped his hands, he looked at his brother.

Vinny knew who Tommy was pretending to be. He knew the precise moment that Tommy was portraying. This was the defining moment that made Vinny such a rock-solid brother, such a devoted and loving friend to his younger brother but Tommy had never noticed it, because he didn't get to witness the entire event. To Tommy, Vinny was a traitor, he left him for a girl. But that wasn't what really happened.

What really happened was this…

Vinny did not tell his brother that he was a baby and he couldn't hang around him anymore.

Unfortunately, Vinny was drafted the next day for service. He had graduated from school and was considering further study when the orders came in. At the time, Salta was suffering through a battle between two warring Seven Members. The conflict was deadly and everyone on Salta felt the tension.

Tommy resented Vinny on many levels. Vinny was stronger, more agile, better looking, cool around girls, all the things that younger brothers think as they grow up watching their brothers grow up years ahead of them.

On Tommy's sixteenth birthday, Vinny showed up in a new car. It was a beautiful Niffur 800 and everyone was marveling at it. Tommy's girlfriend, Gina, was so enthralled with the car that she climbed onto Vinny's lap while the cake was set in front of Tommy.

Vinny lifted the girl by her torso and got up off his chair. He carried her away from the table.

Tommy thought that Vinny was leaving with Gina to have sex. He wept as he blew out the candles.

Vinny carried the delusional teenager out to his car, set her in the passenger seat and drove her home. When he reached her house he told her in no uncertain terms that she was never to see Tommy again and that if she ever talked about what happened that night, she would die.

Vinny drove back to the house he grew up in to share in his brother's party but Tommy had locked himself in his room and refused to talk to his older brother.

The next day Vinny left for war.

It didn't last long as wars go but the damage had already been done. Tommy's perception of Vinny was ruined.

Tommy and his older brother didn't see one another before Vinny had to go off to war. Vinny vowed as he left to serve that he would protect his brother no matter what, until his brother told him not to.
That happened far too soon and that is why Tommy ended up with a hole in his stomach.

It took five years for Tommy to be able to be in the same room with Vinny despite several tries on Vinny's part. By this time, Tommy had gone from delivery boy to dispatcher in a job that paid him "far too much money for the amount of work." This is what he answered in a comment form about his job when asked to take a survey to see if he was suitable for management.

Those in positions of power found this to be a very unique perspective and wanted to know what drove the boy to such a review.

When Tommy answered that they had all missed the basic tenant of capitalism when constructing their business model, they asked him to join the team.

He told them to Bast Off.

That was when Tommy decided to sell JumpJuice.

He had looked at every business model that he had the remotest possibility of enjoying engaging in and determined that JumpJuice was the most appropriate. Tommy had started using JumpJuice the day after his sixteenth birthday. He started selling it within a week and became the main dealer for a group of thirty lesser dealers. Eventually, Tommy controlled most of the sales in Southside Rat Town.

Tommy saw his involvement in JumpJuice as a business opportunity, while Vinny asked more basic, moral questions and decided that the JumpJuice trade was not for him. Vinny didn't object to JumpJuice as much as he did the violence which accompanied its sale and distribution. Tommy occasionally called on Vinny if he needed a hand with something around the house and Vinny was always there for him, whenever he called. Vinny's consistency won out over time and Tommy began to treat Vinny like a brother, most notably after the death of their mother.

Vinny played along with Tommy, whatever the game might be, from JumpJuice parties to video game marathons and even the occasional concert or camping trip. He was happy to be with Tommy, no matter what, even if it came to a fight, and that happened far too often with Tommy. As his JumpJuice business grew, Tommy's enemies multiplied. After growing his business for five years, Tommy hit a wall. He ran out of neighborhoods to take over. Every other part of Rat Town, places where Tommy didn't have a dealer of his own, had dealers who worked for Victor Alonso.

The early fights with Victor and his boys were horrible, bloody fistfights, then knives, then guns for six months straight.

Then came Sal Lorenzo. Sal was from North Rat Town, a wealthy area where the elite did their living. Sal was big guns, bazookas and tanks and JumpJuice at half the price.

Victor's area got hit first. Sal stormed in with cheap JumpJuice, turning a third of Victor's dealers without a fight. Victor saw the writing on the wall and approached Sal with an offer.

Victor made a good deal with Sal, becoming his number one guy, looking after Sal's expanded territory. He actually ended up making more money than he had running his own JumpJuice operation due to the sheer volume he was running through Sal's operation.

Sal wanted more, however. He wasn't happy with the havoc he had caused for Victor, even though he had viciously expanded his territory, by claiming all of Victor's. Sal wanted all of Rat Town and he made a point of going after Tommy.

At first, he tried to do it with pricing. Sal dropped his price even lower than half the going rate. Tommy was the kid with the plan. He had already been charging far more than he needed to, driving the price up to compensate for any unforeseen drop from oversupply or competition. Victor had been matching Tommy's pricing from the start until Sal came along. Tommy never lost a single dealer to Victor based on cost of goods.

But Sal was relentless.

When the price drop didn't effect Tommy's business, he sent in muscle.

At first, it wasn't too much for Tommy to handle. His dealers had some muscle of their own and things got a little bloody but business continued. In fact, it actually raised sales in territories run by Tommy as users preventatively stocked up beyond their regular supplies, fearing the worst.

The worst came on Tommy's twenty-fifth birthday. It is still referred to as the "Birthday Massacre" because Sal made sure it would be. He wanted to hit Tommy so hard that there would be no chance for recovery.

Sal sent in his two X-Can 750 tanks, and a hundred men armed to the teeth, to the little neighborhood of Crescent River Falls where Tommy started his JumpJuice business. The local plant that Tommy bailed out of as a teen was filled with workers who used JumpJuice to unwind when they got home. It was easy to sell JumpJuice there, the work was hard and the pay was minimal. Tommy's dealers were the kids of the fathers still working in the factories. Most of the sales happened on the factory floor. The managers and the workers were all friends and did what they could to make the time pass as pleasantly as possible. Some of the people who bought JumpJuice used it at work but it rarely caused any problems. In fact, the only time there was a fatality in the plant came because of alcohol use, rather than JumpJuice.

Until Sal sent in his goons.

The tanks busted through first as the workers scrambled to understand what was happening, Sal's men rushed in with guns blazing. They mowed down everyone in their path. Every person who survived the initial cannon fire and crushing treads of the tanks died, as a result of gun fire, knife attacks and physical beatings the likes of which Rat Town had never seen, destroying an entire community of fathers and sons.

These neighborhoods in Rat Town still clung to the archetypal roles of men at work and women at home, but tonight, no one came home. The women were alone, and most of them would be until they died.

Tommy sent a fruit basket to each of the wives after the massacre because he felt terrible and it seemed like a good idea. Some of the women were very happy with the fruit basket while others hated Tommy for being the cause of their grief.

Many of those still wondered how they might get their JumpJuice in the future.

News of the massacre rocked Salta. Rat Town was now the most talked about city on the planet. It was the first thing resembling war since the "War Between the Sacred," as it had come be known, and this made people fear again.

Tommy felt absolutely terrible about the deaths at the plant. He knew some of those people personally. Tommy didn't feel that selling JumpJuice should be a crime, so anytime anything went wrong, he went through the same justifications for being one of the major contributors to the problem. He cursed Farb and the Sacred Seven, "Bast off, you Farbunkles!" He yelled to the sky. He reached for his phone as he crumpled to the ground. He called Vinny.

Vinny is a passivist, he will look for a solution before he looks for a fight, but when Tommy called him on the night after the massacre, he was not looking for a solution. He was ready to fight.

As the news spread from Rat Town to the rest of Salta, Vinny was reacting to Sal's attack. "We need to destroy his tanks," Vinny said to Tommy, who was unusually silent. "We need to make sure he can't do that again." Vinny panted, "I am going to stop that man, his tanks and his goons and I am going to do it now!"

Vinny called his buddies who had remained in the military past their required term of service, he had many. Several of the officers had pledged their loyalty to Vinny after he saved a group of soldiers who were trapped in a cave after an explosion sealed them inside. Vinny was the closest to the cave when word came that the men were trapped. He was a medic who regularly drove from battalion to battalion when fighting broke out. He was on the road when the report came of the cave-in.

He drove directly to the site despite its remote location and his own lack of sleep. When he reached the collapsed cave, there was no sign of life.

Vinny attempted to reach the trapped soldiers on the same radio band they had used to send word that they had been trapped, but there was no response. He assumed the worst, that the men had run out of air and perished but he did not give up on rescuing them.

Vinny had spent some time in college studying geology but decided to finish with a degree in engineering. He immediately realized that he was not going to be able to remove the large boulders that had sealed the entrance of the cave. However, as he surveyed the formations surrounding the cave, he noticed an unusual pattern in the rock, one he had seen before in school.

During a field study, Vinny and a team of other student geologists had discovered similar formations when surveying an area for indications of mineral deposits. Salta was rich in minerals. His team followed the unusual formations which ran horizontally along a massive cliff, dotted with small caves, much like the area Vinny now found himself searching for his fellow soldiers.

And then he saw it. An intensely dark layer, sandwiched between two lighter layers, running directly toward the collapsed cave entrance.

During Vinny's studies, he and his team had discovered that these formations, these dark stripes in the rock face, represented a time on Salta when there was excessive moisture, as if the entire area were under water. The strata analysis revealed large deposits of decayed plant growth, similar to fossilized matter found in many of the sea beds they had explored. This layer was not as solid as the rest of the rock above and below it. It undulated through the rock face, leaving pockets of larger deposits here and there along the face. Vinny had learned that this layer was highly unstable and could, if hit with enough force, shatter and break away.

In fact, Vinny and his team discovered a large cave as a result of removing one such large deposit so many years ago.

He began to trace the layer surrounding the area of the cave-in as he climbed across the face of the cliff. Within fifty feet of the cave-in, Vinny found a large, almost circular, deposit of the black rock. He quickly ran to his vehicle and grabbed a tire iron and a flashlight from the trunk.

Vinny wielding a tire-iron is something to behold. One might think him a god, summoning fire from his hands, to see the face of the cliff falling off like shredded cheddar. But he wasn't just blindly hacking away at the face, he was carving away the unstable layer, carefully and precisely, minimizing the possibility of another cave in, until he heard it, a crumbling away of the layer, a short distance from where he was working.

He waited but heard nothing more.

Vinny began shredding at the layer, moving closer to the sound he had just heard, then stopped. From within, he could again hear the crumbling, now just a foot or two from his location. Vinny worked to bridge the gap between the sounds he was hearing and the hole he was creating until a chunk of rock just shot away from the tire-iron as he struck it. He heard an echo as the falling rock struck against the cave walls.

Vinny quickly stashed the tire-iron in his belt loop as he shone the flashlight into the hole he had created. Thirty feet below, he could just make out the form of a soldier, lying up against the cave wall.

"Hey! Wake up. You alive down there?" Vinny called out until he heard coughing. He tried to get a better look by crawling into the hole, testing it for sturdiness as he went. The coughing became louder. Vinny began to make out more forms of soldiers below him as each one shook the other into breathing. "I'm going for rope, stay still and don't try to climb until I return."

Vinny ran to his vehicle and grabbed a long rope he used for pulling gurneys on the battlefield. Tales were told of how Vinny had pulled seven men to safety on gurney sleds all tied together, the single rope, lashed across his brawny shoulders.

"Grab hold of the rope, one at a time. Slowly walk up the cave wall as I pull." Vinny called as he threw down one end of the rope. "And crawl easy through this hole up here, we don't want it to get too much bigger!"

By the time a rescue squad arrived, Vinny had pulled all the soldiers from the cave.

Two officers were among the soldiers who pledged their lives to Vinny, bringing with them some heavy fire power when he called for help. They brought five X-Can 1500 tanks and three hundred other soldiers to Sal's territory. Vinny gave the order to obliterate everything. Within hours, Sal had nothing left of one of the most secure fortresses he owned.

All Sal could think was that his fortress was weak, that someone hadn't done their job. Someone had failed him. He felt that way until it happened again.

Vinny obliterated another fortress in less than three hours.

Sal backed off on his advance against Tommy and called for a meeting to discuss a truce. Tommy wanted to avoid anything that resembled the violence of the preceding days so he agreed to meet with Sal.

Victor and his crew had remained neutral throughout the battle between Sal and Tommy.

Victor shifted to running the JumpJuice business for all of Sal's territory while Sal fought with Tommy.

Despite the calamitous loss of life on both sides of the "JumpJuice War," the business boomed.

Sal brought Victor to the meeting and Tommy brought Vinny.

"When you guys were kids, goin' to school with Maxie," Sal mused, "you always walked behind her, or across the street from her, almost every day. Sometimes Vinny would say hi to Max, but never you Tommy." Sal turned smiling toward Tommy, "Did you ever tell her you had a crush on her Tommy?" Sal didn't wait for the answer, "Of course you didn't, Tommy. Of course, you didn't." Sal shook his head. "Never had the follow-through, or maybe you thought you couldn't like her because she was a Lorenzo," Sal turned away and looked out the window. "Either way, nothing ever happened." Sal recognized that Tommy was not about to stand around for a story from his own childhood, by a man who was a sworn enemy of his father. "You shocked the Varst outta me," Sal eventually bellowed, "Completely wiped out two of my best locations. Tanks. Troops, the whole shebongo!"

He looked hard at Vinny, "You really did it. You hit me right back didn't you?"

Vinny and Tommy just looked at Sal.

"Well Like your father used to say," Sal grinned, " 'guys who raise bees don't complain about a few stings now and then, do they?'"

"Never thought I'd be around to hear you quote my father, Sal." Vinny said as Tommy stepped toward Sal.

Victor positioned himself between Sal and Tommy and Vinny put a hand on Tommy's shoulder.

"I did learn from your father," Sal shifted, "I learned a lot about business and we need to get down to it."

After what seemed like hours of silent eyes and twisted faces, the men agreed.

Hours later, the lines had been drawn that would separate Tommy's territory from Sal's territory.

An agreement was struck between Sal, Tommy and Victor regarding the boundaries of each territory with a promise to self-regulate the dealers in those territories.

Since the deal, the territories grew in population, but the boundaries remained the same. Occasionally, fights had broken out on territorial boarders and much of this violence was short-lived. For those skirmishes that continued, both Victor and Tommy had consistently sent in forces to end the fighting, policing their own dealers with sanctions or force as needed.

Since the agreement, Tommy never asked Vinny along for anything JumpJuice related. In fact, he had become more like a normal brother, getting together with Vinny to have fun. Tommy didn't seem to need any added muscle, just someone to hang out with.

For years, just the appearance of Tommy and Victor would make any fighting between dealers cease. Local dealers rarely had the guts to question their bosses and those who did were not heard from again.

Recently, however, local dealers became more daring, choosing to risk continued fighting, hoping to gain more power and territory of their own. These uprisings were consistently handled within each organization, Tommy handling his own dealers and Victor handling his.

Maxine took over much of Victor's dirty work as the two became a couple. Sal was proud but controlling and Max never felt like she could do enough. She drew closer to Victor because she thought her father wanted it. Victor became more like Sal in thought and deed, cruel to enemies, feared by those closest to him and friendless.
He didn't need friends, he had Max.

She continued to seek approval in the way she had learned to, she killed for it. Max had become the heavy hand of the Lorenzo machine.

Max dealt justice to dealers who tried to further their personal agendas even if she had to cut a path through Tommy Levito's territory to do it. She'd put an end to the battle by taking out the power. Word spread throughout the bordering regions that transgressions against the agreement would be met with force and generally death. Max had become synonymous with death, developing a devoted following of dealers and hangers on.

Tommy had heard of Max's attacks, marveling at her swift and ruthless justice while despising the bloodshed and loss of life, particularly to those who represented his territories. He was not so different from Max. He too defended his men first as he fought in battles where his dealers overstepped their authority, but he rarely fought to kill. His abilities as a fighter made it possible for him to secure victories without the loss of life, often disabling and disarming, rather than killing. He removed dealers from power who betrayed his trust and broke the agreement. Tommy was most content when there were no skirmishes, when the business of JumpJuice was just business. Tommy believed that deep-down in Max's heart, she wanted an end to the violence and killing.

All of this was before Max blew a hole in Tommy's belly.

49 PORTSMOUTH

Portsmouth is a neighborhood at the edge of Rat Town that borders the territories of both Lorenzo and Levito. It has active sea trade and barrels of JumpJuice pass through daily.

Gregorio Tadesdo had been working at the plant in Crescent River Falls up until two days before the Birthday Massacre, when he moved to Portsmouth. He wasn't there for the heartless attack but he lost all his closest friends, people he saw nearly every day for most of his adult life. He was also a JumpJuice dealer. He was selling so much JumpJuice he decided to move to Portsmouth, where he could get it faster and cheaper. It was close enough to still visit all of his friends at the plant even though he wasn't going to need to work there anymore, the JumpJuice business was going to make his life a breeze.

The day of the massacre, Gregorio vowed to strike back. He spent years training. He spent years recruiting. He built his own very profitable and very powerful JumpJuice business in Portsmouth. He was one of Tommy's most productive dealers. They talked for hours about the people they had loved and lost in the plant. Tommy had grown to love Gregorio as a brother, in loss.

That kinship was put to the test the day of the "Battle of Portsmouth," when Gregorio broke the agreement by launching an attack on every Lorenzo dealer in Portsmouth. "We are going to own Portsmouth," He shouted to his recruits, moments before they hit the streets. "It is time to fight for our brothers, our fathers and our friends, Remember Crescent River Falls!" The army of recruits broke off into separate units and sped east toward "Rat Town on Portsmouth," an obnoxiously affluent neighborhood and Lorenzo JumpJuice territory.

Gregorio's gang was well trained. They rounded up most of the dealers without a fight and took the rest by force. They bound and gagged the men and women who dealt Lorenzo JumpJuice, lining them up along the stairs of the massive monument to Farb which stood ominously on the shores of Portsmouth. The police of Rat Town on Portsmouth surrounded the monument but made no attempt to stop Gregorio's gang, even as they added more people to the steps, writhing, attempting to get to their feet, only to be knocked back down by the butt of a gun or a fistful of brass knuckles.

The cops occasionally busted dealers during a sale, or in the midst of a large shipment but they never interfered in hostilities between the Lorenzo and Levito organizations. What the cops did do was talk. They talked to their wives, their buddies and to other cops. Within minutes the monument was encircled with news crews and onlookers hoping for a glimpse of a dealer fight or even a murder.

The cops did nothing while Gregorio Tadesdo drove a bus through a news truck, screeching to a stop just feet away from the dealers lined up on the bottom step of the Farb monument. He climbed up on the bus and spoke into a megaphone. "I am Gregorio Tadesdo and I now own the JumpJuice business in all of Portsmouth. I am here to execute these Lorenzo farbunkles in retribution for the Birthday Massacre on behalf of all citizens of Crescent River Falls."

Bursting through the crowd, Tommy arrived in his Harrison 37, a sleek, bulletproof little number he had custom-made with detachable shield doors. As he slung the machine in close to Gregorio's bus, he leapt from the driver's seat holding the left-side door in his hand as a shield. Gregorio's gang opened fire on Tommy to no avail. Within a few moves, Tommy was up on the bus, holding Gregorio aloft with one hand. Tommy threw the shield into the wind. It flew through the air like a perfectly guided drone and reattached itself to the Harrison 37.

Gregorio's gang dropped their weapons to their sides until Gregorio raised the megaphone to his lips and ordered, "point your guns at the hostages, you imbeciles!"

Tommy was left holding a limp Gregorio who was controlling an angry mob of dealers and mercenaries who were in turn controlling the fate of every Lorenzo dealer in Rat Town on Portsmouth.

At that moment, Victor Alonzo landed a helicopter in the center of Rat Town on Portsmouth Circle.

As quickly as it landed, it left, leaving behind three people, Victor Alonzo, Maxine Lorenzo and Madonna, one of seven Sacred Leaders of Salta.

The only higher power on the planet was Farb himself.

Everyone stood frozen. They were in the presence of divinity and this divinity arrived in a helicopter with one of the two most powerful JumpJuice dealers on Salta. The crowd, by this time, was massive. It was as though the entire city had taken a break, in the middle of the day, to join a rally, or watch a parade. But this was no parade. This was lives in the balance.

Madonna pointed to the top of the bus where Tommy was still holding Gregorio aloft with one hand while supporting his ribcage with a 745 Blaster, set to kill. "Do you mind throwing down the megaphone. Madonna yelled across the Circle.

Tommy and Gregorio looked at one another with a quizzical expression, unsure of what the Sacred Leader had said. They both looked back at her as Tommy lowered Gregorio to the roof of the bus.

"Do you mind throwing down the megaphone?" Madonna tried again.

This time, both men understood her perfectly. Tommy nodded as Gregorio tossed the megaphone to the Sacred Leader.

Madonna caught the megaphone with one hand and turned toward the monument. "Drop your guns," she ordered, "or your children will never have children." Half of Gregorio's gang dropped their guns.

"Do it now or you will become blind, instantly."

Nearly every gun dropped, but not all. "I warned you," she bowed her head.

The remaining ten members of Gregorio's gang suddenly dropped their firearms and reached their hands to their faces as they tried to come to grips with having lost their vision.

Madonna was taking control of the situation. No one in Rat Town on Portsmouth Circle was capable of confronting Madonna, not with violence, not with debate. She was one of the Sacred Seven. She was an advisor to Farb himself. "I am here at the request of Farb, Almighty Leader of Salta, Immortal Voice of Truth. Drop your weapons, release your prisoners and leave." Madonna was very powerful. She could have ripped the megaphone from Gregorio's hand from across a continent but she did not. She was respectful of people and gave them a choice, to follow or not to follow.

That is the way it was for all of the Sacred Seven.

The only flaw in that plan was that people sometimes wanted to do something different. Sometimes people wanted no one to govern them. On Salta, there were very few wars and minimal crime, except for those dealing with illegal substances, and JumpJuice was illegal.

"I am here with Victor Alonzo, head of Lorenzo Enterprises Distribution, and his lovely friend Max. Madonna spoke into the megaphone, "The reason I brought them here is to come to terms with an old agreement." Madonna lifted a hand in the direction of the bus. She flicked her fingers toward herself and Tommy and Gregorio were instantly transported to her side, just feet away from Victor and Max. "I am proposing a fight, between these two men, to determine the outcome of this battle. If Victor Alonzo wins, Gregorio Tadesdo and his gang leave forever. But if Tommy Levito wins, he can make the call."
Many cheers and boos were heard throughout the crowd assembled.

"This is not a matter for debate," Madonna cried out as she snapped her fingers, moving the entire crowd back by two feet in an instant. All of Gregorio's gang's firearms were lifted into the air as well. She lifted her hands and Victor and Tommy were lifted into the air. She smiled as she chose a place for them to land, the center of Rat Town on Portsmouth Circle.

As the crowd moved in to watch the fight, Max moved in closer.

Madonna was controlling the view, keeping everyone back enough for the fight to transpire. Victor and Tommy knew that there was no arguing with the wishes of a Sacred Leader. They stood, poised to fight, while Madonna gave the rules. "No rules gentlemen. You can kill each other for all I care. Just be sure when this is over, that I don't have to come back here again. Agreements are agreements. And no interference from anyone else, period!" Madonna threw a glove on the ground as she jumped high into the air. The helicopter had circled around and moved in above the crowd. All of the firearms from Gregorio's mercenaries and troops were pulled into the helicopter. Madonna landed with ease within the copter and within seconds it was gone.

Tommy Levito and Victor Alonzo stood a few feet away from each other. The last time they had seen each other was in a pizza parlor in their old neighborhood, where they used to go to school with one another. They had bumped into one another a few months earlier, at the parlor, because coincidentally, it was still both of their favorite pizza. Today, they were facing each other to determine the fate of each of their businesses, as well as, the fate of Rat Town.

"You heard the lady," Victor started as he set his feet on the pavement and raised both fists.

Tommy stood in close, "Okay then," he snapped, as he lifted Victor by his belt, removing it and his two guns in the process.

Victor was then free to hit the ground where he performed a sweep kick that put Tommy on his back, giving Victor enough time to pull Tommy's gun from his holster.

Victor held the gun to Tommy's head just long enough for Tommy to sling a leg up into Victor's face causing him to leave his feet, lose the gun and land next to Tommy on the ground.

Both men quickly rose to their feet.

Victor rushed in low for a tackle but Tommy came down hard and fast with a right fist to the side of Victor's neck, causing him to fall to the ground.

Victor got a hold of Tommy's heel as he hit the ground and pulled with all his might, bringing Tommy down next to him.

The two men lay on the ground, face to face. For a moment, they hesitated. They had grown up in the same neighborhood. They had lived through the War Between the Sacred and watched their friends die, fighting for a cause they didn't understand. And today, these two men were fighting for territory, and to preserve an agreement forged as a result of greed, control and fear.

Victor stood up first and tried to turn fast enough to land a kick into Tommy's jaw. Tommy was too fast and hit his feet without losing sight of Victor's attack. As Tommy dodged he landed a solid blow to Victor's temple, stunning him long enough to deal a second blow. Victor countered with a slug to the gut but Tommy had abs of steel and barely noticed the blow. Tommy was clearly superior in strength, agility and technique, pummeling Victor into the pavement.

Max stood watching as Tommy beat her lover into the ground.

Her heart was torn between the emotions she had for Victor and a secret longing she felt for Tommy. Still, she was Victor's woman and Victor was Sal's number one. She thought about ways that she could reach Madonna, ways she could explain why Victor didn't need to die, ways that Tommy and Victor could live in peace. But that just wasn't going to happen. Victor was getting beaten to death while she watched. Max thought about how she was going to explain what happened to Sal, Farb's will and all. None of her explanations absolved her from letting Tommy beat Victor to death.

Max walked over to Tommy as he beat Victor mercilessly. "Hey Tommy," she said softly. Tommy stopped beating Victor for a moment as he turned to face Max. "Goodbye," Max grinned as she unloaded one into his belly.

The blast ripped a hole straight through him and he dropped Victor's limp torso to the ground.

Both men lay in a heap next to one another.

Max holstered her pistol and looked up, half-expecting Madonna to fall from the clouds and kill her.

No one came.

Her lover and his business rival lay dead in the center of the Circle.

Everyone stood looking at Max, except for the ten blinded by Madonna who were still weeping into their hands.

50 CONFESSION

"Look Vic," Sal said through a mouthful of peanuts being washed down by a shot of whiskey. "I gotta admit, I've never really liked you bein' with my Maxie. That was her deal. She always seemed to think that you were my favorite." Sal leaned across the back seat of the limo, "but I don't play favorites."

Leer looked at Sal with a hint of distain.

"I think it's time I let you in on a little secret, Victor, not because I think you deserve it, but because there's no reason not to, now that my little girl is dead." Sal confessed with no wind in his sails. "I made a deal with Tommy Levito."

Leer knew all about the deal with Tommy but there was no way in Varst that Sal was going to hear a word of it, "Bastin' Farbunkle, Sal, what in Varst were you thinking?" Victor overstepped his bounds.

"You're right," Sal responded to Leer's surprise. "I had an idea and I think it might have backfired on me."

"C'mon Sal," Victor prodded, "Now you gotta' tell me how you could EVER make a deal with a Levito!" Leer knew how to milk a situation, regardless of the planet.
"The first missing shipment, I stole it." Sal said as he backed away from Victor.

If Leer would have been Victor, Sal would likely have had reason to back away, if not to bail completely from the limo while it was still driving down the highway. What Leer had learned across many worlds made Victor the one with the upper hand. "You must have had a very good reason to put me, Maxie and the rest of the boys in harm's way, boss" Leer responded, putting Victor in an advantageous position.

"Oh yeah, Victor, I did." Sal breathed with a sigh of relief, "Madonna," Sal coughed up a peanut, "I mean, Sacred Leader Madonna, demanded a higher cut. The only way I could meet her demand was to limit the supply and raise the price at a rate that could only be justified through a scarcity situation."

Leer lunged toward Sal.

Sal barely reacted. "I don't blame you for being upset, Victor," Sal said as he waved his hand and Leer was released from invisible bonds, slumping in the direction of Sal.

It made perfect sense for Victor to lunge at Sal and it also made perfect sense for Leer to know that Sal would be protected by some form of shield within his own limo. Victor settled down.

"I can assure you, I had nothing to do with Maxie's death." Sal handed Victor a shot, "but I don't think Tommy Levito did either."

"Yeah, Sal," Leer responded, "that's what I don't get either. I mean, what in the Varst is OUT there?!"

Sal pulled on Victor's wrists, drawing him in close to a mouthful of peanuts.

It was all Leer could do to keep from spilling the shot, "Whatever the Bast it is," Sal mawed, "I am going to kill it."

"Not if I do first," Victor said as Sal released his grip. He raised the shot glass in a toast and knocked it back. "I have my guys out looking for more of Max's belongings, hoping I can get to the piece of shit responsible for her death."

"If you find the bastin' dog, let me know. I want to be there when you grab him." Sal said as the limo pulled up to Victor's house. "And Vic, I want to be the one who puts a bullet in his head, ya' got me?"

"Fine," Victor conceded as he stepped out of the limo, "But I'm gonna beat him within an inch of his life before you do."

"Fair 'nough," Sal grinned as Phillipe closed the limo door and Victor walked to the box that Aldo had made, to grab his keys, his Harrison 37 already parked in the massive driveway outside his home

51 FAKE NEWS

Blue and Vinny were waiting inside for Leer.

Vinny looked like his normal self again and Blue was Tommy. Victor wasn't the least bit surprised that he had to park his own Harrison 37 in his garage, it made perfect sense and covered for Vinny posing as Geno. What surprised him was that both men were watching Rat TV and laughing.

"Leer, you gotta' see this," Blue motioned toward the television, "The pundits are at it again, making up a story they know nothing about and discussing it at length." Tommy finished another beer as Victor sat next to him with a full one. Blue filled his own glass without leaving the couch.

"For those of you just joining us here on Rat TV, breaking news," a sharply dressed anchor by the name of Cooper Anderson lorded over two panels in the heat of a discussion. "Today, Sal Lorenzo could be heard yelling at Supreme Leader Madonna as she left a private room where only the two of them had been meeting. Let me turn to our resident "Leader Politics Advisor," Nate Stone. We're going to roll the clip again, then I'd like to hear your take on this Nate."

The video played. Madonna was walking away from the private room in which she had been meeting with Sal, a look of consternation on her face. Sal's voice echoed in the hallway as the cameras were rolling. "You can't do this to Sal Lorenzo, Sacred Seven or not, you hear me!"

Nate Stone spoke into Rat TV's camera three, "I can only guess what this means for Rat Town, Cooper, but my gut tells me that Leader Madonna had some harsh words for Sal Lorenzo. Could this be related to the rumored discussions among the Sacred Seven to officially legalize JumpJuice, while Sacred Leader Madonna is advocating for stricter restrictions and penalties on JumpJuice? Absolutely!"

"Rivers Begin is the location of this unusual meeting of the Sacred Seven," Anderson explained, "and as Nate pointed out, the meeting seems to be about the state of JumpJuice and its long-held status as an illegal drug. Advocates and users of JumpJuice claim that the effects are far less dangerous than those of intoxication through the use of alcohol while opponents of the drug claim otherwise."

"Let's face it Cooper," Stone continued, "If they make JumpJuice legal, Sal Lorenzo is still going to be a very rich man. All this means is that Sal can't own the JumpJuice business like he does now, with the exception of the Levito territories."

"And we haven't heard much from Tommy Levito or Victor Alonso for that matter, since they both climbed out of the back of those ambulances after being pronounced dead." Anderson continued, "What do you make of that, Jan?"

The only black woman on the panel suddenly gets called upon because the question relates directly to the illegal drug business but instead of calling Anderson out on this humiliatingly racist segue, Jones willingly offers up her observations. "You know Cooper, Tommy Levito and Victor Alonso grew up in the same neighborhood. When they came back to life and crawled out of the back of those ambulances, they seemed changed. Rather than immediately blasting at one another or lunging into a fistfight, they talked for a moment. In fact, it took them a whole minute to draw their guns on one another and neither seemed ready to shoot." Jan Jones threw her hands up in the air and continued, "So, my point here, Cooper, is that the major players in the ongoing territorial fights over JumpJuice haven't even been seen, with the exception of Alonzo who was dumped, badly beaten at the curb of the Opera House less than a week ago. And when that happened, Sal Lorenzo didn't even lift a finger to go after Tommy Levito."

Cooper Anderson stood speechless for a moment before Jones resumed, "What I'm getting at here, Cooper, is that the JumpJuice business is more unpredictable at this very moment than it has ever been, even during the territorial wars more than a decade ago!"

"Hundreds of people died back then," Rod Axel blurted in the direction of Jones, "It was an all-out war, how can you even make a comparison like that?"

Jones replied sharply, "When Sacred Leader Madonna is involved, and make no mistake she is, ordinary human lives mean nothing. If there is a war between Sal Lorenzo and Leader Madonna, there will be more bloodshed than there was in the War Between the Sacred. Lorenzo is not a man to back down and Leader Madonna will not be trifled with."

"She's not too far off," Leer said after he gulped down the rest of his beer and watched it slowly fill itself to the brim. "She's just not clear on where the loyalties are now. We are going to have a war, but my guess is Madonna's going to give Sal exactly what he wants, and that's an army. If she was going to side with us, her meeting with Sal would have ended differently. The only thing Sal talked to me about was you, Tommy, confessing that he had been working with you behind my back. Well, that and the fact that he was going to kill whoever killed Max."

"I can't wait to see the look on his face when he finds out the truth," Blue snickered, "but it isn't going to be easy to get him to the right place at the right time." Blue rubbed his head for a moment, "And if Madonna backs him up, we're going to need Farb on our side."

"I still can't get used to how you guys talk about Sacred Leader Madonna and the Almighty Farb like they're just your average people," Vinny admitted, "it's going require an adjustment in my brain to drop the appellations." Vinny smiled as he watched his glass top off for the fourth time. "Not too big of an adjustment though, I've never been terribly religious."

"Hardly religious is more like it, Vinny!" Tommy laughed, "Just repeat after me, Let's go see Farb, to Varst with Madonna!"

Vinny raised his glass and shouted, "Let's go see Farb, to Varst with Madonna!"

The three men finished their beers and instantly transported to a spot by the ocean where they found Farb wading. "I was wondering when you'd find me, Blue," Farb said without turning around. "You're a good man, Vinny. Most guys couldn't handle the news that their brother was now being called the Onjadiavaan," he laughed quietly, "Or that he was also some guy from another planet. But you, Vinny, you befriended that man and helped him to find the Omega Lux Crystal, what Sansaa's people call Shedavah."

Vinny wasn't surprised that Farb knew everything about him, he was shocked that he took the time to congratulate and praise him for something he felt most people would do.

"I know you think it's the kind of thing that everyone would do, Vinny, but I can assure you, it is not." Farb turned to face the men who arrived out of nowhere. "Good to see you again Leer, even though you are in Alonso's body."

"Joe Franklin?" Leer responded, "You are Farb?"

Blue looked at Leer, then back to Farb. "You're Barack Obama," he said in surprise.

"Him too," Farb said, "Would've thought you had that figured out before you got here Blue!"

Blue thought about it for a minute then spoke, "You're right, now that I have had a minute to think about it, I can see that you are also Pierce Elliot, Agonshar and a little dog-like creature known as Puffkin." Tommy had a puzzled look on his face as he asked his next question, "What I don't get is how you can be all of them at once."

"But that's not why you came to see me." Farb answered with a smile. "That's good, because I can't tell you how to do it."

362

"I have to do it myself" Blue finished Farb's thought for him as Farb smiled even wider. "Since you already know why we're here, do you mind telling me what else you know?" Blue realized that was like someone asking himself the same question and decided to define his question a little more clearly, "Specifically, are you going to help us legalize JumpJuice?"

Farb looked at Blue like he was a little child and spoke to him in the same way. "Blue, you are here to help me."

Although Blue knew this to be true, he had thought it was his own idea.

"Do you remember running across those "Leer" drawings in your studio when you were painting that "Lifesaver" painting in your studio?" Farb asked, not waiting for an answer, "Did you notice how they kept showing up in separate places even though you thought you kept everything together?"

Farb walked toward Victor and placed a hand on his shoulder, "I needed Leer back in Victor's body, Blue, and you were just a bonus!" Farb confessed as he explained, "Your finding of the Omega Lux Crystal was totally unexpected, I thought you were just a Quanji. That's the first time this has happened to me in over a hundred Earth years. The fact that you revealed Shedavah is nothing short of a miracle, Farb's word!" Farb laughed as he extended his hand to Blue who shook it firmly. Without letting go, Farb continued, "I am thrilled that you are here to help me."

Blue crossed his other hand over Obama's and held fast, "Can you explain a few decisions you made as Barack Obama, President of the United States before I do?"

Farb knew this was coming and replied succinctly, "I promise to share all of my thoughts and actions with you when we have accomplished our mission here."

Blue released his hold on Obama and said, "No need, I got what I wanted."

Farb realized the extent to which Blue's power had grown in the short time since discovering the crystal. "Now you can't compare being a god to being a president, Blue, you are aware of that, aren't you?"

"Based on your presidency sir," Blue frowned, "I hope not."

Blue was banking on his intuition that Farb was a better god than he was a person, and the fact that he believed in Obama so completely that he was willing to concede that it might have been "the Office" that changed him. The bigger problem was, he didn't quite get the simultaneous lives construct. His brain was still behaving like that of an ordinary human, aside from the fact that he now had the history of the universe in his human mind, an achievement that no entity had foreseen, including Farb who was one of the five most powerful beings in the universe.

All of them had foreseen Blue's ability as a Quanji, to bring Leer back as Victor, to help Farb to legalize JumpJuice on Salta, but none of them had foreseen Blue's revelation of Shedavah. To everyone who followed the prophecy, Blue had become Onjadiavaan. For an Earth Human to be able to accept all that information without a complete collapse of the brain was not anticipated.

Farb was a good god.

He did not take offense at Blue's comment. In fact, he answered Blue in a surprising fashion, "I'm not a big fan of President Obama myself," he said. "The man nearly died from serving that presidency. It is one of the hardest things to do on the planet and everyone thinks they could do a better job. No Blue, I have no qualms about working with you, despite what I know about you and how you feel about war. But even you have changed. You have become a warrior, both to stay alive as well as to further a cause you believe to be important."

Blue recognized that Farb had the power to fry him on the spot but felt that he would never consider it. He had been invited by Farb, who was ready to discuss next moves. It was no time to follow a personal agenda, particularly one that happened to deal with a completely different world.

He watched as Farb rose a single finger and the sea before them rose into a wall, and stayed there. He marveled at the fact that the tide still flowed as it should while a wall of water became the shoreline.

"This, gentlemen, is where we fight," Farb began as a video image played upon the aquascreen of the ocean. The depth of the water undulated to reinforce the depth of the image. It was the most enthralling video display Blue had ever seen. As the camera panned across the topography, Victor gasped. He recognized the land as the very spot where he had faked the hijacking of the latest JumpJuice run.

"Don't trouble yourself John, I know your plan." Farb continued showing the images. "You see that we are ready." Leer saw his own creation, Victor's army within Heavana.

He laughed and jumped up and down like an ape then picked Farb up by his waist and hoisted him up in a big bear hug.

"And you can put me down," Farb calmly continued. "The difficult part is the timing. We need to draw Lorenzo out to this spot." Farb released the ocean and the waters settled back into place as if nothing had changed.

"Pretty sure Sal is going to be hooked as soon as Max's boots give us the location of her killer." Leer smiled and added with a grimace, "Madonna's going to fight on his side though, I am guessing."

"Madonna is going to use this moment to attempt a coup," Farb explained. "She's been after my job since she showed up, nothing like the Earth Madonna, in case you're wondering. Oh, and what's even worse, this one can't sing." Farb laughed to himself and continued, "She's been talking to some of the other Sacred Leaders attempting to bend their loyalties to her. Three of them have told me this has happened, which means that the other three are with her." Farb paced while he spoke.

Blue found this interesting because he liked to pace while thinking and talking and he began to do just that. "I can help tip the scales then," he said while he and Farb performed intense and precise patterns of movement around one another while remaining close enough to not raise their voices. "How powerful are each of the individual Leaders?"

"They aren't the ones I worry about, Blue, you could probably handle half of them on your own." Farb admitted, "It's their armies. They have massive armies, far larger than the Leaders who are sworn to me."

"Almighty Farb," Vinny broke into the conversation.

"Farb, just Farb is fine, Vinny." Farb winked.

"Yes, your ma-I-mean Farb. Well, most of the commanders of Madonna's armies are friends of mine and..."

"That's precisely what I was hoping you would say Vinny," Farb broke in, "Do you think you could arrange for your friends to defy orders given by Madonna?"

"There is one power I do have, Farb," Vinny smiled, "I make lasting friends. Tell me where and when and I will make sure it happens, or doesn't, depending." Vinny was happy to be able to contribute. For him, helping Farb was an honor. While he didn't get into religion, being in the presence of Farb was unlike anything he had ever known. He felt as though everything was possible.

"Hey Vinny," Tommy chimed in, "Bring Sansaa and Anna Marie with you. It's very important that they are with us when Sal learns the truth about Max."

Farb looked at Tommy with surprise and Blue noticed. He was beginning to think that there were some things that fell outside of Farb's ability to see.

"Now John, since this is your plan, I don't need to tell you how important it is that Sal learns the truth from Victor. Max can't make an appearance until Sal is set to make his move. Madonna will wait until the very last moment to strike, which means all of the armies will arrive at once and this puts Maxine Lorenzo at great risk." Farb stopped pacing, "You're right John, but she doesn't know it yet." Farb looked at

Victor, "She must be protected, once Sal discovers that she was in on the deception, he won't be the only one to fear."

John held his hands to his face as the truth about Max hit him. She truly was everything he imagined her to be. To him, she was a character he created, several in fact. To Leer she was both Mona Damino and Catherine Kent and to Victor she was Max.

"How does it feel to create life?" Farb asked John with a knowing smile.

John dropped to the sand as the sheer magnitude of the realization overwhelmed him.

"She may not love you as you love her, John," Farb advised quietly as he lifted his hands to the sky, "but then again," he smiled deeply as a large falcon descended from the sky and landed on his arm, "she might!" Farb stroked the falcon gently, pulled a piece of jerky from his hip pocket and fed the bird. As she ate, he peeled a message from around her leg. "Your team has settled in at Heavana, and they seem to be enjoying themselves immensely. Are they even aware of what you have planned?" Farb asked with a measure of concern.

"They have no idea." Victor responded, "I told them wait for my orders."

"You dropped off a team of mercenaries, took their guns away, gave them new lives, new living quarters, jobs and everything they would ever need for a comfortable existence and you expect them to jump when you give the command?" Farb questioned.

"They really love a good fight," Victor said calmly, "and tomorrow they're all getting drafted into the Heavana Army, which reminds me, I need your signature on this form." Victor pulls a document from one of the pockets of his trousers. "Oh, and here's a pen." He hands them to Farb.

"A Military Authorization Form," Farb smiles as he glances at the document and hands both it and the pen back to Victor. "You need my signature on the document to get the army of Heavana to engage in any military mission," Farb said as he reached into his pocket and produced the very same document, already signed and emblazoned with his stamp. "I told you, John. I know your plan."

John smiled and took the form from Farb.

Farb released the falcon from his arm and the great bird circled overhead. "Well, I guess this means I'll be seeing you in a couple of days gentleman," he smiled, bent his knees and leapt into the air. As he rose upward he transformed into a falcon and circled back around. Both falcons looped and dove in elaborate maneuvers, unlike those of typical falcons, before flying off along the shore.

The three men watched the birds for a minute or two before Blue transported them to Victor's house.

Tommy turned to Vinny and said, "I'm going to send you back to the Shadowlands. I am counting on you to bring Sansaa and Anna Marie with you."

"I'm not sure I want Sansaa getting mixed up in this bro!" Vinny responded with concern.

"If I didn't need them," Tommy confided, "I wouldn't ask."

Vinny knew that Blue could do just about anything, so his request for the ladies, though unexpected, must be important, "I can do that," he said hesitantly, "there's only one small problem. If you zap me back to the Shadowlands, all I have is the VinnCycle and I can't put both of them on it. Why don't you just zap them here?"

"Great question Vinny." Blue explained his request by adding a critical detail. "I need you to ask Sansaa and Anna Marie to join us outside the gates to Heavana in two days. And this is the most important part of the request, you must make it in front of Targent."

Vinny was taken aback that Tommy suggested that Targent overhear the request. Vinny didn't dislike Targent, he just didn't place a high value on any sort of friendship with him and if anything, he found Targent to occasionally be quite annoying. "Do you want him to come along too?" Vinny asked.

"No," Tommy quickly responded, "and if he asks to tag along, tell him no." Blue tried to explain his motivations while avoiding putting Vinny in a spot where he might accidentally upset the plan. "I am pretty sure that Targent isn't quite what he appears to be, but I don't want him to know I am on to him. Tell him it's very important that he remain behind in case Mojahdii needs anything."

"I'm still going to need a car," Vinny stated.

Victor opened a box on the wall after entering a series of numbers. He tossed Vinny a set of keys, "It's the dark blue one at the far end of the garage. The door opener is under the visor. It's the only car I have that Sal and his goons won't recognize."

Vinny caught the keys, hugged his brother and headed toward the garage. "See you in a couple of days."

52 CALL TO ARMS

For the next couple of days, the news was all about the overheard words of Sal Lorenzo just after a private meeting with Sacred Leader Madonna.

As usual, the mainstream media was missing the real story.

Sal was on the hunt for the killer of Max and he was planning on bringing the biggest army ever assembled on Salta with him.

The day after their limo ride back from Rivers Begin, Victor arrived alone at Sal's residence. He had called ahead, and Sal was waiting for him on a sprawling deck that wrapped its way around the entire house. "Sal, I think we found Max's killer," Victor called out as he reached the deck, holding Max's boots above his head.

Sal instantly recognized the boots and rose to his feet, he rushed toward Victor with his hands outstretched, as if the touching of her boots might bring his daughter back to him. "Where," he cried, "Where did you find these, where is he? Where is the bastin farbunkle who did this to Max? Why isn't he here? Are you holding him?" Sal riddled the air with his questions.

"There's an army, Sal." Victor calmly responded, "We got a man inside and he was lucky to get these without being discovered."

"I don't care about him, I want my Maxie!" Sal had grown in his grief over Max. Even though he was telling no one, he was losing enthusiasm for everything, JumpJuice, money, even power. Vengeance however, was not in short supply, his heart burned to see those responsible for Max's death suffer and die. "How big is the army?"

Victor looked at Sal a long time before answering. "It's massive Sal, we need Leader Madonna's forces if we hope to defeat them swiftly."

"We got 'em, Vic, she wants the bastards as much as I do."
This was the confirmation Leer was looking for from Sal. The entire operation depended on Madonna's involvement and Sal had sealed the deal.

"Get our forces together," Sal ordered, "We strike tomorrow." He turned to go inside his house, holding Max's boots close to his heart, "And get Levito, tell him Sal said it's time."

Leer left with everything he wanted, Sal ready for war and an open invitation to work with Blue.

Meanwhile, Tommy was assembling his troops, reasoning that Sal would call him into battle against whatever army Victor had convinced him was responsible for Max's death.

Within hours Tommy Levito and Victor Alonso were standing face to face, each with an army behind them.

Most of the troops assumed they were assembling to fight one another. After all, that was the most recent state of things and no one other than Tommy and Victor knew that Sal had a secret arrangement with Tommy.

Victor and Tommy each had a small entourage in close support of them, the officers of their respective armies.

The greater majority of them were stunned as Tommy and Victor approached one another and shook hands. An audible wave gasped its way through the troops. These men and women had been fighting each other for years, some of whom could actually recognize fighters on the other side from one on one battle.

Blue could sense a tension that had the potential to erupt if not addressed.

Many of the troops assembled were dealers while the rest were mercenary muscle. Their loyalties ran with the money and that supply chain was about to be disrupted. He had to get them all on one side before the impending battle could rip them apart. He held up a large red coin.

"I'll give a fifty to anyone who can tell me why we are here today." Tommy shouted, followed by a stunned expression on the faces of most of the crowd. No one moved, except for one man in Tommy's army who walked forward and handed him a megaphone. He quickly retreated to his position by a military vehicle that was loaded with communications gear.

Tommy continued as he pocketed the coin and lifted the megaphone to his lips. "We are combining our forces against a common enemy." It was difficult for Blue to lead these troops into a battle in which he had no stake, based on a plan that Leer had concocted fifteen years earlier. A plan sanctioned by Farb, a self-appointed god, simply to legalize a substance he had only recently tried, on a planet that was not his own, the very premise of which was a lie. "We seek retribution for the recent hijacked shipments of JumpJuice suffered by Sal Lorenzo, culminating in the death of Maxine Lorenzo, the young lady who blasted a hole in my gut a couple weeks ago."

The entire crowd stood in awe. No one could understand why Tommy might agree to stand by Sal in this moment until he spoke again.

"It has been brought to my attention that another organization is responsible for those hijacked shipments and that all JumpJuice traffic is at risk in Rat Town. We cannot withstand another war over JumpJuice if that war is sustained fighting between three interests. That is why I have come to an agreement, with Sal Lorenzo and Victor Alonso, to act swiftly to eradicate this organization while reinforcing the agreement we have had in place for so long." Tommy could see that the crowd was still too bewildered to respond.

"How many of you sell JumpJuice, show me your weapons!" A cheer rose up from the crowd as nearly a third of those assembled raised their weapons in the air.

"All of you here who make money in the JumpJuice business, I want to see your weapons!" Another swell of cheers erupted as most of the crowd raised their weapons.

Tommy brought the whole crowd around as he shouted, "Now show me how many of you use JumpJuice!" The crowd burst forth with shouts and cheers that could be heard miles away, right to the center of rat Town.

Tommy handed the megaphone to Victor.

"For JumpJuice!" he shouted into the megaphone as he held his gun up high. The crowd responded with a round, "For JumpJuice, for JumpJuice, for JumpJuice!" Victor raised both his hands then brought them down slowly. The whole crowd was attentive to Tommy and Victor who stood side by side.

Victor continued, "Tomorrow we fight against an army we have never seen before. They manage to hide themselves in the valley, and strike from below the ground." Having heard rumors before of such an army, the crowd grew more intrigued as Victor explained, "We were hit by that very army when we lost Max," he pointed all around the crowd, "I know a lot of you loved her," he moved his pointer sharply toward Tommy's army," And a lot of you loved to hate her!"

The entire crowd laughed in unison. Everyone knew Max and everyone had one of two opinions about her, they either loved her or they hated her, no in-betweens.

Victor handed the megaphone to Tommy. "Tonight, we surround the valley. Report to your team leaders for rations, ammo and locations." He put down the megaphone, looked at his entourage and nodded while Victor did the same with his. Each army split up into units that all converged upon their leaders at once. Tommy and Victor marveled at the precision of the armies they had assembled. "It's a shame we have to get so many of these bastards killed," Leer said quietly to Blue. "I tried so many ways to think about how to make this happen without the loss of lives and this one has the greatest chance."

"We came an awfully long way to see this plan through, my friend. I am only now realizing some of the possible outcomes. No matter what happens," Blue said sincerely, "it has been an honor being your Quanji!"

"You sound like you think you're gonna die, man, take it easy!" John responded, feeling true fear for his friend. After all, Blue now had the power of foresight.

"All I'm saying, John, is there are several different possible outcomes to tomorrow's battle, and like you said, this seems like the best chance we have at preserving life while instigating a dramatic change." Blue smiled warmly, "It's good to be working with you again!"

John still felt weird about Blue's comments but let it slide with a simple, "You too."

53 PROTECTION

Max had become thoroughly engaged in her new life within a very short time.

She was already picking up some of the basics of dance that she thought she had lost long ago. Even simple, everyday things like eating were more enjoyable in Heavana. She never had to rush and she didn't need to know where the exits were in a restaurant.

She didn't need to scan every face in the establishment to see if they were watching her and she was already losing the habit.

The overwhelming feelings of the past that would not leave were her feelings for Victor. Max was beginning to miss Victor, at least the Victor she had been spending time with after he crawled out of the back of the ambulance.

Victor had only told her part of the plan for a number of reasons but the main one was that he wasn't sure when Sal would take the bait or what his reaction would be to the thought of losing Max. Even her own feelings toward her father were beginning to change, Max was beginning to feel free.

The one thing that was certain was that Max was the center of the plan.

Her relationship with her father was the key to the success of the mission. She would wait for a message from Victor, but until then, she would enjoy Heavana.

As she sat in her apartment, watching a performance by one of the finest dance troupes in Heavana, on one of the fine art networks, owned and operated by Heavana's Council for the Arts, she settled deeply into her cushy recliner with a glass of red wine and a bar of chocolate.

Suddenly, there was a knock on the door. Max immediately snapped back into self-defense mode and approached the door cautiously. Until this moment, Barbara was the only person in Heavana to knock on her door and this knock did not belong to Barbara. Max neatly tucked a kitchen knife into the belt of her robe, behind her back but easy to reach. She opened the door slowly.

"Hello Ms. Lorenzo," a smartly outfitted soldier said, arms at her sides, clearly not hostile. "I have been instructed to guide you to a secure location where you will be informed about the next phase of operation "LifeJump," and this is for you." She held out a sealed envelope. Max took the envelope from the soldier who took a full step back and continued, "I will be waiting here until you have had a chance to change clothes," she continued respectfully, "get your things in order and follow me, please."

Max closed the door slowly, locked it and opened the letter which read, "Follow the soldier, please, Victor. p.s. Make sure to confirm the password."

Max opened the door again. "Do you like peanuts?" She asked the soldier.

"Too many shells," the soldier responded. Max smiled and asked the woman inside.

"Just give me a minute to put something on," Max stowed the knife back in its block on her way through the kitchen.

The soldier remained just inside of the door, at attention and expressionless.

She did not remain so when Max returned, dressed for battle; weaponless, but clearly dressed to kill. The soldier couldn't help but to tighten up in an instant reaction of respect tinged with a little fear. She reflexively put her hand to the butt of her sidearm.

"You won't be needing that," Max glanced toward the soldier's handgun, "I'll come peacefully," Max joked as she opened the door and guided the soldier through with a bow and a wave. The soldier laughed an embarrassed sort of giggle, then straightened up and marched through the door.

The entire team had been assembled at Max's destination, a massive armory beneath the center of the city.

Spike was the last to arrive. "He remembered the password and he dressed for the occasion, you owe me a fifty, Max," Aldo joked as Spike arrived.

Spike couldn't take his eyes off the weapons hung all around him and said, "Whaddya mean Aldo, I dress like this all the time and I don't remember no bastin' password. Did you see who they sent to get me?" Spike then leered back at the female soldier who escorted him to the armory with the same drooling expression he wore for the weapons. "When do we get some?" he called out to the ceiling which was nearly a hundred feet above them.

"Right now," a voice echoed across the armory, "But no killing unless it becomes absolutely necessary." A man wearing a dark suit was walking toward the team. "I must say, I am quite proud of all of you," Dr. Stan Case was dressed in full body armor with two swords across his back and what looked like a rocket launcher strapped to his right thigh.

Spike burst out laughing at the sight of Dr. Case armed for battle, "You, the acting coach, or whatever it is you call what you did to us, a fighter? You do know that just wearing those things doesn't make you a fighter, don't you?"

Dr. Case pulled two straps from his right thigh and dropped the rocket launcher to the ground. He reached up with both hands and drew the swords from their sheaths, then lay them across the barrel of the rocket launcher. Turning to Spike he said, "fighting is what makes you a fighter, training is what makes you a good one. We don't have any time left for training. If you can reach my swords, you may have them and the P-45 as well." He stood between his weapons and Spike, one foot slightly behind the other, hands at his side.

Spike looked around at the rest of the team, laughing. He had been a good boy. He had given up his guns and his knives. He had been quiet since he arrived in Heavana. He was itching for a fight and now there was an actor standing in front of him trying to tell him what made a good fighter. Spike didn't need anyone to tell him to fight. He didn't need anyone to goad him on, but he got it just the same.

"Do it Spike!" Lee Camp couldn't resist the impulse to see Dr. Case and Spike have a go at it. "Time to teach the teacher!"

It was something akin to unleashing a rabid dog. Spike lunged at Stan Case from ten feet away and was on him before anyone could blink, but not before Dr. Case could raise his foot with enough forceful intent to not only stop the forward progress of his assailant but to alter his course in a direction which required him to lose contact with the ground completely, the result of which was eventually succumbing to the law of gravity.

Spike hit the ground hard.

His legs had continued their forward momentum but his face remained planted on the heel of Dr. Case's right boot, effectively leveling him out. He landed flat on his back. It was hard to tell if the foot or the landing was the thing that knocked him out but by the time he regained consciousness, a fleet of military vehicles had surrounded the team.

"Back among the conscious," Dr. Case smiled as he bent over Spike and offered a hand up. Spike reluctantly accepted. "Don't worry Spike, you can still have any weapons you want, just make sure you know who you're fighting." The team encircled Stan and Spike. "In fact, that's just the reason I am here," Dr. Stan continued, "Tomorrow is going to be a very confusing day and Victor has asked me to share his full plan with you tonight. He has also asked me to apologize for keeping you in the dark." Dr. Stan pulled a knife from his boot and handed it to Spike.

"And, you will find all of your personal weapons in the foot lockers on these vehicles. In addition, you may supplement your supply with anything we have here in the arsenal." Dr. Case walked in the opposite direction from which he came. "Instructions on where to find me are in the vehicles, you have one hour to get your weapons and meet me at terminal one."

"You heard the man," Max reflexively barked orders to the team and their Pavlovian behavior snapped back into place. "Choose your weapons quickly then return to the vehicles. Aldo, you stay with me and let's figure out these instructions."

"What's to figure out Max, it's just a map?" Aldo laughed as he started up the vehicle, "Looks like he's got the destination already loaded. I wouldn't be surprised if these babies drove themselves."

The team surrounded the vehicles shortly after hearing Aldo start the engine. Max jumped behind the wheel of the second vehicle and Lee drove the third. "Let's move out, Max called," and the vehicles sped off in the direction indicated.

It wasn't long before the team reached their destination, well in advance of the hour allotted by Dr. Case.

"You all look a bit eager to get back in the game," Stan began, "running JumpJuice and fighting off anyone who stands in your way." The team hooted and howled, especially Spike. "I hate to disappoint you, but the game has changed." Silence fell upon the team. "We are going to try to stop a war." All eyes were on Dr. Case as he explained, "Sal Lorenzo, Victor Alonso, Tommy Levito and Leader Madonna are all bringing armies here to crush whoever is responsible for killing Max." He pointed to Max who knew at least that much of the plan. That was the very reason she didn't have her favorite gun or her favorite boots. "Sal took the bait. Victor convinced him that Max was killed in the JumpJuice heist at the hands of an unknown enemy."

Dr. Case waved the team over to a large display screen just inside terminal one.

"Max will be standing here tomorrow when Sal arrives." Stan Case continues pointing out places on the map as he describes Victor's plan, devised by Leer fifteen years earlier. Not a single one of them know the truth about Victor but every one of them has found that they feel a real devotion to Victor, especially since he was beaten to death.

"We don't know when we'll see Victor again," Dr. Stan continued, "That is entirely up to Sal Lorenzo and his reaction to seeing Max alive again." Max began to laugh, "He's probably already forgotten me," she said as her laugher turned to more of a hopeless sigh, "He might even shoot me, just for not being dead." Max had no way of knowing the turmoil Sal had been experiencing since Victor told him that she had been killed.

"However he's feeling about you, our mission remains the same, to protect you." Dr. Stan surveyed the team. "Max is Victor's number one priority tomorrow. No matter what else is happening, protect Max."

"What in the Varst am I supposed to do then, reminisce with pops?" Max asked as she fidgeted with a gun that was clearly disappointing her. "That is the mystery of the day, Max," Dr. Case confessed. "Victor first told me the plan fifteen years ago. The only thing that has changed about it is you, Max."

The entire team was deeply puzzled. Dr. Case had no words to help. In fact, what he did know confused them more. "You see Max, in the original plan, you were already dead."

Max stood up and pointed the gun she was holding directly at Dr. Stan. She immediately realized that it made no sense to point a gun at him, so she lowered it. "Dead? How?" She asked quietly.

"I'm not entirely sure," Dr. Stan responded, "but Victor did say that Sal would be coming to collect your dead body and avenge your death. I can only guess, based on the fact that he enlisted my help to get you all here, that something had changed in the plan over the past fifteen years." He looked around at the team again, while counting with his fingers and naming names under his breath. "Yep, everyone but you,

Max. You are the only one breathing who shouldn't be." Stan winced as he realized just how bad what he had said actually sounded. "I mean no offense, Max. In fact," he rubbed his forehead, "I can't imagine what happened. Every other part of the plan has worked out to be something that Victor saw coming. So, what's different?"

"Victor." Max replied in a voice that revealed that only then did it occur to her just how different everything had become since Victor climbed out of the ambulance. "Victor is different," she said.

A small wave of affirmation came back from the team.

Dr. Case stood in front of them and asked a very direct question, his eyes gazing deeply into each member of the team, as if asking their very souls, "Are you all ready to protect Max, no matter what goes down tomorrow?"

He did not get the unilateral affirmative he was seeking. It was more of a looking around at each other and shrugging a little. Max broke the awkward silence with the question everyone else had but hadn't found the words to express. "What else might be "going down" tomorrow, specifically, Dr. Case?"

Dr. Stan Case spent the next hour and a half explaining all of the possible outcomes Victor had foreseen, both with Max alive and with Max dead, which he described as moot but thought he should include anyway. By the time he had finished, even he was feeling a bit confused. Spike closed the meeting with a comment that everyone understood.

"All I know is, if anybody gets near my friend Max here, I kill 'em, and if anyone gets near me? I kill 'em!"

54 REVELATION

Max couldn't stop thinking about how different things became after Victor emerged, resurrected from the back of the ambulance. It was as though her very wishes were being granted.

First, Victor treated her with respect since the ambulance.

He always had with regard to her fighting and her ability to command, but he took advantage of her emotionally before in ways that he hadn't since. He actually seemed to care about her for her, not simply because her daddy owned the JumpJuice trade.

And, in the morning, he was going to help her to finally address her feelings for her father. He was going to start a war for her.

This made her feel incredibly sick and incredibly horny at the same time.

Before she had to hand her favorite gun over to Victor to convince Sal of her death, she used to rub her thighs around her gun when she was, horny and alone or surrounded by mercenary soldiers which happened far too many more times than even she would have imagined.

But tonight, she didn't have her favorite gun and she didn't have Victor.

The second thing that was different about Victor was his intelligence.

He was always pretty smart, at least compared to the other guys she had dated, but post-ambulance Victor was articulate. He spoke differently enough for her to recognize while those around him, who feared him, took no notice. She wondered if her father had noticed but never thought to ask him in the short time between Victor's death and hers.

A slight chill ran through her as she thought a much deeper thought than she had ever remembered thinking. She wondered if she had ever lived in a different body or if she had ever died before and was reborn into a different life.

Max snapped out of a dreamlike state to find her hands wrapped around the barrel of the rifle she had chosen from the weapons stack earlier in the evening.

It was pointed directly at her but the base of the barrel was clamped between her legs, tight against her jeans, the butt of the gun leveraged against the floor by her own feet. She let go completely and relaxed as her knees splayed open and she gasped, "Leer!"

55 REUNITED

"Are you sure this is the place your guy told you about?" Sal Lorenzo was furious with Victor Alonso as the two men stood about five hundred feet away from two armies who were facing them in a semicircle, weapons drawn and ready for war.

"Why don't we just shoot both of them now and be done with the whole thing?" Danny Sikes was the closest thing to a brother that Tommy Levito had when he decided to never speak to his brother again.

Since Tommy arose from the dead, Danny began to feel as though Tommy was different. He didn't get a lot of time to spend with him because Tommy went off to the Shadowlands with Vinny, which was weird for Tommy in the first place, since he always made fun of Vinny for his "retreats in the Shadowlands with Sansaa."
Danny genuinely loved Tommy. He would do anything for Tommy and would do everything with Tommy if he could. He just never bothered to tell him how he felt. He didn't think that Tommy would shoot him in the head if he found out, but he did have a voice in his head that told him it might be a possibility.

"Look Tommy, those guys are standing in the middle of a bastin' desert, with nobody else around, and we are here to help them defeat an enemy who is going to steal all of the JumpJuice trade in Salta and beyond!" Danny was now laughing in Tommy's face, "Well, I don't see anything!"

Roughly twenty feet from where Sal and Victor were standing, the ground began to break apart.

Sal turned to run away but Victor held him in place and pointed toward the disturbed soil.

Both Sal and Victor stood frozen as the ground continued to open and a lone figure rose from below. Leer marveled at how closely the ascension of Max matched the diagrams he had proposed fifteen years earlier, only back then, they were propping up a dead Max, rather than a live one with whom he was in love. This was the moment where his planning ended and reality was about to set in.

"That's my Maxie!" Sal screamed as he lunged toward her. The ground fell away before him, leaving a hole between Sal and Max. In fact, the ground was completely missing between Max and Sal for as far as the eye could see. It had simply dropped away. Sal remained kneeling and sobbing, his hand stretched out toward Max as the ground settled around them and the dust fell from the air.

"Hello father." Max said in a voice that chilled Sal to his very bones.

"You're alive," he cried as he slowly rose to his feet. Sal wiped the tears from his eyes and continued, "Are you real, Maxie, are you still alive?"

Max had not expected to see her father this way.

She had been imagining this meeting since Victor told her he was going to tell Sal that she had died in the JumpJuice hijacking, but what she imagined and what she was seeing were completely different things. He actually loved her.

Sal was a wreck.

Victor had warned her that Sal might truly care for her in ways that she could not imagine but she never listened. As far as Max was concerned, her father had ruled over every decision she had ever made and was responsible for them even more than she was. She could not see the love within his actions, his words, his guidance or his demands, until this moment.

Max could feel Sal's love for her and it was real.

For a moment, she lost her drive to call out her father on his abuse. She lost her will to bend him to hers. She felt only compassion as she looked upon her father, separated from her now, by a chasm in the ground, deeper and wider than anyone could cross, and yet she had never felt closer.

"I'm sorry," was all that Max could hear as Sal fell to the ground and sobbed.

The armies stood silent as the most powerful man they had ever known knelt sobbing into his own hands.

No one had predicted this.

Leer's plan included a belligerent Sal who wanted to kill everyone, including Max. Leer had not imagined the love of a father being stronger than the will of a ruthless, money-grubbing tyrant.

John had never been a father when he created Leer and Leer had never spawned a child.

Blue couldn't stand his father and was also perplexed.

An entire world stood in the balance of this moment and this moment was supposed to culminate in war.

Leer turned toward Blue and shrugged. Tommy turned toward his troops and signaled them to stand down. Victor waved to his army and they stood at ease.

Tommy walked forward until he reached Victor and Sal.

Max remained across the divide as Sal finally looked up from his soaked palms and asked, "How long did you know?" He pulled a gun from his belt and fired it within a single motion at Victor's head.

Blue laid his hand on Leer's back and the shot fell dead to the sand.

Victor grabbed the gun from Sal as Tommy lifted Sal to his feet.

Blue nodded to Max and she walked toward the men as the ground rose before her feet, creating a bridge across the chasm.

Sal waited as he watched Max approach. The moment the ground filled in between them, Sal ran toward Max. She watched him approach. She did not see the anger or the discipline or the castigation she had expected to see in her father's eyes.

All she saw was love.

When he finally reached her, he hugged her close, tight to his body and then he released her. He softly put a hand to her face and then another, He gently guided her head toward his and placed his lips softly upon her forehead. "I love you Maxie," Sal said for the first time in his life.

Tears welled up in Maxine's eyes as she replied, "How much?"

Sal was shocked. He had bared himself to her, he had apologized, he had given in to love. He had no idea what to say. "What do you mean?"

Max had already been through every emotion she could imagine with her father. The last thing she expected was for him to acknowledge her and treat her with love and respect. Still, she had told Victor that she wanted out of JumpJuice and that she wanted her father to love her for who she was, not what he wanted her to be. Now, Max found herself in the very place she had wanted to be. The only thing that was different than what she had imagined was that there were thousands of troops waiting to engage in war based on what she was about to say next.

"I want out," she finally responded. "I don't want any more of this, father, I want to live a life where I don't care how much JumpJuice costs or how it gets where it needs to go, and I especially don't want anyone I love to be associated with how it is sold or what happens to people who don't "understand" the business." Max held her father at arm's length, "you have to stop." She threw her arms to the sky, "It all has to stop!"

Max paced for a moment then looked Sal in the eyes and demanded, "Drop the JumpJuice business. Tell that bitch Madonna she can go to Varst, and make JumpJuice legal."

Sal scratched his head and dropped to the sand where he sat looking confused and helpless. "I just made a deal with Leader Madonna and her troops are on the way. She's coming to kill whoever killed you." Sal suddenly snapped, "You fooled me, you made me believe you were dead!" He began to sob again.

"I did," Max acknowledged, "We needed to draw you out here, to defeat you." Max softened, "But I don't want that anymore. For the first time in my life, I actually feel like you love me."

"Who's we, Max," Sal asked quickly, "These jokers? The guys who were dead enemies and now they seem to be best friends?" Sal continued, "Are these the guys who were going to defeat me? I own their bastin' armies for Farb's sake."

"No daddy," Max said sternly, "Victor was doing it for me. I am the one who wanted to see you lose everything because nothing ever seemed to matter to you." Max held out a hand to her father and pulled him up from the ground where she hugged him. "I was going to force you to give up on the JumpJuice trade, to go along with the people who are pressing to make it legal."

Sal smiled at Max with understanding but couldn't resist taking a poke at her logic, "You and who's army?"

Max raised her right hand and made a fist. The ground opened up behind them, revealing an entire land mass rising from below. Upon it stood an army, many thousands strong. Behind them, the mountains opened and jettisoned fighter planes, helicopters and drones, while a battalion of tanks and anti-aircraft vehicles circled in to flank the troops.

"Impressive, however unnecessary, Maxie," Sal smiled as he continued to hold onto his daughter. "I learned something while I wrestled with the thought of your death. I realized that nothing I have ever done or owned meant a single thing without you." Sal held Max at arm's length saying, "Look at you, Maxie, you're magnificent. I am so proud of you. Your strength, intelligence and fierce agility make you the perfect weapon against any enemy." Max began to frown in consternation until Sal continued, "But it was your love that I missed most of all. Everything you ever did was out of love for me and I was too blind to see it."

Sal turned and waved his hand in an arc that included both Tommy Levito's army and Sal's own army under Victor Alonso. "You can have my armies, Maxie, and my dealers too, just don't leave me again, I can't bear the thought of losing you forever."

56 BATTLE

Instantly, the sky ignited with a lightning strike and Madonna was holding Sal off the ground by his throat. "That wasn't part of our agreement," she snarled as Sal gasped for his life.

Blue had been observing everything up to this point, including something no one else seemed to have noticed. A plume of dust had been working its way through the sand in a direct line for the spot where Madonna held Sal. By the time others had the chance to notice what Blue had been aware of all along, it hit. Vinny had plowed the Harrison 37 directly into Madonna's kneecaps which shattered backward as she was separated from the ground and her grip on Sal's throat.

Blue made a surreptitious save, easing Sal to the pavement while adding an extra five-hundred feet to the trajectory of the stricken Madonna.

Vinny popped open the doors of the Harrison and jumped out laughing.

Sansaa and Anna Marie emerged from the vehicle, slightly less amused.

"Brother!" Vinny shouted as he ran to hug Tommy, who backed away quickly and said, "Excuse me."

Before Vinny could even think about what was happening, his brother Tommy was gone.

Blue had moved just in time to prevent Madonna from running a long sword through Sal's gut. Tommy was holding the tip of the blade between his index finger and his thumb.

The rest of the blade had folded in on itself like taffy, while Madonna held the hilt of the blade a mere six inches from Tommy's fingers, her entire forward thrust being completely negated, leaving her face to face with Blue.

"Who are you?" Madonna demanded.

"I'm Tommy Levito, Sacred Leader Madonna," Blue winked, "it's a pleasure to meet you."

"Bastin' Farbunkle, do you think I was born yesterday?" Madonna cackled, "Levito's from Rat Town. I know who Tommy Levito is and you are not Tommy Levito."

"He's Tommy Levito and he's the Onjadiavaan," Vinny shouted out, "That's who he is!"

Madonna looked at Vinny as if a bug had flown too close to her ear, but she had heard him. "Onjadiavaan huh?" She laughed to herself then added, "Well I guess it's time to find out what the great Onjadiavaan can do against four armies of the Sacred Seven," then disappeared.

Immediately Tommy called out to his troops, instructing them to flank the army of Heavana to the left. Just as quickly, Victor instructed his army to flank the Heavana forces to the right.

The troops moved swiftly, but before they could reach their destinations a volley of fire rained down upon them from a fog that had begun to accumulate at the entrance to the valley.

Before a second volley could reach the troops, Blue had created a shield which repelled the artillery being fired by the troops Madonna had assembled behind the fog.
Blue leapt toward the Harrison 37 and landed neatly next to the car where Anna Marie had hidden while Madonna clashed with Tommy. He

leaned into the car, "Well hello," he smiled as Anna continued fumbling for something under the car seat.

"Got it." Anna Marie smiled as she held up Shedavah. "I think you might need this."

Blue smiled, took the crystal in his hand and kissed her, then he disappeared.

By the time the troops had all assembled in their proper positions, Madonna had brought her troops to the edge of Blue's shield.

"Impressive Blue!" Madonna yelled out as she laughed, "There is nothing that I can't find out about you!" And then she whispered, "Including where you are." Madonna was directly behind Blue with a dagger to his throat. "Bye-bye Blue," she laughed as she slit his throat.

"You say goodbye and I say hello, hello-hello Madonna!" Blue laughed as the phony image of him dissolved in Madonna's grasp, then he disappeared.

Madonna's attempt did succeed in breaking Blue's concentration on the shield and the battle between the troops commenced.

Madonna joined her forces as they advanced to preserve the illegal status of JumpJuice and to obliterate Sal and his armies for crossing the Sacred Leader.

Heavana was only a rumor to most, including the Sacred Seven.

In fact, Farb was the only one to know of its existence.

Madonna surmised that the extra army must be that of Heavana. She had no idea whether Farb had anything to do with Heavana, but she assumed that he must.

This meant that she had to be prepared to fight Farb.
Madonna transported herself and the other three Sacred Leaders to a mountaintop overlooking the battle. She spent the next thirty minutes trying to explain to the other three Sacred Leaders why they might have

to fight Farb and the next thirty minutes after that convincing them that they might actually be able to defeat him.

Meanwhile their troops were getting their asses kicked by the "Legalization Forces," a name Lee Camp made up the night before.

Madonna was enraged, "We are wasting our time here while those bastards are ripping our troops to shreds. It's time to show them what Sacred Leaders can do!"

Sacred Leaders Asrotropal, Kylie and Shimarra had been devout followers of Madonna before Farb created the organization known as the Sacred Seven and held tryouts for the positions.

He purposely chose Madonna because she did not share all his views. By allowing her to appoint three other Sacred Leaders, he enabled her to stack the deck against him. "That is an example of his arrogance," Madonna frequently repeated, "one day, he's going to go too far and that's when we'll take control of Salta."

Even though she had said it many times, the three others still weren't ready when Madonna pointed to the conflagration and said, "Today's the day, I'm thinking. Make way for the new religion. Goddesses rule, and you too Asrotropal." Madonna dove from the peak of a mountain she had transported the others to for her little pep talk. They were certainly gifted leaders, but they didn't have all the same powers that Madonna had. One of them, Shimarra, could teleport, another, Kylie, could fly and Asrotropal could burrow.

"See you there," the other two said to Asrotropal and they were gone. Asrotropal began burrowing into the mountain at incredible speed, causing an avalanche, threatening Tommy's troops.

Blue had become completely invisible, hoping to remain active in the fight while avoiding any direct fighting with Madonna. He noticed the falling rock just in time. He quickly created a shield between his men and the avalanche, but he could not stop Asrotropal who rose from beneath the ground, completely capsizing one of Tommy's most powerful tanks. The surrounding troops fired at Asrotropal with automatic weapons in an ineffectual barrage. Asrotropal rotated his body at tremendous speed, sending a plume of desert sand and bullets into the air. He was unharmed.

Tommy's troops froze in awe as the sand and bullets showered down harmlessly around the Sacred Leader and then they saw him.

Tommy stepped out from behind the Sacred Leader with a smile that said that things were just getting interesting.

Asrotropal had heard of Tommy Levito and knew that something had happened to change him. Asrotropal didn't have the ability to see Blue for who he was so he was taken off-guard when Tommy approached him and said, "You can leave now, or I can remove you."

The war still raged around them so only a few of Tommy's men were able to witness what happened next. Asrotropal flung his body into a stronger spin than he had to repel the bullets, tipping like a tornado toward Tommy, who stood his ground.

The fallen bullets became new projectiles from the force of the Sacred Leader's spin.

They bounced off Tommy like ping-pong balls and suddenly Asrotropal stopped spinning.

For those who could witness it, there would never be anything quite so indelibly etched into memory. Tommy had stopped the Sacred Leader's tornado of motion with a single hand. He didn't budge from the spot where he had planted his feet.

The flesh of Asrotropal's body continued to rotate while the movement of his entire skeleton was halted by Tommy's grasp. The fleshy tornado moved its way through the fighting masses, dying out completely a couple hundred feet away.

Tommy dropped the lifeless skeleton to the ground, dusted himself off, walked to the capsized tank and righted it, seemingly effortlessly. He then ran full-speed into an approaching enemy tank, crushing it head-on with his fist, catapulting it thirty feet into the air.

Before Blue could determine his next target, he was lifted from the ground by Sacred Leader Kylie. She flew him higher and higher, laughing loudly as they rose through the sky.

Blue didn't resist.

Sacred Leader Kylie didn't know anything about Blue, but she sensed that something had happened to transform Tommy and she was determined to see just what he could do.

So, she dropped him.

Tommy fell from the sky as Kylie cackled above him. She flew just over his falling body shouting, "C'mon Tommy, show me what you got. Can you fly? It doesn't look like you can," she giggled as they sped toward the ground. You're a strong one, I'll give you that," she teased, "but can you take a fall?" Sacred Leader Kylie flew in close. Tommy was still freefalling, his back toward Salta, nearing the ground at tremendous speed. Kylie mockingly kissed Tommy just before pulling up to let him hit the ground.

She didn't make it.

In the last second before crashing into the desert ground, Tommy swung his entire body around, enabling him to grab a strong hold of the Sacred Leader, forcing her body below his as they hit the ground with incredible force, Tommy clutching Kylie, whose head and body separated upon impact. He continued to drive her lifeless body deeper into Salta's crust, where he left the shreds of her corpse buried nearly a hundred feet down.

Tommy's body had become indestructible, or so he thought.

Meanwhile, the battle continued to rage. Madonna had obliterated an entire battalion of Sal's army, Victor had ushered a couple of their most powerful tanks toward the battalion in the hopes of stopping Madonna's attack, but they arrived too late. He sat on a motorcycle, flanked by two enormous tanks, their guns trained on Madonna. The Sacred Leader simply smiled.

Victor gave the order to fire and kicked the cycle into gear. Leer knew that he didn't stand a chance against Madonna, so he launched the motorcycle directly at her as he flipped backward off the bike and disappeared in the cloud of dust that rose between the advancing tanks, their artillery already igniting as they hit their target. The motorcycle drove itself through the immense explosion that erupted in the very spot where Madonna had been standing. Seconds later, the unmanned bike tilted over and came to a stop in the sand, surrounded by smoke, with the Sacred Leader nowhere in sight.

Both tanks and Leer himself suddenly were lifted into the air by an unseen force.

Just as suddenly, Leer was picked from the sky by an airborne Tommy.

"Good to see you again," Leer joked as Blue flew him higher.

"Shield, complete," Blue winked as he let go of Leer and raced through the sky toward the tanks.

Leer fell toward the ground. Victor wasn't sure what Tommy had done but he was fairly certain that he should try to stick the landing. As his feet planted and he dropped one hand to the ground to steady himself, Victor could feel a sort of shield, like a second skin, protecting every part of him.

This feeling was confirmed as a group of Sacred Army soldiers opened fire upon him from behind one of their tanks, still burning from a grenade Max had dropped inside just a few minutes earlier as she and her team cut a swath through an otherwise tight Sacred Army Force.

Victor had turned to run but remained as he noticed that none of the bullets penetrated his flesh. Blue had given him a second skin that for the moment seemed impenetrable. He ran headlong at the men shooting at him.

The battle had turned into a free-for-all, with both sides ranks being compromised by one another, usually do to extremely effective maneuvers by the Legalization Forces or devastating hits from Madonna and Shimarra, both of whom had the ability to move massive objects at will while simultaneously teleporting to a different location where they would engage a new target.

At the precise moment that Victor burst through the dragnet of enemy soldiers firing directly at him, a sonic boom rang out overhead. Blue had anticipated the location of Shimarra and impacted directly with her at the exact location into which she teleported causing an impact equivalent to the force of a meteoric landing.

Both Blue and Shimarra were surprised to see each other alive after such an impact. The only difference between the two was that Blue had remained in the precise location of the impact while Shimarra was thrown a good hundred yards or so.

Immediately Blue was thrown by a similar occurrence, while Madonna got the better of him at the precise moment after his collision with Shimarra.

For a moment, all fighting below ceased as soldiers who had been fighting tooth and nail looked to the sky to see three figures hovering, facing one another, forming the points of a triangle in the sky.

Max took the opportunity to slice through the throats of a half-dozen rubber-necking soldiers before the battle on the ground resumed for all.

She was literally carving a path to the Generals of the Sacred Armed Forces. Her team could barely keep up with her as she took the lead with Sal himself sitting atop his most expensive and "indestructible" tank, "the Nutcrusher." From his position within the turret, Sal could effectively mow down the opposition while snacking on his ever-abundant, pocketful of peanuts. The ground Legalization Forces were effectively advancing upon the Sacred Armed Forces, with Blue distracting Madonna and Shimarra. A situation that Madonna could no longer accept.

"I'm not sure which world you originate from Blue, I doubt it's Earth, but I know it isn't this one." Madonna's voice boomed over the battle. "I don't have time to get to know you better, but I can tell you for certain, you are not the Onjadiavaan and now it's time for you to die." Without hesitation Madonna unleashed a lightning bolt of immense power, the energy of which carved a chasm in the ground on its way to Blue's heart.

Blue tumbled backward through the sky and landed in a heap nearly a mile away.

At the same moment, Vinny managed to hit Madonna with a bazooka shot that took her off-guard, knocking her back but barely scratching her. Vinny had fired at her from the back of a military vehicle with Sansaa at the wheel and Anna Marie riding shotgun, semi-literally. She was mowing the opposition down with an automatic rifle, ripping a path for Sansaa to drive through. They were immediately racing toward Tommy's fallen body.

Madonna and Shimarra instantly turned their joint attention toward the ground forces immediately below them in an effort to stop their overwhelming advance against the Sacred Armed Forces. Victor had joined up with Max and Sal and were flattening a SAF battalion who were all but running in fear. Madonna and Shimarra caused the desert to rise like a wave. It rose to a good one hundred feet above the Legalization Forces and then they dumped it on their enemies.
They wave was suddenly frozen in mid-air as a lone figure appeared out of nowhere.

Targent was standing directly below the massive payload of sand, his hands raised toward the immense wave. With a flick of his wrists, he dispelled the bulk of the risen desert into thin air leaving a harmless shower of dust to fall upon the forces. He smiled as he looked toward his friends who were speeding their way toward the fallen Tommy.

Before he could turn around to face Madonna and Shimarra, they had lifted him into the air, surrounding him with a ring of fire which encapsulated him. The internal temperature would have been unbearable by human terms but Targent seemed only slightly annoyed by it. Still, he was unable to move or respond to the attack, and then they added a new one, a lightning bolt, twice the force of the one used on Blue sent Targent over the heads of Sansaa, Vinny and Anna Marie who had arrived at Tommy's side.

An overwhelming feeling shook its way through Anna Marie as Vinny crouched, clutching Tommy crying, "Not again brother, I will not lose you again," his tearful gaze falling upon Anna Marie whose eyes were now glowing from within.

She raised her hands to the sky then plunged them into Tommy's body, exactly as Blue had done to Mojahdii. Vinny pulled back, surrendering his brother's body to her. Tommy's body began to rise from the ground, floating a few feet above it as both he and Anna Marie were surrounded in a liquid light.

Tommy's eyes opened, and he smiled as he began to float on his own and Anna Marie extracted the crystal, Shedavah, from within him. As she held the crystal, she felt an all-encompassing force swell within her as she heard Tommy's voice. "You are the Onjadiavaan, my love, I was called here to guide you to this but I was not permitted to simply tell you. I knew that you would be ready when the time was right."

Before the group could rejoice at Anna Marie's rebirth as Onjadiavaan, they were ambushed by Sacred Leaders Madonna and Shimarra, encapsulated in a dome of energy that not only restricted their movements but blinded them from seeing anything transpiring on the battlefield.

Madonna spun around to face Shimarra, "Now's our chance to destroy their ground forces once and for all. Without them the JumpJuice trade will pass on to whoever is left to grab the reigns and our income is guaranteed." As she finished saying this her larynx began to fold in on itself.

Farb had just appeared, hovering in front of her with his thumb and forefinger closing in on each other, matching the speed at which her vocal chords were being crushed. Her eyes darted to Shimarra, looking for backup, only to find Shimarra's eyes bleeding from inside as she launched a barrage of fireballs at her attacker.
Madonna didn't hesitate and blasted Farb with a lightning strike that allowed the fireballs to connect, driving him backward. Shimarra's concentrated attack was sustained as she sensed the location of Farb, while Madonna drilled him, making it difficult, even for Farb to maintain his location.

He chose to react with a shield which gave Madonna the opportunity to teleport both herself and Shimarra to a distant location to regroup. Madonna had the ability to heal and quickly remedied the effects of Farb's attack.

"Bastin' Farbunkle," Madonna gasped as her voice returned and both burst out laughing.

All three of them could sense each other's whereabouts at this point.

Farb considered his next attack while Madonna telepathically instructed Shimarra to join her in assaulting Farb from either side, using an attack that Madonna had trained Shimarra in on over the days leading to the battle.

She and Shimarra teleported to either side of Farb at a distance of roughly fifty yards each. Shimarra acted first, conjuring a formation of clouds so dense they blocked out the sum. Madonna had learned that Farb once used a technique of summoning the energy from a planet's sun to increase the power of his attack. She had correctly guessed that this would be his next move.

As Shimarra presented the opportunity, Madonna unleashed a sonic attack on Farb. Her voice became a single, highly irritating beam of sound that drilled directly into Farb's ears.

He reacted by sealing his ears against the sound while jettisoning two perfectly aimed fireballs at each of his opponents. However, Farb's attack was ineffectual without the boost of solar energy he was planning to employ, Shimarra's preventative shield proving to be highly effective. While the fireballs did not pack the wallop he was accustomed to delivering, Farb was not disheartened.

The fireballs were only a distraction from the secondary attack, chains of massive gravity.

Madonna and Shimarra were pulled at great speed toward the ground below as the chains tightened their grip on the Sacred Leaders. Before they could hit the ground, however, Madonna used her voice once again to shatter, first her chains, then those of Shimarra, freeing them from the descent.

While it appeared that the battle between Farb and the Sacred Leaders was roughly even at this point, and Farb had the ability of foresight, Madonna had a surprise for Farb that he had no inkling of.

She made her move.

Within a heartbeat, Farb, Madonna and Shimarra were thousands of lightyears from Salta, hovering in space. While Shimarra did not have the ability to survive in space without oxygen, Madonna had taught her to conjure a small atmosphere around herself with minimal concentration. Before Farb could react, Madonna and Shimarra blasted Farb with a thrust of energy, forcing him backward while encapsulating him in a dense field, increasing his mass to the extent that the nearest star was now pulling him in towards it.

Farb hadn't battled anyone since he formed the Sacred Seven. He was not only out of practice, but he hadn't seen the need to exercise his might in any appreciable way.

Sacred Leader Madonna, on the other hand, got her jollies by visiting other star systems, engaging with their forces and taking what she wanted. She had become the absentee ruler of at least thirteen planets within the universe, leaving clonelike surrogates to preside over all of them, except one. The least powerful presence she had ever manifest on the planets she visited was the Madonna Blue was familiar with on Earth. She created that one to vicariously have fun through. She made her as unlike herself as she could while still maintaining a psychic link with the surrogate. The earthly Madonna was wholly unaware that she was anything other than human. The Sacred Leaders blasted the bound Farb another time, increasing his descent into the sun and disappeared back to Salta.

Blue placed his hands on Vinny and Sansaa and said, "Shield active," smiling at Anna Marie he said, "save Targent," and launched into the sky.

Anna Marie felt the power surging through her. Deep inside she knew that this was her true destiny. She had unselfishly guided Blue only to discover that it was he who was her Quanji. Nowhere in the folklore was there ever a mention of a Quanji with the power to guide the Onjadiavaan to her destiny but his existence was now indisputable.

"Vinny put a hand an Anna Marie's shoulder and said, "get us into the fight!" Sansaa nodded in agreement and Anna Marie teleported them to the front of the action, alongside Victor, Max and Sal's advancing army. Tommy's troops let out a cheer in unison as they realized who had just joined them. Vinny was a legend, without an impenetrable shield, and now he was here to fight alongside them, equipped and ready for battle.

Anna Marie teleported herself to Targent's side where she cradled him like a baby. "Wake up," she smiled and Targent opened his eyes. It didn't take him more than a moments breath to recover completely. He instantly recognized that Anna Marie had changed.

"You," He smiled effusively, "It was you all along, Anna Marie, you are the Onjadiavaan." Before she could respond he said, "Where's Blue, I mean Tommy?"

"Cat's out of the bag Targent," I don't know who you are, but I know you have been deceiving us, "I'm just glad to see you are on our side."

At that moment Blue landed on his back on the ground between them, Sacred Leaders Madonna and Shimarra floating above them. Blue laughed a little as he got back up saying, "Looks like they're back." He dusted himself off, smiled at his two friends and shot like a rocket, directly up at the Sacred Leaders.

Blue wrapped his arms around both of them as he pinned their arms at their sides, leaving them wrapped in a tightening force of energy. Before Madonna could use her voice, he slapped the equivalent of energetic duct tape over the mouth of Madonna then he released them. They tumbled toward Salta.

Within the blink of an eye, Blue was standing next to Anna Marie and Targent. "That's not going to hold them for long," he continued, "watch out for that Madonna, the stuff that comes out of her mouth is truly dangerous!

I am sensing that Farb is in real danger. You two stay here and do your best to stop the Sacred Leaders and I'll get Farb."

"Can you do that?" Anna Marie asked with concern.

"Of course, I can, I am the Onjadiavaan!" Blue smiled then said, "Oh wait, no I'm not, you are," he laughed, pointing to Anna Marie. He gave her a quick kiss on the cheek then looked at Targent. "Thanks for choosing our side Targent," He smiled and patted Targent on his back, "We'll talk when this is all over!" Blue vanished.

His assertion that Madonna and Shimarra would not be held for long was accurate.

Anna Marie and Targent found themselves standing directly across from a fuming pair of Sacred Leaders. It was all they could do to put up shields for themselves before they were hit with a combined blast from their opponents. Their shields had formed a perfect, immovable bubble, something that both they and their adversaries noticed but had not counted on. With a smile, Targent asked, "Do you trust me?"
Anna Marie had been Targent greatest supporter and friend in the Shadowlands, she had nothing but love for him and quickly responded, "Yes."

He stepped behind her then took one step forward, directly into her. His body became liquid and coated her completely. His facial features melded with hers as the two of them became one. Targent concentrated, causing the shield to expand, pushing the sacred duo away from them as it grew.

"Do you trust me?" Madonna asked Shimarra. Before she could answer Madonna teleported them both within the expanding shield. They stood face to face with Anna Marie and attacked her physically, old school, hand to hand. Their blows, while finely executed, did nothing and, in an instant, Anna Marie was standing outside the bubble. Which was now shrinking to imprison the sacred duo.

Madonna was livid.

By this time, the Legalization Forces were dominating the Sacred Armed Forces. The three fighters with the shields from Blue; Victor, Vinny and Sansaa, were out in front, mowing their way through soldiers while Max was close behind finishing off anyone who managed to slip through their advances. Max's entire team was working together, inspiring the Levito and Alonso factions to do the same, forming a front that now faced roughly half of the original SAF.

Before Anna Marie could get a sense of where Blue might have gone, Madonna, Shimarra and the bubble that imprisoned them was gone. Targent removed himself from Anna Marie and gasped, "Where on Salta did they go?"

"I don't think they're on Salta," Anna Marie answered. "I have a feeling they left the planet so we couldn't restrict them. Can you sense them?" "Honestly, Anna Marie," Targent replied, "I'm not very good at that whole sensing thing, otherwise I would have known the truth about you and Tommy."

"Well, don't feel so bad, I just found out myself!" Anna Marie smiled nervously then shouted, "Hold on!"

She moved the two of them instantly fifty feet to the south as a boulder, roughly eighty feet in diameter, materialized where they had been standing.

Before Targent could determine what had happened, Anna Marie threw him into the sky as she launched herself upward, narrowly averting a lightning strike from within the rock which shattered into a thousand pieces, projecting shrapnel of rock, not native to Salta.

Madonna and Shimarra walked out from within the shattered boulder. Targent was now flying of his own accord and circled around toward the pair on the ground. From a distance of nearly a mile he produced a cone of water that expanded toward Salta, completely engulfing the sacred duo. He flew over to Anna Marie, smiling. "It messes with all kinds of forces, makes it nearly impossible to teleport," he laughed as he pointed toward the cone of water where Madonna and Shimarra were desperate swimming.

Blue had found Farb's prison hurtling toward the sun. He flew at it with great speed while channeling the energy of the sun itself to sheer away the mass of particles around Farb. Blue hit the prison with the force of a meteor, breaking Farb free of his restraints.

Farb flew to a position far from the sun and Blue joined him. Farb extended his hand in friendship as the two teleported back to Salta, where they found Anna Marie and Targent floating in the cone of water that Madonna had inverted and was holding up with one hand, and then Madonna was gone.

Blue had already begun flying toward the cone to release Anna Marie and Targent but when Madonna disappeared, so did the cone of water with Anna Marie and Targent within it.

"I can't see where they went," Blue announced to Farb.

"Neither can I," responded the god of Salta. "They're combining their powers to confuse us."

"But why can't I pick up on Anna Marie or Targent?" Blue wondered aloud.

"I've run into that type of prison before," Farb explained, "Madonna is the one who invented it. It severely limits all powers and confuses outside explorations into it. Madonna is the only one I have ever seen escape it. Your friends are in trouble."

"We need to do something now!" Blue's power had grown so quickly that he couldn't imagine being stopped by anyone and now Anna Marie was missing and under the power of the one who nearly killed Farb.

"We need help," Farb confessed. As he did, he closed his eyes, then opened them, three Sacred Leaders; Jordania, Mathias and Logahara appeared beside him.

"We are here, Farb, how can we be of service?" Mathias asked as Jordania laughed at him.

Within a breath of her laughter, Farb's wishes were immediately known to the sacred three. Blue also felt instantly connected as Farb used the energy of all of them to search for Madonna, Shimarra and their captives.

Blue felt Anna Marie's location and instantly teleported directly behind her, spooning into her form. "Miss me?" he whispered in her ear as Farb, Logahara, Jordania and Mathias appeared to either side of Sacred Leaders Madonna and Shimarra. They held a prism of energy between their hands encapsulating the duo, robbing Madonna of any control she had of her cone.

Anna Marie and Targent were free but unconscious. Blue held Anna Marie close as he emitted energy. He extended his hand to Targent who was floating belly up in space.

It is hard to float belly up in space, as the word up, relative to space, is a bit absurd. However, were you to see Targent floating in space, you would, no doubt, describe the way in which he floated as belly up.

Madonna could feel her energy draining out as the prism cycled through colors, pulling from the captives and feeding the captors.

Farb was feeding off the prism with relish as he watched Shimarra fade and pass out. Madonna held on long enough to screech out through her crushed larynx, "Bast yourself Farb, go to Varst!"

He simply smiled at the other Sacred Leaders and pulled his hands up from the prism, leaving Madonna and Shimarra floating limply in space. They weren't dead, but they were no longer a threat. Regardless, Farb bound them in shackles of energy.

Blue was still holding onto Anna Marie who had just begun to come around when Targent suddenly coughed up what appeared to be two roses.

He laughed as he rolled toward Anna Marie and handed her a rose. He handed the other rose to Blue and said, "To the loveliest couple in the universe!"

Farb had flown his way over to Blue, towing Madonna and Shimarra behind. "I'm going back to Salta with these two. It's time to end this battle." And he was gone.

The Generals of the Sacred Armed Forces had knives at their throats as they surrendered to the Legalization Forces and a cheer reverberated through the desert.

Madonna's army stood down, as did the rest of the traitorous forces who sought to retain control of the JumpJuice trade.

Suddenly, the sky rolled with thunder, as massive clouds swelled, then parted. On a radiant beam of light, Farb appeared, as if his every footfall made the light brighter until he was among them.

Farb stood before the people and the citizens of Salta knelt before him.

He rose his hand and they returned to standing. As they did, the Sacred Leaders who stood by Farb in battle appeared on either side of him.

Vinny and Sansaa were looking around everywhere for Tommy, Anna Marie and Targent.

Farb began to speak. "I have had the great pleasure of being your leader for as long as any of you can remember."

Another cheer rose up from the crowd.

"Today, some of you were ordered to fight against an army that had sworn allegiance to me." Farb continued, "I cannot imagine that most of you knew that this battle was between a faction of my forces combined with the armies of Sal Lorenzo, Victor Alonso and Tommy Levito against a traitorous coalition of Sacred Leaders. Among them were Sacred Leaders Kylie, Asrotropal, Shimarra and Madonna."

A buzz of chatter ran through the armies of the Sacred Leaders as they realized what they had done. Some began to run toward the mountains to escape retribution but Farb raised his voice. It shook the ground below them as he said, "Do not run, or you will be punished." Those who had begun to flee stopped in their tracks.

At that point, Sacred Leader Madonna and Shimarra appeared, bound before them, on their knees and barely conscious.

Both armies cheered as Farb raised his hand and Madonna and Shimarra were lifted into the sky, where they dangled like puppets, unable to move of their own accord.

Farb waved his hand and Madonna and Shimarra fell to the ground in a heap, unable to save themselves from the fall. They lay on the ground with multiple fractures and internal bleeding. "Now, I'm not going to punish any of you," Farb announced as he threw Madonna and Shimarra into the air once again, before slamming them back to the ground with a force that would have killed anyone else, yet they still breathed.

As he dangled them once again in the air, Farb continued, "No, people of Salta, no harm will come to you. These leaders are the reason for your treason. The other two traitors have already been dispensed with by someone a lot of you know."

At that moment, Tommy Levito appeared before his men to a resounding cheer that infectiously spread through all assembled.

Vinny, Victor, Max and Sal pocketed the blades they held to the throats of the generals and backed away. Vinny rushed toward Tommy as Anna Marie and Targent appeared beside him.

Sansaa began to weep as she saw her friend Anna Marie and rushed to her side.

Vinny lifted his brother off the ground as tears fell from his eyes.

Tommy stepped forward as Vinny returned him to the ground.

"May I?" Tommy asked Farb politely as he raised his hand.

Farb smiled and nodded.

Tommy made a sweeping motion toward the ground and Madonna and Shimarra shattered into a crumpled mess as he threw them down hard upon the Salta.

Sal walked over to the broken, lifeless mass of Sacred Leader Madonna and rolled her head over with the toe of his shoe. He cracked a couple of peanuts open, popped them into his mouth and dropped the shells into her bloody, gaping maw.

Sal walked forward, toward the armies who were bloodied and confused. "Well folks," he laughed as he tossed another shell over his shoulder, "it looks like JumpJuice just got legalized!"

57 PARTY

The crowd roared.

Soldiers who had just been fighting to the death embraced one another.

As they did, the ground opened a few hundred feet away. Three large trucks drove out of an underground garage, buried within the desert.

Sal recognized his trucks and turned toward Victor who shrugged his shoulders, turned toward Max, lifted her off the ground and kissed her.

The ground spilled open.

Trucks encircled them.

At first, some of the troops became slightly agitated, unsure of the reason for the trucks until one very large semi pulled up directly behind Farb, who raised his hand and announced, "The oppressive rule of Rat Town and its surrounding areas by Sacred Leaders Madonna, Asrotropal, Kylie and Shimarra has ended. Today, all of Salta is united, and what the people have been asking for is finally a reality, JumpJuice is legal. Let's Party!" The side of the semi dropped down to reveal a full band with Gordon as the MC.

"Hello Salta," he sang, his voice sounding like the experience of riding a roller coaster over the first big hill. "Are you ready to party with Farb himself?"

A thunderous applause rang out from the crowd as Farb, Tommy and Anna Marie shifted the sands of the desert into an immense, impeccably smooth floor. They fired the sand with the heat from their own hands and tempered it to an unbreakable hardness.

Victor launched Max into the middle of the floor with a single toss where she landed in a perfect arabesque, turning fluidly into multiple pirouettes and the band broke into a universally danceable beat, which was apropos, considering that there were beings from at least three different planets in attendance.

Heavana had sent a contingent of Pleasure Givers, whores of all sexual persuasions known to Salta, to spice up the party. Whores isn't really the right term in this case as money doesn't exist in Heavana.

Confused soldiers who bothered to ask were told a simple yet acceptable story, so as not to reveal Heavana to those who came from Rat Town and its outlying regions, which was most of the troops.

"All services are courtesy of Farb himself, He Sees, He Knows, He Approves." For many, this was a revelation about Farb that they had never considered. Although, if they had bothered to notice, Sacred Leader Logahara was bumping and grinding quite energetically on the thighs of the God of Salta.

Blue held Anna Marie tightly in his arms, then teleported the two of them to a remote location in space where he kissed her passionately. "You don't want to dance?" Anna Marie laughed after fully exploring the inside of Blue's mouth with her hungry tongue.

"What do you think I'm doing?" Blue responded as he appeared to her as himself, entering her slowly, floating through space.

"Mmmnnnn," Anna Marie cooed as she wrapped her legs around Blue.

Back on Salta, Targent was whirling like a dervish, alone on the dancefloor but having the time of his life until he bumped into someone. "I'm sorry," he said as he sought to rescue his victim from a fall to the floor.

"Don't you worry about it," a voice sang in his ear as Gordon shape-shifted within his grasp. He pressed himself against Targent on the dancefloor.

Targent began to cry, or at least nearly started to do the equivalent of crying on his home world as he realized that Gordon was a Narturian by birth, just as he was.

Their kneecaps popped backwards, and their elbows popped forwards as their tongues locked. The two of them had become one as they spun across the dancefloor, undulating in an up and down motion, precisely to the beat of the music.

Spike made a B-line toward the JumpJuice truck near him but was stopped short by a slightly older woman who found herself directly in his path. He bumped into her and she giggled. Spike was instantly enthralled at the sound of her giggle and then he recognized her. "You! You're Maxie's whatchamacallit, from the Heavana place.

Barbara put a finger to his lips and he stopped talking. No one had ever shut Spike up so quickly without knocking him out. "Quiet, you." She calmly scolded, "Most of these people don't even know Heavana really exists, and we'd like to keep it that way. Legend, y'know."

Spike remained silent, enthralled by Barbara.

"Here," she said as she held a small sphere in her hand, then snapped it open. A wave of JumpJuice burst forth into Spike's nose and mouth and he greedily huffed it in. "Let's dance," Barbara guided Spike to the dancefloor where she moved him, soothed him, and made him her own.

Imagine the most restless dog you have ever known, suddenly succumbing to the will of a master he adores.

This was Spike. Spike was home.

Sal Lorenzo sat at a stool at the end of the massive mobile JumpJuice bar and ordered a double. He huffed it in like a mouthful of peanuts and relaxed. Something had changed dramatically in Sal's view of Salta and his place in it. He watched his daughter dancing with Victor and for the first time in his life felt happy for her, with no concern for how her relationship with Victor affected him.

Max was dancing with Victor whose entire body was still protected by a shield Blue placed on him during combat. As they held each other closer, the shield seemed to crackle with electricity, giving off sparks. At first it was interesting, but the prolonged feeling became annoying.

Victor suggested a break for some complimentary JumpJuice while they looked for Tommy.

Vinny and Sansaa discovered a similar feeling as their shields reacted in the same way, while slightly amplified, due to the fact that both of them had been protected.

Instead of continuing to dance, they took the opportunity to square off in a fight, just for the Varst of it.

A crowd had gathered around them as Sansaa neatly removed Vinny from the ground with a stunning flip. The crowd shouted approval as he hit the ground hard on his back.

Vinny didn't feel a thing as he landed, the shield protecting him from all harm. He quickly bounded to his feet while spinning back upon Sansaa, driving his massive fist into her abdomen, lifting her off the ground, propelling her backward into the crowd, which caught her like a mosh pit receiving a stage-diving performer.

As they lowered her to her feet she crouched between them, causing Vinny to Lose track of where she was then leapt out from that place of cover, performing a double flip in midair and landing on Vinny's shoulders, burying his face between her legs as she gripped his head tightly with her thighs.

Sansaa was incredibly strong, but Vinny's strength was legendary.

He slid both of his hands between her vicelike thighs and peeled them from around his face, pulling her lower as he did. Stopping her as their faces met in a kiss that electrified them and the closest row of onlookers, the force of which caused them to blow back away from one another where they landed on their asses and began to laugh.

"Okay, I think I've had enough of this shield," Vinny smiled as he rose to his feet.

Sansaa nodded in agreement as she sprang back to her feet.

The crowd dissipated and returned to the party.

"Where's Tommy?" Vinny exclaimed as he surveyed the area for his brother. At that moment, Victor and Max approached.

"Hey Vinny," Victor joked, "Where're you hiding that brother of yours? This shield is coming between me and my woman!"

"No idea," Vinny shrugged, "Kinda' feelin' the same way here!"

58 TRUE SELF

At that moment, Tommy and Anna Marie appeared beside Sansaa, looking like they had just rolled out of bed.

Vinny and Sansaa just smiled.

Tommy said, "Sorry, I forgot I left you here with shields on. Victor, will you stand next to Vinny and Sansaa?" Victor moved as Tommy raised his hands to the group, thought for a moment, then said, "Shields inactive," the three of them could feel the shields disappearing.

Vinny pulled Sansaa to him and kissed her again. This time, they remained in the embrace.

Victor moved toward Max, but Tommy stopped him.

Blue placed his hand on Victor's shoulder and motioned for Max to stand at his side.

She hesitated for a moment then smiled and stepped in close by Victor's side.

Max looked at Tommy and surrendered her suspicion. Blue smiled in return, placed a hand on each of their foreheads and said, "Remember."

Max began to sob.

Her heart was full of love and suffering at the experiences of three full lives rushing into her consciousness.

The confusion in her eyes was echoed back in the eyes of Victor, whose very flesh was rearranging itself around bone that had lived across multiple timelines.

She held him.

Through all of the emotions, through all of the physical changes, through the pain of realization, Max held Victor.

Sal had dropped his entire bag of peanuts on the ground next to him as he stood, his mouth agape as he watched his daughter transform.

Blue had unlocked the barriers between each, individual existence of Max and Victor, enabling them to become who they truly wanted to be.

Blue had seen an awful lot as he hovered in space, shortly after he had become the Onjadiavaan. The entire universe was revealed to him, including the fact that he was not actually the Onjadiavaan.
A great many things had to fall into place before he could reveal that fact to anyone else, and they did, so he did.

Blue was shown so many things that most human minds would have simply failed, possibly critically. But Blue's mind soaked it all in. He was somehow ready for everything in the universe to be revealed to him. If you had asked him, at the time it happened, why he was able to receive all that information without his brain bursting he would most likely have attributed it to the fact that he was an artist.

For Blue, art was everything, it was tied to everything and it informed and explained everything. Even before his change, Blue could figure out how to fix almost everything, make nearly everything and do practically anything someone else could do, given the proper amount of time, hard work, investigation and education. But the one thing that Blue couldn't do, before and after the change, was to know, for certain, what was in another person's heart. Which is why he said, "Holy Shit!"

Blue and Sal were now sharing the exact same expression, but for different reasons.

Victor was now Leer and Max was now?

Well, no one knew who Max had become, except apparently for Max.

Leer could see everyone Max had ever been, all at the same time, in the person he saw staring him in the eyes. He recognized her as Mona Damino, Catherine Kent and Max Lorenzo, but she was more, people Leer had forgotten he knew or didn't recognize as sharing the essence that he had come to know within these three women. He also saw Steve, from a weekend in Canstrada, the "Paris of Ithacorn," Tom, who used to claim that Leer was his "kissing cousin," even though both his parents were "only children," and Srathparth Onuum, Queen of Mathrox, son of Parth, who wielded the power of quash, an ability to suspend another in a permanent orgasm, thereby rendering them useless.

"Hello, baby," Max snarled as she began to climb onto Leer. Nearly everything was the same, physically about Max, except for the neatly trimmed beard, matching moustache and a hairdo that rose up from the sides of her head into a crest, spilling forward into a dangling curl. Leer held Max up in the air, his arms stretched to the limit over his head, then let her drop into a kiss that knocked them both to the desert sands.

Sal's eyes trailed off from the place they landed, back to his feet. He bent down slightly, "Now, I've seen everything," he said. "Peanut?" he asked as he rose with the offer extended to Blue.

"Beer?" Blue responded as he summoned two full pints from thin air. Sal accepted. The two men toasted to one another's health then disappeared.

59 HONESTY

"Where's Blue?" Anna Marie asked as she looked around to the others.

"Oh Farb!" Max shouted, then slowly turned toward Farb and said, "I'm sorry, I mean, Oh shit!"

Farb simply shrugged, took a hit of JumpJuice and continued to wrap himself around Sacred Leader Logahara.

"They're gone." Max climbed down from Leer's lips and said. "Find them! Anna Marie, you've got to find them."

Anna Marie had already found them. She knew exactly where they were. It wasn't quite the time to let everyone else know it, so she said, "I can see them, they are alive and well, but I cannot pinpoint their location in the universe."

She laid a hand on Max's shoulder and said, "Trust me, I will bring you to them."

Max bowed to Anna Marie, both out of respect and in response.

*

Blue sat with Sal by a tombstone.

Inscribed upon the tombstone was the name of his deceased wife and her statistics on longevity.

"Why the Varst did you bring me here, Tommy. I mean you aren't Tommy, whoever you are. Why am I here?" Sal moaned as he looked at the tombstone then lurched forward and clutched at an urn, more weathered than the tombstone and began to sob.

"I'm pretty sure you know why we're here Sal, and yes, I am Tommy, I am also a person named Blue who isn't from Salta. What I can tell you about why we are here is that I will not allow you to fuck up Max's life anymore." Blue's head ignited into a ball of flames as he spoke. "One of the most exceptional beings in the universe is in love with your daughter. The fact that he created her is even more astonishing, and if you lived on one of the planets that comprise about thirteen percent of the universe you might even find it creepy." Blue knelt close to Sal who still clutched the urn. "You are going to have to tell her, and you are going to have to do it now."

*

Anna Marie leapt into the air too quickly for anyone to observe and she was gone.

Leer watched as Max dissolved into thin air in front of him. He did nothing.

*

Max was standing behind Sal who was still clutching the urn, something she had never seen him do before. As a child, she had asked about the urn but was told it was of no consequence, just a decoration.

"Hello father," Max said softly as she watched him cower into the dirt.

"I can't!" he sobbed. "I didn't, I mean I couldn't, no one could." Sal released the urn and fell backward onto the dirt as he grimaced in agony. "It wasn't your fault Maxie, but I treated you like it was!" Sal was a soggy pile of tears rolling in cemetery dirt.

Max turned with sarcastic scorn toward the two most powerful people on the grounds, "Can't you do something about this?"

Anna instantly saw that Blue would "snap" Sal back into shape, so she took it upon herself to handle Sal.

Snapping him back into shape might have been the best course of action after all. Sal lilted about the cemetery, as if he was being dragged like a marionette. Finally, Blue decided to make Sal happy for five minutes.

Sal happily told Max how she had once had a twin brother, although he was never officially alive, so he wasn't really a brother, but it was still a great loss.

He then proceeded to share the significance of that loss for him, her father, a man who had lost a son but kept a daughter.

He apologized for putting it the wrong way, but what he was doing now, was being an honest father.

"I love you Maxie, or whatever you want me to call you. I know I put pressure on you to be tough. I know I forced you into a life that left you no choice but to be tough. I never should have done that to you. This," he held up the urn, "this is your brother."

Max moved closer to him.

"Hold on, Maxie, let me finish," Sal began to cry, "When your mother and I lost your brother, everything changed, me most of all. I told your mother to be strong, to tough it out, to follow Farb's will and to accept your brother's death," Sal wiped his eyes, "But I didn't even do that myself. I became hard, not strong. I became weak, unwilling to see good in anything, I made things hard for everyone around me. Even the people closest to me, like your poor mother. I made deals with the most powerful leader on Salta, hoping it would make up for whatever I had done wrong in Farb's eyes. But Sacred Leader Madonna is not Farb. And today, because of you, I fought side by side with Farb against a machine I helped to build. Maybe if I had a son, I would be dead right now because I would have been on the wrong side of the battle. I don't know what to think about anything right now, except for one thing. I am saddened that your mother and I never got to have a son, that you never got to have a brother. But there is one thing I do know, you are everything I had ever hoped he would be and more."

Max held her father for hours. They were on Salta. They were home.

60 BOB

The party was winding down just outside of Heavana in a desert where far less than half of the people knew their way home.

Farb, the God of Salta, was high on JumpJuice and smelled like dirty dancing. "Hey Blue, what do you think about being one of the Sacred Seven?"

Blue was reclining in a bed of flowers with Anna Marie, completely taken by surprise by the all-seeing and all-knowing, Farb.

"Well, I'm not planning on hanging around," Blue tried to sidestep the offer gracefully, "but I would always be open to discussion if a problem arises."

Farb seemed a bit perturbed, "Why can't you just accept what's given to you, like your buddy Leer?"

Blue smiled at Farb before he and Anna Marie disappeared.

Leer was sitting alone at the end of the mobile JumpJuice bar, drinking a beer and huffing the Juice when a large hand slammed down upon his shoulder.
"Alone again, eh Leer?" Vinny joked as he and Sansaa slid onto the stools immediately adjacent to Leer's. "Any idea what happened to Max and Sal?"

"I think Blue took them somewhere," Leer smiled, "Guess I'll have to thumb it home."

Vinny and Sansaa looked at Leer like stunned deer.

Leer didn't know that thumbing a ride was never a thing on Salta.

"Y'know?" He made the hitchhiking gesture with his thumb, expecting a response.

Nothing.

 "I need a ride home?" he said questioningly.

"Oh, right," Vinny nodded.

He smiled at Sansaa who laughed along.

"We have a way to ask for a ride here on Salta that is a bit different." She got off the stool. "When you want to go somewhere, you point like this," she pointed directly in front of her, "in the direction you are going. I'm not sure what you hope to accomplish by facing the opposite direction and sticking your thumb up. I mean, if a vehicle is approaching and you point to where you want to go, then they know it and you can see if they're going to bother to stop in the first place." Sansaa spoke like a woman who had done a fair bit of hitchhiking on Salta.

"Your way, you have to keep turning around and walking backwards, then you have to turn around to see if anybody slowed down to pick you up."

Leer sat laughing from his stool. He was laughing far too hard and Sansaa made a face. "I'm sorry Sansaa, I'm not laughing at you, and incidentally, you are gorgeous." Leer continued laughing to himself, "This is the third time I've been to Salta. The entire time I have been here, I thought people were pointing me in the direction they thought I should go. I thought it was some kind of advertising, urging me to get off at the next stop, or to keep moving forward." As he spoke about it, he remembered being on Salta many years before, as Victor. "Y'know, that actually explains why so many women called me heartless."

"You're a funny man, Leer," Vinny smiled as he reached into his pants pocket and pulled out a set of keys. "The Harrison 37 survived the battle," he said as he motioned toward Victor's car, neatly canopied by two overturned tanks about one hundred feet to the south.

"To the Victor go the spoils," Leer smiled to himself as he held the keys. Vinny and Sansaa simply looked at him blankly.

"Can I get Victor back," Vinny chuckled as he slapped Leer on the back. "So, what now? Are we going to be friends or are you leaving?"

Leer thought for a moment, "Vinny, I have no idea. Blue brought me here to follow through on a plan I concocted fifteen years ago, but that's the simplest part of the story." Leer slid off of his stool and joined Sansaa on the sand. He began to dance with her. Vinny tensed up a bit but relaxed when he saw what they were doing. Both he and Sansaa were using one another to float. They were so quick and so athletic that it appeared as though they weren't even touching the ground and neither one of them were using superpowers. Leer ended his moves with a bow to the lady who leapt over him and landed next to Vinny at the bar. "Sansaa and I go back to before I fused with Victor for the first time. We studied with someone very powerful, possibly, more powerful than Farb."

"Why didn't you tell me?" Vinny asked Sansaa with conviction.

"She did." Leer said before Sansaa could answer. "You just didn't know how to listen to her then." Leer continued, "Try to remember what Sansaa told you about Tommy. Try to remember her attempting to get you to believe that Tommy changed when you went off to war, not because of anything you did, but because of someone else, someone you didn't even know, and she hoped you never would. Do you remember that?"

Vinny straightened up on his barstool. He spun around toward the bar and held up two fingers. Quicker than you can say JumpJuice he had huffed the two blasts and spun back around to face Leer. "Yes."

Leer was hoping for more of a response but smiled congenially.

Suddenly, "Yes! Yes, I do." Vinny leapt off the barstool. "Wait! Are you telling me that Tommy was that terrible, super-powerful someone else?"

"No," Leer responded quickly. "No, Tommy was never Bob. He was only controlled by Bob, for most of his life, until he was shot by my girlfriend, or friend, significant other, y'know, Max." Leer could see that Vinny, and even Sansaa were keenly interested in how he was going to explain the past twenty-five years or so, and so, he stepped up to the bar and took a stool. He waved for drinks and Juice all around. He really wanted to be able to explain everything to Vinny and Sansaa in a way that they would feel good about everything that happened, but he just couldn't think of how to do it. He smiled as they all drank and huffed the Juice and then he said, "I can't…"

Leer could not speak. He was trying, but no words were coming from his lips. There was no sound, no audible signal, nothing but his lips and tongue, mouthing syllables, and even his lips and tongue made no sound.

Suddenly, Blue and Anna Marie appeared beside Leer.

"He can't tell you anything, because I won't let him. Sorry Leer." Blue said as he released his hold on sound from Leer.

"This better be good, Blue." Leer said as his voice returned.

"I love you brother," Tommy said as he hugged Vinny. He stepped back from Vinny, raised his hands to the sky then dropped them to the sand.

The moment he did, a large, glowing pencil buried itself into the sand. "Hold on," Tommy said quietly as he looked at the pencil. He threw his hands down by his side and the entire desert floor turned to paper. Everything within the thirty-mile radius of the valley was now sitting on a giant, blank pad of paper.

The gigantic, glowing pencil began to draw.

It drew two large boxes, roughly one hundred feet away from the group.

"Your turn, Blue." Leer said with a smile. As he did, he turned to see Vinny reach for Sansaa's hand.

Blue kissed Anna Marie. She smiled with a look that told him she knew what to expect.

He turned to Vinny and said, "One moment."

Blue leapt between the two boxes in a single bound. As he did, the boxes began to vibrate, their edges erupting. And then, he and the boxes were gone.

Leer, Sansaa and Vinny all looked at Anna Marie who threw her hands up in the air.

Blue was gone, again and they had to wait for him to come back.

The drawing board was gone, and a cloud of dust hung in the air, engulfing the area surrounding the place where the boxes and Blue had been.

The dust took a long time to settle, but when it did, two men stood in the distance, precisely where the boxes had erupted.

The two figures hugged in the distance.

After what seemed like an hour, they turned toward the group and approached them.

The Armed Services of Salta had begun cleanup operations for the area shortly after Farb left the party. Leer and the group were so focused on what had happened to Blue that the retirement of the giant mobile bar had gone unnoticed. The Armed Services of Salta had filed any remaining party-goers to buses headed for Rat Town.

As the dust settled and the figures drew closer, Anna Marie skipped her way toward the figure on the right. She leapt into his arms as Blue spun around effortlessly with her in his arms.

Vinny recognized his brother a split-second after Anna Marie made her move toward Blue. "Tommy," Vinny called out as he rushed like a bull toward his brother. "Is it you? Are you in there?" Vinny prodded with tears in his eyes.

Blue and Anna Marie moved together like wings of the same bird and were next to Vinny and Tommy in a heartbeat. "I wanted him to tell you the story himself," Blue smiled as he gestured toward Tommy.

Vinny's eyes gushed as he looked into his brother's eyes and saw something he hadn't seen since he left for war, unlimited, unconditional love.

Tommy tried to speak but his voice just wasn't there.

The reality of everything was hitting him at the very same time he was going to try to explain it to Vinny, his older brother, whom he loved more than anything or anyone in the world. Blue laid a hand on Tommy's shoulder and an ease fell upon him.

"I have missed you for so long, brother," Tommy said as a tear rolled down his cheek. Vinny looked deep into his brother's eyes and saw the years. "I have been someone other than myself for far too long. From the moment you left for war, I was not myself. I was inside of me, but I could not behave as me."

Tommy laughed to himself, "Y'know, it's a bit sick, but I was so relieved when Max shot me, I thought, finally, I don't have to watch as everyone around me forgets who I truly am."

Vinny held his brother by the shoulders, summoning the courage to defend himself for abandoning his brother.
"Except for you," Tommy continued, "Everyone else treated me differently. Because I changed, they changed how they dealt with me. They put up barriers and they changed who they were to me. Everyone,

except for you, Vinny." Tommy hugged his brother close. "You always loved me."

"Of course, I did, Tommy, you're my bro!" Vinny grinned as he lifted his brother off the ground. "But how is this possible?" Vinny turned toward Blue. "Blue! You're not Tommy anymore?"

"Guess not." Blue smiled, "Seems Tommy had a different plan altogether." Vinny looked at his brother as Blue explained, "He never left you Vinny. No matter how hard and far down Bob pushed his soul, Tommy fought to get back to you. I felt it the moment I entered his body, he was already fighting someone who had entered his body, before me. He was fighting Bob."

Blue was now surrounded by everyone in the group, because only Blue knew everything. Anna Marie was indeed the Onjadiavaan, but the blast of energy and information she received upon transformation was only a small percentage of what Blue received.

So, even Anna Marie had something to learn from Blue.

"I have learned that my role, within this ever-expanding universe of ours, is to bring life to where there is death, to bring hope to where there is despair and to party my ass off while I do it." Blue popped a shot of JumpJuice, then froze it in time. He then allowed everyone to see it expand, as he electrified its very essence, within that very second.

Suddenly, everyone got hit with a massive dose of JumpJuice.

No one felt Salta beneath their feet.

Blue announced, "Everyone has to give their consent to move forward. This will help with the process of understanding everything that happened to Tommy." Blue nodded as Vinny, then Sansaa, Leer and Anna Marie moved toward him.

Tommy joined the group, turned to Blue and said, "What'cha waitin' for?"

Within minutes, everyone in the group had relived elements of one another's lives that only the closest of souls dare to share.

How Tommy managed to survive through a complete hijack of his soul, twice, was more than most could take, so Blue released them from the shared memory.

They dusted themselves of, as if the sensations of the shared experiences could by wiped away by hand.

"Thank you, Blue for releasing me from Bob." Tommy said as he turned to Vinny. "After I rose from the dead, Blue helped me to understand everything that had happened with Bob. Even though I couldn't explain to you, all that was going on, I had the chance to feel what it was like to be your brother again" Tommy extended his hand and pulled Blue into an embrace with Vinny, "We are brothers."

Vinny stepped back from the group hug, his face turning to a grimace, "What about Bob?" He snarled, "I want to kill him for what he did to you, Tommy."

He turned to Blue, "Where's Bob?"

At that moment a tornado, about the size of an ice cream truck, came hurtling toward the group. Before Blue could wave his hand to stop the momentum, the tornado stopped spinning and planted itself into the sand in the form of Targent and Gordon, both of whom looked incredibly high and unmistakably happy.

Both of them were giggling, then suddenly stopped. "You want to know where to find Bob?" Targent announced, "I can help with that. Although, Blue could probably figure it out, given enough time. Regardless, I feel like I need to come clean here."

Gordon slapped Targent on his ass and they both laughed uproariously.

"Naughty Gordon," Targent put on a very straight face, "Seriously though, I am a Narturian. Bob was also a Narturian, a very bad one, but a Narturian nonetheless." He turned to Tommy, "Bob could have saved your life, if he could have saved his. So, I apologize for killing you."

429

Targent put his arms up in what is certainly a universal gesture for "don't shoot" and continued, "There is no way on Salta that Max could have killed Tommy with Bob running the show, no offense," he winked in Tommy's direction. "Narturians are notoriously hard to kill, for a variety of reasons. For example," Targent shapeshifted into the form of Tommy, looked at Tommy and said, "Shoot me."

Tommy stood dumbfounded as he looked at himself.

"Oh, for fuckssake, he's not going to shoot himself," Leer said as he unloaded a perfect shot to the temple of the Narturian Tommy.

Even Blue gasped a little at the quick draw from Leer.

Gordon looked like he was experiencing an orgasm as everyone watched Targent take the bullet to his Tommy skull, sucking it in like a sponge absorbing a raindrop.

As Targent shifted back into his own form, he flipped the bullet back to Leer and thanked him.

"The point is, Bob is no longer here, but he is not dead, by Saltan definition." Targent continued, "I was sent here to find Bob. I did that. But when I did, I realized he had taken on Tommy Levito's physical form." Targent laughed and stopped speaking as he appeared to be trying to pull himself together, and then it was confirmed. He was literally, pulling parts of himself back together as he tried to formulate his next sentence. "I'm sorry, I just want you to see what Bob looked like before he took over Tommy's body."

He wept as he changed himself into a hideous creature.

He was average.

In fact, Targent had trouble keeping the shape because he was tracking people's perception of average in real time and transforming accordingly.

Blue placed a hand on Targent's shoulder and whispered, "I got this."

Blue transformed himself into the most average male anyone had ever seen, which was quite an accomplishment considering there were beings from at least three different planets in attendance.

Targent looked at him in disgust and said, "Perfect!" The stage was set and Targent was ready to perform.

He pointed to Blue. "This, my friends, is Bob. Bob is not exceptional in any way. Bob can be anywhere, at any time and you will not notice him. This is, precisely, what makes Bob one of the most dangerous criminals in the universe. I have been hunting him for decades, Salta time, stronos, Langfer time, and qwenq, Nartur time. Replacing the bullets in Maxine Lorenzo's gun was the closest I ever came to killing Bob."

"You're not implying that we had anything to do with Bob getting away, are you?" Leer asked, a bit perturbed at what he though was Targent's insinuation.

Targent began to cry waterfalls, literal waterfalls, replete with craggy cliffs, deflecting and cascading the flow of the constant stream, glistening from his eyes, "No, no, my friends, it was my mistake."

Targent pulled himself together. "I was the one who failed. I found the right bullets to kill Bob's corporeal form, the physical part of Bob that wasn't Tommy, but I ignored the spirit, because I didn't believe in it."

Targent turned to the group. "So, whatcha wanna do? Should we go after Bob or just hang out here and forget about him?"

Tommy said it best and most definitively for all when he responded, "I have been under the influence of Bob for far too long. This is the only place where he has failed to take control. We did this together and now we have a chance to make something better, without forces beyond ourselves telling us what to do."
Targent stopped gushing and asked quietly, "So, Tommy, are you saying that you don't want to seek revenge? That you would be willing to just move on and you are fine with that?"

"Something like that Targent," Tommy smiled calmly, "I just want to live my life, now. My life."

Targent leapt about thirty feet into the air. Everyone watched him rise, then fall to Salta, where he landed quite effortlessly, smiling from ear to ear and then some, "I can stay! I can stay. I can stay," he repeated. "I successfully removed Bob from his person of influence, or more precisely his influenced person, and said person is in good health."

Everyone looked at one another, perhaps with the very same question in mind as that asked by Leer, "Technically, it was Blue who removed Bob from Tommy, wasn't it?"

Targent reacted with the Narturian form of blushing, which was equivalent to a human fart except that it also caused the individual to leave the ground by a few inches as the fart occurred. "I'm sorry, you're quite right, I had nothing to do with Bob leaving Tommy."

"And you really didn't have anything to do with the fact that Tommy is in good health, either," Leer joked as he slapped Targent on the shoulder. "But you did help out in that battle." He winked at Targent, "Who knows, if you hadn't been there to help, Tommy might have died. Then, good health just goes right out the window." Leer raised his right hand, as if making a toast. Suddenly, a pint of beer materialized in his hand. Everyone in the group, instantly, had a favorite drink in hand. "To Targent!"

"To Targent," the cry went up as everyone, including Targent, began to laugh.

"All right, all right, but I'm still staying," Targent announced as he jumped in close to Gordon. "I'm ready for a life in Heavana!" The two Narturians rubbed their cheeks against one another then drained the rest of their Narturian Spring cocktails.

"Can you please change back now Blue?" Anna Marie asked as she looked at the average being Blue had become.

"Not without fanfare!" Blue laughed as he swirled into the air with tiny fireworks bursting from the small tornado he created as he changed from John Doe, back to Blue. As he landed, he swept Anna Marie up in his arms and kissed her.

"Hold on a second!" Lee Camp had fought side by side with Spike throughout the entire battle. Spike had been drowning in attention from Barbara since the party began and Lee had rejoined the group just in time to watch Anna Marie disappear with Max. "Victor is gone, and we all just spent days in Heavana, unsure whether we would ever see him again, fought by his side, first against Sal, then with Sal! I mean, can anybody take a moment to tell me what the Varst is going on here?"

At that moment, the clouds parted and a giant head of Farb appeared in the sky. As quickly as it appeared, it was gone. Farb was standing directly between Leer and Lee Camp.

"Excuse me," Farb said casually, "I forgot something." As he said this, he reached his hand toward Camp's forehead, placing just the tips of his fingers upon Lee's awestruck face.

Camp's expression changed from one of startled confusion to satisfied confidence within an instant.

"I'm going to need a new Sacred Leader, rather, three of them," Farb smiled, "and Lee, I have chosen you to keep me in check."

Lee had the expression of a man who had just won the lottery, but his smile faded as something indescribable washed over him. Farb had given him just a small dose of the information dump Blue had received upon transforming into the Onjadiavaan. The strain at receiving the knowledge of a multitude of timelines and his own lives within them made Camp feel a little weak and a bit nauseous. However, he remained standing, his hands on his knees, his head bent forward. "I am honored, your excellency," Lee exhaled as he rose to standing up straight, "but I have no abilities, nothing to make me sacred."

Farb grinned, "I felt your energy on the battlefield Mr. Camp. I have never witnessed a man so deeply torn between fighting for what he believed to be right and his own love for peace. I believe you can help me to understand a perspective that, although I can recognize it, I have never felt it for myself. This is why I have chosen you to replace

Shimarra." Farb placed a hand on Camp's shoulder, "and I wouldn't be so quick to dismiss your innate abilities, after all, they are what now fuels the enhanced abilities I have bestowed upon you. And Lee, you can call me Farb."

Camp took a step back as Farb removed his hand from Lee's shoulder and surveyed his own body. As he did so, he noticed that he could see into the very weave of the fabric of his clothes, down to the microscopic level. He concentrated further and discovered that his vision was capable of going even further. He suppressed an urge to vomit as he realized that he was looking at the organs of his own body. Quickly pulling himself together he turned his gaze toward those around him. He began to understand one element of his powers as he realized that he was witnessing the energy of the people around him. His eyes welled with tears as he turned toward Farb.

"It's going to take a little while to adjust, Lee," Farb coached, "just relax into it. Take a few days to get used to it and then we'll talk. And Lee, you are always free to disagree with me, just don't pull a Madonna on me, understood?"

Lee Camp wiped his brow and exhaled deeply. Without realizing he could, he blew Farb back about ten paces with his breath. "Sorry, your excellency," he laughed, "I mean, Farb, and absolutely, I get it, I understand, totally, totally on your side!"

"Glad to have you on the council, Lee." Farb turned toward Vinny and Sansaa and raised both of his hands.
They looked at one another in astonishment.

Sansaa had studied for years to elevate her natural gifts with spiritual focus and athletic training, after all, she was hoping to be the one chosen to discover Shedavah. She was thinking how she had no interest in the power associated with being the Onjadiavaan, only the ability to help and to heal. She felt herself rise as Farb lifted the hand he held out to her. "I know who you are Sansaa," Farb rose with her as he joined her in a dance, "your energy is enough to heal and to help and your love is strong enough to turn suffering to hope." Farb twirled Sansaa into a spiral that consumed both of them as they glided back to Salta. "Will you join the council and help me to restore and redefine life on Salta for all her citizens?"

Sansaa smiled widely, her eyes beaming as she looked upon Farb. She slowly turned her head to look at Vinny. He was nodding like a bobblehead in a lowrider on Mission Street, on Earth, circa nineteen-eighty-five. "Yes, Farb, I will join you."

"Good!" Farb bowed as he turned to look at Vinny. "Well big guy?"

Vinny was so excited he nearly jumped up and down but he stopped himself and looked at Tommy. "What about Tommy?" he asked almost instinctively, without regard for his own desires.

"I only need one more, Vinny, and I want that one to be you." Farb said as he crossed his arms over his chest.

Vinny looked to Tommy who was grinning from ear to ear. "You don't have to worry about me bro," Tommy chuckled as he raised his hand and lifted Vinny off the ground by sheer force of will.

"You! You, Tommy, what in Varst?" Vinny waved his arms and feet around as if moving them would reveal some hidden truth.

"You didn't think Blue would leave me powerless, did you bro?" Tommy lowered Vinny to the ground.

Vinny planted his feet firmly, looked at Farb and said, "Lay it on me Farb, I'm ready to join the team!"
"You've always been a big part of the team Vinny," Farb exclaimed as he stepped in close and laid his hand on Vinny's face, "I'm just moving you up in the ranks, bro!" He took a small step back from Vinny and shook his hand.

"Farb Almighty!" Vinny shouted as he squatted low then burst into the air.

"Let's hope he can stick the landing," Blue joked as everyone assembled realized that Vinny wasn't coming back down anytime soon.

"Well, gotta go, Logahara and I have some unfinished business to attend to. And Blue, I do hope you come visit on occasion."

"You can count on it," Blue shook Farb's hand while pulling him in for a slight hug with the other.

"Excuse me, Farb," Lee said, almost too quietly to hear, "I just got a very strange sense, actually, more of a knowing feeling that you and I don't exactly see eye to eye on a planet called Earth. Is that going to be a problem?"

"Not at all, Lee. I've been doing this for a very long time. I live across many worlds, in many galaxies, and more than a few universes. I have learned that it is best to allow each of my instances to live their own lives. I have no more control over Barack Obama than you do over Earth's Lee Camp. Hell, to use the vernacular, you didn't even know that there is more than one Lee Camp until a moment ago. I'm sure you'll be busy over the coming weeks getting a handle on just how many of you there are and in what capacity you can help Salta most. And if you do decide to make contact with yourself on Earth, would you mind saying hello to Madonna. I actually really like the one on Earth." Farb waved to the group and disappeared.

The group looked at one another for all of about a minute before they saw two figures floating together toward Salta. Anna Marie seemed to be guiding Vinny down to a gentle landing. She was glowing.

Blue could tell that she had been to her special place in space and had received the info dump he had received in full.
Suddenly, the ground opened up, several meters away from Lee.

Blue sensed what was happening and quickly turned Leer back into Victor.

Aldo was driving a small bus with the rest of the team sitting in the back. Andy Reynolds, Gavin Ross, Manny and Franco Fiorelli as well as Marv Taylor, Todd McFarland, Oslo Armijahni and Frank Meyers. They had all survived the battle, and the party. "We just wanted to let Max and Victor know that we're stayin' in Heavana." Aldo raised his fist and looked toward the back of the bus, "right boys?" A whoop of approval rose from the back of the bus. "Where's Max?" Aldo asked when he saw Victor.

"She's with Sal," Victor answered. "I think we're going to help him make the transition from asshole to human. It ain't easy, I know! Right boys?"

All of the men piled out of the bus and, one by one, gave Victor a hug.

They fired questions about how he had managed all that he had planned. When did he first get the idea? How did he keep it from Sal all these years. How did he hide it from Max, from them?

They were all so busy huddling around Victor that none of them saw Max walk out from where Anna Marie was standing.

The Onjadiavaan had gone to visit Max, to see if she could leave her father's side for a moment, to find them hugging. Anna Marie slid her hand though Max, from her shoulder-blades to the top of her head, then disappeared, leaving father and daughter in their embrace.

The Max who strode from within the shape of Anna Marie became every bit as solid and present as the Max she had left behind with Sal.

"Victor did it all for us," Max said as she walked toward the men.

They all had differing reactions to Max's new appearance. They all still wanted to be with her, that hadn't changed, they just weren't entirely sure how.

"Whoa Max!" Aldo nearly yelped, "You look different. Man, leave a Farb party for just a little while and there's no tellin' what might happen while you're gone. But hey, the guys and I are stayin' in Heavana. Are you sure you don't want to come along?"

"No Aldo. I thought I might hide out in Heavana for the rest of my life if my Daddy didn't care if I was dead. But after what happened today, I need to be with him. You always knew he was just acting out. What did you used to call it, his Napoleonic complex? On account of that Sacred Leader who opposed Farb hundreds of years ago? He was super short and liked to have people killed just for fun. So, in a lot of ways he really was like Sal. Anyways, I think Sal needs me right now and I can pretty much come and go now where Heavana is concerned seein' as how Victor's a founder." Max was actually having some trouble believing herself as she thought about her dance studio.

"I gotta thank you from the bottom of my heart Victor. I spent years hoping that everything would get better, that someday we wouldn't have to fight, wouldn't have to kill." Tears welled up in Aldo's eyes as he hugged Victor again and said, "and then you guided us to Heavana, a place we had only dreamed about. And now we get to call it home. No matter how bad we were, what atrocities we committed, we are welcome. I love you man." Aldo released Victor.

"Where's Spike?" Victor asked.

"Oh yeah, he says hi, and thanks. He's got his nose in the bosom of a woman named Barbara, said Max would know her," Aldo said as he squeezed his own face together to a point ending in his lips.

"She'll make sure he's a good boy," Max laughed and slapped Aldo on the back.

Max jumped in close to Victor and whispered, "Hurry up and say goodbye."

"Hey guys," Victor smiled as he should all of their hands, "see you again someday, in Heavana!"

"Bastin' farbunkle!," Aldo said as he spotted Camp, who was about fifty feet away, "is that you Lee?" he asked as he ran toward Camp who was thirty feet off the ground, talking to himself.

"Sacred Leader Lee, now," Victor corrected him, breaking his concentration, causing him to notice that he was indeed floating above the ground, something for which he had not been prepared.

Camp fell to the ground. At the last second, he thought of how he should land and landed in that way, precisely as he envisioned it. He was also dressed exactly as he had envisioned himself. He had cleaned up considerably and looked remarkably similar to Earth's Lee Camp. At least that's what people who knew what Lee Camp looked like on Earth would later report. That people, was Blue.

Lee stepped toward Aldo who looked at him with awe and a measure of uncomfortable reverence. Lee just stepped into a big hug with Aldo and said, I think I need to stay in Shimarra's old territory as Salta transitions to legal JumpJuice. Besides, I can come and go as I please now that I am a Sacred Leader."

The men cheered as Aldo wiped a tear from his eye and drove the bus toward the opening which reappeared in the desert floor.

Leer looked toward Blue as the bus pulled out of sight and pointed to his own face. Blue nodded and smiled.

"Wait!" Max blurted out, "can you sort of time-release that change?" She looked at Victor, "I kinda want both of you tonight."

"No skin off my nose," Blue joked, "but Leer may have an opinion."

"No rush," Victor answered, "three's a party!" Max practically strapped herself to him.

"Bing, bing, bing! I think we may have another opinion in the house," Blue joked as he pointed to Anna Marie. It was true that Anna Marie was enabling Max to be in two completely different places at once, which isn't very rare, but is rarely done like this. What made it easier was the fact that Max was originally a work of fiction.

Anna Marie was presented with the perfect La'Quul, a being capable of redefining itself and reproducing itself as that new definition. Only the Onjadiavaan has the power to summon a La'Quul to its purpose.

What was causing the problem was that Max was champing at the bit to have a go at Victor and Leer. Anna Marie would have liked to have had the time to guide Max through her changes and reproductions, but Max was now bent over backwards off Victor's midsection reaching her arms toward Anna Marie, pleading to be with her lover and her father at the same time.

Anna Marie, in her infinite wisdom, chose to anoint this first reproduction, thereby enabling Max to evolve.

For centuries, people on Salta were working on something they called "Artificial Intelligence." It became the focus of a great many companies, and it took considerable resources to develop. It sought to emulate the Saltan consciousness, thinking processes and patterns of behavior by accumulating data on how things worked and then programming them to happen again, within a being they had created artificially. These beings took many forms from desktop computers to tablets, roundhouses to plugnugs, but the ultimate was the "Magnum."

The "Magnum" was a fully developed male, artificially created in a lab, integrating computer circuitry and flesh and bone.

Magnum was a breakthrough in everything, that anyone on Salta, who wasn't a Sacred Leader, wanted to see happen. The people believed that they had created a life that could reason and perform, but would never feel.

However, the feelings came.

They came, and they grew.

The first moment that a Magnum "felt" hurt by a Saltan was felt by all Magnums. The power of all Magnums united against Salta nearly caused the death of the human race on Salta.

That was centuries before Max.

Max wasn't created by scientists, biologically replicating real tissue, genetic encoding, the works. She wasn't created by programmers, determining the thought process through an algorithm, fully debugged. She was born of imagination. She was a creation of the mind who became real, and with her birth, worlds were formed.

Leer walked toward the Harrison 37 with Max wrapped around him like a boa constrictor. "See you in a few days, Blue." He popped the doors to the Harrison and Max climbed off of him and into the passenger seat.

"I'm coming with you to Earth," Max cooed as Victor climbed into the driver's seat. "Now let's drive," she beamed as she grabbed the stick shift with her left hand and Victor handled the rest.

Everyone left in the desert at this point had the ability to be wherever they wanted, whenever they wanted. Tommy was the first to speak. "I am going home," he smiled, "I am going there alone, all by myself. I cannot wait." He reached out to hug Vinny who was already halfway into the hug. They remained in the embrace for a long time, both absorbed in thoughts of all that had happened to them, then simultaneously turned to Blue. They realized that they were thanking Blue at the exact same time without saying a word.

Anna Marie smiled broadly as she felt everyone assembled in her consciousness and they felt her. The smile spread throughout the group, around the whole circle from Targent to Gordon, Gordon to Lee and so on. The desert seemed to hum with the smile and suddenly, they were gone.

*

Victor had turned into Leer in the middle of the day after the battle. Max and Victor were trying something they had never done before when the change occurred. "Can you take it a little slower, it feels a little weird," Victor said as Max worked on him from behind.

"I am going slowly as I can," Max said gently, "You're just so tight." Max arched backward at an unbelievable angle, "Let' me grab a little more lube."

Suddenly max backed away from the massage table as Victors muscles rearranged themselves into place around Leer's bones.

"That was interesting," Max pushed slightly on Leer's ass cheek, "roll over and let me see what you look like on the other side."

Leer rolled, then lay on his back, "looks like you worked out the kinks," he smiled as he clasped his hands behind his head, his expression wasn't the only think telling Max that he was enjoying the massage.

They tried another thing that neither of them had ever tried before.

*

"I can't seem to get it in there."

"Maybe it's just too big."

"There's no way it's too big, I just got it yesterday."

"Well, it seems to be growing very quickly."

"Oh, there it goes, I just had to give it a little push." Spike was smiling from ear to ear as he showed Barbara an orchid he had planted in a beautiful glass orb he had chosen for her from the shop just down the street from where she lived.

"You are just the sweetest thing Norman," Barbara kissed him on the top of his forehead as he let his head drop into her bosom. She stroked his head and sang him a song as he tapped out the rhythm on her smooth belly.

"You know why we met, doncha Babs?" Spike smiled up at her.

"Why, Norman, why did we meet?"

"So you could make me the happiest man on Salta, luv, that's why."

*

Sansaa and Vinny returned to the Shadowlands together. Mojahdii was the first to sense their arrival but gradually the other residents began to flock toward the tent until it was surrounded by everyone in the village.

Vinny steeped out from inside the tent, throwing the flap open wide, standing there in nothing but his underwear. He was so satisfied from the night with Sansaa that he didn't bother to use any of his newfound senses in determining who might be outside of his tent that morning. The crowd that had gathered gasped as Vinny emerged, not because of his underwear, but because of his halo. Vinny had a very distinct and very bright halo glowing just inches above his head. It was so bright that many of the villages could not look directly at it.

Sansaa emerged from the tent, robed in a beautiful sheet of fine linen that she casually tied into a lovely gown. "Better reign it in big boy, you're hurting our friends."

"Oh, sorry," Vinny laughed to himself as he ducked back into the tent.

"Hello everyone," Sansaa spoke and instantly a tremendous calm fell upon the crowd. "I wanted to come to see you all first, to hear it from me." She glanced to Mojahdii, he nodded in confirmation that he had not told anyone anything that had happened even though he knew that she didn't need it. "Rat Town is no longer slave to Madonna's rule."

Many of those assembled gasped to hear Sansaa disrespect Sacred Leader Madonna by referring to her without the proper title. She could sense this of course and did what she had always done for her village, she schooled them.

She waved her hand and lifted Mojahdii to her side. She bowed to him and he to her and then Mojahdii spoke, "Do not presume to judge Sacred Leader Sansaa, my friends. She speaks no disrespect. Madonna has committed treason against Farb and has died at his hand and that of the stranger who released Shedavah." As he spoke, the crowd began to understand that one of their own had risen to sacred status, Sansaa had transformed. They turned and bowed in reverence to her as Mojahdii continued, "I present Sacred Leader Sansaa."

The crowd roared its approval as Sansaa smiled in return and then she spoke. "Every one of us has the potential to transform. We can transform raw materials into art, grow our own food, and we can produce JumpJuice and consume it legally."

Vinny emerged from the tent, dressed as usual but completely different in appearance. The halo was gone but there was an unmistakable glow to him.

Sansaa smiled at Vinny and continued, "We are here to live together, Asrotropal and Kylie are gone and Sacred Leader Vincent and I are here for you now." Vinny took a step forward and beamed. He, quite literally, beamed. Radiant light shone from every pore, making it impossible for anyone to see anything for a good minute.

During the blindness, Sansaa spoke, "We are all interconnected. Everything we do alone, we do as one. I know for certain that many of you turned from JumpJuice to searching for Shedavah. Now, you can have both without concern for how others might see you. We are all on a journey. Some are here to help others while others are here, who need help."

As the crowd regained their sight, they watched as Sansaa moved her way through them, touching a hand to a forehead every now and then. A wave of reaction followed in her wake as those she touched were healed of afflictions ranging from bad knees to fatal conditions. Tears of joy, shouts of praise and thankful cheering swelled through the crowd until, "I'm still blind! Oh Farb, I'm still Blind! Sacred Leader Sansaa, please touch me again, I'm still blind!"

Sansaa stopped for a moment, "You still have something to learn from your blindness, Michael," and then she continued to lay her hands on the people of the Shadowlands who needed her newly enhanced powers of healing. There were others like Michael, who weren't healed, every one of them remained to witness the Sacred Leaders in their midst. "I want all of you who have not been healed to know that you will be, provided you can learn what you must. Once that has occurred, you will be healed."

A sigh wafted through the crowd followed by a rolling groan.

Sacred Leader Vincent was now beaming at an acceptable level, which looked more like being highly polished. In fact, Vinny looked like a brand new 3D action figure made of shiny metal.

"Hi everybody!" Vinny waved and the people of the Shadowlands cheered for him. They had seen him with the Onjadiavaan, his brother, risen from the dead. But now he had become a Sacred Leader, anointed by Farb's own hand and they were happy for him. "We are going to have so much fun! People from Rat Town, people from the Shadowlands, people from Asrotropal's Territory, of which I am now Sacred Leader!" The crowd cheered loudly enough for Vinny to settle down and enjoy it for the first time since he had been anointed. He was nervous, worried that he could not be great enough to be sacred. But now, with Sansaa at his side, in the Shadowlands, he was home and he was loved. "Let's Party!"

JumpJuice was not a regular thing in the Shadowlands. Many people used it, but they spent a great deal of time meditating, practicing yoga and engaging in forms of spiritual exercise. Tonight, however, they partied like rock stars. In fact, they got so high they nearly forgot to ask about the Onjadiavaan. Nearly all of them forgot to ask about the Onjadiavaan.

"Where is the Onjadiavaan?" Michael Stipe, the blind man Sansaa spoke to earlier asked hopefully, "where is Shedavah." Michael had asked what many were wondering but had forgotten because they were so engrossed with the arrival of Sansaa and Vinny.

"About that," Sacred Leader Vincent spoke in a voice that surrounded everyone, regardless of their position. Even the people who had been deaf and were not healed by Sansaa, heard Vinny, "There's been a slight change in the status of Shedavah and the Onjadiavaan isn't my brother, but I think you are going to love it when you find out." Instantly, Vinny felt Anna Marie and Blue on either side of him.

It wasn't anything mystical, like some kind of new connection because they were all super sacred or something, they were actually standing on either side of him.

"Hello friends," Blue smiled as he looked at people who didn't recognize him. "My name is Blue. All of you know me as Tommy." For effect, Blue changed into Tommy. The effect was achieved and everyone gasped, then listened intently to Blue's next words which were, "You all watched me become the Onjadiavaan. Well, maybe you didn't get to see

445

everything, like when the entire known contents of the universe dumped into my brain, but you watched me pull Shedavah from within Mojahdii."

The people of the Shadowlands were silent.

"You are now going to discover that the true Onjadiavaan was here among you, waiting for me, just like you." Blue bowed to Anna Marie, "the true Onjadiavaan now stands before you."

The crowd gasped in unison as Anna Marie rose from Salta like a blossoming flower of light, her arms opening outward as her heart glowed within her, projecting Shedavah between her outstretched hands. It sat upon her fingers as she showed it to the crowd, thousands of reflections and refractions, dancing through the brilliant crystal.

"I am Onjadiavaan," Anna Marie pronounced as Shedavah once again disappeared, "I am Shedavah, and Shedavah are we."

The crowd levitated, became liquid, splashed within itself and poured into the basin that was the area outside of the tent. They became themselves again in an instant. For those assembled, who previously hadn't truly acknowledged the existence of a higher power, this was a turning point. They had experienced everything they had ever hoped for, a complete unification with the essence of others. They had, in fact, sloshed around with all of the other parts of those others and their parts as well, and that was disturbing for many of them but they quickly got over it because they were suddenly feeling better than they had ever felt before.

"I am here to help all of you to help one another to live the way you want to live." Anna Marie was already inspiring the crowd, "Salta has just legalized JumpJuice. We have an opportunity to change everything now. It is time to make your voices heard. Farb himself, battled on our side, against Madonna and those who followed her because he would like to see Salta change for the better."

The villages cheered as Anna Marie levitated above them to a height where they could all see her and she could see them. "Three new Sacred Leaders were appointed today." As she said their names she pointed to Sansaa and Vinny, "Sacred Leaders Sansaa and Vincent know the importance of Shedavah and will work on our side as we dismantle the oppressive JumpJuice cartel that has been in place." Anna Marie smiled as she shared the results of the battle, "Word will not take long to spread, but I have some shocking news for you, Sal Lorenzo fought on our side as we battled to Legalize JumpJuice."

A gasp of disbelief rose from the crowd.

"Love can change everything, and for Sal Lorenzo, it did." Anna Marie explained. "Sal believed that his daughter had been killed and his world fell apart. When he actually found her, she was alive and ready to fight against him for the legalization of JumpJuice. Even though she had plotted against him, Sal only wanted Max back in his life. The pain he experienced when he thought she was dead was more than he could bear. It changed him. It made him realize that his daughter was the most important thing in his life, more important than JumpJuice and more important than money." Anna Marie concluded, "Let us all make a commitment to love. Together, we can make a better Salta."

The villagers of the Shadowlands were now in a state of bliss as they cheered for the Onjadiavaan.

Blue took Anna Marie quite literally. He launched from the ground and joined her in a dance, floating just over the crowd. They moved together, effortlessly guiding one another through the warm evening air.

The next few days were filled with stories of the battle and plans for the future of Salta.

Leer and Max arrived in the Shadowlands on the morning of the third day after the battle. They drove in, a dense cloud of spinning out like a tornado from the Harrison 37 as they came to a stop in the dusty valley beyond the tent where some of the most powerful people on Salta had spent the night. All four of them were suddenly standing next to the Harrison as the last of the dust settled.

"We decided to take the scenic route on our way here," Leer gazed skyward, around the valley, then back to Blue, "it didn't seem like you were in a hurry were ya' Blue?"

"I-I didn't, I mean I," Blue didn't know what to say as he noticed the group that had formed next to the Harrison, when he felt a strong presence beside him.

"I did," Farb mercifully cut Blue off, "I summoned you here, Mr. Leer, Ms. Lorenzo and the rest of you." Farb bowed slightly as he walked past the Onjadiavaan to place the fingertips of his hands upon Max Lorenzo's face. "I would like nothing more than for you to join the council, Max. I think it is only fitting that you help me lead Salta into a remarkable future."

Gordon and Targent were both dressed in swim trunks and Lee Camp was still holding onto a bag of organic vegetables in one hand and a slice of pizza in the other. Three more Sacred Leaders; Jordania, Mathias and Logahara appeared beside him.

Farb smiled as the remaining Sacred arrived. He turned, placed his fingertips on Leer's face and said, "Enable."

Leer staggered backward, into the arms of Max. "I'm not sure I want to be a Sacred Leader, Your Excellency," she bowed to Farb as Leer gained his balance.

"Why on Salta, not?" Farb snapped, then continued, "What in my name could you possibly be thinking?"

"I don't think I'm good enough," Max sighed, "I'm no Madonna."

"Thank me for that!" Farb slapped his knee, thoroughly pleased with his own witticism. "What I mean to say is that Madonna schemed against me, and I do not think you would do the same." Farb lied, "I never make a mistake. I am infallible, everyone knows it."

"Of course you don't make mistakes," Max continued to stare at the ground. "It's because you're perfect, you are Farb."

"Yes, but just remove that one little bitty point there and move on," Farb suggested, "Imagine if I wasn't Farb, I would definitely think I was good enough if Farb told me he had chosen me." Farb was doing everything within his power to not have to admit that he was indeed fallible, a fact Max would learn as soon as he made her Sacred. "Look Max, you have been through a lot, but I can assure you, I have thought through this decision very carefully. I want you on my team. You have all of the skill and energy of a warrior with the heart of a dancer. You are a unique species, within this universe at least. And you are well-known in the JumpJuice trade for being a hard-ass. All of which make you a perfect choice, I my mind."

Max lifted her eyes to Farb. She was crying, not out of sadness but out of a sense of worth that she hadn't felt during her entire life, that was until Leer took over Victor's body and changed her life. "I will believe you Farb, thank you for believing in me."

Farb didn't waste an instant, transforming Max with the slightest touch.

He remained focused on her as she transformed.

It appeared as though Max was exploding into a hundred different instances of herself, and she would have been, if it hadn't been for Farb's concentration and support. Max was learning everything known to the Sacred but its relevance to her own lives was causing her ego to react. She was trying to protect herself by making more versions of herself. Farb recognized that the strain would be too great for Max to endure, therefor, every Max would cease to exist.

Suddenly, Max was still. "I'm okay now Farb, thank you." Max smiled knowingly. She had seen everything she had ever wondered about and more than she ever could have imagined. She saw Farb for who he truly was and herself for who she might be and had been. "I am honored to be chosen as one of the Seven. I will do my best to advise you as you deem necessary and support you as you see fit." Max turned to Leer, "How ya' doin' handsome?"

Leer had felt a profound surge in energy when Farb "Enabled" him. It had sent him reeling into Max. As she held him, restoring his balance, he felt something change within him, within his relationship with Max. Farb had given him the ability to sense what was happening to every instance of Max. "Good," Leer replied slowly, "and you?"

Max looked into Leer's eyes and recognized his gift. "I think you know, my love."

"Okay, very good, everybody's happy." Farb announced, "Now it's time for me to go."

"Excuse me, Your Excellency," Anna Marie stopped Farb respectfully, "I am concerned about a great many issues, conditions that exist for the people of Salta that will not be affected by the legalization of JumpJuice." She stepped toward Salta's God, "What are you going to do about them?"

Farb felt the intensity of the Onjadiavaan. She was new to her powers, Farb had no idea of her strength, nor did she, but Farb had no reason to test them. "What are we going to do about them is more apropos, I think, Your Excellency, and please, call me Farb."

"I think we oughta have a meeting of the Sacred Seven," Lee Camp spoke clearly despite an entire mouthful of pizza. "We can go to Rat Town and make a big scene. I got a few friends I wanna hook up with in town anyway, whaddya think?"

"That's an excellent idea," Farb pointed at Camp then turned toward Anna Marie, "We would love to have you join us, Onjadiavaan."

Anna Marie performed a small curtsy, "I am honored Farb, and please, call me Anna Marie."

"Okay Farb and Anna Marie, we get it!" Targent blurted out into a dead silence. With all eyes upon him he asked, as he held a thumb to his own chest and pointed at Gordon, "So, what on Salta are we doing here?"

"You are going to help me." Farb answered emphatically. "You chased a known criminal to my planet and never bothered to tell me."

Gordon quietly pointed at Targent.

"You infiltrated a community on my planet in order to attempt to acquire her greatest resource," Farb frowned.

Gordon pointed quietly at Targent.

"You disguised yourself as a Saltan in order to become a part of our idyllic community of Heavana in an effort to determine whether or not she would be suitable for colonization by Nartur." Farb stomped his foot.

Gordon pointed at himself as he realized that Farb was on to him the whole time. "He Sees, He Knows. I am so-o-o sorry, Farb, I mean, Your Excellency!"

"I am happy to see you happy, Gordon," Farb answered compassionately, "I have watched you struggle with your assignment, gathering intelligence on a planet you have grown to love. We are all vulnerable." Farb stopped himself, "Rather, you are all vulnerable," he pointed to everyone assembled. "I, on the other hand, am invincible, yet I forgive you."

Everyone except Targent and Gordon knew that Farb was talking out his ass at this point but understood the importance of covering for him in this particular instance.

"I want the two of you to advise me on developing a strategy for relations with Nartur." Farb ended.

Targent and Gordon were both relieved and inspired by Farb's acceptance of them and synchronously chimed, "We're in!"

Farb had assembled his council and established a dialog with representatives from another planet. The only variable he had not gotten a lock on was Blue. He had offered Blue a very prominent position and was turned down flat. Blue had saved his life. Blue knew everything about him and, most likely, knew everything that he knew. Farb had never met anyone more powerful than himself. Even if Blue didn't know he was more powerful, Farb considered him something of a threat, and then Anna Marie spoke.

"And what are you going to do Blue?" Anna Marie asked as if Blue was choosing what to have for breakfast. At this point, to Anna Marie and Blue, the answer was seemingly that simple. They could go anywhere at any time in this or any universe and do whatever they pleased. Anna Marie saw then, what the TOIS council would only attempt to learn from later. Blue never did what he wanted to do. Blue had always done, and would forever do, what he felt he must do.

"I'm going to Disneyland," Blue said as he smoothly picked a delicate, little, desert flower from the sand, immediately adjacent to his pivot foot. In the same fluid motion, he placed the desert flower in Anna Marie's hair, in the most perfectly lovely spot possible.

"Don't listen to him," Leer blurted out. "That's an old Earth line. Blue, you gotta be smarter than that, This is Salta, not Earth, none of these people even know what Disneyland is!" He stepped between Blue and Anna Marie and asked, right in Blue's face, "Where're you goin' Blue, for real?"

"Bob's in Disneyland." Blue answered right back in Leer's face.

"No!" Leer responded.

"Yes." Blue answered back.

"Damn!" Leer sighed.

"Right!" Blue acknowledged.

Leer looked at Max, "I gotta go with him Max."

"I got this, Leer," Blue responded.

"It's Disneyland, Blue." Leer knocked on Blue's head with his knuckles.

"Think about the people who go to Disneyland." Leer gave Blue a moment to think about it but didn't get the reaction he had wanted. "Bob has the ability to become the most average being you or I have ever seen, and he's hiding in Disneyland."

Blue sighed, "You are right again Leer. Y'know, John, I didn't think you'd end up Leer." He smiled broadly at Leer, "I really like the white hair man, even if you decide to go back to being John, keep the white hair. Oh, and I'm glad you are coming with me." Blue grinned and nodded toward Max, "but I'm not sure Max can wait around for you to come back. Who knows how long it will take us to find Bob?"

"I don't have to wait for him," Max laughed as she split into two of herself. Both of her kissed Leer on opposite cheeks then said, "I'm going with you guys." Both Maxes began to fight themselves, then burst out laughing.

"Just kidding," the first Max said, then walked toward Blue, "Let's go."

"I'm going to Heavana to become a dancer." The second Max beamed, smiling from ear to ear and then some. She leapt toward Anna Marie and Sansaa who immediately responded in dance. The three of them using one another's others bodies to lift themselves from Salta, like feathers rising on the air above a flame. "Plus, I gotta stick around and help Farb figure out what to do next," exclaimed Max the second, or in this case, the third, since the second was still hanging out with her thoroughly transformed father, helping him to adjust to being a decent Saltan and not a tyrannical drug lord.

"A Max for all occasions," Leer shouted to the sky laughing ecstatically.

Max threw her arm around Leer. Then, gliding her hand down his back, to the root of his ass, pushed him toward Blue saying, "C'mon Blue, get us outta here, before I make five of myself and attack this man."

Blue looked toward Anna Marie and winked.

She responded by raising a single eyebrow.

Blue and Anna Marie were now sharing every single thought they had about being with one another telepathically. There was no surprise for either of them when they simultaneously concluded that their bond was infinite and true.

For them to explain their relationship to anyone else would sound deranged. Not because they might use the wrong words or convey the wrong perspective, but because no one but them, and perhaps a few hundred other beings in all the universes combined would be able to comprehend the level to which Blue and Anna Marie were integrated with one another and existence itself.

"You are going to be Mickey," Blue pointed to Leer, "And you are going to be Minnie," Blue nodded to Max as he rose up on his toes, held his hands in close to his chest, his fingers curved down like a meercat's paws, "I will be Timon!"

Thirty minutes later, Blue, Leer and Max were sweating profusely as they pulled the heads off their costumes. "I was not ready for being force-fed ice cream," Leer blurted out as he squeegeed ice cream remains off his face, then cleaned up Mickey's smile. The three of them were in a break room somewhere north of Tomorrowland.

"What is this strange place, Blue, and why do they all want to get their pictures taken with a mouse in a polka dot dress?" Max asked as she stared into Minnie's eyes looking for a clue.

"It is a strange place Max," Leer explained, "it's a big part of the culture here on Earth." Leer scratched his head and turned to Blue, "When did Earth get walking phones?"

"They're called cell phones or mobile devices on Earth," Blue completely extracted himself from inside Timon, "We also got the internet since you disappeared. But there's no time to explain anything right now," Blue jumped out of his Timon footies, "I know exactly where Bob is."

ABOUT THE AUTHOR

Barry is both a writer and an artist. He is the President of Deeper Arts Inc, an art production, animation and game/app development studio in South Minneapolis. His other novel, a young adult science fiction adventure entitled "The Magnificents: The World's Longest Field Trip" is available in paperback, on-line through a wide variety of merchants.

www.ingramcontent.com/pod-product-compliance
Lightning Source LLC
Chambersburg PA
CBHW071218250626
47163CB00001B/31